LIVING IN THE PRESENT

Edgar Banks, unsuccessful, loveless and alone, decides to commit suicide. But before going he wanted to give a farewell present to life. Brooding over the most obnoxious people he knew, he decided to murder the worst man among them, and so die with the knowledge that he had left the world a cleaner place. LIVING IN THE PRESENT describes, with all the gusto and sense of comedy displayed in the author's first novel HURRY ON DOWN, Edgar's strange Odyssey, to Geneva, a Swiss Alpine resort, the shores of Lake Maggiore and back to London in pursuit of his fantastic objective—and also another objective which life forced on him in his wanderings and which by a strange development in his story became in the end attainable.

By the same Author:

HURRY ON DOWN

LIVING IN THE PRESENT

A Novel

by

JOHN WAIN

London : SECKER & WARBURG : 1955

Made and printed in England
by
William Clowes and Sons, Ltd.
London and Beccles
and
first published
1955
by
Martin Secker and Warburg Ltd.
7 John Street
London
W.C.1

Faith is the consciousness that moral values and spiritual experiences have a sacred character.

GEORGE LA PIANA

Them that die'll be the lucky ones.

LONG JOHN SILVER

GEORGE'S

I

THE moment he decided to commit suicide, Edgar began to live in the present. It was, for him, a novel sensation. Always, during the twenty-nine years he had lived, there had been some menacing tomorrow, some nagging yesterday, which between them had contrived to smother today, to render it haggard and pock-marked with worry. But from this moment, seven o'clock on the evening of February 7th, all that was over. He had decided. No more tomorrows, during the brief time that remained to him; and yesterday, deprived of its all-powerful ally, would be insignificant.

He took out a clean sheet of paper and unclipped his fountain pen from his pocket; but before beginning to write, he rose from his chair and switched on the second bar of the electric fire. No need for economies now; when next quarter's electricity bill arrived, he would probably be beyond the reach of all industries, nationalized or otherwise, for good. Probably, but not certainly, for he had a task to perform before leaving, and he was in no hurry. No one is who lives in the present.

He unscrewed the cap of his fountain pen and wrote at the top of the paper: REASONS FOR THE SUICIDE OF ME, EDGAR BANKS. At that moment there was a loud knock on his outer door. Putting his pen down with a sigh, he went and opened it. Standing outside was a stocky dark-haired young man with a curious smile, half obsequious and half mocking, on his rubbery face. It was the occupant of the flat below.

"What is it, Flannery?" Edgar asked.

"You wouldn't mind lending me a few glasses, I suppose? Some extra people have turned up at my party. And if you're

1

not playing your records we could do with some of them, too."

Flannery looked at Edgar in a contemptuous way as he spoke, implying that he knew Edgar would be fool enough to lend him the glasses and records, and despised him for it. Edgar turned away without answering, went into the sitting-room, and, taking up his pen, wrote immediately under the heading:

1. *Because this world contains people like Humbert Flannery.*

He looked at the words critically for a moment, then crossed out "people like." One was enough. Meanwhile Flannery had followed him into the room and stood warming his hands at the electric fire. His family, in changing their name from Vogelbaum, had adopted that of Flannery with the object, doubtless, of adding to the sorrows of Ireland. He looked at Edgar and sneered amicably.

"Shall I get the glasses out of the cupboard?"

Edgar stood up.

"Flannery, I want to tell you how much I detest you and the blasted parties you're always having. And how much I hope, every time I hear the row coming up through the floorboards, that the party will be a flop and you'll run out of drink when it's too late to go out and get any more, and just sit there hating one another and end up by cutting one another's throats from ear to ear."

Flannery crossed to the wall-cupboard and took out eight wine-glasses. "Where are the records?" he asked. He was a man who always got what he wanted and saw no sense in pretending to be grateful. Picking up a tray, he put the glasses carefully on it.

"There's something about you that always makes me feel unclean," said Edgar.

"It's because you are unclean," Flannery answered. He leered. A keen amateur student of psychology, he felt it his mission in life to bring other people's slumbering anarchic instincts to the surface. His own were on the surface already.

"The word 'unclean' has no meaning, coming from you," said Edgar. "You wouldn't know cleanliness if you saw it."

"I've never seen it," Flannery said simply. Catching sight of the gramophone records on top of the bookcase, he put them

2

under his arm. Then, feeling strong in possession of what he had come for, he turned his greasy satyr's face towards Edgar.

"All alone tonight? Where's Phyllis?"

"Go to hell."

"Thanks for the loan," said Flannery, moving toward the door. He shut it behind him. Edgar heard his voice a moment later, as he rejoined the party, raised in mocking exultation. Then, after a short lull, a new sound floated up. It was his own record of Fats Waller playing "Short'ning Bread". Mingled with the strains came the occasional high sharp crash of one of his glasses being broken. Wearily he resumed his writing.

2. *Because Phyllis has finally left me.*

Not that even this made much real difference, he reflected; they had so obviously been drifting apart for months, and the pretence, kept up for form's sake, that they would marry one day when they were "quite sure" about their feelings for each other, had become steadily more perfunctory and more seldom brought up in their conversations. His function in her life had been, it was increasingly obvious, to provide a diversion, to keep her amused until the "right man" should happen along. Still, it was a measure of his failure, in this as in everything else, that she had tired of him even before any such thing had happened. As far as he knew, there was no one on her horizon who at all resembled this mythical "right" man, who would, for a woman so easily bored and so little capable of any depth of emotion, clearly never materialize at all; but she had decided, evidently, that she preferred even solitude, even having no man at all, to a continuation of their scrappy and unappetizing liaison. She was quite right, he felt bitterly; how could she live with him when he could not even live with himself? Still, she had been *somebody*, and it was no use pretending that their coldly ill-natured telephone conversation of the previous night had not been a disagreeable shock. It was one of the nights when she usually came round to cook his supper and share his bed, and after waiting till half-past nine he had dialled her number, but he had known even before the ringing began that she would not come, that night or any night. Not particularly important in itself, the episode had provided the half-hearted push that sent him over the edge, for it had taken away the last thing that he could even pretend to be living for.

3

Scowling gloomily, he wrote:

3. *Because I am a schoolmaster.*

This was self-explanatory. He had never entertained any high hopes of his profession, but at least in the first few years there had been the faint altruistic glow of having chosen such obviously unpleasant work, that had, besides, the merit of being socially "useful" in a rough-and-ready way; but this had now been damped down, leaving only the complex emotions typical of the economic slave: self-pity, resentment, and a willingness to feel, or pretend to feel, moral disdain for those who had succeeded in netting more of the goods of this world. Sometimes, indeed, he had experienced waves of sheer incredulity, lasting for days on end. Surely it was some hideous dream: he could not really be sitting there, resting the leather-patched elbows of his jacket on the littered desk in front of him, with "1679 Habeas Corpus Act passed" on the blackboard behind him and a roomful of idle, vicious and bored urchins in front? There was the door, and beyond it the street, with buses going past; all he had to do was pinch himself, wake up, and pass out into reality. And then Stimms, the headmaster, would send for him, and pompously read out, with frequent pauses and meaning glances over his spectacles, some foolish letter of complaint from a monomaniac parent. "My son, Snivelling Sam on the back row, does not seem very happy at school, and I wonder if perhaps his form-master," &c., &c. This was the only reality to which he ever passed through the classroom door. Sweat broke out all over Edgar's body as he thought of how much he hated Stimms. Hurriedly he wrote the next item on his list.

4. *Because loneliness is particularly hellish in London, and I live in London, and I am lonely.*

There were hundreds like him, he reflected, in this dreadful city. But then, there were also hundreds of suicides. There was no sense in trying to blink the fact that modern life had got out of hand. Millions of people had to live in London, and London had grown, by accident, without anyone noticing or being able to stop it, into a sewer that engulfed and poisoned them. A gust of laughter came up from Flannery's party, and a girl's voice cried, loudly enough for him to hear the words, "You're hurting me."

You're hurting me, too, he said to the wall. The flat-dwelling system made it all the worse by locking you in a cell where you could hear other people, of the loathsome type who found this sewer congenial, enjoying themselves in their nasty and noisy way. As for living in the country, rooted in some tightly organized society "close to the soil", he had tried it. You might as well be dead properly if you were going to die and not keep your heart beating and pretending to be alive. Good morning, vicar. How's the postman's rheumatism? I've ordered up the firing-squad for both of you, please be ready at six tomorrow morning.

Well, but if London was hateful, if rural life was a living death, surely that did not exhaust the possibilities? There must be hundreds of other ways of living; why be so drastic as to give up and walk out of human life altogether? He paused for a moment, then slumped back in his chair, his face split by a huge yawn. The subject was too boring. He had thrashed it out in his mind over and over during the past three years. Of course there were hundreds of ways in which his life might be revolutionized, in which he might begin again with nothing about him that recalled the failure of his first attempt. He might, for example, devote his evenings for a couple of months to learning Spanish, and then apply for a post somewhere in Latin America, and sink himself without trace in some God-forsaken hole such as Tucumán, or be the one white man in some starving village among the Andean peaks. He could take a course in cookery and sign on in the galley of a rust-dappled tramp steamer. If suicide was his object, why not go along to a circus and volunteer, for five pounds a time, to put his head in a lion's mouth, until one evening, startled by the flapping of a newspaper or the distant yap of a fox-terrier, the animal involuntarily tensed its jaws and neatly decapitated him? Yes, there were so many ways of "starting again", but none of them went deep enough. Wherever he went, whatever he did, there would always be the insupportable ennui and pointlessness of human life. He was well aware that his list did no more than scratch the surface; all these annoyances and drawbacks would have been bearable enough if there had been any discernible meaning to the jigsaw, anything "to live for", as the phrase had it. But the root of the trouble was his blankly unalterable conviction that, for him, there was no point in going on. He dragged himself out of bed in the morning, cleaned his teeth, knotted his

5

tie, went to work, shovelled food into himself, paid his taxes, waited in shops to buy things like soap, biscuits, and envelopes; and he had, ultimately, no idea of what he was doing it *for*. He did not try to erect this sense of futility into a "system"; indeed, he was English enough to feel a savage contempt for modish philosophers who went about preaching a profitable brand of nihilism, blandly informing their fellow-creatures that they were already in hell and there was no point in struggling against it, meanwhile making a good living and enjoying life hugely. If the fools were sincere, why did they not take his way out and leave their carcasses for the solemn crows? In any case, as far as Edgar could see, life was, on the whole, very substantially "worth living" for the great mass of mankind. They had no more beliefs and no more hope than he had, but they seemed to derive a pleasure, or at any rate a dour satisfaction, from the mere process of "going on" that was beyond him to fathom.

Altogether the idea of suicide had tumbled into his mind without shock or surprise, merely as the logical result of his attitude toward life. There had been no violent break with any former pattern of existence. He could not say, for instance, that he had at any time held any definite, comforting beliefs which he had now lost. Religious beliefs, for instance, had never entered into the picture at all; he belonged to the second generation of universal agnosticism, so that the very people who had, in his childhood, gone through the motions of inculcating those beliefs had been patently unconvinced and their efforts perfunctory. He had been taught Scripture at school by a master who had "offered" Scripture, in addition to physical training and arithmetic, as a means of getting a job; indeed, there was a fairly obvious, though not overt, understanding that the subject was only kept on the curriculum because it counted toward the School Leaving Certificate. In common with millions of his coevals, it had never happened to Edgar to meet anyone of the slightest intelligence who gave the impression of seriously believing in religious doctrines; the very parsons had been either perfunctory or apologetic about the whole business. And what else was there, what else could there have been? His was not a creative nature that could find a way of life in any of the arts; and beyond that there was only the hog-trough of politics. Nowhere was there the slightest hint of an answer to the question, "Why go on?"

He was aware that certain influential thinkers and writers, sharing this sense of the lack of an ultimate purpose, had answered that the secret lay in personal relationships. A small, cultured minority, living for the most part on money that someone else had sweated and cheated to earn, they averted their eyes from the plague-ridden jungle around them, and concentrated on various fantastic elaborations of the simple basic emotion of human friendship. When members of this group happened to be "literary", their habit of endlessly analysing simple actions and motives had given their work a degree of etiolation that had always seemed to Edgar as meaningless as the complex courting rituals of certain insects. As for the published diaries and memoirs of certain well-meaning ladies of this species, whenever Edgar had happened to glance at them they had moved him only to splenetic laughter. The thing was so obviously viable only if you were too civilized to grasp the nature of human life at all, and then only if you lived in a money-cocoon which you could pretend to be unaware of, while firmly drawing the attention of everyone else to it. Even at this moment of defeat and withdrawal, Edgar felt a certain pride that he was human enough to inhabit a world where fire burnt, water made you wet, a blow from a clenched fist would knock a man down and a spade blister his palms. He saw no reason for cluttering up the earth's surface any longer, and he was willing to take himself off.

Flannery and his guests began to bawl out some drunken chorus. Maddened, Edgar seized an empty milk-bottle and hammered on the floor, but they evidently heard nothing. Savagely he pounded down the stairs to Flannery's front door, lifted the flap of the letter-box, and yelled with all the strength of his lungs, "For Christ's sake shut up!" The choir faltered, then continued with redoubled energy.

Standing on Flannery's mat, worn out with rage and frustration, Edgar lifted his clenched fists above his head. Then, suddenly, a glow of self-confidence suffused him. What did it matter? He was going, leaving it all, and besides, he had his secret; his great and magnanimous resolution. Putting his shoulders back, he strode up the stairs to his own flat. "Never mind being negative," he said to the electric fire. "That's all over. We're going to think of the positive side of it now."

Full of calm and well-being, he took out a bottle of sherry that

7

Flannery had fortunately overlooked. The glasses were all gone, so he poured some into a tea-cup and sat down to sip it and consider his wonderful and secret idea. It had come to him in the same instant as his decision to commit suicide, and he had luxuriously deferred brooding over it until he had disposed of the less pleasant, but necessary, task of defining his reasons for leaving the world. But now he was free to revel in it, to enjoy the power and magnificence it would bring him; free to live in the present.

Taking up a second sheet of paper, he wrote neatly at the head: LIST OF CANDIDATES FOR THE ROLE OF BURNT OFFERING. He laughed aloud with joy as the words formed themselves under his hand.

For his idea was as simple and beautiful as the idea of death. If he was to leave his life unfinished, and confess thereby that it had got into a tangle that he could never hope to sort out, it was clearly his duty to make some farewell gesture to life before going; for he loved life, though he had failed at it. And what better gesture could he make than to remove some blot from the surface of the earth by taking one hateful being with him into oblivion? He had no need to fear any punishment—it would be simple to make an end of himself before they came to catch and hang him—and he could use this immunity to despatch someone who rendered the sacred mystery of life hideous and offensive. All he had to do was to provide an answer to the question, "*Who is there, among my acquaintance, of whom it could truthfully be said that the world would be a cleaner place without him?*"

Mentally Edgar passed in review the people he disliked. In place of the acute nausea this process usually brought on, he felt now a radiant calm and satisfaction. "One of you bastards is in for it," he chuckled joyfully, rubbing his palms together. He picked up the fountain pen.

For a few minutes he was lost in thought. The trouble at first seemed to be an *embarras de richesse*, for the death of almost everyone he had come in contact with in the last few years would be, from some points of view, an excellent thing. But gradually he became aware of the real problem. Not one of them was really worthy of the dignity. They were petty, evil and stunted, but not dangerous enough. Furthermore, this thing, to yield the right kind of satisfaction, must be conducted on a high moral level. It was not enough for him, personally, to dislike the victim; this, after all, was a farewell present to life, on the eve of his departure. It was to be both his apology and his justification.

"DEATH DESTROYS A MAN," he wrote in large letters on the still virgin paper, "BUT THE IDEA OF DEATH SAVES HIM."

It was for him to see to it that the idea of death, his own imminent death, should save him from all suspicion of pettiness and personal vendetta. And this immediately ruled out most of the people he would have liked to exterminate. Stimms, for instance. There he sat, like a puffed-up toad behind his ornate desk, too stupid to conceal the fact that he relished every tiny gratification of that power-instinct which drove him along through life. "I don't like having to draw your attention to this, Banks," he had said only the other day, "but the situation in the profession has changed a good deal since you came here. It's what they call an employer's market now. There are several hundred Arts graduates out of work. So one doesn't have to, if you get my meaning, put up with what one can get, not any longer. If a man is, shall we say, a bit idiosyncratic about things, a bit inclined to drag his feet when it comes to putting his shoulder to the wheel for the good of the school, well, he's what they call expendable, in the present state of affairs." And he had vibrated with pleasure at this chance to crack the whip. Musing over a long line of such incidents, Edgar was inclined to write the name of Stimms on his list, but he made, after all, no movement. Abolish Stimms, and someone exactly similar would spring up out of the mud, for the system which manufactured such articles could replace an infinite number of murdered Stimmses; and what, in any case, did any of them matter?

It was the same with everyone who occured to him. There was Francis Jollet, with his pallid obscene face balanced on his pole of a body; Jollet whose fish's eyes, incredibly debased and debasing, never took on any glow of human warmth even when he was edging his way to the elbow of some flea-bitten little celebrity at a cocktail party. And yet, what was Jollet's crime against humanity? Only that he was without the feeble sparks of a moral sense that kept most people, even most people in the circles he frequented—the seamier side of the theatre and ballet world—from giving up their last rags of decent humanity. If nature had endowed Jollet with a sexual coldness and deadness that enabled

9

him to feel no repugnance at being all things to all men and most things to most women, at least he had shown gratitude by turning this negative gift to practical use.

Besides, Jollet was not anti-life in the sense that Edgar had in mind. He stood for obscenity, and obscenity is at least a form of life, compared with the kind of utter destructiveness which haunted Edgar as an ideal enemy.

"I must work at this," he said aloud. "I must lay down canons."

"Who is anti-life?" he wrote. "Who is he at whose approach everything vital becomes stupefied, values change places, love becomes pride of possession, courage becomes aggressiveness? Who is at war with the power that makes trees grow and wounds heal?"

A great burst of shouting came up from Flannery's party, and the cold rage in Edgar's heart forced him into action. From a box under the kitchen sink he took a hammer and a ball of string. The hammer had a tiny metal ring at the end of its handle, so that it could be hung up. To this he tied one end of the string, and, opening the window, unrolled the ball until the hammer hung level with Flannery's lighted and uncurtained window. Then he began to swing it steadily to and fro.

Three times the hammer, which was not a heavy one, banged against the glass without breaking it. All was going according to plan. Then the window was suddenly drawn up, and a man's arm reached out and grabbed. Edgar swung the hammer away, but on the return swing it crashed violently into the upper part of the window, shivering it into tiny pieces which fell, like frost shaken from a pine tree, in the light of the lamp-post on the pavement below.

"What the ruddy blazes are you playing at?" came a throaty roar from the street. "Drunken beasts," he heard a woman's voice through the mist. Startled into immobility, Edgar stared down at the two figures.

Then a girl's arm came through the open part of the window and grasped the hammer. "I've got it! I've got it!" she cried in a high unsteady voice which he recognized. Twisting round in the window, she looked up at him. It was Phyllis.

"Let go my hammer, please," he said.

"You let go," she said slowly. Speech was not easy after a couple of hours at Flannery's parties.

10

How utterly senseless it all was, and how emblematic of the life he had decided to leave behind! In a petty way, she had betrayed him by coming to hold revel with that loathsome mob in the room below, so soon after their parting; in a petty way, he had tried to interrupt their fun, and it had brought them together in a doubly petty way—no, it was pettiness *squared*; he holding the string, she the hammer, while the dank London air gnawed at their bones.

"Phyllis," he said, feeling utterly foolish, holding the string in a tight straight line. "Phyllis, this may be our last conversation together—don't you want to say anything to me?"

She coughed deeply, as if about to vomit. "A parcel of bloody drunks," shouted the man on the pavement. Phyllis dribbled out a white ball of spittle which fell gracefully down towards him.

"Do' want convers-ation," she said. "Want the hammer. 'Shbeautiful hammer. Shmine. I found it!"

"Keep it," he said. "Keep it for a souvenir."

"I'll take it—bed with me. Shouvenir," she said, looking up at him again.

"You know what you can do with it," he said, and let the string fall. He shut the window.

WHO IS ANTI-LIFE? asked the writing on the paper. "I am," he said heavily, staring down at it. DEATH DESTROYS A MAN, it said in capitals, BUT THE IDEA OF DEATH SAVES HIM.

"Then let it save me," he said. "Let it save me soon."

He put his coat on and went down the stairs.

The restaurant had been crowded earlier on, and now, though it was almost empty, the heat and the stale smells of tobacco and human breath remained as a testimony to the existence of a peak hour. Soon it would be closing, and the two blousy waitresses were frankly allowing their fatigue and boredom to appear as they dumped platefuls of twice-cooked inferior food before the moody late-comers; they had even given up crossing out from the menu the dishes that were "off", but this did not inconvenience Edgar, who knew by long experience that there would be, at this hour, nothing "on" but corned-beef rissoles, a spoonful of greens boiled to rags and tasting of soda, and perhaps a chunk of waxy ice-cream to follow. He settled spiritlessly into a corner seat.

How glad he felt, as he looked round, that he would soon be

11

free of it all! This place, with its rough-cast yellow walls running with condensed moisture, its rickety tables covered with dirty cloths and surmounted by furry sauce-bottles and squalid overflowing ash-trays, presided over by a couple of slatterns whose off-white aprons blended perfectly with their pasty cheeks, seemed to typify his whole environment. London was full of places like this; so were the provinces; while as for the country towns and villages, they did not rise even to this parody of communal feeding; in any town with less than ten thousand inhabitants, there was, after eight o'clock, nothing to put in your belly except the lukewarm beer of the local pub. And the point of these horrible places was a subtle one; what made them so repulsive was not simply bad management, not simply the docility of the poor wretches who fed there, but a deeply-rooted moral idea. This is what you get for not having a home of your own. If you don't like it, why aren't you sitting in a semi-detached villa with a plump smiling little wife—or a thin scowling one for that matter—serving up your dinner straight from the half-paid-for gas cooker? It serves you right, the horrible restaurants muttered in chorus, all up and down England: *it serves you right*.

"Tykin' the rissole?" asked the fatter of the two waitresses, lounging up to his table.

"Can't I have a boiled egg instead?" some perverse instinct prompted him to ask in reply.

"On'y rissoles on," she said indifferently.

"Welsh rarebit? Any form of cheese dish?"

"Rissoles," she said, making the word sound like an obscene expression of contempt.

"Oh, all right," he said with a weary explosion of breath. She stumped away.

What was the use of keeping himself alive anyway? The rubbish he was about to swallow would keep him moving and breathing for a few more hours in this hell, and what for? But there was his resolution, he thought, and brightened as its powerful magic worked. That was worth keeping alive for. He thought of Samson's end, but the story had never appealed to him; to slaughter a whole templeful of people was surely wasteful. There must have been one or two decent ones among them who had not deserved to die. The whole thing was too redolent of the bitter tribal warfare that seemed to be the main preoccupation of the Old Testament. "The Good Book," he murmured aloud, and smiled wanly. Crash! There's a couple of thousand tons of masonry for you! Bang, wallop—this is the best we can do till the bombing plane gets itself invented! No, no; his way was better. And yet it had something of the same sacerdotal quality; he would murder for high motives, in defence of life.

The waitress had placed two rissoles, looking like half-warmed gobbets of donkey's dung, in front of him. He took up his knife and held it poised over them. Stonehenge. When the sun falls across the victim's breast, the priest will strike.

"Let's carve him as a dish fit for the gods," he said aloud.

Then, as if to parody the shaft of sunlight he had imagined, a shadow fell across his plate. It flickered away, and another followed it. Two newcomers, on their way to a table, had passed between him and the nearest lamp.

"There's no doubt that the time is absolutely ripe," one of them said in a voice he recognized. "Sir Rufus is absolutely determined to act soon."

Years ago, casting about in his mind for an adjective that applied to this voice, Edgar had decided that "wet" was the best one. It sounded as if the man's vocal chords were vibrating in a bath of saliva. Being also rather high-pitched and finicking, it was altogether in accord with the man's name, which was Rollo Philipson-Smith.

Philipson-Smith sat down with his companion only two tables away. His proximity had the same effect on Edgar as a sore thumb: the more he wished to ignore it, the more insistently it thrust itself upon his consciousness. If his food had been worth concentrating his attention on, things might have been different; but even the sight and sound of Philipson-Smith were preferable to, or at any rate no worse than, the taste, temperature and texture of the rissoles. Poised between the two, Edgar perceived more clearly than ever the advantages of suicide.

Not that Philipson-Smith did not do his best; that had to be conceded. Endowed by nature with a degree of repulsiveness rarely met with even in London, he had made every effort, not, indeed, to mitigate this repulsiveness, but to stylize it in the manner that would show him to what he considered the best advantage. His figure was ill-proportioned, with absurdly short legs, but he held himself stiffly erect so as to give it some approach

13

to dignity. At thirty, his hair was already thinning, and of an undistinguished colour, but he had it carefully cut so as to sweep back horizontally above his ears, and finish in a neatly-combed roll at the back of his neck, giving him something of the look of an Oxford "blood" of the Oscar Wilde period. His hands were hideous, with short spatulate fingers, but he manicured them carefully and wore a tastefully designed signet ring. He had, it was evident, no natural taste in clothes, but he had taken pains to study minutely the clothes of men he wished to resemble, and to discover the names of their tailors.

It was also evident that this care had begun early in his life; he had the unmistakable facial cast of a person with projecting front teeth, yet his teeth did not actually project so as to be visible when his mouth was closed. Obviously his parents had been sensible enough to consult a good dentist, who had fixed a wire round the teeth to hold them back while his face had not yet taken its final shape.

Yes, everything that could be done for Rollo Philipson-Smith had been done. And yet it seemed to Edgar, as he studied the man covertly between forkfuls, that this had, after all, not been sufficient. It was impossible, for instance, to do anything about his eyes, which were very small. Sunk deeply into his face, much too close together, at the top of his rather flat nose, they conveyed a suggestion of the orang-outang; a resemblance that Philipson-Smith might have carried off better had he possessed the physical strength and agility of that creature. Further, the orang-outang is not normally clean-shaven; Philipson-Smith was clean-shaven, in the technical sense of that word, but nature had been too lavish of the dark stubble that formed about his jowls, so that a mere two or three hours after shaving he developed a dark smear about the lips which made him look, through no fault of his own, treacherous and ill-conditioned. The effect, Edgar decided, was as if some practical joker had crept up on Philipson-Smith as he took a nap in an armchair, and laid on this sinister shading with a soft lead pencil. Amid the dark shadows his mouth seemed unnaturally conspicuous, which again was a pity, for it was unpleasantly moist, and pouted in a way that suggested petulance and undisciplined sensuality. He wore suede shoes, and had two slits cut into the back of his jacket to indicate that he came of the propertied class who were accustomed to ride horses.

14

Finishing his second rissole, Edgar decided that he had been right to dislike Philipson-Smith. Years ago, when Edgar had first come to live in London, they had met several times at parties. Philipson-Smith at that time had thought of himself as a poet, or at least proclaimed at every opportunity, real or fancied, that he so thought of himself. He had contributed now and again to the smaller and less strictly edited literary magazines. Edgar had occasionally seen these contributions, but had never found much to admire in them. They made lavish use of the more esoteric stage-properties of Roman Catholicism (Philipson-Smith called himself an Anglo-Catholic, but he was not above allowing a certain confusion of the two to appear in his work; he would, it was understood, have liked to "go over", but he knew how converts were regarded in the Catholic circles to which he aspired, and he preferred the safe, if limited, dividends of the native branch, which was sufficiently chic for all practical purposes). The general import of his poems was always that the religion to which he claimed to adhere was a fashionable and exclusive secret society, well furnished with passwords and signs which were intended to be unintelligible to the rabble. By adopting a sufficiently haughty attitude towards modern agnostic civilization in general, and the poor in general, and the poor in purse most of all, and then spicing the mixture with a generous sprinkling of quasi-symbolic images, of which the Fish, the Bird, and Bread were his three overworked favourites, his poems managed to create a vague but (to some tastes) satisfying atmosphere of mystery and preoccupation with Higher Things. In a very literal sense, these Higher Things did actually exist for Philipson-Smith, who had realized early in life that to have the reputation of an esoteric religious poet was an invaluable aid to social climbing. Of late years, having ridden as far on the moving staircase of poetry as it would take him, he had quietly abandoned it. But even during his brief poetic career, his bardic pretensions had failed to conceal his essential lack of sensibility exactly as now, under Edgar's scrutiny, the signet ring failed to conceal the vermicular flabbiness of the finger it encircled, or the careful arrangement of the hair to atone for the ugly shape of the skull beneath.

His companion looked several years younger. He had sandy hair and a long, bony face which ended, surprisingly, in a weak chin. He appeared to be drunk, but it may have been only his general air of vacuity and silliness which gave this impression.

"A'm naturally in seepathy with Sir Rufus on a' these matters," Edgar heard him say. "Wha' we need is a retairn, eh, a retairn . . ."

"Yes, yes," cut in Philipson-Smith, evidently despising the man and tolerating him only as an audience. "All we have to do is to make one determined effort, co-ordinated throughout all our international centres, to . . ."

"A retairn," continued the Scot loudly and stubbornly, "to the tradeetional, eh, the tradeetional vairtues." He passed his hand meditatively over his receding chin as gravely as if it had been a long jutting one.

Watching this pair, Edgar tried to reach a final decision as to which of them he disliked most. Without much hesitation, he decided that it was Philipson-Smith. For one thing, he knew him, and had positive proof of his arrogance and love of bullying to add to the already convincing testimony of his appearance. Then again, his Scotch companion was so obviously contemptible; with all the heavy persistence of his race, he lacked its courage and solidity, and this rendered him less dangerous than a man of energy and decision—evil energy and misguided decision—like Philipson-Smith. It was clear from their conversation that Philipson-Smith needed a jackal, and, having found a candidate for the office, had invited him out to dinner in order to discuss some concrete proposal with him; it seemed that he was offering to get him a job in some kind of organization.

The waitress had at last shambled as far as the table where the two sat. Philipson-Smith looked up at her coldly.

"We'll have a bottle of wine—let me order that to begin with," he said.

"We're not licensed," she muttered, stifling a yawn.

"Well, you can send out for it," he snapped.

She showed no sign of having heard. Edgar prepared to enjoy the spectacle of the two of them fighting it out. He pushed his empty plate to one side and leaned forward with his elbows on the table.

"Did you hear what I said? Let me see you send someone out for a bottle of wine before I order anything to eat."

"We don't serve nothink like that 'ere. No wine," she explained, not without a certain kindliness, as one might explain some obvious point to a child or a senile person.

16

"Listen," said Philipson-Smith quietly and dangerously. "Never mind what you do and don't do. I came here for service and I want service. It's perfectly simple for you to send out for a bottle of wine, and that's what you're going to do—understand?"

He held her eyes with his own, and exerted the full force of his will upon her. For an instant she wavered.

"I s'pose Bert could go," she said irresolutely.

"Never mind who could go," said Philipson-Smith, pressing his advantage. "I don't want to learn all the details of how you run the business. I want a bottle of wine on this table, and I want it within ten minutes."

"Sauce!" exclaimed the second waitress in the background.

"Naw, there's sarce here a'ready; it's wine we want," said the Scotchman to her. He smiled in enjoyment of his own brilliance.

"Bert!" shouted the first waitress plaintively. "Bert!"

A tall, thin youth of eighteen, with pimples and a dirty apron, came out of the kitchen. A waft of hot air, laden with the vile smell of the horse-oil they were using for frying, came with him.

"Wancer boller wine," said the waitress, pointing to Philipson-Smith. "Wabbout you gonnout geddi?"

"Cor sufferin' Moses," Bert cried. He seemed thunderstruck. "Me go out, *me*? Wabbout my perishin' assma? Sryne-in'. Srynin' like sufferin' bleedin' Niagara." He looked plaintively from one to another of the company. "I got assma, perishin' bad assma," he said to Philipson-Smith.

Edgar had never until that moment seen anything so evil as the look that crossed Philipson-Smith's face. His lips tightened and receded, not far, but far enough to expose the tips of his teeth, and his eyes became pin-points of rage and hatred, glaring at Bert with terrible venom. In an instant Edgar understood the full extent of the depth and darkness of Philipson-Smith's hatred of modern democratic civilization. In the eighteenth century he would have been able, unchallenged and unpunished, to strike Bert across the face with his riding-whip. In the middle ages, a few words to the local dictator would have sufficed to get him beaten and set down to cool in the stocks, to teach him that the lower orders had no right to suffer from asthma. In the nineteen-thirties, if they had been citizens of the right country, Bert would have been chained up in a concentration camp, with Philipson-Smith marching up and down swinging a whip. But here and now,

17

in England, they had to settle it man to man. Philipson-Smith was two stone heavier than Bert, and in better physical shape through not having to spend his days and nights in a stinking kitchen. He rose from his chair and seized Bert by the front of his thread-bare pullover.

"Get outside and fetch that wine," he growled. "Go on, outside. You're employed here, you understand? You're employed here to serve the customers." He doubled his free hand into a fist and drew it back in menace.

With a rush of blood to the head, Edgar jerked himself upright. His chair clattered to the ground. He stepped forward and took hold of Philipson-Smith's elbow, gripping it hard.

"To hell with that caper, Smith," he said harshly. "You can't send an asthmatic kid out in the pouring rain."

Philipson-Smith swung round.

"So you're here, are you?" he sneered. "And kicking into your own goal as usual. How d'you think we're ever going to get any decent service out of these scum unless we're firm with them?"

"Aye, the scum," put in the Scot drunkenly from where he sat.

"I'm not saying you haven't got some right on your side," said Edgar. "The service in this place is bloody awful, the food's filth, and they make a silly fuss about going out to get anything to drink to make it seem palatable."

"Sauce!" muttered the second waitress again. She could get a lot out of a vocabulary of one word.

"But that isn't the way to go about it, throwing your weight about like a bloody bully," Edgar went on fiercely.

"Ah, that's typical of you and your damned softness," shouted Philipson-Smith. "It's no good trying to look for any co-operation from men like you. I tell you, Banks, things'll be a lot easier when all your type are——" he paused.

"Behind barbed wire? Or in front of a firing squad? Which were you going to say?"

Two views of human conduct faced each other on the shabby carpet of the restaurant. One, fiercely sure of itself; the other already undermined, ready to give up, planning even now to abandon the struggle, yet twitching into movement by a reflex action in the face of this challenge.

"Mister Charley! Mister Charley!" called the first waitress in a high aggrieved voice.

18

Edgar relaxed. The proprietor of this place, whose Christian name or surname, no one knew which, was Charley, had been the heavyweight champion of the Notting Hill district a decade earlier. Physically, he stood in the same relation to Philipson-Smith as Philipson-Smith did to Bert.

The kitchen door swung open on its worn-out spring, and out padded a bald-headed man with the arms of a gorilla. A cloud of stinking air danced attendance on him like a boxer's second.

"Oo's makin' trouble?" he rumbled placidly.

"'E set on me," whimpered Bert, "Jes' fer I didn' wanner go outside in the perishin' rain, me with me perishin' assmer always worse this timer year."

Gorilla faced orang-outang between the tables.

"'Sright, 'e set on 'im," confirmed the waitress. Her colleague, silent, framed the word "sauce" with her lips.

"Outside, mister," said primate to primate.

"I'll lodge a complaint about the service in this place. I'll get your catering licence revoked," said Philipson-Smith.

"Out bloody *side*," said Mr. Charley. He indicated the door.

Philipson-Smith turned to Edgar. Beneath the dark smear on his cheeks, he was white with frustrated rage.

"I'll leave you to your friends," he sneered.

"You won't be lonely," said Edgar. He nodded towards the weak-chinned moron still sitting at the table. "You can take your crocodile-bird with you."

As Philipson-Smith started for the door, the Scotchman stood up and followed him. "It's naething but what I'd expect fra a lo' of bluidy degenerits. Bluidy English," he said over his shoulder.

"You keep your ruddy sauce," said the second waitress, revealing an unexpected ability to build a connected sentence round her favourite word.

Mr. Charley and Bert went back into their inferno, and Edgar settled down at his table with a mixture of emotions. It had been an unsatisfying experience, for he felt so little inspired by the party he had defended. After all, it was a fact that the place was a sullen, horrible hole, the food was hog-wash, the waitresses were cows, and Mr. Charley and Bert, though shining angels by comparison with Philipson-Smith, could by no effort of the imagination be described as verray parfit gentil knights.

19

"Those that I fight I do not hate," he murmured, "And those I guard I do not love."

But even as he formed the words he knew that they would never do as a summary of the case. It might be true, or at least arguable, that he did not love Bert, Mr. Charley, and the waitresses; but it was demonstrably untrue that he did not hate Philipson-Smith. He had a quick mental vision of Philipson-Smith's face, expressing in its malignant scowl everything that had for two thousand years been recognized as hateful, every cruelty, every denial of human justice and wisdom.

Impatiently he stood up, paid his bill, hurried into his coat, out, and along the soaking streets. Arriving at his flat, he burst into the living-room without waiting to take off his wet coat. There was still a confused murmur of noise from Flannery's party, but as he seized the paper some chance caused a sudden hush to fall, as if the moment of solemnity must be observed.

Edgar wrote: "1. Kill Philipson-Smith. 2. Kill self." He paused, his brow creased with thought, then added, "3. Remember stop milk."

II

"Is that you, Mr. Stimms?" asked Edgar into the telephone.

"Speaking," came the familiar toad's croak.

"This is Banks. I'm afraid I shan't be coming to school for a bit. I'm ill."

"I'm sorry to hear that, Banks," said Stimms, meaning (and conveying) that he was sorry to hear that Edgar was not going to the school, not that he was sorry to hear he was ill.

"Well, don't say it as if you thought I ought to wait till the holidays to be ill," Edgar could not help retorting.

There was a short pause, as if Stimms were wondering whether to rebuke Edgar for his insolence, and then deciding to make allowances for him in case he had, for instance, a high fever that made him not quite himself.

"What is the nature of your illness, Banks?" he asked.

"The doctor hasn't diagnosed it yet," Edgar answered.

"But what's the matter? What are your symptoms?"

Edgar had not intended to bait Stimms at all. Indeed, the whole business of going to the trouble of lying to him, a thing that would in future be strictly taboo during the last few days or weeks of his life, had been out of respect for the headmaster's feelings. The sacrificial victim, marked down for murder, should be murdered; but the others should be treated with tolerance, even with a kind of distant kindliness. Their little concerns, their tiny insect-bites, did not bother him any longer.

Nevertheless, it was hard to shake off a five-year habit of intense dislike of Stimms. During those years, the impulse to kick Stimms in the stomach had been so frequently aroused that it had finally taken its place among his reflexes. Not his natural reflexes, such as shutting his eye when a speck of dirt entered it, but his

21

acquired reflexes, such as swerving his bicycle towards the correct side of the road on hearing a motor-horn. It was just as automatic and just as difficult to restrain.

"What's the matter? Why don't you answer my question?" came the voice of Stimms, reduced to a thin mechanical parody by the hateful instrument.

"I was vomiting," Edgar explained.

"I didn't hear anything."

"I was vomiting silently. I'm one of the rare people that can."

"Do you mean your stomach is upset?"

Edgar was getting tired of this inquisition. He had done his best for Stimms.

"Excuse me, but I'll have to ring off now," he said politely. "There's a policeman coming to arrest me for vomiting in a telephone box."

"How can you be well enough to go out to a telephone box?" asked Stimms keenly, revealing the grasp of significant detail that had got him where he was. "Besides, I thought you had a telephone in your own place."

"So I have," said Edgar. "I'm using it now. It was the other day I vomited in the telephone box. Now a policeman has come to my own flat with a warrant to arrest me. He's standing beside me now. *That's right, sir,*" he said in a deep voice, "*I'm just going to take him off to the station. Come along o' me, young feller,*" he added, turning slightly away from the mouthpiece. "But officer, I'm too ill to go out," he said in his own voice, making it sound pathetic and appealing. "*You looks all right to me,*" he said in the deep voice. "*It's my belief he's shamming, sir, trying to avoid arrest,*" he added into the mouthpiece,

A wordless cry came along the wire from Stimms. The whole thing was rapidly becoming too much for him. Edgar's imitation of a policeman was feeble and unconvincing, and his whole story obviously fantastic; but on the other hand it was utterly impossible for Stimms to reverse the habits of a lifetime so far as to believe that a member of his staff would deliberately trifle with him on a Monday morning at nine o'clock. There was only one solution left open; he himself was going off his head, or, at the very best, having a nightmare.

"Take your hands off me!" cried Edgar in a voice that conveyed both fear and menace. "*Now then, now then,*" he said,

22

"you'd better come quietly or it'll be the worse for you." "This is an outrage!" he cried, banging the telephone receiver against the wall several times to indicate that a struggle was going on, and also to produce an unpleasant sensation in Stimm's eardrums. "Let me go, *No, come along o' me*, I appeal to you, Stimms," he shouted. "Ring up Scotland Yard at once, ten Downing Street, House of Commons, Fleet Street, anybody—don't let them do this to me, it's totalitarianism! *Will you come quietly or do you want me to use this*? You wouldn't dare, *ha, ha, wouldn't I*? Don't let them do it, Sti——" he shouted, then collapsed heavily as the imaginary truncheon thudded on the side of his head. He was so wrapped up in his performance that he actually crashed forward on to his face after leaning inertly on the wall for a few seconds. The telephone receiver swung limply to and fro above his motionless body. A faint quacking indicated that Stimms was saying something, but the victim of the outrage was past caring. He lay still, imaging a dark stain spreading over the carpet. . . .

Then, suddenly, the face of Rollo Philipson-Smith flashed into Edgar's mind. Startled, he stood up quickly, replaced the still twittering receiver, and stood grimly considering. His grotesque play-acting was all very well. He could afford to fool about in that way because the reality he was guying did not exist in England. And the reason it did not exist was because men like Philipson-Smith were, for the moment, kept under. His mind went back to the scene in the restaurant. "Sir Rufus is determined to act soon." Whoever this Sir Rufus was, Edgar had a swift and horrible clairvoyance about this action of his. He knew, irrationally but with absolute certainty, that it would involve, at some stage, such actions as clubbing a man on the side of the head as he struggled to shout into a telephone.

He went into the sitting-room. Lighting a cigarette, he stared gloomily out of the window at the February sleet, his face set and grim. What is the nature of your illness? The doctor hasn't diagnosed it yet. His little joke had left a nasty taste behind it, the taste of Philipson-Smith.

"Dear Philipson-Smith," Edgar wrote,
"I am sorry that we should have had rather an unpleasant little scene in the restaurant on Saturday night, particularly as I have hoped for some time that we might renew our acquaintance

23

and improve it somewhat. I think we see eye to eye about many things ('Like blistering hell we do,' he said aloud), and as for the points on which we don't altogether agree, it would be pleasant, wouldn't it ('NO') to talk them over and see where our difference lies. ('I'll poison you like a rat,' he said, 'like the slimy rat you are.') Would you care to drop in to my place one evening and have a drink? ('I've got something that'll just suit you.')

"I feel that you have interesting views, which I have never entirely understood, and if you felt like discussing them with me, you would at least have an attentive audience."

Edgar paused and thought of the scene; Philipson-Smith's corpse, sagging limply over one side of the armchair, with the glass still clutched in his ungainly hand; and himself dead likewise, sitting bolt upright on the sofa, staring across with sightless eyes as if listening carefully to a detailed argument. It was all so neat. Philipson-Smith would never suspect that the brandy was poisoned, because he would put the poison in the *bottle*. Then they would both drink a fatal dose in the same instant. His own dying pangs would be comforted by the sight of this evil being undergoing the same torment. There were, of course, more painless ways of committing suicide, but he felt it to be fitting that he should not condemn Philipson-Smith to anything he was afraid to undergo himself. There would be something cowardly, and unworthy of the high dignity of his task, in leaving his enemy to squirm on the carpet in agony while he himself took a nice comfortable overdose of barbiturates. No, they should both go out through the same door.

Absent-mindedly, he wrote in conclusion, "Looking forward to poisoning you." Then, realizing what he had done, he tore up the paper with a weary sigh and began again. It was a humiliating letter to have to write once, let alone twice. All this crawling, these falsehoods! But any other way was useless. As it was, he had decided to write rather than telephone, because he knew his voice would have failed him and refused to utter the necessary amount of flattery and apology. He knew well that Philipson-Smith, who thought in terms of power, associated only with people who were rich and powerful enough to give him a horrible pleasure in abasing himself before them, or else pliable and insignificant enough to abase themselves before him in turn. Of equal companionship he knew nothing. Since Edgar could obviously not qualify for the first of these categories, there remained nothing for him but the second. Already, his carefree ideal of living in the present was beginning to seem less easy. For a moment he was tempted to throw up his noble resolve, and devote his last days to a debauch instead; he could draw out what remained of his money—it was enough to last for a few weeks— and spend it on drink and women. Shrugging, he dismissed the base impulse when it had barely risen in his mind. That would be to allow the idea of death to *destroy* him. Better far to go out like some hero of Elizabethan tragedy, with the body of his enemy— his enemy and life's—safely pinned, like a beetle on a piece of cardboard, where he could see it.

He wrote the letter out, correctly this time, and, having sealed and stamped it, went out to the post. As the envelope fell into the engulfing darkness of the box, to lie there safe and warm and irretrievable, he felt a shiver pass through his body. It was done! The rest of his journey was short and plainly marked; he knowingly, and the enemy of life unknowingly, were tied together, moving in step, steadily, the way that they must go.

Meanwhile, time hung heavily. Until Philipson-Smith chose to answer his note and come along to be poisoned, his days were without occupation. He went out for aimless walks, but the vile weather in the dingy, noisy streets always drove him indoors again after a few minutes; sometimes he would pick up a book and try to read a few pages, but there seemed no point in such activities; he did not want to be bothered with thrillers or anything else that promised pure entertainment, and as for serious reading, from which he might hope to learn something, to gain in human wisdom, what was the point of it? He already knew the few simple truths he needed to know; it would be folly to waste his last few days in amassing knowledge and experience as if he were going to live for another forty years.

On the third morning after sending the note, the postman came and went, bringing no answer, and Edgar sat dejectedly by the electric fire, with his breakfast cup and plate unwashed on the table, staring gloomily out of the window. He felt like a man in the condemned cell; and, indeed, in one respect the comparison

25

did hold good, for he had given someone else the power to fix the time of his death. He could not turn the key and come out, to walk his last hundred yards, when it suited him; Philipson-Smith must be, unknowingly, the gaoler who came for him on the last morning, bringing with him, in his own detestable person, the whole retinue—prison chaplain, governor, doctor, chief juror and guards. This train of meditations did little to raise Edgar's drooping spirits as the rain blew in gusts against the pane.

At about half-past twelve, as he was listlessly preparing to go out and get a meal, his bell rang. Someone down in the street had read the card and pressed the correct button. Taking his overcoat, he hurried down. Perhaps it was a note from his victim, delivered by hand. He was surprised, on opening the door, to see a tousel-headed urchin whom he recognized from school.

"Please, sir, Benton said to deliver this," the boy squeaked.

"Thank you, Jenkinson; wait a moment for the answer, will you?"

He opened the envelope and read the note.

"Dear Mr. Banks," it ran,

"We are sorry to hear of your indisposition, which we trust will soon be terminated, and permit of your return.

Yours sincerely,

R. T. Benton.

P.S. I suppose it is now inevitable that we suspend our arrangements for Saturday night."

Edgar turned back to Jenkinson.

"Please tell him it'll be all right for Saturday, and that the arrangements aren't to be altered," he said. "Off you go now, and don't forget."

"No, sir," cried the lad. He turned on his heel, extended his arms at a slight backward angle from his body, so as to represent the swept-back wings of a supersonic fighter, and scampered rapidly away. A high-pitched whine arose from his four turbojets as he banked steeply, gaining height at the rate of four hundred feet per second, and circled to avoid an approaching pram. Refuelling in the air, he passed from view round the corner of the street, headed for his first base in Greenland. Beneath him the pitiless waters of the arctic sea lay in wait as far as the eye could reach.

26

Edgar walked on towards the restaurant. He was touched, undeniably touched. This Benton was a Sixth Form boy, the leading spirit of a small group of awkward, shy, argumentative youths who represented the school's intelligentsia. They were naïve beyond belief, ignorant beyond comprehension, and given to taking refuge in a jarring pretentiousness. The note he held in his hand contained the whole essence of their gaucherie, with its stilted phraseology, a mixture of business English and prim, spinsterly words like "indisposition". And yet, in its blundering attempt at delicacy—putting the request, its real object, in a P.S. as if it were an afterthought—the note also conveyed the clumping, bull-calf brand of decency and genuineness that never failed to go to Edgar's heart. It was his habit, once a month during term, to invite these half-dozen louts up to his flat, to drink coffee and wrangle over questions that interested them. These evenings were always a mixed experience for Edgar. On the one hand, of course, they were a bore, and naturally so, for the conversation was dogged by every possible disadvantage—ignorance, social awkwardness, invincible silence on the part of some and exaggerated loquacity on the part of others. On the other hand, he found them deeply sustaining and soothing. It seemed to him, though he freely admitted the possibility of his being wrong on both counts, that he was doing something for these youths which was vitally necessary, and that as human material they were worth saving. Very few of them would be going on to the University; all they had before them, for the most part, was a couple of years in the Army and then the dreary, stifling round of an existence divided between office and suburb, in which only two problems would be counted as "real"; at the office, how to push out the man next above and grab his job; at home, how to keep up with the neighbours in appearances. In a few months they would be branded on the forehead and lose all disposition to question their fate, but just at this moment they had reached that critical stage in their growth when they had expanded without finally hardening, when their minds, adult in capacity, were juvenile in receptiveness. It had seemed to Edgar that by seizing this opportunity, even so feeble and uncertain a hammer as himself could work on their hot iron. He might be able to give them just that spark of subversiveness and enquiry that would turn, before it was too late, a few of the robots into men; one or two of the waxworks in the endless dreary Madame Tussaud's of modern England might begin to move and speak, and it would be his doing. It was an uncertain, intermittent faith, and certainly not enough to provide a positive incentive to live, or balance out the numbing weight of item 3 on his list of reasons for suicide. But it was the one tiny scrap of something positive that his wretched *métier* afforded him, and, while he waited for his Sydney Carton's guillotine, he could be worse employed than in keeping it going.

Accordingly the next Saturday evening he forgot his feverish impatience at still not having heard from Philipson-Smith in the pleasure of sitting in the centre of a clumsily eager circle of disputants. This evening, to his relief, they had kept off religion and politics, and the conversation concerned itself with knowledge.

"What it always seems to me," mumbled a stocky black-browed youth whose chief value to his Alma Mater was as a full-back, "is, that you can't know *everything*. You've gotter *select*. There's a lot of things you might spend years finding out about, and then, at the end of it, what it seems to me, is, you might find you might of spent that time better on something *else*. It isn't all the same amount of *use*, it seems to me."

"Ah, yes, but what do you call *use*? Useful for what?" put in a thin fair boy whose keen face and restless eyes gave him a false appearance of shrewdness; actually he was merely argumentative. "How can you know before you know something whether something's going to be useful to know; eh?"

"Well, it seems to me," the full-back grunted, imperturbably, "that you can look *round*, you can make a *selection*, you can say, this is going to be in my line, this other's going to be in someone *else's* line."

Edgar cut in, to keep the conversation from stagnating: "But aren't there any basic disciplines? Isn't there anything that we all ought to know about?"

"Classics," said Benton firmly. As the one boy in the school who had elected to devote himself to Latin and Greek, he was as touchy about their superiority to all other studies as any faithful member of a declining church.

"It seems to me you were bound to say that," said the full-back in his strong bass voice. "What it seems to me, is, you've decided, this suits *me*, *I* want to know what these men thought and what

28

they did. So everybody's gotter decide the same. Now *why*. Tell me *why*." He looked at Benton amiably, yet as if preparing to seize his knees and throw him to the ground.

"Well, because it's all *based*, don't you see," cried Benton. He put down his coffee cup and leaned forward eagerly. When he matured he would be a handsome man, and already one could see, round the pimples, the good bone structure of his face. "All our civilization, it's *based* on what the Greeks and Romans . . . take law, take philosophy . . . look at architecture," he ended lamely, fighting to put his thoughts in order.

"Well, but what about mathematics?" said a boy who had not yet spoken. "Isn't that just as fundamental?"

"For technology, yes," sneered Benton.

"I don't think Jackson meant that," Edgar interposed again, to keep the peace, for 'technology' was a word of abuse in Benton's mouth. "I think he meant that if a knowledge of the ancient world is necessary because it underlies other kinds of knowledge, the same can be said of mathematics. And I think he's right."

"Well, but look here," began Benton excitedly. They all began to talk at once.

"The Greeks had mathematics; how d'you get round that?"

"I'm not *trying* to get round it——"

"Come, they must have known enough maths. to be able to build—to calculate the stresses and all that."

"What it seems to me, is——"

"The Greeks didn't have a symbol for zero."

"You can easily get along without knowing——"

"I didn't say they *couldn't* build. I said——"

"You can't have any mathematics worth knowing if you haven't got a symbol for zero. Anyone knows——"

Edgar looked, covertly, but with a flush of genuine pleasure, from one eager face to another. The evening was a success; he had been afraid at first that this might be one of the times when the talk refused to flow, and they broke up lamely at ten o'clock with nothing to remember from the occasion. But this was something worth having.

Their voices, impatiently running on in chorus, mounted higher, then were suddenly hushed as the bell shrilled.

As he went down the stairs to the street door, Edgar wondered who this could be. What a curse if it should turn out to be Philipson-Smith, calling for a sociable evening just when it would be impossible to murder him!

But why would it be impossible? What better setting could one ask for? he suddenly thought as he went down the second flight of stairs. On the contrary, it would be the ideal opportunity to arraign the criminal before a jury of the younger generation, to prove his guilt, sentence him and carry out the execution there and then. The boys would take a good deal of persuading, of course, before they would agree to sit by and watch a double death; but he did not doubt his ability to supply this persuasion. What a cue for oratory it would be, with the prisoner surrounded by a ring of intent, serious young faces, and the full-back leaning his back against the locked door to make escape doubly impossible. "It rests with you, gentlemen," Edgar rehearsed as he went down the third and last flight of stairs, "whether, in the face of his hatred of everything that it will be the business of your lives to foster and love, this man shall be allowed to continue his dangerous and unhappy existence."

He opened the street door. It was Phyllis.

"You must have rung the wrong bell," he said. "Flannery lives on the floor below me, don't you remember?"

He looked at her. She had done her hair differently, sweeping it back and gathering it into a tight bunch which stood out at the back of her head. She had also made up carefully, producing a smooth matt effect which gave no indication of whether it was human skin or linoleum that lay beneath. Her finger-nails and lips were painted some dark shade that looked purple in the lamplight.

"No, it was your bell I wanted to ring," she said, enunciating clearly and in a lofty, disdainful manner. "I want to come up and take some things I left behind in your flat."

Panic filled Edgar's chest and rose to his throat. Phyllis and the boys upstairs would never mix; it would be an inconceivable disaster to allow them to confront one another, with him as the only common factor. There would be no chance of passing her off as a relative or a casual acquaintance. He knew Phyllis's temperament too well for that; she would extract every ounce of pleasure from the humiliation she could cause him.

"Don't bother coming up," he said, trying to speak casually,

30

but revealing in his thick, anxious tone that it was terribly important to him. "I'll send you the things. I'll post them tomorrow morning and you'll get them on Monday."

She stared at him. He saw in her eyes the dawning realization that some accident had put her in a position of power.

"I'll come up and take them now," she said firmly, and walked past him into the narrow hall.

For an instant, as she brushed past him, he was tempted to grasp her wrist and hold her back. Surely it would be simple enough to put her out by force and slam the door? The idea died, of course, as soon as it was born. She would make a scene, and probably scream; Flannery would come out and throw all his energies into making the situation worse and worse. Probably it would be his idea of a joke to go into the witness-box and testify that he had seen Edgar commit an indecent assault on the girl. And even if he got her outside the door without incident, she would ring and ring at the bell. It was hopeless.

She marched on ahead of him, up the three flights, and he gloomily followed. Her hair was brown, and it struck him that the bun at the back of that erect, unforgiving head was very similar in size and shape to a boxing-glove with a heavyweight's fist inside it. He derived no pleasure from the comparison.

At the top of the second flight she turned and faced him, calling a halt so as to begin the process of putting him through his torture.

"You seem very anxious not to let me come up," she said. "Can I have three guesses? Is it a visitor?"

He was silent.

"I think that's right for guess number one," she said with cool enjoyment. "Guess number two—it's a *female* visitor. One you're rather anxious to impress. Still right?"

Edgar saw a ray of hope. There was just a chance, if he played a desperate game, of coming through this business.

"Look, Phyllis," he said, "I'll confess. It *is* a woman, but not quite the kind you think. I'd much rather you didn't come up, because, well, it would be very awkward. Not awkward for her, but awkward for you."

"Awkward for *me*? Why? What sort of woman is it you've got in?"

"It's a tart," he said.

31

She had been about to go on up the stairs, but now she halted and turned round.

"She's taken her clothes off and she's sitting by the electric fire," Edgar went on, speaking in a low, urgent voice.

Phyllis was taken aback. She leaned against the wall.

"*All* her clothes?" she asked in a frightened whisper.

Edgar nodded with a sorrowful impressiveness.

"Oh, you *men*," said Phyllis hotly. "You beastly, horrible men. You're all alike. You're all beastly, horrible *pigs*." She seemed about to burst into tears.

"I wouldn't go in, honestly," he said. "She might turn ugly. She hates being interrupted. I do too, don't you? I can't work with anyone looking over my shoulder."

"You beast," she whispered. "You degraded beast. To think— to think I let you——"

She stopped and whimpered softly. Edgar seized his opportunity.

"She's a powerfully built girl," he said. "She was a lady wrestler before she took this up. She'll tear you in pieces."

Phyllis suddenly straightened. "I'm not afraid of any horrible common prostitute," she snapped. "And I'm not afraid of you, either. I came here to get the things I left, and I'm not going without them." She turned to mount the stairs.

He took her wrist. "Phyllis," he said. He was sweating like a mule. "Phyllis, don't go in there. She'll use her nails on you. I couldn't protect you."

"You ought to be able to *control* her," she flung at him over her shoulder, dragging her wrist free. "She's your *servant*. She's here to do what you *pay* her to do."

She stamped up the remaining stairs. The door of Edgar's flat was open. She pushed through it and burst dramatically into the sitting-room.

The youths looked up at her in shy surprise, then awkwardly stood up. Curiosity and timidity were mingled in their glances.

Edgar came in.

"Miss Johnson, gentlemen," he said. "A friend of mine. She's called to pick up some things of hers."

Phyllis looked at him coldly and savagely.

"Very funny," she said. "Ve-ry funny."

At any rate, he had given her a shock, and drawn the first blood. But any consolation this might have brought him was very quickly swamped by the realization that she would now be more than ever determined to humiliate him. She stood still for a moment, collecting her wits, then stepped into the centre of the stage and began to act.

"Please do sit down, gentlemen," she said. "I'm terribly sorry—I seem to have interrupted a stag party."

Her manner combined two elements, both equally jarring to Edgar. The "I-trust-you-not-to-hurt-me-I'm-a-weak-female" manner was thinly smeared over a basic manner of brazen sexual provocation.

"I won't interrupt you for long," Phyllis went on. "I just had to call and pick up some things I left here." Turning to Edgar, she cooed, "You don't mind if I go into the bedroom, do you, Edgar?"

"I hardly think you'll find anything of yours in there," he tried, foolishly, to bluster.

It was the perfect opening for her, as he could see as soon as the words had left his mouth.

"*Don't* you?" she said in exaggerated mock surprise. She swept her glance round the circle of mute, staring adolescents. "You understand, don't you?" she appealed to them wordlessly with her eyes. "You see how pitifully he's trying to bluff?"

Part of the trouble was that she had dolled herself up so hideously, thought Edgar. After all, when he had first met her and had been attracted by her, she had been relatively simple in dress and behaviour. He had soon discovered the corruption and egotism that actually underlay this simplicity, but by that time he was in the net. And now, for this display, she had turned herself out in a way that transferred these qualities to the surface for all to see. It was too horrible.

Phyllis walked slowly, with a good deal of hip-play, to the bedroom door and disappeared. The youths stared, guiltily fascinated, at her back. Their faces showed the dreadful mixture of emotions common to their time of life—concupiscence, intense curiosity, equally intense guilt and fear. As the bedroom door closed behind her, they dropped their eyes, unable to meet each other's looks or Edgar's.

"Ah, these women," said Edgar. "Every time they call to see you they leave something behind, if it's only a copy of *Vogue* or an empty powder-case."

33

His words rang out falsely. The full-back had turned scarlet; Benton, by contrast, was very pale and looked in danger of a heart attack. Still, they tried to rally and assist him in keeping up the pretence that Phyllis had just looked in to pick up a few casual odds and ends, left behind on a social visit.

"My sister," Benton said in a tight, strained voice, "leaves her umbrella behind at every party she goes to. Always leaves it behind. She just doesn't seem to be able to remember——"

"Edgar," Phyllis called from the bedroom. She opened the door and looked out, drawing her face into an expression of pathetic bewilderment. "I thought I'd left my *best* pyjamas here. I can only find my *old* ones." She seemed to imply that after being cad enough to seduce her, he had taken her best pyjamas out and sold them for the price of a bottle of whisky.

"For God's sake," said Edgar roughly, "Have I got to be responsible for everything that any scatter-brained woman leaves in my flat?"

Wrong again, hideously wrong. He had given the impression that his flat was a second-hand clothes store of intimate garments left behind by a succession of misguided women. Once again, Phyllis had tricked him into leading with his chin, and she knew it.

"I don't know anything about that," she said, sweetly reasonable. "I'm only asking about *my* things." She disappeared into the bedroom.

Edgar drew a long breath. "Let me make some more coffee," he said. "I'm afraid there's no more fresh milk, but I've got a tin of condensed."

Hastily he strode into the kitchen and began messing about with water and saucepans. He made an unnecessary noise, encouraging the gas to roar and the taps to splash, and generally trying to impose a barrier between himself and the painful scene in the sitting-room. Hearing Phyllis call, "Where are my slippers, Edgar, please?" he even hummed a few bars of some popular tune, exactly like an over-acting character in a bad farce pretending not to hear someone speaking.

When he took the coffee in he knew at once that the worst had happened. Phyllis had completed her packing, rolling the articles in a sheet of newspaper. But instead of going she had taken a seat on the sofa next to Benton.

"Oh, good, some coffee!" she cried as Edgar entered. "I'm just

34

ready for some . . . Edgar, you don't mind if I stay and drink a cup of coffee before I go?"

It was a good thing, Edgar thought swiftly, that he had not yet prepared the poisoned brandy for Philipson-Smith. He felt at this moment that he would certainly have given Phyllis a dose, and that would have imported an element of the haphazard into his carefully-laid plans.

"What do you say, men?" he asked with false brightness. "Shall we let her stay and join in the discussion?"

Idiot, he could not have said anything more calculated to increase their embarrassment. They mumbled with their eyes on the carpet.

"Discussion?" she cried. "Oh, do tell me. Was it something terribly important?"

"We were talking about knowledge," muttered the boy who had spoken of mathematics.

"Ah, knowledge, knowledge," Phyllis said dramatically. "What a wonderful thing it is at your age—so many kinds of knowledge, of experience, just *waiting* for you."

It was quite clear what she meant. Edgar felt as if he had a tight rubber band round his throat, and that it was shrinking at lightning speed.

Phyllis turned her eyes on Benton. She had obviously picked him out as the most suitable prey.

"Don't you think," she said in a low, serious voice, "that the most valuable knowledge isn't always to be found in books? That it has to come from—from life as well?"

The poor lad was hypnotised. "Life," he said huskily.

"Yes, life brings us such wonderful lessons, doesn't it, often?" she said. Then, after a pause, "But perhaps you don't know that yet. Perhaps life hasn't started to show you what it's capable of."

"Oh, take him to the bedroom and get it over—we'll wait," Edgar felt like saying. Actually he was incapable of speech or movement.

"I better be going," said the full-back, standing up. There was a general shuffling of feet.

"Oh, *please* don't," cried Phyllis in mock distress. "You'll make me feel I've *driven* you away. . . . It's so seldom one gets an opportunity to discuss the things that *really* matter. . . ."

They looked at her hesitantly, indecision in their faces. But the full-back was getting into his overcoat.

"Got a long bus ride home," he said.

His action led the others to break away also. One by one they stood up, drank the last of their coffee, put on their coats. Edgar stood on the hearthrug, utterly miserable. His last session with them was in ruins, his reputation in their eyes utterly soiled. Not even the news of his death, when it reached them, would quite redeem this. "Queer chap, old Banks," they would say. "A bit of a one for the women, y'know. I dare say it was that drove him crackers in the end. Did I ever tell you about that puss we found in his place one night? She was a bit of all right," and the story would circulate, with additions, till it became added to the smoking-room repertory. As middle-aged men, sitting in hotel lounges with business cronies, they would still be recalling how Phyllis had chased Edgar round and round the sitting-room, screaming that he had ruined and then deserted her.

They were ready to go. He could not meet their eyes. "I'll see you down the stairs," he said tonelessly.

"Wait for me. I'm coming too," said Phyllis, gathering up her parcel. She took Benton's arm; Edgar saw Benton wince, yet not entirely with revulsion. She had got her claws into him, the boy would be sophisticated and ruined at an early age, and it would be his fault, his fault.

They clumped down the three flights, silently. Phyllis, holding on to Benton's arm, came last. *I ought to feel sorry for her,* he thought. *She's reached the age when she's attracted to young boys, her days of real happiness are over.* He tried to feel sorry for her, but without success.

Looking back, he saw her slip a piece of paper into his hand. "My telephone number," she said. Benton looked shell-shocked. But Edgar knew that after a struggle, a struggle which might go on for days or weeks, he would dial the number she had given him.

He opened the door and let them out.

"Good-night," he said.

"Good-night, Mr. Banks." "Thanks awfully, sir."

"Thanks for letting me come in, Edgar," Phyllis said smugly.

Their footsteps died. Standing at the foot of the stairs, Edgar felt an unfamiliar sensation; something was missing.

Then he remembered. It was the first time they had left without fixing the date of their next meeting.

On a freezing evening, ten days after sending his note, Edgar, in desperation, stood beside the telephone. It was clear that circumstances left him with no choice but to submit to one more humiliation. To accost Philipson-Smith by this means was a hateful thought because it involved exposing himself to the risk of frightful snubs and general offensiveness: still, what else could he do? Even though the telephone, with its horrible inhumanity, gave all the advantage to the aggressor, and his role this evening was defensive, even sycophantic. Muttering a curse, he dialled the number as the clock struck eight.

For a long time nobody answered, and he imagined the telephone standing on a heavy oak chest in the hall, near the front door, while the life of the household went on upstairs and some rickety old maid-of-all-work toiled up the steps from what had once been the servants' hall. Nearer and nearer she came, approaching the bewildering instrument cautiously—they did not use such things in houses when she was a girl, and in all these years she had never got used to it—and, before lifting the receiver to stop its angry shrilling, one would have said (or was it a trick of the half-light?) that she swiftly crossed herself, and her withered lips moved to mutter, "The houly mother of God save us from hurt and harm." Edgar's face took on a sympathetic expression as he imagined the poor, superstitious old drudge. His quarrel was not with her; he did not want her to be frightened of the terrible vengeance he carried. In his mind's eye he saw her bony fingers tremble slightly as they reached out to pick up the instrument and receive one more of the messages that were never for her.

Cheated once more by his over-imaginative habit of mind, he felt suddenly humiliated when the voice of Philipson-Smith flooded wetly along the wire, enunciating the number of his telephone.

"Oh, ah, this is Banks here," he began miserably.

Philipson-Smith seemed to have nothing to say to this: at all events he remained silent for so long that Edgar decided to speak again. As he did so, however, it became clear that Philipson-Smith had merely intended a long and insolent pause, for he began to speak at the same instant as Edgar, with the result that they both stopped again, foiled.

After another long pause, Edgar said, "I was just wondering if you'd had my letter."

37

"I believe so," Philipson-Smith drawled. Edgar could imagine his simian eyes gleaming with pleasure at this unexpected opportunity to indulge his love of bullying.

"I must confess," Edgar said in a voice that shook slightly, "that, considering the letter was a perfectly courteous one and consisted of an offer of hospitality, I had half expected you to reply to it."

"I had half intended to," came the luxurious reply, released word by word. "But it seems to have slipped my mind."

Edgar took a grip on himself. The main thing to do was to force a decision, and get the man to say he would come, as quickly as possible; he must spare himself any more of this writhing in anguish, or he would begin to scream insults and threats into the telephone.

"Well, that's quite understandable," he said in a bluff, friendly manner; his voice, of its own accord, became deep and resonant, giving a Dingley Dell effect of hearty openness. "Anyway, I thought something of the kind must have happened, and I just thought I'd ring up to see if you'll give me the pleasure of entertaining you round at my place one night "

Philipson-Smith paused for so long that the only charitable conclusion would have been that he was trying to take out a cigarette, and that for some reason the cigarettes had slipped sideways in the packet and it was difficult to get at them; and that after getting the cigarette into his mouth he had trouble with his lighter, shaking it and even laying down the receiver so as to adjust the flint. When he spoke again, Edgar half expected him to mumble slightly, in the manner of a man with a cigarette in his mouth, but there was no change in the cold, distinct articulation.

"I'm very busy just now, Banks I don't often get an evening free. And if you don't mind my being frank, I don't think it would be much of a pleasure to spend it with you."

Edgar played his last card.

"This isn't just a social call, you see," he said. "I—I'm conscious of feeling rather, well, rather confused. I've always held rather definite opinions, but just lately I've felt, well, in need of some kind of really clarifying discussion. I rather have the feeling that you, holding equally definite opinions of the type I've never understood until now, not that I understand them now, but, well . . ."

His voice tailed off, and he waited tensely. Probably the thought of making a convert to his loathsome credo was the only bait by which Philipson-Smith could be tempted.

However, all he said was, "I'll send you some pamphlets to read," in the tone of one who is about to replace the receiver.

"There's no substitute for a straight exchange of ideas," Edgar cried anxiously.

Philipson-Smith hesitated.

"I don't think you're worth it, Banks," he said coldly, "but if you really want me to shed a little light into your mind, I daresay I could look in for an hour next Saturday."

Two more days to live. Thursday night, Friday, Friday night, Saturday, then death.

"I'm so glad," he said. "You'll be alone, won't you? I don't think I could stand that Caledonian gent."

"You're referring, I suppose, to my friend Mr. McWhirtner," said Philipson-Smith. "No, I'm inclined to think I shall come on my own. About nine."

"It's very good of you to spare the time."

"Only an hour, mind," said Philipson-Smith curtly.

"Oh, certainly," said Edgar. "I wouldn't dream of detaining you," he added politely. His voice had almost finished the second syllable of "detaining" when the receiver at the other end was brusquely laid down.

Edgar went into the sitting-room and stood quite still, staring out of the window as if studying the architecture of the house opposite. In a detached, clinical way, and without the slightest wavering of his resolution, he noticed, suddenly, that he was afraid.

III

EDGAR had not received a scientific education, and now that it was time to prepare for Philipson-Smith's visit, he realized what a handicap this would be. Whether or not such an education would have been a "preparation for life", it would certainly have been a much better preparation for death than any of the knowledge he actually had. However, he reflected, his education had been of the old-fashioned kind, of which the basic assumption was that intelligence was transferable; mental adroitness gained from the study of any one subject could be applied to anything else that came to hand. He set himself, therefore, to transfer his intelligence to the subject of how to cause death by poisoning.

After pursuing, and abandoning, various impossible schemes for deceiving a doctor into giving him a prescription for some deadly drug, he decided to fall back on poisons which could be bought for household purposes. A childhood memory came to his aid: *spirits of salt*—wasn't there something called that? His mother had used it for cleaning, and he had always been told to keep well away from that bottle on the grounds that the stuff was some kind of terrible acid. Sulphuric, was it? No, hydrochloric acid, that was it. Well, if hydrochloric acid, mixed with brandy, could kill a man, Philipson-Smith and he were both goners. Then there was arsenic. But how did one get hold of arsenic? And how ought one to mix these things—in what strength, and how disguised?

Time passed as he sat listlessly ruminating over these questions. Suddenly—a couple of eternities had passed, but still it was sudden—Saturday morning arrived. Only a few hours were left for his preparations! Spurred by panic, he hurried out to the public library and read up poisons in the *Encyclopædia Britannica*.

Yes, there it was: spirits of salt *was* hydrochloric acid, and definitely described as a doer of no good to the human animal. Arsenic was there, too, and in a moment of engaging candour the great work of reference let slip the information that certain kinds of fly-paper contained a lot of it in their gum, and that intending murderers had been known to soak off this gum, thereby obtaining a "strong solution" with enough arsenic in it to put an end to anyone's worries. Under the hostile stare of the library clerk, he shut the volume with a snap, exulting. No harm in firing off both barrels. He would get a bottle of brandy, empty out about a quarter of it, and top it up with spirits of salt *and* the solution from half-a-dozen fly-papers. Insecticide, plus a cleaning agent, were two very appropriate things for Philipson-Smith.

Were they appropriate for him too? Oh, no doubt, no doubt. Whether or not, he must die in the same manner as his victim: honour demanded no shrinking from that.

"Spring-cleanin'?" the young lady in the chemist's asked him as she handed over his purchases.

"Yes," he said, unsmiling, "and I'm doing it thoroughly this time."

Back in the flat, he lit the gas under the kettle in readiness for the fly-papers. It would be a pity if they were of some new-fangled kind that did not contain arsenic. But then whatever they contained would probably be pretty poisonous. And there would be plenty of hydrochloric acid, in any case.

Damn! In his haste and preoccupation, he had forgotten to get a bottle of something to put the stuff in. Turning out the gas, he hurried down the stairs again. It would have to be brandy, of course. Nothing else would be strong enough to mask the flavour, and, besides, brandy had a certain *cachet*. Philipson-Smith might refuse this or that drink, but no one ever refused a glass of brandy. He must do the thing in style and get a really *good* brandy.

Head erect, sauntering stiffly and proudly, he was a French aristocrat going to the guillotine. The wine-merchant, who over the years had served him often enough with cheap African wines, looked at him curiously more than once during their short interview, as Edgar haughtily rejected several good brandies in turn before settling on what was, incontrovertibly, the best. Paying a colossal sum for it, he took the paper-wrapped bottle

41

away reverentially, leaving the man staring after him, little knowing that the rumble of the tumbril and the jeers of a hate-maddened mob ought to have been sounding in his ghostly ears.

Back upstairs again, Edgar worked methodically, almost gaily. The water was heated, the fly-papers were soaked, the hydrochloric acid stood ready in its uncapped bottle. Last came the turn of the brandy-bottle. As the corkscrew bit downwards, Edgar felt that he was already driving a weapon into his own entrails; as the cork popped out, it was no cork, but his own red and reeking heart.

These fancies did not, however, overlay his sense of practicalities. He had paid good money for this brandy, and at least some of it should be put to the use its distillers had intended. About a third should be poured out; he tilted it carefully, pouring into a tumbler. That was it. Now the poison. Half arsenic, half hydrochloric acid, till the bottle was filled almost to the top; almost, but not quite, for he had no new cork, so it was necessary to make the bottle look as if he had had, say, one drink out of it, to see whether it was fit for his guest. The task was complete, the bottle was corked, and his great and noble idea could proceed. When Philipson-Smith came. Until then, he could always fill in time by drinking some of his own brandy. Taking the tumbler, he went into the sitting-room and switched on the electric fire. "Cheerio," he said to himself, softly. He had never drunk neat brandy out of a tumbler before.

At ten minutes to nine the bell rang. As he went down the stairs Edgar tried to feel some appropriate emotion. After all, that one short, savage jab of sound was the signal for the ending of his life, just as certainly as the prison clock striking eight on the morning of a hanging. Damn it, he reasoned, he ought to be feeling *something*: if not fear, then relief—relief that the business had now been taken out of his hands, that the last few minutes of his life would unfold themselves along pre-arranged and entirely unalterable lines. He was annoyed that the expected surge of emotion did not come. Without it he felt blank and empty, shrivelled and without significance.

Going down the third flight of stairs he even tried to analyse his lack of mental sensation. Was it exhaustion? No, for he suddenly felt quite buoyant. The tug of conflicting emotions, cancelling one another out? No, he knew that sensation too, and this was not it. He had to admit that the real underlying cause of his blankness was a little hard pellet of scepticism at the centre of his mind. Until the door opened and revealed Philipson-Smith standing there, until the brandy made a gurgling sound as it poured into the glasses, until the bayonet of pain began to twist in his stomach, there was some little corner of his being, a corner he could not reach, which simply did not believe it. Anti-climax had been so intimately woven into the fabric of his life that he had grown to expect it.

He opened the door with a ceremonious gesture, adopting a stance similar to that of a person launching an ocean-going liner.

The corner of his mind had been right. It was McWhirtner.

"Did you want something?" he enquired politely.

"Arrunt ye expectin' me?" McWhirtner asked. His chin was as small as the cap of a beer-bottle, and his little eyes peered out of their holes like pale mice.

"I'm expecting Mr. Philipson-Smith, who is—or was—coming here by invitation."

"Eh, well," said McWhirtner, "he'll be along. He didnae say precisely whun he'd be comin'. He wanted me to come along furrust and wait."

"So he sent you as his John the Baptist," said Edgar. It was true that McWhirtner would make an effective preparation for the entry of Philipson-Smith, for he created so strong an atmos-phere of mingled boredom and revulsion that the arrival of anyone else, however loathsome, would be welcomed.

"Let's never mind John this and John that," cried McWhirtner impatiently, edging his way past Edgar into the hall. "It's no verra hospitable to keep me standin' ootside on a night like yon."

Edgar looked at him curiously. "You don't really talk like that naturally, do you?" he asked. "I mean, it sounds like an English person who's been listening to Harry Lauder on the wireless."

McWhirtner had already started to climb the stairs. "I want a drink," he said over his shoulder.

"You mean a dram," said Edgar, following him. "Keep the act good."

Then he remembered the poisoned brandy. He must get into the flat before McWhirtner went in and noticed it, or it would be difficult to avoid giving him some. He had no objection to

43

poisoning McWhirtner, but it would be awkward if Philipson-Smith arrived and found his jackal lying dead. It would make him disinclined to accept anything Edgar might offer him to drink.

He quickened his pace. McWhirtner, hearing him speed up, began to bound up the stairs like a stag. No doubt he was thinking that Edgar was trying to get into the flat first and hide something he did not want to share.

The race was conducted in complete silence, save for the agonized panting of the contestants. Edgar did not want to make matters explicit by calling to McWhirtner to hold back and let him go in first; and the Scot, for his part, clutched at the last rags of dignity by pretending that he did not hear Edgar's pounding footsteps behind him. They began on the last flight of stairs almost neck and neck. McWhirtner was in slightly worse physical trim than Edgar, but on the other hand he was driven on by the urgent desire to see what it was that Edgar was trying to exclude him from. He had a deep, obsessive suspicion that it was alcohol. Wheezing like a worn-out carthorse, he lengthened his stroke with a sudden effort and leapt up three stairs instead of his habitual two, thus gaining the advantage of the curve. Edgar thrust his elbow savagely at the wall as he ran round the outside, but the added impetus was not sufficient, and it was McWhirtner who breasted the tape as they thundered over the threshold and reeled, utterly spent, into the sitting-room.

There, hideously obvious in the circle of lamplight, stood the occasional table with the brandy bottle on it.

McWhirtner's eyes had evidently misted over with the effort, for he seemed to be still unaware of the incriminating object. He stood leaning against the mantelpiece, passing his hand over his forehead, while great glassy beads of sweat formed at the roots of his sandy hair. For one insane second, Edgar wondered whether it would be possible to move forward and gather up the bottle unobtrusively, slipping it under his jacket, before McWhirtner became himself again.

Ridiculous, of course. Nobody had ever hidden alcoholic drink from McWhirtner, and they were not starting now. Before Edgar could take a step in the direction of the table, he moved. Sitting down, without haste, in the armchair, he reached out and put his bony hand round the neck of the bottle. When he had it safe, he spoke.

"No bein' a Heilan mon masel, I'm mebbe unaccustomed to climbin'. Ony road, I found your stairs a wheen steep. Quite poot me oot o' breath. Wi' your kind permeession, I'll be takin' a drap oot o' this bottle."

Edgar forced himself to speak. "I'd rather you didn't, if you don't mind," he said.

McWhirtner's only answer was to turn his pale eyes to Edgar's face and sneer gently up at him as he pulled out the cork.

"Put that bottle down," said Edgar roughly.

"This isnae what they call English hospitality, is it?" McWhirtner asked. He was enjoying the situation immensely. His reading of it was, of course, that Edgar thought brandy was too good to be given to an uninvited guest, and that the sight of it disappearing down his, McWhirtner's, throat would plunge Edgar into torment. This thought, combined with the immediate prospect of getting some free brandy, gave him intense pleasure. At the same time he despised Edgar for not being clever enough to have hidden the bottle before coming down to open the door.

"Don't be a damned fool, man! You mustn't drink that!" Edgar shouted. McWhirtner calmly poured out a glass; but, before beginning to drink it, he asked, to prolong the agony, "And why not? Were ye savin it for some special purrupus?"

"Because it's poi——" Edgar began, and stopped.

"It's poy? What d'ye mean, it's poy? That's no wha' it says on the bottle," said McWhirtner. He raised the glass to his lips.

Edgar darted forward and punched at the hand that held the glass. Its contents spilled out. McWhirtner made a violent effort to save it, lost his balance and crashed heavily down on the hearth. It was not in his nature to let go of the bottle in his other hand, but, by a reflex action, he flung that hand out to protect himself. The bottle smashed on the tiles.

"There, ye clumsy bastard!" he shouted. "Ye've gone and lost the bluidy lot because ye're too damned mean to give a man a dram!"

He was torn by conflicting emotions. His joy at seeing Edgar's brandy spilt, before Edgar himself had drunk any of it, was matched by his chagrin at not having slaked his own alcoholic thirst. He took out his handkerchief and began clumsily to mop up the shining liquid.

45

"Oh, don't be such a damned fool," cried Edgar. He caught McWhirtner's wrist and jerked him on to his feet.

"Ye've spilt it. Ye've broken the bottle and spilt it," McWhirtner said stupidly. Blood trickled from a small cut on the palm of his hand.

Edgar felt despair washing over his mind. His chance was ruined. Philipson-Smith would come and go unharmed; he could not murder him in any other way, with the bread-knife or by strangulation, because this detestable sot would be there to join in the struggle, or to run out bawling for help as they fought over the carpet.

"All because ye're so bluidy mean," McWhirtner cried. "Ye can't offer a man a drap to drink on a freezin' night." His joy at the loss of Edgar's brandy was losing its battle against his dipsomania.

Edgar felt weary and defeated. Sadly, he took out his wallet.

"Here's a pound note, McWhirtner," he said coldly. "Go out to the pub on the corner and get a bottle of wine. If there's any change left over, get yourself a whisky with it," he added.

"Go oot yoursel'," McWhirtner muttered stubbornly. "You're the host."

"No," Edgar said flatly.

There was a short pause while McWhirtner's pride fought with his realization that if he did not go out to get some wine, Edgar would not go either, and there would be nothing to drink. He took the pound and went silently through the door and down the stairs.

Edgar sat, crumpled, in the armchair. What a fiasco; Philipson-Smith, by his insulting gesture in sending this moron round to precede him, had protected himself better than he could by hiring a squad of detectives. If McWhirtner had not smashed the bottle, things might still have gone according to plan, for Edgar would certainly not have hesitated to hand out a glass to the Scot as well; in hunting big game one does not scruple to tread on a woodlouse. But the blundering drunkard had served his purpose admirably. And now, what lay before him but an agonizing evening in which he would be both insulted and bored, and worse still, left alive at the end?

McWhirtner came back. He had uncorked the bottle before bringing it away from the pub, and had already drunk a third of its contents. Before speaking to Edgar he poured out two glasses and set the bottle down on the table.

"So ye want to lairn somethin' aboot the Movement?" he asked, squinting cagily and stroking his tiny chin.

"Save it," said Edgar. He did not care to hear a garbled version; did not, in fact, care to hear any version. But now he would have to. Oh, damn his luck!

"Weel, I can tell ye one thing before Rollo gets here," said McWhirtner. "Sir Rufus has made Rollo his Publications Editor. We're startin' up a monthly magazine. An me," he tapped his chest drunkenly, "me, I'm the Leeterary Editor."

"That'll sink it," said Edgar indifferently.

"Sink it!" shouted McWhirtner truculently. "Mebbe ye don't know I'm one o' the best livin' Scots poets!"

He began to fumble in his inside pocket, and produced a dog-eared wad of typescript.

"It's regional, regional, ye see," he said. "We're no' in seempathy wi' this effete English culture. We're after a retairn, a retairn,"

"To the traditional virtues," Edgar put in wearily.

"Ay, the tradeetional vairtues," McWhirtner cried. He unfolded the sheets of paper. "Noo, I'll just read ye some of ma poems."

He began to read in an unintelligible monotone. Edgar tried to avoid paying attention, and indeed would have been unable to follow if he had tried, for the verses were in a bastard literary dialect whose sole object seemed to be to replace every English word by a Scotch one, without reference to period or region. Nevertheless, enough of the remorseless drawl filtered through to make him realize that McWhirtner, like Philipson-Smith, did, in his own fashion, make the best of himself; for it was obvious that his poems, if written in standard English, would have been immediately recognizable as clumsy, sentimental trash.

So intense was his boredom that it even swamped the struggling mixture of emotions within him. All he was capable of realizing was that Philipson-Smith—and, for that matter, he himself—had been, for the time being, reprieved. He must have patience, and wait for his next chance.

After a quarter of an hour, the bell rang. Its note seemed to be a sardonic parody of the more challenging, but misleading, summons it had made earlier. Taking the wine-bottle with him so that McWhirtner should be spared the temptation to empty it while he was out of the room, Edgar went downstairs.

Philipson-Smith glanced at his watch as he came over the threshold. "I'm afraid I can only stay half-an-hour, after all," he said.

"Never mind," said Edgar. "It was considerate of you to send Will Fyffe round. I've been enjoying his company."

"His name isn't Will Fyffe," said Philipson-Smith brusquely. "And if you're disposed to start sneering at the kind of thing he represents, I can tell you straight away that we shan't get very far."

Edgar choked back the retort he wanted to make. He must propitiate Philipson-Smith if there were to be any hope of seeing him again and getting a chance to cut his throat, poison him or shatter his skull with a platelayer's hammer.

"Anyway, do come up," he said. Turning, he led the way up the stairs, keeping the wine-bottle in front of him to hide it. Inside the flat, he poured out a glass for the enemy of life, handed him the cigarettes and mustered an amiable smile.

"I understand from McWindbag that you're a member of some kind of organization or party," he said, trying to simulate polite, though intense, interest. "Is it a secret, or can I ask you about it?"

"As far as I can see," said Philipson-Smith calmly and insolently, "there are only two possible motives you could have for asking me questions about the Movement. One is to try to get into it, the other is to get information that will be useful in opposing it. Either way you're wasting your time. You can't get into it because at this stage we're not looking for recruits—and when we do we'll hand-pick them. And as for opposing it, you might as well realize from the start that it's going to be irresistible—utterly irresistible."

There's another motive, Edgar thought as he sat silent and impassive, *and it isn't anything like the ones you think, but it's going to teach you what it means to be handpicked yourself.* Looking across at the orang-outang face, he felt suddenly happy. His choice had been the right one, and that, after all, was the most important thing. It did not matter whether he succeeded in killing Philipson-Smith the first time, or the first half-dozen times, for that matter, as long as he killed him. The most terrible thing would have been to kill the wrong person, someone who was not utterly and eternally hateful.

"As for its being a secret," Philipson-Smith went on disdainfully, "if you were more awake to what's going on you could have read quite a lot about it already in the ordinary newspapers. They don't know much, of course—only what we've released—but if you'd kept up to date with them you'd know at least the main intention of the Movement—and that it's irresistible."

Perhaps the best way, Edgar thought suddenly, would be to hammer a peg through his temples like Jael the wife of Heber the Kenite in the Good Book.

"As far as I know anything about *your* opinions," Philipson-Smith went on, "you could more or less say that the Movement stands for the exact opposite in every particular."

He smiled as if he had made a joke. His voice was wetter than ever this evening, as if the liquid that bedewed his vocal chords had thickened to the consistency of sewing-machine oil.

"If you had to name one single objective as paramount," Edgar said to keep the conversation going, "could you pick one out?"

"Strength," said Philipson-Smith. "As we see it, there's too much weakness in the post-war world—*our* side of the world at any rate. Too much vacillation, too much pandering to the populace. We need a ring of authoritarian governments, dedicated to the ideal of sharpening the quality of life in the western countries, through an unflinching pursuit of strength."

He was obviously quoting from some idiotic manifesto, doubtless composed by Sir Rufus. It was clear that, whoever this sinister figure was, Edgar's intuition about him had been right.

"I seem to have heard something like that doctrine before," Edgar said musingly.

"That's right," Philipson-Smith cut in witheringly. "Trot out the catch-words—say it's Fascism. They're doing that already, your friends on the Left."

Edgar had no friends on the Left, but he let it go.

"We're not frightened by words, as you are," said Philipson-Smith hotly. The dark shading on his jowl seemed to have grown several degrees darker in the few minutes since he had entered. "Of course as soon as you see a movement which isn't afraid to talk in terms of national strength, you start yapping about Fascism. Well, we don't care. If it comes to that, there are several countries today that could learn a lot from the pre-war Fascist governments."

49

"Yes, and several that could teach them a thing or two, but what has that got to do with us?" Edgar retorted. He fought to keep down his mounting irritation; if he quarrelled with the man now, it would be so much harder to fulfil his mission.

"I can see I'm wasting my time," said Philipson-Smith. He stood up to go.

"Come, come," said Edgar. "A little opposition, in a friendly spirit of enquiry, ought not to——"

"Enquiry be damned. I don't know why you ever professed this sudden interest in hearing about the Movement, but I can see I was acting from mistaken kindness in coming round. I don't see why I should waste any time on your kind anyway. You're on the way out."

That's true, Edgar thought, *but when I go out, you're going too, so why hurry?*

"Look," he said in a conciliatory tone, "if I and my kind are on the way out, why don't you show some generosity to a beaten enemy?"

Philipson-Smith looked at him. His eyes, at the top of that flat nose, looked hot enough to burn a man's finger.

"Because you're not beaten yet," he said. "Unfortunately."

Before Edgar could answer, there was a knock on the door. He went and opened it. Flannery stood on the mat and gave him his satyr's smile.

"Go away and rob a church," said Edgar. "I'm busy."

Flannery came in, pushing Edgar gently to one side. "I've run out of cigarettes," he said. He went into the sitting-room and crossed towards the mantelpiece to help himself from Edgar's box. Passing in front of the visitors, he gave them a sardonic bow.

"Who's this?" Philipson-Smith asked Edgar, contriving to suggest that he had not come here to be insulted by a procession of Edgar's doomed and decadent friends.

"I'm a neighbour," said Flannery. "If you've got anything to ask me, you may address me directly—I can talk."

Suddenly McWhirtner stood up. He faced Flannery across the hearth, staring at him bitterly and intently, then raised his hand and pointed at him like a man in an old recruiting poster.

"Ye're a Jew!" he said loudly.

The slight shrug with which Flannery responded gave the answer, as it was intended to, without words.

"A bluidy Jew!" said McWhirtner more loudly than before.

Edgar looked at Philipson-Smith, expecting him to control and rebuke his minion. But he was sitting stiffly, bending slightly forward in his chair, and did not move. His face had gone completely impassive, as if to indicate that, while McWhirtner's action was not such as he himself would have undertaken, he was restrained by his principles from doing anything to interfere.

Flannery looked sardonically across at McWhirtner. Centuries of patience and cynicism were suddenly there in the lines of his face.

"So it's beginning again, is it?" he said softly. "And so soon?"

McWhirtner leaned forward, hands on hips. "I'll gie ye a piece o' advice, Mister Jew," he said. "Get packin' before we catch up wi' ye."

Flannery shook his head, but the ancient, sardonic smile did not leave his face. Edgar had never seen him smile like that till now.

"We made that mistake before," he said. "Too many times. In future we'll stay and fight it out."

Philipson-Smith spoke.

"So you'll fight, will you?" he said. "Well, you've got an ally in our host here. You'll make a good team, you and Banks."

"I don't need any help from Banks," said Flannery. He took five cigarettes from the box and put them in his case. "I'll give you these back tomorrow," he said.

"Ay, gie them back," sneered McWhirtner. "He'll be doon to collect 'em if ye dinna. He's that mean he'll smash a bottle o' brandy so as not to gie a mon a drink."

Flannery did not answer. He went to the door, turned, and looked steadily at the two visitors before going out, as if making sure that he remembered their faces.

"You'll recognize us again, I think?" said Philipson-Smith.

Flannery bowed. "If I don't," he said, "I'm sure you'll advertise your identity loudly enough."

He went out.

"Come on, let's be going," said Philipson-Smith. He stood up. Edgar made a desperate effort. A little lying, a little duplicity now, and he would safeguard this precious opportunity to be avenged in the name of mankind.

"Need you——" he said, and stopped. It was too much. His

51

disgust and anger would not let him go on. He suddenly realized that, although he liked Flannery as little as ever, he would die on the barricades, if ever it came to that, to protect him from these two.

"All right, go," he said wearily. They collected their overcoats. McWhirtner poured out and drank the last of the wine.

"Could you——" Edgar forced himself to utter the words— "drop in some other time?"

"Impossible," said Philipson-Smith curtly. "We're off to Geneva tomorrow night, and we'll be there indefinitely."

"Och, we wouldnae come even if we were stayin' at hame," added McWhirtner.

They went out. The little pools of poisoned brandy, lying there in the curved pieces of broken glass, glinted up at Edgar as he stood alone on the hearth. It seemed to him that they smiled, like Flannery, with an ancient, cynical patience.

He went to bed, and lay smoking cigarettes and staring at the ceiling. Sleep was out of the question. He felt as if the contents of his mind were slowly shaking down and packing more densely together, like objects grouped in the hold of a sinking ship. Obviously he had expected the whole thing to be too easy. He had thought this task could be performed in a few days, whereas this first failure went to prove that another quality besides determination had to be added to the mixture: perseverance. Well, why not? He was his own master, his few savings were there in the bank, there was no hurry. Out there in the sitting-room, everything was as it had always been; no corpse lay contorted on the carpet, no tiny sticky glass, clutched in a stiff hand, awaited the forensic analyst. But Philipson-Smith was already dead, of that Edgar was certain. He had taken his decision, and nothing should hinder him. As for himself, he occupied a hinterland between life and death; he had still the living man's power of action, and with it the tranquillity and freedom of the dead. The thought calmed him, and towards dawn, with the light still burning and the heaped ash-tray on a chair by his side, he slept.

When he woke, it was nearly eleven o'clock. Without pausing to take thought, but acting as if he had never been to sleep at all, he got out of bed, put on his dressing-gown, and, going to the telephone, dialled Philipson-Smith's number.

"He's not at home, I'm afraid," said a woman's voice. Its tone and inflexions were sufficiently like those of Philipson-Smith to indicate that this was his mother. Edgar wondered, for an instant, how she would react to the news that her son was dead.

"It doesn't matter, madam," he said. "It's just that there's an important message that's going to be handed to him personally when he gets to Geneva to-morrow morning. This message will be brought in by a man in a grey coat and black scarf who'll be sitting in the hotel lounge from ten o'clock till noon. Will you tell him that?"

"It's from Sir Rufus?" she asked anxiously.

"We don't usually mention names over the telephone," he replied sternly, "but since you've said it, yes, it is."

His shot in the dark had gone home; he had presumed on her knowing vaguely that her son was working for the Movement. Now it was time to play the last trick card, the old Sherlock Holmes stunt.

"And I just wanted to make sure that the address he gave us is the right one," he said.

"My son will be in at five o'clock, just before he sets off for the airport," she cut in. "Wouldn't you rather——"

"Madam," he said impatiently, "I'm telephoning from Heath Row myself. My plane leaves in twelve minutes for Bombay."

He felt rather anxious about giving her all these details that she could check on, but as long as he got the address it wouldn't matter if she found out that the message had been a fake. Now for the Sherlock gambit.

"According to our Sub-Central office he'll be staying at the Hotel Biarritz," he said, bending his head downwards a little as if reading from a notebook.

"Oh no, there must have been a mistake," she said. "The address he's left me is the Hotel Thyssen."

"Spelt?" Edgar rapped out masterfully. She spelt it.

"There's been some inefficiency here," Edgar said in a bullying tone. "It's my duty to tell you, madam, that if this inefficiency is traced to your son, he will not escape the usual penalties."

He rang off, and went to make some tea. He was still drinking it at noon when Flannery knocked on the door and came in.

"Here are your five cigarettes," he said, inclining his head with a touch of mockery, but not smiling. He put a paper packet on the table.

53

"Keep them," said Edgar. "Cigarettes are cheaper where I'm going."

"Where are you going?"

"Geneva," he said.

Flannery went out, leaving the cigarettes behind. They were of a more expensive brand than the ones he had borrowed.

IV

As far as Calais, Edgar's journey had been uneventful, allowing
him leisure for meditation of a lofty and melancholy nature; and,
knowing that Life very seldom stands that kind of nonsense for
long, he began to wonder, as he walked down the ship's gangway,
how soon something farcical, disgusting or terrifying would begin
to happen. He need not have concerned himself. As the packed
herd of passengers shuffled and butted its way into the long
customs-shed, harassed by barking porters and cowering under
blasts of sound from a fresh set of loudspeakers, he found himself jammed shoulder to shoulder with a woman carrying a baby.
Normally he would not have given the woman a second glance;
she was evidently in her early thirties, but beginning already to
acquire the bloated pallor that Nature sends to blondes when they
marry and settle down. Her hair was, in theory, scraped up on to
her head in a tightly-disciplined coiffure; in actual fact most of
it had escaped from the clips and was waving feebly at the back
of her neck in strands, some long, some short, with a fluffy mass
at the lower edge which was too short to have reached as far as
the clips anyway and ought, to make the effect anything like a
success, to have been shaved off. Having vaguely taken in these
details in the instant when he first jostled her, Edgar would have
paid her no more attention than if she had been a lamp-post he
had brushed against; but the baby, whom she was carrying in
the crook of her one free arm as negligently as if it had been a
leg of mutton, somehow managed to get one tiny hand free, and,
reaching out, seized a button on Edgar's coat. He tried, gently, to
detach the little fingers with their slivers of soft finger-nail, but
the baby clung on fiercely, with almost epileptic strength. The
crowd swayed onwards for a few yards. Edgar had surrendered his

larger suitcase, but he was still carrying a small hand-case, and he had to change it over to the other side so as to keep as narrow a space as possible between him and the woman, to prevent the baby from being dragged away from its mother and trampled underfoot. They halted, and, putting his case down, Edgar applied both hands to an attempt to prise the dimpled fist off his button, but there was no purchase for his fingers. He turned his head to speak to the woman, but she was talking over her shoulder to a little man with thinning hair, dressed in a black overcoat. A space cleared in the crowd for an instant, and through it Edgar was able to glimpse two more children, a boy and a girl, holding on to the man's hands.

The crowd bumped forward and thrust the woman closer to Edgar. The baby, seeing its chance, brought its mouth up to the button to suck it, and to this end relaxed the grip of its fist. Then, with another swing of the pendulum, it was jerked away again, foiled. Edgar felt a momentary relief at being free, but immediately realized that his last state was worse than his first, for the mite paused only to inflate its lungs before letting go with a piercing shriek that echoed up and down the crowded shed like the cry of a macaw in the jungle. The mother, still with head turned towards her mate, joggled the child up and down absent-mindedly, but the screams continued with unbelievable violence. Slowly the queue jiggled on; Edgar was trapped with the baby's shrieking, contorted face never more than nine inches from his ear. They halted, held up by some obstacle at the head of the procession, and the baby began to thrash about like a newly-landed conger, yelling with frustration and rage. In desperation, Edgar sidled up to it with the coat button extended between his finger and thumb, but it was useless; either the baby was too stupid to grasp what he was trying to do, or the original cause of its grievance had been forgotten in the violence of the paroxysm. Its face became dark and mottled, and a new note—a savage rasping like the filing of metal—was added to the wild, high screaming. Edgar wondered feverishly what possible new noises and contortions the child could have produced if it had been impaled. His head swam with the din. He plucked nervously at the woman's sleeve.

"Can't you do something, madam?" he shouted above the racket. She turned and looked at him with clear, cow-like eyes.

"Do something? What about?"

56

"The baby," he yelled. "It'll be having a fit or something in a minute!"

She smiled unconcernedly. "Oh, I don't think so," she said, looking down at the struggling little animal. "It's good for them to cry a bit, you know. It exercises their lungs." The baby, as if to confirm this statement, paused for a second and then began a new series of shouts on a different note. Its little throat was so rasped out that the voice sounded hoarse and deep, like a bargee's. Edgar flinched.

"It's not natural for them to be quiet all the time," the woman went on, looking at Edgar rather severely, as if he were selfishly trying to get the baby to behave in an unnatural manner to suit his own comfort. "He's healthy, that's all," she said, looking down at the purple, screwed-up face.

The crowd broke up, and Edgar thankfully moved over to the appropriate table. Casting a backward glance, he saw the baby suddenly relax and collapse over its mother's arm as if dead.

The douanier perfunctorily scribbled a chalk mark on his suitcase, and he dragged it off the table, only to have it wrested out of his hand by a porter in blue overalls and chin to match. Muttering with annoyance, Edgar set off for the platform where the train was standing, and waited, chafing with impatience as the minutes passed. Finally the man re-appeared, at the far end of the platform, nonchalantly wheeling a trolley. Beckoning to Edgar, he took his case and dumped it in the corridor through the nearest open door.

Edgar climbed aboard. The porter followed and silently stood beside him, watching while he took his case into a compartment and lifted it on to the already crowded rack. Before sitting down he turned to the man and handed him a huge tip. The porter looked incredulously at the paper money, unfolding it carefully, as if he could not believe that anyone could be so miserly.

"Pas beaucoup," he said at last.

"Vous n'avez pas fait beaucoup, alors," Edgar replied harshly.

The man turned his back, then suddenly whipped round. For an instant Edgar thought he was about to make a fight of it. Then, just as they were glaring at each other, a small fist thudded into Edgar's solar plexus and a shrill voice cried, "I've got a bigger pen-knife than you!"

Turning, he saw a small boy standing beside him. In one hand he was waving a huge clasp-knife with a tarnished and (mercifully) blunt blade. With the other, doubled into a fist, he was battering at Edgar's ribs and stomach. Sitting on the seat behind him were the woman with her baby, the husband in his black overcoat, and the little girl.

"That man's got a funny chin," cried the boy, turning his attention to the porter. "He's got a funny chin and a funny face!" He threatened the porter with his knife. The man backed away, muttering terrible obscenities, and got off the train.

Edgar sat down. This was the last compartment he would have chosen, but, having put his suitcase on the rack, he felt trapped; particularly as the boy had, in a sense, placed him under an obligation by driving away the porter.

As he settled into his seat the mother gave him a heavy, indifferent glance, not without a slight flavour of suspicion, as if at any moment he might utter some criticism of one of the children. The father, on the other hand, screwed his worried little features into a smile. It was a peculiar smile; appealing, timid and rather guilty, as if to say, "I admit that I am, in a sense, responsible for this lot, and, while determined to put a bold face on it—after all, it is socially useful to produce a family—I realize, between man and man, that this calls for a certain indulgence on your part." Edgar replied with a smile that was intended to absolve the fellow from all blame, and to reassure him that things would come right in the end. "They'll grow up and leave you in peace one day," he nearly said.

The train began to move, and the paterfamilias evidently felt his tongue loosened by the exhilarating effect of motion. He leaned forward slightly.

"Always a relief to get the crossing over, isn't it?" he said.

"They were very good on the boat," his wife cut in stonily before Edgar could reply.

"I wasn't thinking of the children, dear," he said, turning towards her. "I just meant that it's—well, it's always a relief," he ended lamely.

"They were as good as gold," she said. "Better than you thought they'd be."

"Oh, well, I always do look on the black side," he said, glancing across at Edgar with the same smile as before.

Edgar, feeling it was time he spoke, opened his mouth, but the little girl, who had been staring purposefully at the paper her father carried rolled up in his hand, suddenly cried shrilly, "I want to see the pictures!"

Apologetically the man unrolled his paper. Edgar could see that it was one of the non-illustrated weeklies. "There aren't any pictures in this one, darling," he said.

"I want to see the pictures," the child said, enunciating clearly as if afraid that he had not understood.

"Daddy hasn't got any pictures in his paper, darling," he repeated.

Her under-lip began to turn outwards and downwards.

"No pictures," the poor devil babbled in an attempt to save himself. He rapidly flicked over the pages, showing her the immobile, colourless print on each one.

She began to scream wildly. Edgar lit a cigarette to steady his nerves.

"Yooooooo show me the pi-ictuuuuuuuuuuuuuuuuures . . . Yooooooo . . ."

"Why don't you show her the pictures, Bob?" asked his wife indifferently.

"There aren't any. There aren't any in this paper," he shouted above the screams. The baby, out of sympathy, began to join in with short, powerful blasts of the foghorn.

Edgar sat back, appalled but fascinated. He wanted to see how they would get out of the difficulty; whether, indeed, they would get out of it, or whether the racket would go on all the way to wherever they were going. The husband looked wildly round for inspiration, then suddenly seemed to remember that he had an illustrated paper among his luggage on the rack. He stood up and began dragging the smaller cases down, while the noise exploded round him like well-directed flak.

It was interesting to note that, meantime, the woman showed no sign of strain. It was evident that her hearing was normal, for she showed awareness that the children were crying; now and then she leaned across and made some inaudible but probably soothing remark to the little girl, and all the time she carelessly joggled the baby up and down as she had done in the customs-shed. It was not that she could not hear; it was simply that her nerves had been exposed to this kind of thing for so long that, as a protective measure, they had finally atrophied, leaving her in the state of lethargy which Edgar had already noticed in her conversation. She was like a person permanently dosed with quarter or half grains of barbiturate.

Frantically the husband opened one of the cases on the seat, and, standing with his back to Edgar, began burrowing in it.

"I'll get Mopsy out," he shouted in a high-pitched voice. Edgar did not know what Mopsy was, but it must have been something the little girl did not require, for the noise actually intensified and became mingled with desperate choking sobs. The words, or a version of the words, "Don't want Mopsy," could be distinguished from time to time.

Hitherto the son and heir had been silent, occupying himself with the cutting of deep perpendicular slashes in the seat-cushion behind him. Now, finishing his task, he folded his knife and fastened it to a clip on his belt. Then he looked up and saw his father rummaging in the open case. At once he hurled himself down the length of the compartment, cannoning violently into his father's ribs, and dived both hands into the disordered interior of the case.

"I want a sweetie," he shouted fiercely.

Taken by surprise, his father stumbled slightly, trampling heavily on Edgar's foot. In an instant the boy had seized the suitcase and emptied out its contents on to the floor. A paper bag lay exposed on the top of the mound.

"Roger's sweeties!" he shouted in triumph.

"Nancy's sweeties," corrected his sister, leaning forward and snatching at the bag. She managed to get one hand round his wrist, preventing him from putting his hand behind his back; expertly he grabbed at her hair with his free hand and pulled her down on to the floor. Bawling, they grovelled like cats amid the spilt contents of the suitcase. The boy was the elder and heavier, but the girl had plenty of fighting spirit and could reasonably hope, Edgar thought, for a decision on points.

"Oh, Bob, you are careless," said the woman. "You've let all the things fall out. Do pick them up. And they can both have a sweetie," she added, revealing once more that she could see and hear, though she could not feel, the raging strife that was going on around her.

Meekly the husband gathered up the bag's contents and stuffed them back in some sort of order. Sweets were handed out,

60

unwrapped and sucked in silence. Even the baby, feeling strange new peace enveloping it, allowed its noise mechanism run down and come to a halt with a series of fretful snarls.

The head of the family was obviously very tired. As he sank back on the seat, closing his eyes, the blood seemed to drain from his face and leave it as white and empty as a ping-pong ball. Edgar felt genuinely sorry for him; with his purple-ringed eyes and crumpled clothing, he made the long-drawn-out trials of parenthood, parenthood on a small income, vividly real. This morning, and the morning before, and the morning before that, he had been awakened by one or other of his offspring jumping on his belly in the pearly dawn. To-night, and the night after, and the night after that, he would be kept awake by frenzied yelling, or pushed out of bed to go and heat milk or carry vessels containing urine. His wife had evidently once been a woman, but now . . . Edgar pictured her sprawled in bed like a dead seal. And yet, and yet . . . these people had something in their lives, something important which he could not see but whose presence he could feel.

The wide landscape of France was slipping rhythmically past them, and for a few minutes, Edgar, forgetting that he was a self-doomed man with no energy to spare for frivolities, stared out of the window, enjoying the fact that everyday objects were different from those he was accustomed to. The railway engines and rolling stock were different, the telegraph poles were different, and in the streets between the different houses one caught glimpses of differently dressed people riding different bicycles and pushing different carts. This made Edgar happy.

"It's time to take the children along to the restaurant car and get them some tea," came the mother's voice, cutting into his somnolence. He looked across at the father to see what his reaction would be. The man opened his eyes with an effort, and a look of utter hopelessness came over his face. He lay back against the cushions, his eyes open and staring, but made no movement.

"They ought not to have tea any later than half-past four," she said in the same dead, unconcerned voice.

The man's eyelids flickered like those of a lizard. He passed the tip of his tongue over his lower lip. Edgar watched with intense, covert interest. It seemed that the victim was on the point of rebelling. He half expected to hear him come out with some desperate defiance, such as "Take them yourself." Actually he said, hesitantly, "Tell you what. I'll just go and have a cup myself first. I don't quite feel up to taking them until I've had a chance to pick myself up a bit."

"All right," she said indifferently. It was obvious that she did not, in the ordinary sense, nag him. It was just that she had narrowed her life to one purpose, and bore towards it with fantastic pressure. He could not oppose her remorseless drive without being crushed or broken.

He stood up thankfully. Edgar's mind worked at speed. If he could arrange to be in the compartment when the family went to tea, he would know a short interval of blessed peace. As far as getting his own tea was concerned, he could have it either before or after they did. But if he had it after them, it would mean staying in the compartment now, in the absence of the husband, and exposed both to the devilry of the children and the semi-hostility of the mother. He stood up.

"I think I'll follow your example," he said with a polite smile.

The mother, from where she sat, shot him a look of increased suspicion, as if she expected him to take her husband to the restaurant car and drink him under the table and then fling him off the train. It was not a rational suspicion, merely the deep, instinctive distrust of the child-ridden mother, who sees in every outsider, male or female, a threat against the security of the family.

"Don't be long, Bob," she called warningly.

"I won't," Bob said as he opened the door into the corridor.

"They mustn't have tea later than——"

"Half-past four, I know," he cried, almost jauntily, stepping out of the foetid compartment with the stride of a free man. Edgar followed his swaying back down the strung-out coaches.

The next dawn found Edgar stretched out sleepless in his *couchette*. The rhythmic thrust and roll of the train had its usual weird effect, lulling the mind into a trance-like somnolence while at the same time making real sleep difficult to achieve. The other passengers snored, groaned, twitched and now and then shouted incoherently in their sleep. An American woman in the bunk below him had already cried, "Get out, Henry," three times during the night; her husband, from the bunk opposite, lay awake and listened in a purposeful silence that seemed to indicate that his

62

Christian name was not Henry. At least, Edgar thought, it was better than if she had cried, "Come in, Henry." He surrendered his mind to a long drifting reverie; connected thought was impossible. He thought of the city of Geneva lying in the first grey light, awaiting them; he had never been there, never even thought about the place much, except as the scene of permanent international wrangling, and here he was taking his carcase there with no intention of bringing it back. The Swiss police were probably very efficient, and he had no intention of delaying his own self-destruction after finishing Philipson-Smith; the thought of being picked up and sent home to England for trial, carefully guarded and his life preserved for the hangman's rope, was far too distasteful. There must be absolutely no delay; as soon as the job was done he must put himself beyond the reach of punishment.

Punishment! Now that he came to think of it, had he not heard somewhere that there was such a thing as a divine edict against suicide, and a punishment reserved for it in some future state of existence? For a moment, as an experiment, he deliberately tried to frighten himself. What if it were true, that there really was a place called Hell, and that you could be sent there without reprieve for resigning the job before you reached retiring age? Lying in the swaying bunk, within touching distance of the uncomfortably sprawled, cramped bodies of five fellow-creatures, all enclosed in a dark, stuffy metal box, it was momentarily easier to imagine Hell; but even so, Edgar could not keep the picture before his mind's eye. Try as he would to force the idea into his consciousness, it always slipped through immediately, like an unsuitable coin put into a London Transport ticket-machine. It was true, of course, that Hell existed; he had peered into it from time to time since his earliest days, and for the last two or three years he had lived in its suburbs and paid visits to its centre so frequently that it would have been cheaper to take a season-ticket; but *that* Hell was, ultimately, manageable; it had an exit, which he had discovered and through which he was about to make his way. Once again he tried to frighten himself with visions of the other, the traditional Hell, but the various illustrations he had seen of it, mostly in infancy, had entered too deeply into his mental vision of the infernal state and made it ridiculous; the devils with toasting-forks kept swarming into the centre of the picture and reducing the thing to farce. "All right, come in,

Henry," the American woman cried. Her husband clambered grimly out of his bunk, put on a flowered silk dressing-gown, and went along to shave.

Geneva, Edgar thought. Well, why not? It was for several reasons a very suitable place to die. For one thing, it did not seem to be a place where anyone went if he could help it. Edgar did not remember ever having heard anyone say, "I wish I could get a job that allowed me to live in Geneva," or, "What a nuisance having to come away from Geneva, where I was so happy." In that respect it was a city of death. Yesterday, for instance, he had talked to the paterfamilias over their tea, and it had turned out that the poor downtrodden wretch, tired of struggling to make ends meet as a cashier in a provincial bank or whatever he had been, had managed to net a job in some international organisation and was transplanting his entire life out here. But somehow the prospect of earning some five times his previous salary had not seemed to fill the man with elation. "It'll be better for the wife and kids, of course," he had said reflectively, staring out of the window with his tea-cup arrested in mid-lift, "but there are some things I'll——" he had left the sentence unfinished, but had turned his head and looked directly at Edgar for an instant, and in his eyes Edgar had seen the rest. Miserable as his life in England had been, it had been *his*, and when the new anonymous, vagrant, prosperous life swallowed him, what tiny seeds of reality and character he still had left would wither immediately. Of all the sacrifices he would make for his family, this was the hardest, and no one would ever thank him for it; they would only say how lucky he had been to get such a good job. The physical death that Edgar was seeking was no more absolute than the spiritual death of Crabshaw—for such, he had confessed, was his name—and it seemed to give Geneva a symbolic fitness for the deed that must be done.

The American came back, shaved. He shook his wife curtly. Edgar imagined that he would start divorce proceedings immediately, citing this Henry as co-respondent. "Wake up, Claire," he cried sternly. "We have to change at Lausanne." She opened her eyes. "Did you sleep well, Henry, honey?" she asked him; Edgar felt disappointed, yet relieved, that his fantasy had no basis and the man's name was actually Henry. But in that case, why had he behaved so angrily? Then he remembered; it was because she had said "Get out, Henry," three times and "Come in Henry," only once. Melancholy and disillusioned, his drama-loving nature cheated once more by the commonplace truth, he began to search for his clothes.

Then it was Lausanne, and the train halted to hand over the visitors it had brought to Switzerland, like a kind uncle giving out Christmas presents. The chill, airy station, eerily silent and inhumanly clean, seemed to drain the passengers of individuality as they alighted singly or in groups on the neat platform, and to infect them instead with its own passionless efficiency. Like the figures in an old silent film, they stumped at grotesque speed down one platform, over a bridge, on to another, and into the right train, which immediately began to click smoothly along through the spruce and boring landscape. Edgar suddenly felt hungry in a curious, mechanical way, as if his body were a cleverly designed machine which had begun to falter through lack of fuel. He made his way to the restaurant car.

The Crabshaws were already there, and Bob gave him so friendly and pathetic a smile when he walked in that there seemed no choice but to join him. Immediately he regretted it, for he had slept badly, and half an hour with these children would be all it needed to drain out the last ounce of his vitality. Between them they acted as a sort of unofficial bodyguard for Philipson-Smith, by robbing his assassin of strength.

Somehow the meal proceeded. During most of it, Mrs. Crabshaw was breast-feeding the baby behind a newspaper; it was an English newspaper, and Edgar would have liked to read the headlines, but she was holding it upside down. This had the good effect of silencing one-third of the available noise apparatus, but unfortunately the other two seemed aware of the additional responsibilities that now devolved on them, and set themselves to be more objectionable than usual by a minimum of fifty per cent. each. In this they were successful, having the advantage of the terrain; there was always a jug of milk to be tipped into the lap of some adult, always a fried egg to be crushed in the fist, the hand to be then opened and pressed on to the back of an adult's hand, and so forth. Edgar was sitting next to the boy, and he determined from the start that while a certain amount of nervous agitation could be sustained in the cause of human friendliness, physical hurt he could not and would not incur. Dedicated to his

65

high task, he must keep himself intact. In the intervals of carrying on a disjointed conversation with the Crabshaws, he steeled himself to ignore the marmalade smeared over the dial of his wrist-watch, the sausage thrust up the open end of his tie, the toast crumbled down the back of his neck, and other more or less routine attentions; but he kept a sharp though unobtrusive look-out for any signs of actual violence. The boy's clasp-knife hung from his belt as usual; probably if the worst came to the worst, and his other manœuvres left Edgar more or less unhurt, he would unclasp it and openly stab him, trusting to the law to spare his life because of his tender years. Edgar decided that if he saw Roger's hand moving towards the clip that held the knife, he would whip off his jacket and throw it round the boy's head and shoulders, at the same time using his weight to pin him in the corner until armed help arrived.

"Of course, the children are a great comfort," said Mr. Crabshaw, eating with his left hand because his daughter was holding his right and making patterns on it with mustard and salt. "It means that we can take a family atmosphere with us wherever we go, and after all, home is where the family is, I always say."

The newspaper fluttered; behind its protective screen, Mrs. Crabshaw was gently shaking the baby, as if to get it to feed more quickly by encouraging the milk it had already swallowed to run down to the bottom of its stomach.

"That's what I always say, too," said Edgar. He poured out a cup of scalding hot coffee, then noticed the boy looking fixedly at the steam rising from it. Obviously he was wondering if the coffee were hot enough to give Edgar a second- or third-degree burn if it were poured down his chest.

"Of course educating them isn't going to be easy," said Mr. Crabshaw. He pulled out his handkerchief from his breast pocket; a shower of corn flakes, stealthily packed into the pocket by one of his children, cascaded on to the table. "But there are nursery schools run by the international community there, quite un-officially, you know."

Edgar's nerves were keyed up to an almost unbearable pitch. At any moment, the boy would launch a sudden lightning blow at his coffee-cup, splashing the almost boiling contents on to him. He must be ready to counter this blow without seeming to anticipate it.

66

"I believe the teachers are mostly Americans," said Mr. Crabshaw.

"He's had enough now, Bob. Give me his powder and pins out of the basket," said Mrs. Crabshaw, lowering the newspaper and revealing that she had adjusted her clothing to the demands of normal social life. Mr. Crabshaw turned to burrow in some kind of receptacle under the table.

Immediately the boy saw his chance. With no parental eye on him, he acted with diabolic skill and perfect timing. Edgar had been watching his hands, expecting him to deliver a normal open-handed blow at the cup, which had just been refilled; actually he simply jerked up his elbow, striking, not the cup, but the lower and forward part of the hand that held it.

Edgar was outwitted, but even so he was not entirely taken unawares. He had hoped to apply a corresponding counter-stress to make the coffee fly into the boy's face, but there was no longer any chance of bringing off such a refined riposte. He simply jerked his arm galvanically forwards and upwards, at the same time flicking his wrist as violently as possible.

The coffee shot out of the cup in a graceful pillar which gave the illusion of solidity, like a small brown waterspout. Whether the effect would have been the same if they had been sitting in an ordinary dining-room, or whether the fact of their being in a moving vehicle had any effect on the physics of the thing, Edgar could never afterwards be sure. At all events, the flying cylinder of liquid curved backwards, spread itself out into the shape of a pigeon's wings, and fell, more heavily than its actual weight appeared to warrant, on the heads and shoulders of the two people sitting at the table behind them.

Even the boy Roger was nonplussed at the uproar which immediately arose. There was a shrill female cry, accompanied basso-profondo by a male voice uttering a volley of oaths in a language which Edgar recognized as Dutch. The boy shrank into his corner, making himself appear as small as possible; he looked too tiny and frail to have thrown the coffee so high, even if the wide-eyed frankness of his features had not declared any such offence utterly impossible. Mr. and Mrs. Crabshaw sat motionless, staring with horror at the two faces which appeared over the back of the seat behind Edgar.

The Dutchman was a powerfully built man, but Edgar noticed

3*

immediately that he was not in outstandingly good physical condition; he looked as if years of over-eating had robbed him of the elasticity of movement necessary to inflict real damage on his opponent in a brawl. He had been eating porridge, and the shock of receiving the baptismal assault of scalding liquid had caused him to blow, or otherwise eject, the contents of his mouth both downwards, over his stiff grey beard, and upwards, in some curious fashion, so that his cheeks were dappled with it almost to the eyes.

The female face belonged to a young woman, but past her first youth; though rather puffy and with a poor complexion, it was decidedly more attractive than the Dutchman's face, not only as being free from porridge, but also as wearing a tolerant, even good-humoured expression under a surface of quasi-comic exasperation.

If the Dutchman knew any other language than his own, the violence of his emotion had driven it from his mind. The young woman, however, spoke in a language he understood.

"Jeeze, brother," she said to Edgar. "You certainly are a messy feeder."

"I'm so sorry," Edgar said politely. He stood up.

"I can't think of *any* liquid I like down the back of my neck," she said plaintively, "but coffee's one of the worst—even this hair-wash they call coffee over here."

The Dutchman produced his handkerchief. With it he wiped most of the porridge from his face, leaving only a few flecks close to either ear.

"Seem's like this guy's got a use for his handkerchief," she said, looking at him with a certain distaste. "And I've left my own back in the compartment."

Edgar felt ashamed of himself. He produced his handkerchief to lend her; but before he could do so, the boy Roger had leaned forward, snatched it, and slipped it through the window, which was open about an inch. Holding it for an instant in the slipstream, where it billowed out like a flag of truce on a wind-swept battlefield, he released it. It vanished, and he looked up at Edgar with a triumphant smile.

"Roger, don't," said his mother perfunctorily.

"Relation of yours?" asked the young woman, indicating the boy.

"Only in the sense that we're all the sons of Adam," said Edgar bitterly.

"How do you do, Mr. Adam?" she said to Crabshaw.

The Dutchman sat down, muttering. Edgar passed his paper napkin to the young woman, and she carefully wiped the back of her head and neck. Mrs. Crabshaw settled down, evidently feeling that first things should come first, and began to polish the baby's buttocks like a small pair of shoes. Mr. Crabshaw, crushed and uncertain of what role he should be playing, picked up the newspaper which had guarded his wife's modesty and pretended to read it. In his nervousness he was holding it upside down, but this now made no difference to Edgar. He had had enough of the whole scene. Standing up, he signalled to the attendant that he wished to pay his bill.

The girl also stood up. "I guess we'll regley la nott and vamoose, hein?" she said. There was something frank and appealing in the way she said "we". Edgar felt as if they had breakfasted together, even, in a curious way, as if they had spent the night together in his stifling, swaying bunk. Throwing hot coffee over a person is an action that naturally makes for intimacy of one sort or another, but this was something extra, something that proceeded from the character of the girl.

They paid their bills. Edgar wondered for a moment whether it would be a chivalrous gesture to offer to pay hers for her, as he had been the means of interrupting her meal, but she had produced a leather wallet and paid before he could muster the resolution to do so. They got out of their seats.

"Awfully sorry—afraid it was partly my little boy——" Mr. Crabshaw muttered, seizing his last opportunity to apologize before they departed. Evidently he had seen the crime from the corner of his eye.

"Gee, that's all right, Adam," she said with a wide smile. "What's a few blisters on the back of the neck between friends?"

Their eyes met. Mrs. Crabshaw looked up from the baby in her familiar manner, half hostile and half indifferent. For a moment nobody was watching Edgar, and he took advantage of this to dip a dessert-spoon in the honey and daub it over Roger's curly head. The boy began silently fumbling for his clasp-knife, his features full of a grim determination to finish Edgar once and for all.

69

"And we *are* friends, aren't we?" the young woman went on. "Say, I like your kiddies. I'd like to see some more of them. What hotel are you staying at?"

"The Hotel Familial," he muttered in confusion, "just for a bit—till we get settled——"

His wife looked at him as if, but for her habitual lethargy, she would have kicked him under the table.

"And you're staying there too, aren't you?" she said, turning to Edgar. "Don't tell me, I know you Briddish always stick together."

Edgar had in fact no hotel reservation at Geneva, and he was too confused to know how to answer. In any case it was time to go; the boy was working his clasp-knife open and glancing up at him murderously.

"Yes, yes, Hotel Familial," he said hastily.

"Well, that's just dandy," she said. "I guess I'll check in there myself."

She turned and led the way between the tables as if she expected to be followed.

For the next half-hour Edgar was in a state of miasma. He found himself accompanying the young woman down the corridor of the train; her compartment was only half filled, and he found himself sitting in the vacant seat next to her, smoking and chatting; he learnt that her name was Mirabelle something-or-other and that she was employed by a newspaper; he stood beside her on the platform as they collected their luggage; he crossed the road to the Hotel Familial with her, the Crabshaws straggling across behind them; he stood at the desk, signed the book, collected his key, and finally sat in his room, with his unpacked suitcase beside him, staring at the clean counterpane, the long window, the bedside telephone. He was here, installed, and all he had to do was to find Philipson-Smith, murder him, and then commit suicide. It was easy.

Before ten minutes had passed, he heard a knock on the door. He opened it. Mirabelle stood there.

"Say, this looks mighty comfortable," she said, peering past him into the room. "My room's just down the corridor, did you know? We're all going to be so cosy and on famee together."

He looked at her in alarm.

"Well, come on, Don Hwarn," she said, glancing at her wrist-watch. "What about taking me out to see the sights? We'll have a highball and then it'll be time for lunch."

Dumbly he escorted her out into the scurrying street. At first he was nervous and awkward, wondering just where this was supposed to be leading, but her complete absence of strain, and her general assumption that they had known each other for twenty years on the most intimate terms, finally unfroze him and he realized that he had been talking animatedly. What helped, of course, was the fact that she was not beautiful; rather short and shapeless, with a wide mouth, he felt that she offered no disturbing challenge; felt, indeed, rather ashamed of even considering the thought. Obviously this was simply American friendliness; the ruthless way in which she had picked him up did not "mean anything", as it would have done with a European woman.

After lunch he recollected his stern purpose. He had not come to Geneva to sit chatting with wide-mouthed American newspaper women.

"I must go back to the hotel," he said. "I've got some enquiries to make."

"Gee, you're getting down to business early," she said. "Me, I usually give myself a day doing nothing when I get to a new place, just soaking up the atmosphere. It pays off, you know, in newspaper work."

"That may be," he said, "but mine isn't newspaper work."

"O.K., don't talk," she said, grinning. They went back to the hotel.

"I'll leave you to your Top Secret activities, Mr. Sherlock," she said, going towards the lift. "My room's number one-oh-one if you want me."

"If I want you?" he could not help asking, startled.

"Yep," she said, signalling the lift. "If you want me for anything."

She opened the gates and got into the lift. Edgar felt that he needed to think. He sat down in the foyer, staring in front of him.

An hour or so later, his thoughts were reduced to order and a rough plan of campaign was sketched. Before thinking things out, he had vaguely supposed that the first step would be to find the Hotel Thyssen and begin shadowing Philipson-Smith; but

71

now it was clear that that side of things could easily wait. The most important question, after all, was not how to get hold of his victim, but how to dispose of him when found. His first task was to discover the nature of the city, their battlefield and their common grave. Before making any rigid plans, he must take a long, slow walk through Geneva, with his mind loosely receptive to influences and ideas. Some concrete suggestion would come to him on the wind.

He pushed through the swing doors. The short winter afternoon was already declining, with the pale sun ready at any moment to lower itself into a chill bath of mist and fizz out. The streets, even in the centre of the city, were relatively quiet, for there were several hours yet before the shops and offices closed and released a home-scurrying throng, and it was no weather for loungers. Down the long street from the Gare Cornavin to the lake, Edgar had plenty of leisure to meditate without keeping a strict eye on where he was going; the way was clear except for the women scurrying like spiders out of one shop doorway and into the next. And once he set foot on the bridge that led over the narrow strip of lake to the old city, it was as quiet as a walk in the country.

In spite of the cold, Edgar slowed down to a saunter as he came to a bridge, and looked about him, avid for the dominant impression, the fugitive idea.

Without doubt one impression over-ruled the others. The lake; that was the focal point. Everything led the eye towards it; the skin and nostrils were everywhere and always conscious of the mist it never ceased to exude; the neon signs were mockingly held in its black mirror, their dramatic shapes wriggling like feeble hooked fish; to get from one part of the city to another, one had continually to cross it. In summer, no doubt, when sky and water were blue, the lake was an inexhaustible source of gaiety to the town; now, in the sorriest season, it dragged the spirits of the whole place down to a level never reached by any city inland.

Edgar finished crossing the bridge and stood beneath the trees. Idly, in the fading light, he read a notice put up by some kind of public authority. It was one of a series explaining what different kinds of wild fowl visited the lake at each season of the year, with advice on how to recognize them. He turned and faced the mist-hung field of grey liquid, wondering how any wild creature could be anything but repelled by it. It looked colder and wetter

72

than any water he had ever seen. Away on the other shore, the stark trees looked like the rigid hands of drowning persons, held up above the surface for an instant longer than was necessary.

From that moment Edgar understood what he had to do. As the mercenary soldier hired by life to oppose its enemy, he was provided free of charge with his weapon. His instructions were plain; Philipson-Smith must make the acquaintance of that grey water. He must drop into it, soaking it into his clothes and hair, drawing it into his lungs, belching and bubbling it as he died.

It would not be difficult. His victim would be unaware even that he was in Geneva. He would shadow him, creep up on him unawares. Then, even if Philipson-Smith were a good swimmer, he would never be able to swim when his arms were pinioned by his sides. As they would be, of course, by Edgar's arms. Even if he tried to float on his back, he would never manage it when he was dragged downwards by a heavy weight. As he would be, of course, by Edgar's weight.

It would not be pleasant; even the poison he had expected to swallow was less daunting than this quietly lapping water. At least it would have left him dry, in his own warmed and lit sitting-room; in his own comfortable chair, even, unless he had squirmed so much as to fall out of it. But the principle still held; he must not, could not, sentence the accused to any torment he was unwilling to inflict on himself. One had to die somehow, and a big gesture was always worth making. A faint twitch somewhere inside him indicated a vestigial impulse, even at this late stage, to give it all up and start life afresh; but it died immediately. Was it really so much worse to fall into cold water and choke yourself, than to drag on for forty years longer and then choke yourself in exactly the same manner with pneumonia—without even the comfort of having taken your fate into your own hands?

It was night suddenly. He shivered, and crossed the street to a café, deeply hankering for a few minutes of warmth, light, alcoholic drink, and the proximity of ordinary human creatures, the unconscious, the unthinking, the doomed, those whom the idea of death had not yet saved, whom death would not yet destroy.

73

V

Moodily, Edgar sat the next morning in a café. Outside, the wide street had an air almost festive as the sunshine glinted on the windscreens of the swooping Citroëns and Volkswagens; it was a sunshine peculiar to the Swiss February, still retaining the thin clarity of winter but with a hint of new warmth and intoxication. Yet Edgar stared coldly and with dislike through the plate glass. He had been in Geneva for a whole twenty-four hours, and Philipson-Smith was still alive, still free to go about spreading his venom.

The waiter approached, his snow-white apron marking him as Swiss although his atrabilious expression was international. One would have thought that he, and not Edgar, was a frustrated murderer. Edgar ordered a cup of coffee. He spoke tolerably good French, modulated his voice politely, and assumed a fairly pleasant expression, but this did not satisfy the waiter.

"Yes, siree!" the waiter shouted. "Amur-rican, hussell!"

Edgar looked up at him in surprise and murmured, "Je suis anglais."

"Amur-rican cawfee, mess prodockshon!" cried the waiter. He moved away between the tables.

Through the window, Edgar saw Mirabelle walking determinedly along to the bus stop. She had evidently finished her prescribed initial period of atmosphere-soaking, and was in earnest this morning. Even at this distance he could see that her whole demeanour had altered.

He wondered why he disliked her so little; almost liked her, indeed. She was a successful journalist, a fact which in itself was proof of a good deal of ruthlessness and coarseness in her nature; she was entirely lacking in the keep-yourself-to-yourself attitude

74

which he had been brought up to equate with politeness—indeed, she had moved her cup and plate and joined him at breakfast, a thing he normally detested. And yet there remained her utterly disarming absence of humbug, her real good humour, and the almost hypnotic way in which she managed to create an atmosphere of intimacy. Neither asking nor inviting personal questions, she managed to convey the impression that they already knew all about each other. Even amid his gloom, at breakfast this morning, Edgar had been aware of the same strange sensation that he had felt in the restaurant-car of the train. He had been unable to shake off the feeling that they must have spent the night together.

"Beezniss, Amur-rican seestim!" shouted the waiter, placing a cup of coffee on the table. Eyeing him wearily, Edgar mentally resolved not to come to this café again. He was so powerless against the man, who was obviously consumed with bitterness against the United States and also afflicted with some kind of paralysis of the memory, leaving him with no knowledge of any other foreign nation.

He sipped his coffee. How should he fill in the long hours? Of course, as soon as darkness fell, he would have to station himself in or near the Hotel Thyssen; but until then, he had a wearily long stretch ahead of him. Ah, well, there were always the cinemas. He sank into a long reverie, feebly struggling to impose some order on the myriad new impressions he had lately received.

Between preoccupation and fatigue, his mind was working very slowly this morning, and he now noted, with an almost scientific detachment, that his eyes had been staring at a familiar object for several seconds without, as yet, having produced any mental reaction. He sat quite still, allowing the enormous time-lag to tick away, analysing his delayed reaction with a kind of frightened pleasure. Suddenly it all clicked into place. The familiar object, which was about four feet from the ground on the other side of the plate glass, twisted itself into a hideous grimace, conveying hatred and revulsion mingled with a brave defiance. It was the face of the boy Roger.

Edgar shrank back. His mind suddenly racing, he realized in a flash that if the boy was there on the pavement, his mother would not be far away, and in all probability the little girl and the baby as well; and that, having no one to talk to in this strange city, Mrs. Crabshaw might very well bring the whole spawn of hell

75

into this place to plague him while she allowed herself the pleasure of talking English for half-an-hour or so.

Too late. She was there, her eyes following the direction of the boy's pointing finger; she was at the door, she was walking over to his table; he was finished.

"Good morning. Sit down, Roger, dear. Leave that alone, Nancy. Keep still, Roger, don't do that to the table or the gentleman won't give you any nice Ovaltine. Don't do that to the window, dear. *No*, Nancy, you *can't*. I hope you don't mind us joining you, it's a relief to see an English face."

"Where's the baby?" Edgar asked. His question was motivated by fear lest she should suddenly produce the infant from some hiding-place, but he managed in the interests of politeness to keep this fear out of his voice, so that he sounded full of kindly interest in the baby, even disappointed at not seeing it there.

"Oh, he's sleeping, poor little mite," said Mrs. Crabshaw. She seemed rather animated this morning, and capable of uttering quite long sentences, provided, of course, that they related to the children. "It's all tired him dreadfully. And there's a very nice chamber-maid—Hortense, the dark one, do you know her?— who says she'll keep an eye on him while I take the others out for a bit. She'll see to him if he wakes up. She speaks English, you know."

Edgar did not see what difference this could make to the baby, but he said nothing. For the next five minutes the conversation involved itself in a thicket of "Don't want narshy old Overtine" and "The gentleman won't give you *anything* AT ALL if you do that to the table."

Suddenly, turning to Edgar, Mrs. Crabshaw said, "My husband's spending the morning at the Palais."

Edgar wondered if she meant that he had gone to a dance, then remembered.

"Is that where he's going to work?" he asked.

She nodded. "But he's not starting this morning. He's just going to be shown over. Roger, put that *down* or the gentleman won't bring you *anything*. That American woman, the one that's staying at our hotel, she's going too. What do you think of her?"

Edgar hesitated, wondering how to reply non-committally, or at best how to make her understand that Mirabelle was not the kind of girl who broke up marriages, but rather cemented them.

76

Before he could answer, however, the children began to fight, savagely and with deafening shrieks, using the salt-cellar and sugar-basin as weapons.

"Forty-Ninth Pairer Lell!" shouted the waiter, approaching them. "Amur-rican, Seevil War!"

"Two Ovaltines, please, and a coffee," said Mrs. Crabshaw, looking at him over the heads of the struggling children.

"A. Brum Lincunn, Gawd Awmighty!" the waiter shouted. The boy Roger began to throw lumps of sugar at him. One struck the back of his neck as he turned away, leaving a small pink mark.

"I shall be glad when we get a place of our own," said Mrs. Crabshaw. "Of course it was all a bit sudden, getting this job, and the pay was so good we couldn't hesitate, but I must say I hope we'll get something soon and not have to live in hotels. You never know *what* sort of people you'll meet." Her mind seemed to be still running on Mirabelle.

The waiter came up with Mrs. Crabshaw's order. Edgar expected him to shout something derisive about America, but instead he lowered his voice almost to a whisper, and, as he set down the tray, hissed in a blistering undertone, as if it were a frightful obscenity, "Hairy S. Truman."

"And Truman Capote to you," Edgar replied. They glared at one another for a moment, but the tension was broken by the boy Roger, who seized his sister's mug of Ovaltine and threw it in a blinding shower over Edgar's face and head. By the time handkerchiefs had been produced, the sticky, hot liquid wiped from his eyes, nose and hair, and the waiter despatched for a fresh supply, all thoughts of an international *fracas* had melted away.

"There ought to be some kind of a housing scheme," Mrs. Crabshaw said. "Oh, dear," she added, looking through the window with an expression of deep concern. Her habitual half-drugged air of indifference had given place to something almost approaching animation, as if her ruined nervous system had received some very strong stimulus which, for a moment, had recalled it to normal activity.

Edgar craned to see what she was looking at. Immediately he froze rigid with horror and despair. Words were beyond him, but a low animal moan escaped his lips. If Mrs. Crabshaw had been distressed at what she saw, Edgar was cruelly stunned.

In animated conversation, walking towards the door of the restaurant with the evident intention of entering, were Mr. Crabshaw, Mirabelle, Philipson-Smith and McWhirtner.

Sickened by the evident determination of Fate to ruin his plans, Edgar sat immobile and sullen. As the door swung open and the quartet, laughing and chattering, walked over to their table, he barely raised his eyes. Surely this was a dream—surely there are some accidents so grotesque that they *cannot* happen?

Mrs. Crabshaw was hardly any more pleased by the turn of events. By a typical manifestation of the psychology of a woman with young children, she hated Mirabelle because she was a woman, and Philipson-Smith and McWhirtner because they were men. They represented different, but equally dangerous, lines of attack on the citadel of the home. It was essential that nothing, neither a rival female nor the intrusion of male society and its freedoms, should come between Bob and his family duties for ten years at least.

Mr. Crabshaw knew this, and he manœuvred so as to remain at the rear of the cortège as it approached them, staring down at the floor as if looking for something he had dropped. Philipson-Smith stationed himself slightly to one side of the others, evidently in the hope of conveying that he happened by chance to be going in the same direction, but was not particularly pleased at being in their company. Only McWhirtner was evidently enjoying himself. He had his arm hooked through Mirabelle's at a rather unnatural angle, as if she were pulling away from him and he restraining her by something like force.

At first neither Philipson-Smith nor McWhirtner noticed the identity of the man sitting next to Mrs. Crabshaw. When they did, it was with different, but highly characteristic, reactions. McWhirtner gaped, his chin not so much dropping as receding into the corrugated skin behind it, and his pallid eyes staring; then an expression of ludicrous triumph came over his face as he realized that here was an unexpected opportunity to resume baiting Edgar over the episode of the spilt brandy. Philipson-Smith, for his part, immediately assumed an expression of weariness and disdain, without any intermediate stage of surprise; as if Edgar were the kind of nuisance that was likely to crop up at any point in space or time, causing every unpleasant emotion except that of shock.

78

"Well, gee, how nice to find you two together," Mirabelle cried. Then, catching Mrs. Crabshaw's stony glare, she added, "But I'm afraid this looks like intrusion—I didn't mean it that way. Why, honey, if you want to be by yourself with your husband, all you have to do is say so," she went on almost pleadingly.

"No, no, that's all right," Mr. Crabshaw called out with sudden violence from his place at the rear of the scrum. It was obvious that he was panic-stricken at the thought of being left alone with his wife. There was an instant of silence, during which Edgar looked sullenly from Philipson-Smith to McWhirtner and back again. Mirabelle was temporarily nonplussed, Mr. Crabshaw was staring out of the window as if trying to read the licence plates of passing traffic as part of a medical examination, and it looked as if the social occasion lay in ruins before it had even begun.

Fortunately, however, the children were present, and therefore no silence, awkward or otherwise, could continue for more than two or three seconds. The little girl, catching sight of her father, squirmed out of her chair, pushed it over backwards with a clatter on the tiled floor, and cried piercingly, "Daddy! See me dancing!"

Lifting up her skirt till it seemed she intended to drag it over her head, she began to strut backwards and forwards.

"Hoorah!" Mr. Crabshaw shouted. "Hoorah for Nancy!"

It was clear that the main feature of her dancing was the continual accompaniment of paternal cheering. She tottered to and fro, grasping the edge of her skirt in dimpled fists, and he stood with his hands clasped and raised above his head, shouting in an odd, strained voice, "Hoorah! Bravo Nancy!"

Their tongues loosened, everyone spoke at once. McWhirtner said he wanted a drink, Philipson-Smith asked Edgar what he was doing in Geneva, Edgar asked Mirabelle where she was going to sit, Mrs. Crabshaw said, "Put that down, Roger," Roger said something not fully audible, Mr. Crabshaw cheered wildly, and the waiter shouted "O.K., Chicago!"

After a few minutes of Bedlam, order was restored by (of all people) McWhirtner, whose alcoholic thirst was acute enough to import a compelling persistence into his clamour for something to drink. The waiter at length allowed himself to be dissuaded from his original intention of providing the whole party with a bottle of Coca-Cola each, and with savage mutters of "Eye-bal", went off to get something more suitable; chairs were found, and the bizarre assortment of humanity found themselves seated round the table. McWhirtner was next to Mirabelle; Edgar worked himself into a place opposite them, between Mr. and Mrs. Crabshaw, which he chose with the two-fold motive of preventing a domestic scene and avoiding the proximity of Philipson-Smith; and the children squirmed from one chair to another, now and then darting forward to knock an ash-tray on to the floor or tear a menu-card into fragments.

Conversation seemed at first likely to lag, but, with the appearance of a couple of bottles of wine, the blessed influence of the grape made itself felt. Either they all talked more, and more amicably, or the wine made them think that this was the case, which amounted to the same thing. Edgar took out his cigarettes and handed them round; he was pleased to see that even Philipson-Smith accepted one and murmured something that might have been interpreted as "Thanks". This was a help; the more friendly, on the surface, their relations could be made, the better the chance of accomplishing the essential manœuvres towards his object without arousing the man's suspicions. He sat back, drawing on his cigarette, with a feeling that things were going with unexpected smoothness.

All at once, however, his illusion was mercilessly shattered. Philipson-Smith leaned forward, eyeing Edgar across the quiescent figure of Mr. Crabshaw, and spoke in a voice that relentlessly cut through the general chirp of conversation.

"You didn't answer, did you, Banks, when I asked you what brought you to Geneva?"

Edgar looked desperately across at Mirabelle. She was watching him without expression, obviously waiting for his answer. He had read of characters in novels who, when asked awkward questions, looked at the wall as if expecting to find the answer written there. He looked at the wall as if expecting to find the answer written there. It was watching him without expression, obviously waiting for his answer.

"What's the matter?" said Philipson-Smith mockingly. "Is it something you don't want to tell me?"

Dragging on his cigarette till the cork tip singed, Edgar looked at him. Go on, tell the swine one more lie; one more lie, and then live in the present.

"I've taken an executive job with the Whirlwind Helicopter Company," he said. "I suppose you've heard of them."

"No, I haven't," said Philipson-Smith shortly.

"I'm surprised," said Edgar, trying to whip surprise into his voice. "They're advertised pretty widely. The object is to allow the helicopter to come into its own, particularly as regards the city-to-city flight."

"Geneva being one of the cities?"

"Oh, *Geneva*," Edgar countered emphatically. "Geneva's going to be one of the *centres*. We aim to operate twelve flights a day from Geneva, going as far afield as Rome and Amsterdam."

"What kind of helicopters are you using?" Mirabelle asked innocently.

"Piaseckis," said Edgar. "Biaxial forty-seaters." He looked at her for a long time, hoping that it would be possible, without actually adopting a conspiratorial expression, to convey to her that he was lying and induce her to start making things easier for him, instead of more difficult.

"Piaseckis? I thought the Sikorsky VS-300 was the most successful," Mr. Crabshaw unexpectedly put in.

"They're not finally adapted for civilian use yet," Edgar said flatly, beginning to sweat. What an uncomfortable lot the bastards seemed to know about helicopters!

Philipson-Smith leaned forward still further. His mouth opened, evidently to ask Edgar some fresh, searching question. This time it would stump him, for he had now unburdened himself of the fragmentary information he had on the subject. Even the bit about the Sikorsky VS-300 was pure invention, and it was not a theme on which he could go on improvising for long.

Fortunately Nancy selected this as the best moment to climb into Philipson-Smith's lap and begin trying to pull his hair down so as to hide his eyes. In this, Edgar had to admit that she showed a sound grasp of the æsthetics of the situation, for Philipson-Smith's eyes had begun to smoulder in an ugly way, full of incredulity and contempt. Mr. Crabshaw leaned across and tried to pull Nancy away, which had the effect of making her cling to Philipson-Smith and scream loudly. This in turn brought a loud, ironic cry of "Starzan Stripes!" from the waiter, who was still

81

determined to regard every incident among the group, however trivial, as evidence of the imminent downfall of the United States. Evidently the situation was saved, for the moment at least.

For the next forty minutes the conversation staggered on in this manner, like a windjammer lurching from squall to squall. But if this period was trying, it was at least fairly coherent and controlled. Looking back afterwards on the events of the day, Edgar saw clearly that the beginning of his real débâcle was the departure of Mrs. Crabshaw at lunch-time. Even though her presence had involved the presence of the children, and therefore a degree of nervous tension so high as to impart some flavour of hallucination to the most ordinary events and impressions, she had nevertheless represented a kind of sanity—though this did not become apparent until she had gone.

Her departure was marked by one of Bob's minimal gestures of rebellion, recalling the time when he had elected to go and get a cup of tea by himself in the train. The battle, though no more than a quick skirmish and never declaring itself overtly, was interesting enough to engage the attention of everyone present, so that all other conversation ceased for the moment.

"It's half-past twelve, Bob," Mrs. Crabshaw called out suddenly, over-riding the conversation. When he did not answer, she added, "That's the time they said was the best time for lunch at the hotel."

"Oh, yes?" said Mr. Crabshaw, politely, as if the subject were one that interested him but did not, so far as he could see, have any bearing on him personally.

"The children had Ovaltine, and I had coffee; here's the ticket on the table," she went on, cleverly conveying that the alcoholic liquid of which both he and she had consumed their part was exclusively the concern of the drunken riff-raff into whose company they had had the misfortune to be thrown. She stood up.

"Right you are, dear, I'll see to it," Mr. Crabshaw replied, not moving from his place at the table. He smiled at her as if to wish her a pleasant afternoon till they should meet again. Edgar, studying him, admired the naturalness and conviction he was putting into his part, but felt a scarcely-suppressed edge of nervousness beneath the surface.

The audience naturally expected Mrs. Crabshaw at this point

to move into the open with some such words as, "Well, aren't you coming?" But in this they overlooked the largely unspoken nature of the conversations, and particularly the quarrels, of married people. Mrs. Crabshaw produced a sudden diversion by turning her attention to the children, about whose necks she wrapped brightly-coloured scarves, and whose hands she thrust into gloves. By switching her attack to another part of the front in this way, she perceptibly increased Bob's nervousness and rendered him more open to her next thrust, which was, "It's always best to be punctual when you're staying in an hotel."

Mr. Crabshaw, like a boxer who has been warned for holding, came out of his corner with his guard up cleanly. "Oh, the *hotel*," he said, with the air of one clearing up a mystery. "I see what you mean, the hotel. I should have mentioned before, dear—I didn't think of going back to the hotel this lunch-time."

"What," said Mrs. Crabshaw, then paused for three full seconds, "*did* you think of doing this lunch-time?"

As Mr. Crabshaw opened his mouth to speak, McWhirtner, for some reason, thrust in. "We'll luik after him, Missus Crabshaw," he said slyly, leering up at her. "We'll see he gets a guid meal an' comes back to ye safe an' sooned." His tone and manner combined to suggest that as soon as Mrs. Crabshaw had left the restaurant he was going to open a suitcase full of heroin, give Mr. Crabshaw a strong dose and then take him to an expensive brothel. He even cast a knowing glance out of the corner of his eye in the direction of the waiter, as if the waiter had the address of the brothel in a small book in his pocket and needed only a little encouragement to reveal it. Watching him, Edgar felt that the degree of utter moral lowness he managed to infuse into the atmosphere was something without parallel; then he remembered Flannery, who, if present, would doubtless have had the suitcase of heroin open on the table by this time, and would need no information supplied by the waiter on how to spend a vicious afternoon. So intense was the impression of spiritual dereliction called up by the combined presence of McWhirtner in the flesh, and Flannery in the spirit, that it blotted out a few sentences of the conversation, and by the time he was capable of paying attention again, Mrs. Crabshaw had grasped a child in either hand and was frankly shooting unspoken menaces at her husband across the table.

83

"There's no call, that *I* can see, for you to go undermining your health by not eating proper meals."

"Ah, but that's just it," Mr. Crabshaw countered, unsuccessfully trying by his manner to suggest a barrister who has trapped an astute witness into making a damaging admission. "There's nothing worse for my health than dragging round doing a heavy afternoon's foot-slogging on a full stomach. I've got to spend the whole time between now and five o'clock down at the . . . I've got to go round all the . . . ." for some reason he did not seem able to specify exactly where he was going; Edgar, once more an enthralled spectator, divined that this was caused not by any duplicity on his part, not by any lack of genuine places that he really was supposed to be visiting, but simply by a partial mental black-out brought on by the strain of the argument. "That's why I thought I'd just stay quietly here and have some cheese and a cup of coffee." The pace of his speech increased and his articulation became increasingly blurred. "Light lunch best from point of view health foot-slogging to do, *coffee and cheese*."

The sudden emphasis with which he brought out these last two words seemed to attract the attention of the boy Roger, who began to chant loudly, "Coffee and cheese. Coffee and cheese. Shiver and sneeze. I made a rhyme then, Mummy, Mummy, I said——"

"Cuppa cawfee, doe-knots!" shouted the waiter, coming towards them between the tables. "Amur-rican, my define!"

"You can have cheese and light things like that when we go back to the——"

"Listen, Mummy, Mummy, listen. Coffee and cheese, shiver and——"

Mrs. Crabshaw, giving up, fell silent; as she did so her habitual state of drugged calm reasserted itself. Her geared-down nervous system was not capable of these flights for more than a few moments, and it was evident as she turned away and took the still chanting children out of the door that she was not, for the moment, angry with her husband for not coming home to lunch. It was not that she lacked the will to be angry. It was simply that the small, bright spring of animation which had welled up from the desert of her personality had dried up as suddenly as it had appeared. Later, no doubt, she would find the means of becoming, for a few minutes, a violent scold; but behind this or any other display of feeling lay lethargy, her habitual state, waiting to claim her. The loose blonde fleece at the back of her neck gleamed almost peacefully at them as she disappeared into the street.

Immediately Edgar's pleased appreciation of this well-acted interlude was punched to pieces, before he had time to savour it in his mind. Philipson-Smith, who had been ignoring the contestants and keeping his eyes sullenly and scornfully on Edgar's face, set down his glass on the table with a sharp, disdainful movement, and spoke wetly.

"It comes under the heading of coincidence, doesn't it, Banks?"

"Comes—under the heading," Edgar stammered, "of what, did you say?"

"Of coincidence," said Philipson-Smith wickedly.

"What does?" Edgar feebly countered. As a boy, he had sometimes played draughts with his grandfather, and when the old gentleman, who always beat him, had deprived him of all his pieces except one, he had sometimes been able to postpone the inevitable defeat for a few minutes by moving that one remaining piece backwards and forwards in a safe corner, while the menacing Kings closed in at their leisure. He was rapidly getting the same feeling now. And yet, damn it all, he thought, he was going to *murder* this man; he was here to hunt, not to be hunted.

"Don't you really know what I mean? I mean the fact that you should turn up in Geneva just when——"

"Will you please for Christ's sake STOP that!" Mirabelle screamed. Startled, they turned and looked at her.

"Stop what?" Philipson-Smith asked.

"Ask him," Mirabelle replied, with a jerk of her head towards McWhirtner. "Ask him: he knows."

McWhirtner looked across the table with a complacent, lubricious smirk. Already drunk, he appeared to take it almost as a compliment, a tribute to his masculinity, that he had managed to shock and offend Mirabelle. Without needing to be told, Edgar knew the kind of thing he must have been doing; squeezing her hand or groping under the table for her knee.

Mirabelle poured herself out a drink and took it down in a gulp. That left the bottle empty, and McWhirtner, to whom an empty bottle represented as great a challenge as an unsullied woman, began urgently signalling to the waiter.

Edgar, drinking fast once more, began to feel that he needed

85

something to eat. His grasp of reality was weakening, and he needed the bite of cheese on his tongue, the bulk of bread in his stomach, to keep him steady. Once more the waiter was summoned, a parley was held, and the man was with difficulty induced to stop chanting in a contemptuous monotone, "Biff stick. French fried p'tayrs"; finally a slab of cheese and some long baton-shaped loaves made their appearance among the litter of glasses and heaped ashtrays on the table.

Later Mr. Crabshaw, having eaten rapidly and heartily of the cheese, appeared to remember his duty towards his absent wife, and said, "I must have some coffee."

Mirabelle beamed. "And what say we have a little Kirsch in it?" she suggested to the company at large. She seemed to have quite recovered her good humour; Mrs. Crabshaw was not there to accuse her, wordlessly, of being a painted Jezebel, and McWhirtner had for some minutes had his hands occupied in feeding himself.

"I got better s'ggeshon," a voice said thickly. "Nemmine the coffee. Less just have the Kirsch."

For some reason Mirabelle and Mr. Crabshaw both laughed when they heard these words, while McWhirtner stopped chewing and stared across at Edgar. Considering carefully, Edgar realized after a moment that the voice that had just spoken was not that of Philipson-Smith, McWhirtner, Mr. Crabshaw or the waiter. Being a male voice, it could not, he thought slowly and logically, have been Mirabelle's voice. Perhaps some intruder, anxious to strike up acquaintance with them, was standing behind one of the chairs. He looked over his shoulder. There was no one there. It must have been his own voice.

But how could it be his own voice when it was so obviously the voice of a rather drunk person? Soberly he worked at this problem for a moment, finally coming up with the answer. He, Edgar, must be rather drunk.

Not too drunk, however, to keep a grip on the basic realities of the situation. Its major strategy was, in any case, very simple: now that he and Philipson-Smith had been thrown together, it was no longer possible to shadow him unseen and make the final assault a complete surprise attack. On the other hand, that part of his original plan could easily be dispensed with. The essential thing was not that Philipson-Smith should be unaware of his presence, but merely that he should be unaware of his intentions. Indeed, he thought suddenly, it was possible that their being brought into contact in this natural, unpremeditated way was a piece of good luck. All he had to do was to stay in his present company, avoiding any awkward questions and taking care not to provoke a quarrel, and sooner or later they were bound to find themselves walking near the lake, with the advantage that Philipson-Smith would be entirely unsuspecting. This, from all points of view, was better than having to shadow him. Edgar had never been a Boy Scout, and had thus missed his best opportunity to become a master of the art of stalking; at the age of fifteen he had felt, with the heedless confidence of youth, that a modern urban-dwelling man had no need to spend his leisure hours learning the tactics of the aboriginal hunter, and that world food supplies, however menaced, would be a long time in sinking to the level at which survival would depend on one's ability to catch a hare with a home-made net and cook it over a wood fire. How little he had foreseen of what life was to bring him! Baden-Powell had, after all, the laugh on Edgar, who, if only he had enrolled as a Scout, would by this time have used his trained woodsman's eye to detect a dozen different ways in which Philipson-Smith could be trapped. From this, sitting heavily at the café table, Edgar deduced a general rule of human conduct: *always assume that whatever the future is like, it will be more primitive than the present. Learn to cut your nails with your left hand, for some day you might not have a right.*

His drunkenness now began to close in on him, but as usual his ratiocinative faculties were the last to go. He knew that, so long as he did not drink any more, he was securely in possession of his mental, if not his physical, processes. Lighting a cigarette, he addressed himself to thinking out the problem of how to turn the present situation to account. By why think it out? Why not simply leave it to chance? After all, it was chance, a chance that would have seemed incredible before it happened, that had put this company round one table. Yes, that reminded him, who or what was responsible? How had it happened?

Impressed suddenly with the urgency of this question, he leaned forward to Mirabelle. "Did you know these two before, or did you meet them for the first time this morning?" he asked. The question seemed rather brusque, almost police-court, in its unmodified form, so he added, "If you don't think me too curious, that is."

"We were just going round the Palais des Nations," she replied. "They don't let you wander about just as you like, you have to wait till there's a guide taking a group round."

"An' we starruted a conversation, didnae we, luvey?" McWhirtner asked her tenderly. He was like a happy bridegroom rapturously telling the story of how he first came to know his bride. He looked at her possessively.

"You can probably imagine how it was," she said to Edgar. "We were hardly in the second room before I was taken into custody by Burning Rabbie here." She showed no surprise that Edgar and the other two should be already acquainted; probably thinking, American fashion, that in so small a country as England everyone knew everyone else automatically.

So the incredible coincidence had turned out to be mere routine after all. Obviously, in their first full day in Geneva, they had all visited the Palais des Nations; Mirabelle and Mr. Crabshaw, having already met, had formed one half of the bloc ready-made, and the link between the two halves had been supplied by McWhirtner's rage to become acquainted with Mirabelle. Edgar began to realize that the Scot, although of so much weaker character than his master, could sometimes sway him by the violence of his appetites; when, for one reason or another, McWhirtner made a sudden lurch in any direction, Philipson-Smith would be dragged along. It had happened in this case, and so the formation of the party owed, in fact, nothing to chance. The very choice of the restaurant had been dictated by the fact that Mr. Crabshaw had arranged to meet his wife there. In fact, the only accidental part of the whole business was the fact that he, Edgar, had chosen that particular place to sit in; and even that was logical enough, for it was the café nearest his hotel.

As he sat thinking, ignoring the conversation, Edgar suddenly became aware of a rubbing sensation on the inner side of his right ankle, a sensation too sharply-defined and external to be produced by his drunkenness. Peering down, expecting to find a dog or cat under the table, he saw McWhirtner's foot slowly scraping backwards and forwards, so that their ankles swished together. Was the fellow insane? His reactions slowed down by the wine, Edgar took several seconds to discover the probable explanation;

then he glanced up again, at McWhirtner's face. As he had expected, it was turned towards Mirabelle with an expression of lubricious affection.

Taking careful aim, for it was terribly important to make this both hard and accurate, Edgar drew back his left foot, leaving his right one there as bait. Pausing, he inched his chair slightly to one side so as to give absolutely free play to his leg; then, with precision and venom, he launched a terrible kick at Mc-Whirtner's right shin.

"Holy God!" McWhirtner shouted. He jumped up, sending his chair over backwards with a clatter, and stood nursing his leg. "There wasnae ony call to dae that, lassie," he said to Mirabelle.

"Do what? I didn't do anything," she said, looking at him in surprise.

"Och, yes ye did," said McWhirtner. "Ye ken verra weel ye kicked me. Holy God," he said again, massaging his shin. Sitting down, he rolled up his trouser leg. The skin was broken, and already it was evident that there would be a large bump and a livid bruise. Edgar felt happy and peaceful.

"Ye ocht to be a bluidy fuitball player," McWhirtner continued, staring reproachfully at her.

"Brooklyn Dodgers! Noter Daim!" the waiter called out from behind the bar. He imitated the motion of swinging a baseball bat.

"That guy's a little mixed up in his games," Mirabelle said.

"He isnae the only bluidy one," McWhirtner grumbled. He drew up his chair again and poured out another drink. "A don't mind a slap in the face,"—he forgot, in his anger, to say "dinna" instead of "don't"—"but a bluidy great kick on the shin's another bluidy matter."

"Oh, shut up, for God's sake," said Philipson-Smith suddenly. Like everyone else, he was beginning to show signs of having drunk too much and too quickly, and the effect in his case was of increased waspishness and misanthropy. Edgar could see that it was going to be hard work avoiding a quarrel with him.

McWhirtner, sulking heavily, drained and refilled his glass. A heavy and dangerous silence fell, and Edgar was afraid that it would be broken by some fresh outburst of bickering, in which case the party would probably split up and his plans would once more be in ruins; he would be back where he started from, only rather worse off. He strained his faculties to think of a remark

89

that would quieten the gusty atmosphere, but before he could think of one, Mr. Crabshaw said, "It's about time I was pushing off."

He said this rather wistfully, as if feeling something more than the normal reluctance to go back to work in the afternoon, and stood up in a peculiarly hesitant manner. It was hard to resist the feeling that what he really wanted was a little coaxing to stay where he was for the time being. Not having a heart of stone, Edgar began slowly searching for the right words in which to express himself, but for the second time in succession he found himself beaten to the post. For some reason it had become terribly difficult to marshall enough words and shape them into a coherent sentence; possibly the explanation lay in the rigid censorship he was having to impose on his own speech, always looking twice at every word before he uttered it in case it should convey something revealing to Philipson-Smith. The combined effect of this inhibition and his slight, but increasing, intoxication was to deprive him of the power of speech almost entirely.

At all events, it was Mirabelle who cried out gaily, "Well, gosh, Adam, there's no need to run away so quickly. It's only twenty of two. We've all got work to do this afternoon, but we can afford the time to stay here and be comfortable for a bit yet."

He sat down obediently and with a thankful smile; but, evidently needing some small show of justification on practical grounds, he said, "I think I'll have another coffee. I don't think there was quite enough Kirsch in the last one."

"Not half enough," she laughed expansively. "We should order another round with double ones in them this time."

Mr. Crabshaw began waving and beckoning, and finally the waiter plodded wearily towards them between the tables, glaring. On receiving the order he stood staring at them for a considerable time, his eyes travelling from face to face, as if they had collectively offered him an insult, and he was trying to decide which one should be assaulted first. When he had at last turned away and left them, they held a short, anxious conference.

"Do you think he takes it as an insult to the quality of the stuff he brought us the first time?" Mr. Crabshaw asked, puzzled.

"No, no, it's something to do with thinking we're Americans," said Edgar. The sentence as it stood was, he felt, rather insulting to Mirabelle, so he hurried on, "he seems to have some sort of deep-rooted . . . whatever it is he's got seems to be pretty well . . . pretty well . . ." his voice died out under the impossibility of getting the words to the front of his mouth in an even flow.

"Maybe there's some tragic personal history," said Mirabelle in a low voice, her eyes wide with sympathy. "An incident like, well, a G.I. taking his girl away from him, or something."

"It's just that he doesn't like Americans," Philipson-Smith interposed curtly, his tone leaving it beyond doubt that, as far as he could see, the man was behaving in a perfectly natural and proper manner. He looked round contemptuously at the others, evidently hoping that his words would be followed by a short, pained silence in which they would suffer embarrassment and confusion. Unfortunately McWhirtner ruined the effect by coming in immediately on his tail with, "Och, there's nae mystery aboot it. It's somethin' ta dae wi' gettin' a bigger teep."

"No, no," Mirabelle cried impatiently. As a journalist, she had an insatiable thirst for human interest stories, and an in-grained habit of making them out of any material, or no material at all if need be. "I tell you I can see it in the guy's face. Why, can't you just picture it! There he is standing on the street, dolled up fit to roll 'em, and waiting two hours—it starts raining, he gets soaked but he won't quit, he loves her, see? Then across the other side he sees his chick walking along with a G.I. One look's enough for him—she's got her face turned away but there's only one chick that walks the way she does. So he goes home, there's his old mother, and she says to him, why, Gustave or whatever his name is, I thought you were going out with Annette this evening. *Annette?* he says. Why, that lousy two-timing little broad, Mom, if you think I'd bother—then he can't go on, can't finish it, and he bursts out——"

"Shhhhh!" Mr. Crabshaw hissed. The waiter was approaching them, holding the tray with one hand and fumbling inside his coat with the other as if for a revolver. As he set down their drinks, they looked at him gravely, full of pity for his sufferings.

However, crushing as the waiter's load of sorrows may have been, it had not prevented him from being open-handed with the Kirsch. As Edgar sipped his portion, it seemed to turn into scalding vapour somewhere in his throat, and rise straight into his brain without any intervening journey through the stomach. Aware that this was an illusion, he was also aware that the sensation of raw, aggressive well-being that surged through his frame was none the less, within its limits, real and immensely helpful. His spirits had been flagging, but now they revived with remarkable force. He glanced sideways at Philipson-Smith, bubbling inwardly with happiness at the thought of how neatly the man's fate had been delivered into his hands; for so, in his new-found exultation, he now read the situation, ignoring its swirl of complexities and cross-currents.

McWhirtner, meanwhile, since receiving Edgar's kick on the shin, had been remarkably quiescent in his attitude towards Mirabelle. Now, however, the pain had had time to wear off, and he had besides, in Homeric phrase, put away his desire of eating and drinking. Looking at her fixedly, he began to scrape his chair sideways until it jammed against hers. Edgar watched him intently, ready to intervene and frustrate the physical advances he appeared likely to make at any moment; but the Scot, evidently mindful of the setback which had greeted his previous attempt, must have decided on a less direct approach. He began fumbling purposefully in the inner pocket of his jacket.

"Ye may know it or ye may not," he said impressively to Mirabelle, "but ye happen to be sittin' next to one o' the best livin' Scots poets."

She either affected not to hear him, or was genuinely sunk in thought, for she made no reply. Undaunted, McWhirtner produced his crumpled wad of typescript.

"It's tradeetional," he said. "Noo, this fairst one is a translation o' a foorteenth-century——"

"Oh, God," said Philipson-Smith loudly.

". . . a foorteenth, or possibly airly fifteenth . . ."

"Listen, for God's sake," said Philipson-Smith urgently. "I'll make you a straight offer, McWhirtner. Are you listening?"

McWhirtner paused, the top sheet of his typescript still held at the ready. Without answering, he looked at Philipson-Smith warily.

"If you'll fold that stuff up and put it back in your pocket, *and keep it there*, I'll stand you a good stiff drink."

"Wha' kind o' drink?" McWhirtner countered, allowing his suspicious squint full play. Once more Edgar was interested to see how the disciple had, as it were, certain well-defined areas of authority over the master, certain predictable periods when there was nothing to be done with him, like a normally reliable transport animal who was subject to natural attacks of wildness or *must*.

"Any kind you like," said Philipson-Smith, showing that he was prepared to concede unlimited ground during this spasm of revolt; he could make up for it, of course, by drawing the rein tighter when it was over.

McWhirtner nodded gravely. "A'll hold ye to that," he said, folding up his typescript and putting it back into his pocket.

Whether Philipson-Smith's next suggestion was motivated by a wish to postpone the moment when he would have to pay for McWhirtner's drink, or whether it arose from some more obscure impulse, Edgar had no means of telling. At all events, he stood up abruptly and said, as if unbearably plagued and bored, "Look here, for God's sake let's clear out of here. I've just about had enough of it."

Again Edgar speculated on the state of mind which underlay his words, noticing that he did not even attempt to get himself and McWhirtner out of the place by themselves. Of course it would have been impossible to detach the Scot from the company of Mirabelle, and therefore, if necessary, the whole party would have to be moved. It was enjoyable to see a really self-willed and authoritarian person hamstrung in this way, and the joke became even richer when one added the fact that by this enforced acquiescence he was actually helping to engineer his own death.

Mirabelle beamed delightedly. "Why, yes, let's do that," she cried hoarsely. "I know a fine comfortable little joint on the other side of the water. Discovered it last night. It's——"

At the words "the other side of the water" Edgar stiffened; his brain surged with the immediacy of the situation, so that he missed whatever was said next. Was it to come already? He had always imagined the assault as taking place at night, and here they were, about to cross the lake in the middle of the day. Still, there was no reason why the thing should not be brought off. There would, of course, be more people about, and quite possibly those people would include some interfering fool who would dive in and attempt to "save" them. But that was a chance he had to take. Standing up, he bunched his fists inside his jacket pockets, and shot Philipson-Smith a look in which he made hardly any attempt to mask the grimness. It was nearly time to throw off the pretence.

It seemed that, during the few moments in which Edgar had been oblivious of the talk around him, Mr. Crabshaw had agreed to the proposal. So it was really coming. There they all were, taking down their overcoats from the pegs, beckoning the waiter, gathering up the scattered bills and working out the amount they had to pay.

Lurching slightly as he drew on his coat, Edgar remembered his share in the reckoning. Snatching out his wallet, he threw down a sum far in excess of what he actually owed, and waved aside Mirabelle's protests. Again the glorious sense of living in the present was flowing through his veins. Let them have those miserable bits of paper! He had done with the whole weary business of accumulating and spending them. It was the time for expansive gestures. Then he realized, as he turned away, that Mirabelle and Mr. Crabshaw were exchanging a sympathetic glance. It was clear that they thought he was drunk, and that his generosity was simply a result of befuddlement. Well, they could think it. They would see soon enough. Anyway, it was true: he *was* drunk, but not in the way they imagined.

Walking over to the door, he turned to let the others catch up with him. He saw Mirabelle hand the money to the waiter, and then pause as if saying something to him; her head was tilted to gaze earnestly up into his face. The waiter stiffened, took a pace backwards, and shouted violently, "Occupez-vous de ce qui vous regarde!" Not at all put out by his outburst, she smiled at him sweetly, full of womanly understanding. Goaded, he flailed the metal tray above his head and hissed, "Leeberty Statch you, phooey!" Nodding sympathetically, she came over to the others and they emerged into the street.

"What were you saying to him?" Edgar asked her.

"Oh," she said dreamily, savouring the situation, "I just asked him if she was very beautiful. Then I told him never mind, he'd get over it one day."

One day, Edgar thought, *a lot of things will be got over one day. But that's the future, and there are two of us here who won't see any future.* Turning again to look at Philipson-Smith, he ground his foot against the kerb-stone and staggered heavily. Mr. Crabshaw and Mirabelle exchanged glances, the duplicates of the ones they had exchanged before. Damn it all, he must pull himself together. Which way were they going, anyhow? They

94

ought to have been turning to the left to go down the Rue Cornavin. Instead, they were moving straight ahead. What was happening?

"Take it easy, Sherlock," Mirabelle said gaily, taking hold of his arm. "Over here's where the trams go from."

His pang of alarm and annoyance at being called Sherlock, in front of the man he had been shadowing, deflected Edgar's attention, for several seconds, from the word "tram". When it penetrated, he stood still, halted as by a sudden onset of paralysis. They were not walking! They were going to sit in some damned horrible tram and be carried safely over the lake without a chance of getting near the water! "Oh, I say," he burst out vehemently. "Surely we—I mean, why not just walk over to this place? It seems silly to go on the tram when it's, when it's such a nice afternoon."

His companions also halted, and, turning, they stared at him in surprise. "A nice afternoon?" Mr. Crabshaw asked gently. Edgar opened his mouth to repeat what he had said, then closed it again, wearily. The rain was pouring down; above them, the clouds were dark and unbroken, the gutters at their feet were flooded. His own hair was beginning to cling wetly to his scalp. Looking round, he noticed yet again the sympathetic exchange of glances.

"Would you like to go back to the hotel and lie down?" Mr. Crabshaw asked kindly. Fury exploded inside Edgar's head.

"NO," he said loudly, almost shouting. "No, I should NOT like to go back to the hotel and lie down. I should hate to go back to the hotel and lie down. If there's one thing I should dislike it would be to go back to the——"

With soothing murmurs of "That's all right, old chap," and "Come on now, take it easy," they led him away to the tram-stop. A car rumbled up, and with infinite consideration Mirabelle and Mr. Crabshaw helped Edgar up the steps, got him into a seat, and paid his fare. Philipson-Smith and McWhirtner, each deriving his own kind of pleasure from the incident, followed, and the tram started.

Edgar stared fixedly at his watch until the dial resumed its normal circularity; then he read the figures. Ten to six. How much longer were they going to stay there? What was it that the others

95

seemed to find so attractive about this place and about each other? As usual, he supposed, it was a complex of reasons that held them together; Mr. Crabshaw was in a frankly escapist mood, putting off as long as possible his formal entry into the new life which he was going to hate so much and which was to rob him of his last shreds of human identity: Mirabelle was in the grip of her own conviviality and her desire to be surrounded by men: McWhirtner was there because of Mirabelle and because they were drinking and idling. Philipson-Smith—here, for the first time, one ran into an enigma, but the leading clues seemed to be, firstly, that he had a certain need for the company of McWhirtner and did not wish to let him slip the collar and go off on a blind that might last for several days, and secondly that he had begun to succumb to lethargy after so many hours of drinking. That only left Edgar himself, and he was there in order to murder Philipson-Smith.

In this way, carefully and stolidly, he worked out the logic of the situation. But ten to six! It was incredible that they should have sat in this tiny, stuffy place for so long. Their own conversation was fragmentary and boring, and there were no other diversions in the place to keep them amused. That is, unless one counted the juke-box. He had been slightly surprised, on entering, to discover that this discreetly furnished little bar, with its deep carpets and convincing display of chromium, glass, and black leather, should have possessed—no, it was too crude to call it a juke-box—an automatic record-player. It was, of course, very different from the vulgar-looking painted metal box found in pin-table arcades; but there, within the smoothly grained wood, behind the polished glass, was the stock of tiny long-playing records, each identified by a neat label outside the case. For some reason, this apparatus had fascinated McWhirtner, whom no one had hitherto suspected of being musical. He had been borrowing coins from Philipson-Smith at a steady rate ever since they had come in, and had by now worked through the entire repertory of the machine. At this moment, its strains once more died away, and McWhirtner once more began to clamour for the loan of a twenty-centime piece.

"Wouldn't it be cheaper to hire a barrel-organ man to come round with you everywhere?" Mr. Crabshaw asked him. "I'm sure it would work out cheaper than twenty centimes a tune."

"Barrel-organ men have monkeys," said Mirabelle, eyeing McWhirtner gravely. "There might be a risk of confusion."

"Och, a bit o' music makes the harrut grow fonder," said McWhirtner. He gazed at her tenderly. "Music hath charrums to suthe the savage——"

"Oh, for God's sake take the money and *shut up*!" Philipson-Smith cut in, employing his unbearable-ennui voice, which by this stage had become more or less permanent with him.

McWhirtner went over to the record-player and started it up again. Whether by accident or design, he had lit on a record of Bessie Smith singing "I Used To Be Your Sweet Mama." The powerful strains filled the small room, mingling with a burst of conversation from a group of hectic young people, probably students from Geneva University, who had just entered.

"Oh, Bed, isn't it Godlam?" Mr. Crabshaw said wearily.

The others looked at him for a moment, and Philipson-Smith, who seldom spoke unless there were a rebuke to be administered, said, "I suppose you mean, Oh, God, isn't it Bedlam."

"You can suppose what you like," said Mr. Crabshaw stiffly, "and I can say what I like. Oh, Bed, it's Godlam," he repeated. "Any objection?" he added threateningly to Philipson-Smith.

Edgar wondered what would happen if they quarrelled and fought, and Mr. Crabshaw killed Philipson-Smith. He supposed the only thing left would be for him to go and commit suicide independently. Unless, of course, he could manage to take the blame, making it appear that he, and not Mr. Crabshaw, had committed the murder. What a curious trial there would be, with Edgar trying to establish his own guilt in the face of all the evidence accumulated by the police. "I put it to you, Gentlemen," he would say to the Jury. "Why, and for what possible motive or combination of motives, should I wish to put my own neck in the noose if I were innocent? No, it is because I am guilty, it is because that guilt is gnawing at my soul, that I cannot see an innocent man take my punishment."

"Ever heard the joke about the man who gave his fiancée a watch?" Mr. Crabshaw asked of nobody in particular.

"I used to be your sweet Momma, sweet Poppa," Bessie Smith sang, "but now I'm just as sour as can be."

"Look at this man, the prisoner," Edgar said to the jury. "A

97

man known to be harmless, peace-loving, a devoted husband and the father of three delightful children. Are those children to become orphans simply on the strength of a mass of loose circumstantial evidence?"

"It was a very nice watch, but it was empty," said Mr. Crabshaw.

"Gee, that's better now they've put the lights on," said Mirabelle. "Well, it looks as if we were in for a nice pleasant evening all together. I don't remember when I've know an afternoon go so——"

"Look, on the other hand, at me," Edgar thundered to the attentive jurors. "A man everywhere considered, and rightly, to have made a sorry failure of his life. A man without ties, without steadying responsibilities. Professionally, well known to be lazy and unreliable. Personally, well known to be negligible. I call the evidence of Mr. McWhirtner on both these points; you have heard the testimony of Mr. Stimms as to my conduct during the years when he was my employer, and you have heard him describe how I inconsiderately, and without any warning, abandoned my duties to drift about across Europe. In the words of the poet, look here upon this picture, and on this. Why should there be the slightest hesitation in the minds of any of you, as to which of us must own to the guilt of destroying a fellow-creature?"

"You had your chance, and you proved unfaithful," Bessie Smith sang. "Now I'm gonna be just mean and hateful."

" 'Why did you give me a watch without any works?' she asked," Mr. Crabshaw pursued.

"What do you say we make the next round black coffee?" Mirabelle asked. "Too much of this wine doesn't agree with your inside."

"Impossible," said McWhirtner, shaking his head slowly. "There isnae ony help to be got fra fluidin' yirsel wi' non-alcoholic swill. The best thing'd be tae switch over tae somethin' wi' a real punch to it. That reminds me, Rollo, ye havenae boght me the dram yet."

"Listen, everybody, before I forget," Mirabelle suddenly cried out. "There was an idea I had . . . I almost forgot."

"Got ideas, eh? Ye arenae the only one, luvey," said Mc-Whirtner fondly. He smiled his tender bridegroom's smile.

"I've had a message from my paper," Mirabelle continued. "I've got to go up into the Alps next week-end, to a little place called Les Glissades. It's very beautiful, I've seen pictures of it," she said solemnly.

"I'll give you the works when we get married," said Mr. Crabshaw. The others stared at him in amazement.

"You'll give me *what*?" Mirabelle asked in a stunned whisper.

"No, no, not *you*," Mr. Crabshaw said patiently.

"Then who?" she demanded on a rising note. "You're——"

"That's what the man said," he muttered drowsily, as if losing interest in the subject. "The man in the story."

Mirabelle looked at him for a moment. "I give up," she said finally. "Well, look, what I was saying is this. I've got a great idea—just great. My paper wants me to get an interview with Earl Hammer—he's an American jazz pianist who's knocking them cold over here just now, on tour—and it seems he's going to be at Les Glissades next week-end. He's difficult to interview, and they want me to chase him up there."

"The police have done their work well," Edgar admitted. "But there are certain necessary limitations to police work. It must needs be impersonal, essentially co-operative, not to say bureaucratic. I will not deny that the evidence they have assembled looks, on the face of it, logical enough."

"Wouldn't it be a lovely idea if we *all* went up there—all together? We could all do with a change and some mountain air and snow. Why, think how the wife and the kiddies would enjoy it! We could all have such a lovely gay week-end."

The students, who had seated themselves at the bar, began making an ill-defined scuffling noise; two of them seemed to be fighting.

"But the police, with their impersonal, bureaucratic methods, must always find that the *human* truth of the situation will elude them. It is the human truth that is assembled here, in this court, to-day; it is the human truth that is plain for you all to see."

Edgar found that Mr. Crabshaw was staring at him solicitously. He flushed with annoyance and began to light a fresh cigarette.

"Sure you're feeling all right, old chap, are you?" Mr. Crabshaw asked. Considerately, he kept his voice low so that the others should not hear.

"Why shouldn't I be all right?" Edgar asked crossly.

"Oh, no reason at all," Mr. Crabshaw said in a tone obviously designed to humour him. "It was just that you—well, you seemed to be moving your lips in a funny way, and looking straight ahead, as if you were talking to yourself."

Edgar fought back his irritation and produced a sickly smile. "Thanks for telling me," he said. "My mind must have been wandering for a minute." Eyeing Mr. Crabshaw, he kept the smile on his face for a little longer, at the same time deciding to let him stew in his own juice if ever it came to a murder trial.

"You can all get away, can't you? What do you say?" Mirabelle appealed to the company.

Edgar, realizing in retrospect the gist of what she had been saying, sat passively, awaiting the decision of the others. It was nothing to him; neither he nor Philipson-Smith would be going; and, probably, the shock of their combined death, and the investigations that were bound to follow it, would rob them of either the inclination or the opportunity to take any week-end trips to the mountains. Nevertheless, it interested him, in a rather detached and Olympian way, to see their reactions. Philipson-Smith was obviously prepared to dismiss the idea contemptuously, without troubling to make up any polite excuses; but, before venturing to do so, he glanced at McWhirtner to see whether his mood of rebellion would extend to cover this situation as well. Most emphatically, it did.

"Of coorse we'll come wi' ye, darlin'," he cried, seizing her hand. "We've naethin' special on next week-end, eh, Rollo?"

They glared at one another for a moment; then, once more, Edgar had the delicious sensation of seeing Philipson-Smith knuckle under. He simply did not dare allow the submerged struggle of wills to come to an open clash. McWhirtner, in the grip of his violent hankering for Mirabelle, would have snapped the bond between them like straw, leaving Philipson-Smith stranded: a masterless servant is enviable by comparison with a servantless master, and they both knew it.

"I'll think it over. I'm not sure what we're doing," Philipson-Smith muttered wetly.

"We arenae daein' onythin'!" McWhirtner shouted, flashing rebellion from his pale eyes. "It's all settled, sweetie," he said to Mirabelle. "We're comin'. An you too, eh?" he added to Mr. Crabshaw.

"Well . . . I have been thinking, already, of getting the family up to the mountains for a bit . . . it seems a good opportunity if we're all . . ." Mr. Crabshaw murmured, half in soliloquy.

"Why, gee, isn't that fine!" Mirabelle beamed. "All of us'll go! And you, Sherlock, you haven't said you'll come, but you *will*, won't you?"

Edgar nodded silently. That conversation was, in fact, the last event of the evening to stay in his mind with any clarity. The rest furnished a good many impressions, but all were in some degree blurred and unreal. Doggedly, wherever they went, he made one of the party; every time they left one place to move on to another, he suggested that they should go on foot, in the hope of crossing the lake; heavily, he sat at countless tables, now eating, now drinking, now smoking, always manœuvring to avoid a clash with Philipson-Smith. Beyond that he was incapable of going. The power of making conversation, or of attending to the conversation that went on about him, had vanished, and with it had gone any sense of direction, or ability to distinguish one bar or restaurant from another. He had the impression that they visited about a dozen places, each more or less similar to the one with the juke-box, but it might as easily have been three or thirty. In place of the usual ordered and arranged sequence of impressions, all he had now was a sense of the monotonous alternation of indoors and outdoors. The indoor periods were further subdivided according to whether the room they sat in was large or small, dim or bright, noisy or quiet; as the evening progressed he became aware that the small and noisy kind moved into the ascendancy.

At length he became, mistily, aware that Mr. Crabshaw was saying, "It's long past midnight; let's get home to bed." Then they were outside; the night air smacked into Edgar's face like a custard pie. Coughing, he lurched against the wall, then pulled himself erect and shook off, not violently but with a certain dignified reproachfulness, the friendly guiding hand that Mr. Crabshaw laid upon his shoulder. A fine rain was falling, mingling with the mist so that it was hard to distinguish between the two; it was as if the spirit of the lake had silently reached out and taken possession of the city. Tired and silent, they began to walk down the gleaming pavement. After a moment's pause at the traffic-lights, while the thin trickle of late-night cars collected into a pool and then dispersed, they were across the wide street and on the bridge.

101

Edgar, breathing carefully through his nose as if air were rationed, worked his way to the side nearest the stone parapet. Philipson-Smith was in front, jolting stiffly along on his short legs while McWhirtner, at his side, kept up a confused flow of conversation. Mirabelle was on Edgar's left, and, beyond her on the outside of the pavement, Mr. Crabshaw. No one was talking to him, nothing was distracting him or going wrong in any way; all he had to do was to leap forward, pinion Philipson-Smith's arms by his sides, and bundle him over the parapet. Already he could hear the deep, plunging splash of their two bodies meeting the water. Only one thing was wrong, and that not much more than a minor detail; McWhirtner, who in the interests of Edgar's convenience ought to have staioned himself on Philipson-Smith's off side, was in fact walking along next to the parapet, as if offering himself for destruction in the place of his master; just as, Edgar reflected, he had unintentionally done the first time.

Never mind; he would stumble out of the way when the surprise came. And when should it come? Now, *now*—they were half-way across the bridge, there was no one else near them, the water down there must be deep and easy to drown in. In another ten paces—no, *now*—no, in another ten paces . . . one, two, three, four, five, six, seven——

On the count of seven, as if it had been waiting for a signal, the stone parapet leaned inwards and banged Edgar in the ribs. At once, like a boxer's other fist, the glistening pavement in front of him bulged upwards, aiming at his jaw. On his guard, Edgar flung his head backwards to avoid the blow; but there was no time to cover up against the murderous right hook of the parapet, and again came the savage jab, flinging him over towards Mirabelle. With a squawk, she clutched at him, but he shook himself free. In spite of them all he would succeed; there, ahead, was Philipson-Smith's back, receding but not yet out of reach. With a convulsive effort he leapt forward, arms outstretched, but the wily pavement, boxing according to the book of rules, only allowed him two steps before reaching up with a tremendous blow to the point of the jaw. It was over, the referee was counting eight, nine and ten, and he was supine on the pavement with the water lapping hideously down there on his left, and the others gathered round him with cluckings of sympathy.

Still not believing it, he was hoisted to his feet, only to find that he could not stand without support. Mumbling incoherently, drawn between contradictory impulses—to laugh, to cry, to shout, to be sick—he allowed himself to be guided along, off the bridge, through the streets, into the hotel under the sympathetic scrutiny of the night-porter, into the lift, along the corridor, through the door of his bedroom. Then the others had all melted away, and it was Mirabelle who was settling him into the armchair, speaking to him.

"What—you say?" he asked her.

"I was only asking whether you'd be all right about getting into bed," she said. "Here—maybe I'd better take your shoes off. It's always the hardest thing."

As she bent and untied his shoelaces he remembered that it was she who had held him, prevented him from falling, guided him home. What force did she represent, what force powerful enough to bring them all together so as to give him his chance, and then to plunge them into a miasma of idleness and self-indulgence which had ended by robbing him of that same chance? He looked down at her, with her hunched, solid body, wide mouth and busy fingers, and knew the answer.

"It's Pleasure," he said. "You represent Pleasure, that's what it is."

She paid no attention, and he thought she had not heard him. But when he found his soiled, irksome clothes drawn off, the wide bed sinking under his relaxed weight, the pillow cradling his head, and her body moulding itself suddenly, eagerly, to the shape of his, he knew that she had heard him, and had understood; or, if she had not understood, had at any rate produced a reading of the situation which, for the moment, he could not choose but accept.

VI

As the little grey train clanked round the mountain's shoulder, brilliant afternoon sunshine flooded through the pane, suddenly, into Edgar's face. Shading his eyes with one hand, he peered down, past the trim metallic flank of the carriage, past the rough log fence, down into the bewildering reticulation of hard light and deep shadow elaborated by the pines in their motionless, tapering arabesque, to where the tiny river savaged its way between the boulders, sinking its little sharp teeth into them like a tiger cub in a terrible rage. He was glad he had managed to escape the others. He could not imagine the person whose company, in the midst of such drama, would be other than jarring; and the presence of no matter which member of his present group of companions could lead only to violence, and that in a very short time. As it was, after enduring the journey from Geneva as far as the stop where they had to leave the main line and take to the mountain railway, he had managed to wander into the town and "forget" the time of the little grey train, so that they had left without him and he was following them two hours later. Now he had the compartment, psychically speaking, to himself; only six hulking youths with ice-hockey sticks, and, at each stop, a clambering-out of peasants carrying sacks, pieces of wood, and tools, and a clambering-in of other peasants, in roughly equal numbers, so that the journey was punctuated every seven or eight minutes by a tremendous explosion of handshaking, sack-shouldering, and roaring of family gossip.

With a steady humming and a rhythmic, premeditated banging over the points, the train crawled onwards and upwards. Edgar felt as if he and it were still the same size as they had been down on the plain, that he was still five feet ten inches tall and the train still about forty-five feet long; but he knew that this was an illusion, that in fact the train had shrunk to the size of the one he used to play with on the living-room floor, and that he himself was barely an inch high, peering through the tiny window at the sleeping cat as big as a mammoth, gazing up in wonder at the cliff of the hearth. There was no other way, they *had* to become as small as that to avoid attracting attention to themselves in such remote and well-bred company: the arrogant peaks, thrusting impatiently clear of the clinging pine-belt, the furious ravines, the slopes where boulders the size of Buckingham Palace lay strewn like a child's marbles. It would never do to be noticed; if spoken to, they must pretend not to understand, or they would say the wrong thing and be terribly snubbed. And so the train became smaller and smaller, buzzing along its gleaming little rails with matchstick sleepers, under its wires strung out on poles as tall and slender as uncut lead pencils.

At last they rolled into Les Glissades, swelling out again to their former size as the station and the village street received them. The young men with ice-hockey sticks appeared first the size of white mice, then the size of chickens, then the size of St. Bernard dogs, then the size of mules, which was their natural size. Edgar took his case and climbed out.

As he approached the hotel where they had all arranged to stay, his mountain-inspired feeling of awe and wonder left him, and was replaced by his habitual mood of sardonic moroseness. This was because of the impossibility of avoiding this place and going to some other hotel which did not contain Philipson-Smith, McWhirtner, and Mr. and Mrs. Crabshaw and their children.

Mercifully, however, none of them were to be seen. They must be out for a walk, in which case all he had to do was to keep his eyes open when he went out and he could easily avoid them. In his haste lest any or all of them should come back and trap him in the Pension, he rushed through the preliminaries, barely glancing at the room where the porter dumped his bag, pausing for no more than a quick impression of the waxed plank floor, scrubbed walls and ceiling likewise of planks, narrow white bed and single window.

Outside again, he dropped the reins and let his mind amble by itself, like a horse that knows its own way, while his body mechanically trudged along a path where the snow had been trodden down to a hard, discoloured pavement. This path led upwards towards the sun. Though it was barely four o'clock, the village street was already drowned in twilight and evening mist, for the sun, blocked by the westward peaks, threw its light horizontally across the valley, so that the eastward snow-fields were like a hard white beach, disappearing inch by inch under a tide of shadow. The sunlit acres of snow reflected the crisp sunlight so powerfully as to make the shaded expanse seem by contrast almost black.

Plodding upwards, Edgar crossed the dividing line and emerged into the hot sunshine. The warmth made him unbutton his collar, the glare sent him fumbling in a pocket for his sun-glasses. He turned and stared about him, downwards to the village, across at the opposite side of the valley, sideways to where it twisted out of sight between fresh peaks.

Immediately he knew what kind of death awaited Philipson-Smith and himself on this leg of the course. The whole setting was compounded of speed and violence. Still as it was, the landscape was a study in frozen speed. Nothing moved, not even a breeze to stir the pine needles; here and there a ski-er, swerving down the mountain like a fly on a man's bald head, served to emphasize the utterly unchanging outlines above and behind his small black body with its queer amphibious-looking feet. And yet every motionless line suggested—and not merely suggested, but consisted of—speed and violence. Every descent was sharp, every sky-line was saw-toothed and dramatic, every pine stretched up on tip-toe, fiercely clutching for a handful of sky, every trickle of running water was whirling downwards with unbearable precipitation.

In this setting, it must be a clean, swift, violent death. One second they must be alive, the next broken to pieces beyond recognition, their spirits freed instantly, with no intermediate stage. Millions of years had passed since the cooling of the furious basalt beneath it had caused the earth's granite crust to contract and buckle outwards into these fantastic shapes, and every minute since then had seen the landscape and all its inhabitants living up to this initial act of violence in their own various ways. The chamois, grazing on the glacier's edge, was ready to jump down a precipice rather than be taken by the hunter; the eagle

106

hung in the sky ready to dive and sweep its shadow across the ground faster than a frightened hare could run; the peasant retreated the other way, into shrewd patience, away from flamboyance, but even he had an accelerated pulse rate and a higher density of corpuscles in his blood. Up here, every movement of the human body was quicker, every breath made the heart bound, every thought was of something hitherto unguessed-at. Edgar felt confident that these conditions were his allies; that Philipson-Smith, this time, would not escape, and that a quick and savage death awaited them both.

The actual details could come later. Obviously the best thing would be to push him over a precipice. In Geneva, with its strangling fog and wet streets, the lake had been inevitable and necessary; here, it was to be death by falling. But this, from a practical point of view, was rather difficult to arrange. He could hardly suggest to Philipson-Smith that they should take a walk along the edge of a cliff. Besides, without doing any actual mountaineering, it was not easy to get to the edge of any drop that would kill a man. In the clarity of the air the huge glacier, scored with deep crevasses, seemed a few minutes' walk away, but of course even its lower slopes could be reached only by a morning's hard walk, and still one would be in perfect safety.

Then he caught sight of the télésiège. He had not, so far, noticed the wires strung up to the inhospitable height and brilliance of one of the neighbouring peaks. But now the machinery evidently began running again after a short interval, and brightly-painted cabins began to float up and down, each gripping the wire with its one steel claw.

Edgar followed the route of the cabins with eager eyes. Surely, as high as that, there would be slopes down which, if once a man started to roll, nothing could save him? It might, for that matter, be possible to travel in the same cabin as Philipson-Smith, and, at the most dangerous part of the journey, to whip the door open and bundle him out, to bounce crazily down rocky slopes until his smashed body, and Edgar's too, fetched up only a few yards above the village street, to be carted away and buried as victims of one more Alpine accident.

The tide of darkness rose to his feet as he stood gazing up at the peak. It would soon be time to go down and endure once more the friction of human relationships, with their endless alternation of farce and tragedy. But this time, it would not be for long.

The bell sounded for dinner, and Edgar, swinging his legs from the bed, stood upright. This had to be faced, and the sooner the better. He went downstairs.

Being the first to enter the dining-room, he was cornered by the proprietress, a big-boned middle-aged woman with a flaming red face, huge gnarled ears, and the loudest voice he had ever heard in man or woman. The window-panes quivered in their frames as she shouted gleefully that their party were to be all together so as to enjoy each other's company. Seizing his arm, she dragged him to a long table in the centre of the room, pulled out a chair, flung him into it as adroitly as a Japanese wrestler, and stood at his elbow bellowing information about the village, the latest weather reports, and her hope that they would be comfortable, while he bent his head like a sapling in a hurricane.

Fortunately, the others entered in a body, so that he was spared the necessity of making conversation to them individually. In particular he had been avoiding Mirabelle; he was still not sure what changes in her attitude to him would result from the events of that night in Geneva, and, for his part, he lacked the strength to embark, at this late hour, on a new and deeper relationship—lacked, even, the strength to reject such developments and fight them off.

They sat down, Philipson-Smith and McWhirtner at the end of the table, where they were screened from Edgar by the impenetrable jungle of the Crabshaw children. The baby was in bed, and, as usual in his absence, the other two seemed determined to spare no effort to lay waste the nervous system of any adult they could get at. Mirabelle, genial and disarming as ever, was opposite him, her manner exactly the same as it had been on the morning when they met.

There was, of course, no conversation during the meal, for the children put up a sound-barrage that made it absurd even to go through the motions of moving one's lips. The only adult who succeeded in communicating anything *viva voce* was the proprietress, who ran into the room now and again to roar, in a voice of thunder, questions about how they liked the food, what they intended to do that evening, and so forth. This was not, however,

108

the only communication that went on, for Mrs. Crabshaw several times found herself with a few seconds' leisure in which to exchange nods and sympathetic smiles with another woman, who sat at a corner table and spooned fragments of meat and vegetable into the mouth of a little girl of about Nancy's age. As plates clattered to the floor, cutlery clashed, shrieks of anger or self-pity scored the air, and various liquids were flung about, the two women rallied one another with eloquent glances. "Keep going, dear," the glances said. "After all, it's what we asked for."

Edgar found the whole spectacle full of interest. It even had, for him, a certain tranquillity; Philipson-Smith and McWhirtner were put out of action, having no recourse but to eat their food as quickly as possible and look forward to the moment when they could get away and sit in the bar; Mirabelle likewise could present no problems; he was secure against immediate physical attack from either of the children, for neither of them was sitting beside him; and, in particular, the contrast between the two mothers was a fascinating one. They represented the two possible types. Mrs. Crabshaw had the cow-like, drugged calm of the mother whose neural equipment has been battered into a self-protective lethargy; the other woman had gone the opposite way, and was in a continual state of hysterical tension. Every time she raised a spoonful of food to the obstinately clamped mouth of her offspring, her hand trembled and her whole body assumed a taut, unnatural posture, while her anxiously puckered face showed that the swallowing of this spoonful, this very one, was to her a matter of life and death. Sometimes she succeeded in getting a little of the food actually as far as the inside of her daughter's mouth; at those moments an eager joy and pride of achievement suffused her face, only to crumple into ludicrous disappointment when the child (as she never failed to do) spat the food violently on to the tablecloth.

By the time the adult members of the party were half-way through their meal, the children had eaten as much as they could be persuaded to eat, and had been in a sitting position for as long as they would tolerate the indignity. In consequence they were "allowed" to get down and run about between the tables. Introductions made themselves, and the little girl from the corner table was merged into the firm of Roger, Nancy and Co.

Her nationality, and therefore that of her mother, turned out to be English.

The sweet was served, and, unable any longer to postpone the pleasure of talking professional shop, the Englishwoman carried her plate over to the communal table at the request of Mrs. Crabshaw. During the re-shuffle of places that followed, Edgar was terrified lest he should be manœuvred down the table and find himself next to Philipson-Smith or McWhirtner, but fortunately the tide carried him even further away from them. In any case they were obviously both eating quickly and casting eager glances at the door leading to the blessed haven of the bar; though McWhirtner, he noticed without surprise, was beginning, in proportion as his hunger for food and wine was satisfied, to turn his eyes towards Mirabelle, who for the moment represented for him the third of life's pressing needs.

The waitress placed Edgar's fruit salad in front of him, the proprietress seized him by the arm and shouted that he was not to forget to put his shoes outside the door in the morning, the two mothers were talking animatedly, Mirabelle lit a cigarette, and the children began running round and round the tables with skull-crushing cries. The combined weight of these diverse impressions was too much, and Edgar's mind turned in upon itself, refusing to concentrate, waiting only, like a city during an air raid, for some sort of lull in which life could begin again. Scraps of talk filtered through, but his mind made no attempt to get them into any coherent arrangement.

"The doctor didn't want me to breast-feed Cecily. He said my milk hadn't got enough fat in it."

"What nonsense! I sometimes think they don't know *what* they're talking about. As a matter of fact they said exactly the same——"

"An whut was ye plannin' on daein' the nicht? They say there's a wheen place where there's dancin'."

"Sorry, Angus, I don't dance."

Zowie. Clatter of a chair pulled to the ground. Feverish screaming renewed.

"—exactly the same to me over Nancy. Not rich enough. But as I told them, I happen to know that the mother's milk is *always* good for the baby."

"Of course it is. A law of nature."

110

"Et messieurs? Dames? Qu'est-ce que vous allez faire ce soir?"

"Och, weel, we could jist sit oot."

"I don't know what you're doing, but I'm going to the bar before I murder one of these kids. A damned disgrace the way this place is run."

"Il y a un bal masque au patinoire."

"I don't sit out, either, Mr. Lauder."

"Och, where's the sense in makin' things sae awkward?"

"Try a soap suppository for her. I'll show you how to make them."

Another chair skidded to the ground. The three children began fighting, bitterly and indiscriminately. Philipson-Smith stalked out to the bar, his too-short legs jerking like a puppet's. McWhirtner continued to talk quietly and intensely to Mirabelle. Mr. Crabshaw sat absolutely still, like a wild animal hoping to avoid being seen. The ladies talked on. Edgar pushed his chair away from the table, measured the distance to the door with a keen glance, and made a bolt for it.

Safely in his room, he climbed through the low window and stood on the balcony. Above, to his left, the solid massif idled majestically in the ice-breeding darkness, needled with starlight. There was no moon, but the light from the stars alone seemed more candid than even the moon's would have been in the marshy skies of home. This was a backdrop for the biggest actions a man could perform, a politely deaf audience for the biggest words he could utter.

Behind him, in the room, he heard a knock on the door. Going back inside, he pulled the long windows shut and called to the knocker to enter.

It was Mirabelle. As she came in she glanced over her shoulder as if afraid of being followed.

"Sit down, won't you?" he said, drawing up the only chair. She sat down on the bed, looking at him.

"I certainly hate to stop you communing, or whatever it is people do with nature," she said, "but I'd be kind of happy if you let me sit here a while. Till the hunt's died down."

"The Highland hunt?" he asked.

She nodded. "Yes, that rube again."

There was a short silence while she fished out a packet of

111

cigarettes, handed him one, and he lit both. Then she began, unexpectedly, to explain herself.

"It's not exactly difficult to see that you don't figure me out any too well," she said, exhaling in a long stream, the smoke cut into uneven fragments by her words. "It's pretty clear that you're thinking, hell, all this guy wants is a lay. Why doesn't she give it him and keep him quiet?"

He opened his mouth to protest, then closed it, for she was perfectly right.

"Oh, I know it seems pretty simple to you," she went on. "I'll be the first to admit that a little horizontal exercise doesn't make much difference to me. It's just one of those things you have to have, like eating and going to sleep. I wasn't one to stand on ceremony, ever since the first time I tried it and found it made me feel fine."

She paused, and he said promptingly, "Yes?"

"But that doesn't mean," the words came out with an emphasis that seemed strangely close to vehemence, "that I can't be choosy. Hell, I may be a tramp, but I can be choosy. A *choosy* tramp, that's me."

She seemed to expect him to say something, but he could think of nothing to say except, perhaps, to thank her for having chosen him, but he did not wish to be flippant. This seemed to be, for her, a serious occasion.

"And when it comes to rat-faced guys that talk like burlesque turns," she continued, "and the stuffed shirts they go around with, for that matter, well, it burns me."

It flashed into Edgar's mind that she might be on the point of asking him to allow her to stay there all night, to be secure against unwanted visitors to her room. He wondered how, in this case, he could explain and justify the refusal he had, inevitably, to give. He could not possibly convey to her, without disclosing his secret, how and why he came to regard himself as a man dedicated to a high purpose, not free to squander his energies on unimportant pleasures.

Fortunately, his intuition had been wrong, and she had no such request to make. A silence fell, for she had said all there was to say. It was his turn.

"Well, stay here as long as you like, Mirabelle," he said. "If anyone knocks on the door, I won't open it."

112

She put her feet up and lay comfortably on the bed.

"It's big of you, Edgar," she said. "And you needn't worry about being disturbed, either. I kind of sensed the other night that—well, that your heart wasn't in it. You get to be an amateur psychiatrist in my racket, but I'd say you were too tough a case for me. It isn't because of another woman, it isn't because you're the kind that doesn't go in for the game. It's something I just don't know about."

"Yes," he said. "It's something you just don't know about."

There was a knock on the door. She looked appealingly at him. "Who's there?" he called.

The door began to open. With a single quick stride Edgar was standing with his shoulder against it. This could only be McWhirtner. Philipson-Smith was perfectly capable of ordering storm-troopers to invade a man's bedroom, but not of opening the door himself without being invited to come in. His code would not permit it; by McWhirtner's code, it would be standard practice.

"What the hell do you want?" he called harshly.

"Yir hospitality hasn't changed, I see: the same harruty welcome," came McWhirtner's voice; he was drunk again.

"Clear off. I'm busy," Edgar said sternly to the boards of the door.

McWhirtner gave an obscene chuckle. "Ay, ye're beesy. The lassie's wi' ye—that's true, ye cannae deny it."

Edgar knew the uselessness of answering; he simply drew the bolt of the door and went back to his chair. They heard McWhirtner's feet shuffling about, as if he were undecided whether to go or stay; no doubt he was bending down to see whether anything could be made out through the key-hole.

The creaking and scraping continued. Edgar and Mirabelle lit fresh cigarettes. From time to time, McWhirtner called out some piece of drunken badinage, such as "Leave it alone, Banks—there's a better man oot here waitin' to take yir place." The minutes passed, and at last there was a silence. It was perfectly obvious, however, that McWhirtner was still there, for the slightest movement over the creaking plank floor could be heard all over the house, and they had heard no receding tread. They sat quietly for some minutes, enjoying the thought that they were comfortably resting, while McWhirtner was irritably standing up in a draughty corridor: but after a while Mirabelle's patience snapped, and she said in a ringing voice, "Well, to the hell with it. I don't care if that bum does know I'm here. Let him stand out there till he gets tired."

McWhirtner still gave no sign of his presence; no doubt he considered it the height of subtlety to keep quiet in the hope that sooner or later they would say something they did not wish him to hear.

"Yes, the poor fool," Edgar said loudly. "Let him stand out there and cultivate the traditional virtues."

They continued to amuse themselves for some time by dissecting McWhirtner's character and commenting on his physical appearance. The stubborn imbecile gave, meanwhile, no sign of life. They were just beginning to tire of this in turn, and Edgar was about to throw the door open and leap out to kick McWhirtner downstairs, when suddenly the silence was shattered into millions of sharp fragments. McWhirtner gave a loud scream of pain and terror; within a fraction of a second a high, childish voice followed on with a ghastly yell of vindictive triumph; and hardly had the twin sounds died away when two other voices, also high and childish, joined in with a silvery laughter that seemed to epitomize the innocent joy of infancy.

Mirabelle, her face set, jerked herself upright. Edgar, spurred by a determination to meet whatever new menace had presented itself as bravely as possible, flung open the door.

The landing was in darkness, but the oblong of yellow light from the doorway revealed McWhirtner leaning against the wall, deathly pale and clutching his right shoulder in his left hand. Beside him, smirking in triumph, stood the boy Roger. In his dimpled little fist he held, triumphantly extended, the clasp-knife. Blunt as it was, its broad blade was streaked with blood. Peeping round the corner of the landing were the two little girls.

What had happened was obvious. As McWhirtner froze, intently listening to the conversation filtering through the door, the boy Roger had crept up behind him and stabbed him with his knife. The two little girls played a passive but important role in this drama; they were the audience for whose benefit the gladiatorial show was laid on.

"He cut me, the little sod," McWhirtner moaned gently. All the fight was knocked out of him by the brutality and unexpectedness

114

of the assault. Edgar felt almost sorry for him, though his sorrow was tempered by the reflection that, after all, it had only been a matter of time before the boy stabbed someone, and, that being so, it was as well that McWhirtner should be the victim. If he died from his wounds before medical attention could be procured, the world would lose nothing except a few jejune and maudlin pieces of pseudo-Scotch verse, while, on the credit side, its supplies of alcoholic drink would be distributed more fairly, its women molested less frequently, and the human total of boredom and irritation considerably diminished.

"The little sod," McWhirtner said again, piteously. He took off his jacket and rolled his shirt-sleeve almost to the shoulder. This revealed to Edgar that any hope of a fairer distribution of the world's liquor supplies was still in the future, for the wound inflicted by the boy's knife, though long, was very shallow. The blade had merely scored down the outside of McWhirtner's arm and ripped off a piece of skin some four inches long and an eighth of an inch wide.

"Oo, blood!" Roger shouted. His eyes shone with the utterly selfless joy of childhood as he contemplated the results of his assault. All his life he would look back on the pure exultation of this moment; not even his first love affair would hold more magic. It would be a pity, Edgar reflected, to spoil it by battering him into unconsciousness.

Voices were heard along the corridor, and Mrs. Crabshaw and the other Englishwoman appeared, clucking at their offspring.

"It's time to go to bed, Roger," Mrs. Crabshaw said firmly. McWhirtner turned on her with a mixture of menace and pathetic appeal.

"Luik at my arrum," he said, holding it out. Several drops of blood were dislodged by the movement and fell to the floor.

"Oh, dear," she said. "Come along, Roger. Bye-byes."

"It was him," McWhirtner shouted. "He crept up and cut me wi' that bluidy knife."

"*Not* in front of the children, please," Mrs. Crabshaw said sharply. "No bad language in front of *my* children, *if* you please."

"But jist luik!" McWhirtner bawled. "Jist luik at my bluidy arrum!"

The other Englishwoman, white to the lips, gathered up her daughter and began to canter away down the corridor. The child, loath to leave the scene of the drama, set up a frantic howling. Mrs. Crabshaw, clutching Roger and Nancy to her waist, stood confronting McWhirtner as if he had tried to kidnap them for vivisection.

"It's true, Mrs. Crabshaw," Edgar could not help saying. "I'm afraid Roger *did* cut him with his clasp-knife."

She turned on him. "Don't *you* start using bad language, too," she said sternly. "The whole thing is because we haven't got anywhere of our own to live. What an upbringing for the children, dragging round these awful hotels, mixing with all *sorts* of people!"

"A wasnae daein' onythin' tae him," McWhirtner wailed. He leaned against the wall, closing his eyes, then suddenly bent forward with a flicker of demoniac energy, and yelled, "The little sod!"

"The little sod!" Roger shouted. "Sod, sod, you're a sod!" he chanted. His sister joined in rapturously.

"*There!*" Mrs. Crabshaw stormed. "*Now* what a fine thing you've done. I hope you're proud, yes, proud, both of you!"

The children continued to chant delightedly.

"Teaching them that *language*!" Mrs. Crabshaw shrilled. "Now they'll be using that word all the time!"

Mr. Crabshaw appeared at the end of the corridor. Taking in with one glance the fact that there was some crisis on hand, he stood irresolute, as if wishing to draw back and be hidden. But McWhirtner had seen him.

"Come and luik at this!" he called. "Come and luik at what yir bairn's done to my arrum wi'out me daein' onythin' tae him!"

Mr. Crabshaw approached, still irresolute. His wife's voice, urging him to be a man and do something to defend his children from the corrupting influences about them, did not seem to add to his energies or to give him a sense that he belonged anywhere in the situation. Then, as he drew nearer, he saw the wound in McWhirtner's arm. Immediately his whole attitude changed.

"Just come in here to the light," he said, propelling McWhirtner through the door into Edgar's room. Edgar felt a faint sardonic amusement at the thought that he had got in, after all. Mr. Crabshaw examined the wound under the electric light, took out a clean handkerchief, washed the arm with hot water and soap, and bound it up.

"I was in the R.A.M.C. during the war," he explained, giving the bandage a final jerk to tighten it.

"Weel, poot yir son in the bluidy Commandos in the next one," growled McWhirtner.

"There's gratitude, I must say," said Mrs. Crabshaw from the doorway. "Bob sees to his arm so nicely, and I don't suppose we'll ever see the handkerchief back, and that's all he can say." Her attitude was exactly the same as if McWhirtner had been the victim of a street accident and Bob had happened to be passing and had given him first aid. Indeed, the parallel was a very close one, for the question of her child's guilt not only did not, but could not possibly, occur to her. She was psychologically conditioned to supporting her children in any circumstances. Edgar began to wish he had come here with the object of preparing material for a treatise on the mental aberrations of mothers with young children, instead of the prosaic intention of merely committing murder and suicide.

"Little sod! I'm a sod!" Roger called over his shoulder as he was led away to bed.

"He's right, isnae he?" McWhirtner said to Mr. Crabshaw. The remark had an epic simplicity that gave Edgar, for a moment, something like a respect for the speaker.

"That'll be all right in a couple of days. Just don't use that arm too much and don't get any dirt in the scratch," Mr. Crabshaw told him. He was interested in nothing but the medical aspect of the affair; and McWhirtner, realizing this, switched his attention to an attempt to play on this professional attitude and turn it to his own advantage.

"I'm sufferin' frae shock," he said, looking narrowly into Mr. Crabshaw's face. "Naethin' short o' a guid glass o' brandy'll dae me ony guid."

"Well, there's no harm in having a drink if it'll make you feel more settled," said Mr. Crabshaw. "You can go down and get yourself one from the bar."

"Gang doon tae the *bar*?" spluttered McWhirtner indignantly. He seemed about to begin threatening Mr. Crabshaw, then evidently remembered that he was playing on being an invalid. His face crumpled into an expression of pain and weariness. "A'm tew faint to gang doon the steers," he said, sitting down on Edgar's bed.

Mr. Crabshaw looked at him dubiously. He had already done his duty by McWhirtner, and seemed to be wondering whether his personal code of ethics would permit him to stave off this black-mailing request for brandy. Edgar could read his thoughts so clearly that, in the manner of Edgar Allan Poe's Dupin, he allowed several steps to be taken and then chimed in orally with the indicated next move.

"After all, it *was* an unprovoked attack, and it *was* your son," he said, his tone indicating responsible fair-mindedness. He did not want Mr. Crabshaw to pay for any brandy for McWhirtner, but on the other hand it was essential, in the interests of abstract justice, that Mr. Crabshaw be reminded occasionally that he had increased the world total of fatigue and resentment by helping to bring the boy Roger into existence.

"Are you sure it was unprovoked?" Mr. Crabshaw asked him, sharply; he was too preoccupied to notice the Edgar Allan Poe effect. "I mean, Roger doesn't usually—I mean, generally he's fairly——" his voice trailed off under the strain of trying to convey a false impression without actually telling an overt lie.

"Brandy," McWhirtner said faintly. He lay back with his head on Edgar's pillow, causing Edgar to make a mental note that he must ask for a clean pillow-case before going to bed, and swung his feet up on to the counterpane. As Mirabelle had all this time been sitting on the bed, this made her squirm into the narrow space between McWhirtner and the wall, where she sat with her knees drawn up, looking profoundly uncomfortable.

Mr. Crabshaw turned and walked out. He did not say that he was going to the bar, but his hang-dog expression, and the briskness of his tread, indicating that he had an unpleasant task ahead and wished to get it over, put it beyond doubt that he would shortly be back with a glass of brandy for McWhirtner.

Mirabelle seemed to be measuring the distance across Mc-Whirtner's body as if preparing to jump across without touching him, and gain the floor. To spare her the trouble of these acrobatics, Edgar said, "You can go to your own room now, McWhistler. When Crabshaw brings the brandy up we'll tell him you're there."

McWhirtner smiled confidently. "Ay," he said. "D'ye see ony green in ma ee?"

Edgar and Mirabelle both looked at him in surprise.

"It wadnae be the fairst time ye've tried to stop me frae gettin' a dram o' brandy, eh, Banks?"

"I wish now," Edgar said slowly and with absolute sincerity, "that I'd let you go ahead that first time."

"A'll bet ye do," said McWhirtner. He stretched luxuriously on the bed and leered at Edgar, savouring what he imagined to be his discomfiture. Then he seemed suddenly to remember Mirabelle, and rolled on to his right side so as to face her, instantly rolling back with a grimace of anguish because it was his right shoulder that bore the fresh stab of Roger's knife. This created a moment's lull in which Mirabelle could stand up, move to the foot of the bed, and step across McWhirtner's legs to freedom. She began to execute this manœuvre, but McWhirtner seemed as firmly convinced of his right to her physical proximity as of his right to a glass of brandy. Swiftly sitting up, he clutched at her waist just at the moment when she was off balance. With a squawk of anger and revulsion, she jerked her body violently forwards. Edgar caught a brief, fevered glimpse of her face turned in his direction with an expression of almost frantic appeal, and her hands flung out before her, and in the same instant he bounded across to the bed, grabbing for her shoulders.

Mirabelle's solid trunk, normally balanced firmly on her rather heavy legs, was not easy to arrest once it began to topple. There was, besides, the fact that McWhirtner, still in a sitting position, had been thrown violently sideways, causing his grip to slide lower, so that he suddenly came to be holding Mirabelle round the knees in a classic Rugby tackle. Edgar, his arms suddenly full of Mirabelle's falling weight, reeled and fell backwards. There was a loud, dry crack from the bed—evidently the wooden frame had broken into two or more pieces—another cry of nervous anguish and fear from Mirabelle, a curse from McWhirtner, and they were on the floor in a tangled heap.

Edgar's head struck the door in a glancing way as he fell, but apart from the ringing head-noises and temporarily dimmed vision which resulted from this, he was unhurt. Indeed, the ricochet from the door had, he saw, caused him to fall in a slanting direction, so that Mirabelle's weight did not land directly on him. Her head and shoulders fell across his chest, but her position in falling concentrated the weight at about knee-level, and he was glad to note that McWhirtner, still clinging to her legs, had been and was being ground into the floor by the threshing weight of her beam end.

Before he could enjoy the spectacle as it deserved to be enjoyed, someone began trying to open the door, succeeding only in pressing its hard edge into the small of his back.

"Stop that! Wait a minute!" he shouted.

"For goodness' sake, what are you *doing* in there?" came the voice of Mr. Crabshaw, irritable and authoritative; evidently he had not yet re-assumed his true personality, and was still Crabshaw the field hospital staff-nurse rather than Crabshaw the down-trodden office worker.

"They're killin' me!" shouted McWhirtner. It was not clear whether he was in genuine terror or merely seizing a possible chance to bring discredit on Edgar and Mirabelle and a larger glass of brandy to himself. "Get off me, ye murruderin' sow!" he shouted to Mirabelle, his voice quavering with a convincing suggestion of hysteria.

Mr. Crabshaw began to thrust hard at the door. Edgar squirmed frantically, goaded by the pain in his back, and at the same time Mirabelle lifted her knees from McWhirtner's collarbone. Slowly they stood up, leaving a clear space for Mr. Crabshaw to enter. He did so, carrying a small glass of golden liquid.

"They hadn't got brandy; it's whisky," he said to McWhirtner.

"It's tae late; A'm deein'," McWhirtner said faintly. Raising himself on one elbow, he took the glass from Mr. Crabshaw's hand and tossed the whisky down his throat. "A'm dee——" he began again, but subsided into a fit of coughing which made him writhe about on the floor; much as a man would do, Edgar swiftly reflected, who had drunk a glass of poisoned brandy.

Mr. Crabshaw shot a curt glance at Edgar and Mirabelle, as if to convey that he would like to investigate more fully the question of their guilt, but must attend to his patient first. Grasping McWhirtner with surprising strength, he swung him on to the bed, which gave two more loud cracks and settled slowly into a pronounced list. Edgar and Mirabelle silently left the room, brushing themselves down and stopping every few paces to feel for possible broken bones. Without speaking, they limped down to the bar, which was mercifully clear of Philipson-Smith, and sat down.

At first Edgar's dominant mood was one of sympathy for Mirabelle. He realized that to be grasped by McWhirtner and to crash down on the floor with his tentacles still round her must

120

have caused her acute mental suffering, not much less than that felt by a person with a horror of snakes when entwined by an anaconda. After a few minutes, however, another impression made its way to the foreground of his mind. He suddenly saw the whole situation here at Les Glissades with a new clarity. Of course! Mirabelle was his one chance of controlling the turn of events, the one lever with which he might displace the heavy masses that lay in his path. Previously, he had been not so much unaware of this fact, as aware of it in a sporadic and not fully conscious way; after all, he must, even in the midst of his incredible blindness and slowness, have registered *somewhere* in his mind that it was only through Mirabelle, and specifically through McWhirtner's lust for Mirabelle, that they had all been swept into coming up here in the first place.

He looked at her. She was taking quick, nervous sips at her drink, at the same time holding the wet, frayed end of her cigarette never further than two inches from her lips, so that she could take in smoke at intervals of only three or four seconds. Nevertheless, as he watched, she seemed to grow calmer. Still not looking at him, she suddenly set her glass down, put her hands over her face, and gave a long shudder. He sat still, not daring to reach out and touch her, wishing he knew whether this was the nervous crisis, after which she would quickly recover, or the beginning of some dreadful delayed reaction.

For a long time, almost a minute, she kept her face hidden, while the frayed cigarette smouldered between the fingers of her right hand. Then, lowering her hands, she straightened up. Turning on her wooden stool, she looked Edgar full in the face.

"Out of character, isn't it?" she asked, her voice quite steady. "You wouldn't think I had anything sensitive about me."

"I didn't say that," Edgar replied.

"No, I said it, and it's true. I come and hide in your room just to keep that monkey's paws off me, and the next thing we're all rolling on the floor like we can't get enough of each other."

Edgar laid his hand warningly on her shoulder, speaking quickly to head her off before she could follow her train of thought.

"Stop that. It's silly to think of the episode in those terms. Did you never slip down and fall in the mud when you were a child, playing? And did you ever reproach yourself for it? No—

you might have been cross that you had mud all over your dress, but you knew it hadn't any meaning—it was an accident. I can see you've had a bad shake-up by being thrown into contact with that obscene oaf, but it's irrational. He can't do you any harm if you don't want him to do you any harm."

"That's a long speech," she said. With one chubby finger she began to trace diminishing circles in the spilt vermouth on the bar counter. "What's the idea of making a long speech like that? You're not going around trying to argue women out of irrational states they've gotten themselves into, are you? Because if so, let me tell you right away that there are better ways of wasting your——"

"Listen," Edgar cut in urgently. "It's true that I'm trying to argue you out of an irrational state, but it's not something I make a habit of. And what's even more important, I want you to do something really big for me. I want you to let yourself be argued out of it *without asking why*."

As he spoke, he wondered idly if involving her as an unwitting partner in homicide were one more technical method of damning his soul.

She held her hands up at about shoulder-height and flapped them forwards, indicating weariness and disbelief.

"Listen, never mind apologizing," she said. "Just tell me what it is you want me to *do*. I'll tell you fast enough whether it's something I'm prepared to do or not."

"Just keep McWhirtner on a string for a couple of days," Edgar said simply, relieved that the discussion had come down at last to straightforward practicalities. "He's in pursuit of you, and as long as he doesn't wake up absolutely to the fact that he'll never get anywhere, there's a handle for me to swing the pair of them about by. It was McWhirtner's reproductive instinct that got us all up here, just as much as your wish for a change from the Geneva atmosphere, I needn't tell you that. It's not much I'm asking. Just don't have a show-down for a day or two. Leave him with enough illusion to keep him running."

"A handle to swing them?" she said, as he paused. "Which way would you be wanting to swing them?"

"I mean just in simple things," he said. "For instance, tomorrow I want Philipson-Smith to go up on the télésiège to the top of the mountain. To fix that it'll be necessary for McWhirtner to go. That means you'll have to go, and probably have to put up with his fairly close company for some hours. You may even have to ride up in a cabin with him, though I'll do my best to spare you that."

She swung round on her stool so that their knees were touching, but it was not intimacy she wanted. It was honesty.

"Spring one surprise on me," she said almost fiercely. "Startle the pants off me. Treat me as if I were a real person."

He stared at her.

"Do you really think I'm so dumb," she said bitterly, "that I haven't noticed that you're casting around for some way of rubbing this guy Smith out? Why, I knew that in Geneva when you tried to push him into the lake."

He looked at her incredulously. "You know that?"

"Of course."

"And you're still willing—to help me?"

She looked up and held his gaze for a moment, not smiling.

"It isn't quite that simple. I wouldn't help you if it was a question of sticking a knife into somebody's back. But somebody, in some way, has *got* to help you. Somebody has got to make you feel less . . ."

"Less what?"

She shrugged hopelessly. "I don't know the word for it. Less *alone*—less bitter about everything—no, those are both wrong. Less whatever it is you're feeling."

For an instant he was tempted to begin talking, to go on volubly, hardly pausing, for a couple of hours, explaining everything to her, making her see. Then, as suddenly, his habitual weariness and blankness engulfed him again.

She seemed to take his silence as ending the conversation, and got down abruptly from her stool. "We'll go up the mountain tomorrow, then," she said in a business-like voice. "I'll go and invite Lauder now. And where he goes, the other one'll go."

He wanted to say *thank you*, he wanted to say *you're good, you're human*, but nothing would come.

"Isn't she ready *yet*?" Philipson-Smith asked, his wet voice drying itself out into a snarl of impatience.

"Evidently not, since she isn't down," Edgar answered curtly. His loathing of Philipson-Smith was mounting as his nervous tension increased, and for an instant he thought he would be unable to restrain his violent impulse to attack him there and then. It would be the work of a second to seize him by the shoulders and swing him suddenly backwards, with one foot stuck out stiffly as a trip, so that he should crash down with his head against the glass door of the proprietress's office. Edgar had a quick, joyous vision of that ill-shaped cranium, with its over-conscious coiffure, bursting the pane into a great star-shaped hole. But he fought down the seething tide of his hatred, silently urging himself to keep still just a little longer. "Release will come soon, release will come soon," he murmured under his breath.

McWhirtner said nothing. He was sitting on a chair near the door, already wearing his overcoat and gloves, immersed in pleasurable anticipation. Although it was three-quarters of an hour since breakfast, and Mirabelle had really no excuse for not being ready to set off, he showed no impatience. Screwing round, he leered up at Edgar with the expression of a fanatical card player who knows himself to have the best hand.

Edgar wondered whether he ought to go upstairs and knock on the door of Mirabelle's room. Perhaps she was there, lying on the bed weeping or shuddering with revulsion at the thought of having to tolerate the close proximity of McWhirtner. Or was she desperately gulping rye whisky out of a flask, like a character out of Raymond Chandler? By what means did she hope to muster up the courage and nervous stability to go through with it?

He glanced nervously at the stairs, and in the same instant she appeared, smiling broadly; even he, who was looking for signs of nervous tension, could discern none. Perhaps she had really been drinking out of a flask.

Philipson-Smith held the door open for her to go out, managing with really enviable address to perform this courteous action in such a way as to make it seem an insult; as if he were a butler who had been told to usher out, and never to re-admit, a guest who had been found stealing the silver. Before Mirabelle could reach the door, McWhirtner rose from his chair and went out ahead of her. Philipson-Smith allowed his mouth to lose a little of its flabbiness—one could never say of him that he *compressed* his lips—with an effect of annoyance; even Edgar was surprised. It looked like a demonstration of bad manners for a children's television show, a sort of *voulu* how-not-to-do-it gesture, to be

124

followed by other demonstrations on noisy eating, crossing the road diagonally, and so forth. Once outside, however, it was clear that McWhirtner had been acting according to a deliberate plan, his aim being to make absolutely certain that he, and not anyone else, should walk beside Mirabelle. He clutched bonily at her arm, and for an instant Edgar thought she was going to strike him, but suddenly she seemed to relax. As they set off, she allowed her arm to be hooked through his, and even leaned slightly towards him, with an attitude of dutiful resignation that suggested a Victorian bride submissively enduring something her mother had told her she wouldn't like but must do for the sake of the bargain.

Philipson-Smith breathed noisily through his nose as they stumped over the powdery snow. Edgar momentarily longed to break off two of the long, tapering icicles which hung like poniards from the eaves of every chalet, and thrust them simultaneously into both nostrils. Then, as the dry air flared in his lungs and sent his blood dancing through its channels, he felt almost gay. What a wonderful day to die on! What a superb job he would make of this murder, and what a pleasure it would be to do it! Beneath these thoughts, he was aware of a third, not quite so sharply defined; he dug for it, and, when it came up, felt slightly disconcerted. It was the kind of thought he had not expected to have any more; had, in fact, deliberately said good-bye to, before ever setting out on this adventure. "What a good thing I lived to see a day like this in a setting like this," the thought said, as nearly as he could translate it into words. "A good thing I *did* fail to kill him in London or I should never have come here and seen this snow, this sky, these mountains." Edgar frowned heavily and pushed the thought back into the recesses of his mind, where his Freudian Censor was waiting to handcuff it. What was this, a Cook's Tour?

As they reached the wooden shed which marked the starting-point of the télésiège, McWhirtner speeded up, dragging Mirabelle by the arm. If alone, Edgar would have been quite prepared to make a race of it, as he had done when they climbed the stairs to his flat; but with Philipson-Smith obstinately strutting along at three miles an hour, he was clearly *hors concours*. By the time they had bought their tickets and passed into the echoing semi-darkness of the shed, McWhirtner and Mirabelle were already in

125

their cabin, and, as Edgar watched, the attendant bent his massive shoulder, gave a heave, and they were off. He saw Mirabelle's face glancing, pale and set, through the window, and felt a pang of stern pity for her sufferings. But before he could allow this emotion to develop, the attendant had pulled another two-seater cabin into place, torn their tickets in half, and locked the door on them. A rocking swing, a dazzling shift from shadow to sunshine, and they had started on their journey.

VII

Surely this must be it. Such close physical proximity to his enemy, such a tension-producing parody of comradely intimacy, *must* be the signal for action to break out at last. Face to face on the narrow, hard seats, as inescapably together as mice in a biscuit tin, they had to shuffle for advantageous positions of knee and ankle, like passengers in a cramped railway compartment. It was not possible to avoid the tangible, physical presence of Philipson-Smith; Edgar found that the aura of the man's personality was, in his present state of wire-drawn hyperæsthesia, curiously concrete in its effect. It was as if waves of Philipson-Smithness were flowing out of his pores like a thick gas, filling the tiny metal box, making it almost impossible to breathe.

As the cabin was drawn steadily upwards on the cable, and the tops of the pine trees began to brush slowly underneath them, Edgar's first impression, after the neural shock of his adversary's nearness had worn off a little, was one of disappointment at finding that the attendant had locked the door. Obviously it was standard practice; another man with a key would unlock it when they drew into the shed at the top of their climb, but in the meantime the company had no intention of allowing them to smash themselves up while on its property. This ruled out not only the chance of killing Philipson-Smith immediately, but also the possible escape from his own death of disgust and boredom; he could not even, if the waves of the fellow's personality proved too strong and rank to be borne, wrench open the door, catch at the branches of some strong tree, and let the cabin sway onwards and upwards without him. Suppose Philipson-Smith actually began to expound his loathsome doctrines? Edgar would be trapped and forced to listen, just as he had been on the brandy-bottle evening. So intense was his apprehension that he squirmed on his seat and jerked his ankles several times as if hit on the knee with a rubber hammer. Philipson-Smith, who had been staring out of the window as if he disliked what he saw there but preferred it to the sight of Edgar, turned to him with a frown.

"Would you mind not fidgeting? This thing's cramped enough as it is, don't you think?"

"Sorry," Edgar muttered mechanically, thinking how queer it was to be apologizing to a man for some minor discourtesy when in a few minutes, or a couple of hours at the most, one would be murdering him. This naturally led his mind to think of practical details, and he realized with a sinking of the stomach that even now, after all his pains, it was by no means certain that he would find the right conditions. The peak, up to whose foot the cable stretched, stood out like floodlit crystal against the blue emptiness of the sky; if he craned a little to one side he could see it ahead; but he knew that the station of the télésiège was not at the top of it, and, for safety's sake, it would obviously be built well away from any steep precipices. Suppose Philipson-Smith were to elect to spend the whole day lounging on the terrace in front of the restaurant? What if it should prove impossible to get him even to take a stroll to some slope where a quick push might send him rolling endlessly downwards? In his nervous agitation, Edgar grabbed at the sill of the open Perspex window, half-consciously hoping that the door might be persuaded, even now, to yield and swing open, so that the work of Life might go forward with no more delay.

"For God's sake, what's the matter with you?" Philipson-Smith demanded, his voice wet and irritable. "Look here, Banks," he went on sternly, "I don't care a damn if you go about acting like a man on the verge of a nervous breakdown, but don't do it near me, understand?"

"How can anybody be near you——" Edgar began, then subsided into a fit of self-induced coughing and spluttering. He had been going to finish "—and *not* be on the verge of a nervous breakdown?" but some tiny hard crumb of rationality, once more, had saved him. A quarrel would mean the end of any hopes he might still have of luring Philipson-Smith to come for a walk and look over a precipice. Choking noisily at the thought of how

128

nearly he had slammed his foot into it, he rolled backwards and forwards on his seat, bitterly conscious of Philipson-Smith's aggrieved stare.

"Oh, for God's sake put a stop to it," Philipson-Smith almost shouted. "My God, Banks, you're practically certifiable, d'you know it?"

Yes, Edgar thought, *they're going to certify me soon. They're going to certify me dead. You too, you'll be dead, too.*

Philipson-Smith's attention was now definitely fixed on Edgar. Any intention he may have had of ignoring the presence of anyone else in the cabin was clearly impossible in the face of his irritation.

"Yes," he said in an altered tone, meditative and savage. "Yes, Banks, now that we seem to have got ourselves a few minutes' privacy, you might as well come clean about your ideas. First of all, I'd be obliged if you'd tell me, if you don't mind, just what you're doing shadowing McWhirtner and myself across Europe in this way."

"Sikorsky——" Edgar began, then stopped. Why bother?

"Sikorsky be damned," said Philipson-Smith hotly. "Don't start that feeble stuff about a helicopter line again. You're following us, I know that, blast you, and I want to know why!"

"You want to know why," Edgar repeated. The cabin had reached one of the steel masts, and at that instant ran over the bearings with a loud *klunk-klunk*. Thirty feet beneath was the shining snow, traced with the marks of skis like a child's scribble in faint pencil. Suddenly he began to laugh hysterically.

"You wa—hoo-oooo, you want to hoooooo, heigh, haha," he moaned. Philipson-Smith's face, seen through a red mist, twisted itself into the same murderous scowl as it had shown to Bert in the restaurant; but this time the only effect it had on Edgar was to bring him to the verge of breaking a blood-vessel with a fresh paroxysm of volcanic laughter. He shudderingly drew in breath, then collapsed forward, head in hands, shaking.

"Shut up, d'you hear, damn you?" Philipson-Smith screamed; more than anything else he hated being laughed at. He clenched his fists and half-rose from his seat, his shoulders hunched against the sloping metal behind him. Edgar gave a long quavering bray of mirth, then suddenly found himself serious again. The desire to laugh had evaporated as suddenly as it had come.

129

"You want to know why I'm following you," he said in a normal voice.

When Philipson-Smith did not answer, Edgar began to talk, fluently and calmly, with the old detached feeling, so familiar to his fantasy-ridden mind, of listening to another person. The theatrical streak in his nature, which made it so fatally easy to convince himself of the truth of any preposterous story, whipped uppermost and began to show itself.

"I might as well come clean, Smith," he said, "though what I'm going to say will be a pretty big surprise to you, and not a particularly welcome one either. It's true that I had some idea of keeping tabs on you and McWhirtleberry, and not altogether for your *beaux yeux* either."

No answer. Before going on Edgar took out a packet of cigarettes and held it out. When Philipson-Smith coldly ignored the conciliatory gesture, he took one out for himself and lit it.

"The fact is, and this must be about the last thing you expected to hear from me," he went on, "I—well, it's difficult to explain, but I . . ."

He paused again, utterly wrapped up in his performance as a man making a difficult and self-humbling admission, sweating with sincerity. He looked appealingly across at Philipson-Smith through the smoke of his cigarette.

"I've been doing a lot of thinking," he spluttered, "and I've finally become convinced that you people are right, and I've been wrong. Very wrong."

Especially wrong not to kick you in the sweetbreads long before now, he supplied mentally, with a momentary lapse from his willing suspension of disbelief; then renewed the attack.

"You see, it suddenly came over me, after talking to you, that I was wasting my life, messing about without any direction. After you left that evening I lay in bed and thought for a long time." (*About how best to murder you.*) "It struck me then that the best thing for me, the only hope, you might say, of getting straight with my own conscience, was to try my best to get taken on in your organization."

An expression of incredulous contempt appeared on Philipson-Smith's orang-outang features. "Taken——" he began in a high, wondering voice.

"Oh, only in a very subordinate position, of course," Edgar

cut in quickly. "After all, I'm of normal intelligence, though I know you don't think so, and I could be trained to be of *some* use, surely? If there's nothing else I'm considered fit for, I'll spend my time going about with a loud-speaker van, making speeches on street corners, chalking slogans on walls, anything you like to set me to."

His stomach gave a great lurch as he pronounced the words, and, looking out of the window at the mountains and the sky, he breathed a silent prayer to life for forgiveness that he had said such things.

Philipson-Smith's face had meanwhile assumed a different expression; instead of an orang-outang, he resembled an astute goldfish that has been offered a poisoned ant's egg. His mouth, losing its mushiness to an unprecedented degree, closed over those thrusting front teeth, and became for the moment his dominant feature. He radiated distrust through the grey smoke of Edgar's cigarette.

"You're certainly right," he said after a pause, "in thinking that any such suggestion, coming from you, is a surprise to me. But not for the reasons you would probably assign. Whatever change of heart, or mind, you may or may not have had, doesn't interest me. And it wouldn't interest anyone connected with the Movement."

He glared challengingly across at Edgar as if expecting him to dispute, or appeal against, this judgment; but Edgar was too exhausted by his recent histrionics, and too sickened by the situation, to do more than say feebly, "Yes?"

"Yes," said Philipson-Smith curtly. "Or rather, no, it wouldn't. Where the surprise comes in is simply in finding out that you have so little sense of the realities that you could deliberately ignore what I said to you that night in London."

Klunk-klunk. They were two-thirds of the way up, and level with the window the topmost branches of the pines were dusted with dry snow. At the foot of the nearest one, Edgar glimpsed the track of a hare. Life, forgive me, forgive me.

"I told you then that we had no need of recruits for the time being. And also that we should know how to hand-pick them when the need arose."

"But it's bad political psychology," Edgar burst out, sweeping himself once more into feeling that he would give up anything, sink to any level of indignity, if only he could be allowed to save his soul by joining Philipson-Smith's party. "It's bad political psychology not to recognize that the converted enemy is the firmest ally if he's genuinely converted."

"Yes," said Philipson-Smith in a dead voice, like an actor being tested for the part of Carl Peterson in a third-rate repertory company. "Yes. If he's genuinely converted." He paused, then, with a sudden violence, snapped: "Who are you working for?"

"Who am I what?" Edgar repeated, outraged, genuinely seething with the emotions of a sincere proselyte who finds the door closing in his face. "What do you, what can you possibly mean?"

"What I can possibly, and do, and intend to, mean is this," said Philipson-Smith, leaning forward like Carl Peterson. "Who is employing you in your bungling and transparent attempts to get inside the Movement for the purpose of sabotaging it?"

"Life is employing me," Edgar said, suddenly, before he could stop himself.

"Life?" echoed Philipson-Smith. "What do you mean? Who or what are you talking about, or have you finally lost your reason altogether?"

"I mean the magazine, of course," Edgar came back with a rush of glibness that gratified him in its futile way. "I'm doing a special series of articles for *Life* on contemporary political movements. It was for that reason that I first began to interest myself in your group. I'm sorry, it was rather disingenuous of me not to have told you that originally. But the point is that it's become, don't you see, retrospectively unimportant. I mean, the original reason why I began to check up on it was because of the articles for *Life*, but as soon as I began to find out more, well, that side of it became dwarfed by the—dwarfed by the——"

"Why didn't the editors approach Sir Rufus in the proper way?"

"Well, because, don't you see," *Klunk-klunk*, "the whole interest of the series lies in the unofficial tone: how it strikes an ordinary non-political observer. Instead of sending a permanent correspondent to interview the people at the top, and get sold the usual rosy view of the party's history and prospects, they hire some ordinary, unpretentious person like myself to string along with the members of the thing, and get a kind of worm's-eye

132

view. . . . Of course, what they didn't reckon on was the possibility of the observer being convinced, and dropping the original idea—I shall certainly be dropping it myself——"

With a final *klunk* the cabin swung into the gloom of the shed. The effect was like the drawing of a thick curtain, and they blinked at each other as the attendant fumbled open the door.

"I'm telling *Life* that I want to withdraw, that I don't want any pay——" Edgar babbled weakly, then felt his voice trail away into emptiness. "Any pay," he said slowly, staring in front of him.

Philipson-Smith hunched his shoulders to get out of the cabin, then, standing beside it, unnaturally straightened them. Edgar, clambering after him, felt like the victim of an ill-natured practical joke, from which the victim, however well he takes it, can expect no increase of popularity.

"Don't bother to lie to me, Banks," said Philipson-Smith gently and sternly, like a bishop who has found that his housemaid is pregnant by the milkman. "You're damned bad at it, and it isn't very funny."

He stalked away, out of the shed door. Watching the sunlight cascade suddenly on to his receding figure, Edgar felt old and tired. "It isn't funny, you're damned bad at it, it isn't funny," he suddenly shrieked with nerve-drawn fury. His voice was drowned by the banging and snarling of the machinery. Very slowly, head bowed, he walked out of the shed on to the shining snow.

The télésiège had only recently been completed, and it was hard not to feel that the mountain was still finding it difficult to get over the shock. In all the millennia since man had appeared on the earth, he had found his way up to this gleaming summit only rarely; none but the hardier members of his species, and they only in twos and threes, had left their tracks in this snow. Then, some eight or nine weeks before Edgar's visit, the apparatus had been completed and declared open to the public: immediately they had swarmed from below like termites, the young and healthy, the old and infirm, the gouty, the rheumatic, the obese, the daring, the timid. Here, above the pine-belt, where the chamois had grazed in safety, the new playground of men already looked as if it had been flourishing for a thousand seasons: but the mountain had not quite got used to it.

133

Edgar, not having any skis with him and not having any idea what he would have done with them if he had had any, kept perforce to the path of packed-down snow that led from the upper station of the télésiège to the restaurant. This irked him, for it was virtually the same thing as being under house arrest in the company of Philipson-Smith; neither of them could move over the deep snow which lay all about, so they would have to stay inside the restaurant, or on the terrace in front of it. He scanned the landscape for any traces of a path along which it would be possible to walk. There was nothing; in any case, to venture on to the ski-ing slopes would have been as foolhardy as walking along the middle of a road full of traffic, for at intervals of two or three seconds the ski-ers were streaming down past the restaurant like diving hawks, suddenly appearing over the creamy brow of the slope at any one of a hundred points. So much skill, so much happy activity, so much light and air and space under the dark blue mid-winter sky: it was an inspiring spectacle. But Edgar was not inspired. He had hoped, vaguely, that the top of a Swiss Alp was the sort of place from which it would be easy to throw a man down and kill him. It just showed, didn't it, eh, how much *he* knew about Swiss Alps.

Oh, well, here was the restaurant, and Mirabelle was bound to be needing some moral support after her ride up in the same cabin as McWhirtner. He went up the wooden ramp and entered the room.

They were all there, in characteristic attitudes. Philipson-Smith had already seated himself at a table on the far side of the restaurant, alone, and was disdainfully turning over the pages of an illustrated paper. Mirabelle was standing at the counter, talking animatedly to a huge man wearing a bright yellow suit. McWhirtner was sitting close to where Edgar stood, near the door. He had a long red scratch running down his right cheek, and his collar was burst open.

"What happened?" Edgar asked him, hoping by a display of insolent curiosity to increase whatever degree of discomfort McWhirtner was already feeling.

"Wha' d'ye bluidy well think?" McWhirtner countered sullenly. "A mosquito ran doon ma face with his skates on."

"That'll teach you to leave mosquitoes alone," Edgar said genially, and passed on towards the counter. He felt a little better.

Mirabelle paid no attention to him even when he leaned on the counter beside her. She was talking in a steady, even flow to the man in the yellow suit. Her companion gave little sign of enjoying her company, but evidently was not quick-witted enough to think of a way of shaking her off.

"And then it came to you—suddenly—didn't it?" she cried.

"What came to me?" the man croaked in an uneasy bass. He stared apologetically down at the empty glass he was twirling between his enormous fingers.

"Why, your sense of the national mood in music," Mirabelle rang out, writing in shorthand. "You suddenly knew what a deep, human need there was for the real, basic musical expression of the spirit of the American people. Their joys, their sorrows, their daily struggle," she explained. Edgar realized that this must be Earl Hammer. He looked at the man with interest. He had a record by him at home. Or rather, he did have a record by him at home, when he had a home, when such things used to mean anything to him, before he began to live in the present.

"Why, that's just how it was," Mirabelle beamed, writing.

"Well, it was like this, lady," Hammer began trying to explain. "It was back in thirty-six. We had a kinda hard winter that year. It was after I quit bein' an attendant at the baseball stadium."

"The background of one of America's native musicians," Mirabelle squawked in delight. "That truly indigenous—no, that won't do—that truly—the ball game—they'll eat this," she went on, mumbling phrases to herself and scribbling eagerly. "My music came to me in the roar of applause that greeted a home run by——"

The big man made a gesture of alarm. "Easy, lady, easy," he begged her. "It was that winter of thirty-six—I'm tryin' to *tell* ya same as ya asked me. I'd quit the stadium. It was while I was washin' the cabs'"

"Washing the cabs?" Mirabelle pressed him, her eyes shrewdly narrowed, pencil poised.

"The cabs," Hammer muttered. He seemed exhausted. "I'm workin' nights, washin' these cabs down, see, and a feller comes in and offers me fifty dollars——"

"Earl Hammer's music rises in all its strength from the labouring muscles of the American people," Mirabelle chanted,

135

writing. "From the dingy garage where he worked eight hours a night——"

"That was no dingy garage," Hammer interrupted, pained. "Real clean and smart, lots of tone. Why, some of them cabs was——"

"Until at last the American people decided that no one could interpret their daily lives like Earl Hammer—only this six-foot-four, two-hundred-and-forty-pound Kansas City cab-driver——"

"Cab-*washer*. There's a difference," Edgar put in.

Philipson-Smith, ashen with anger, came up to the counter. Glaring at the youth behind it, who was washing cups in a stainless steel sink, he rapped on the wood with a five-franc piece.

"Je voudrais du service," he snapped.

The youth looked at him coldly. "Un moment," he murmured, and went on with the cups.

Philipson-Smith began wrangling in a high-pitched, hectoring voice. Edgar, with a heavy sigh, turned away. What with Mirabelle's high-pressure falsification of the simple history of the vogue which had lifted a working man into success as an entertainer, and Philipson-Smith's assertion of the power-principle, he felt a deep hankering to be somewhere else.

But as he crossed the room, a sudden fountain of sound began to dance and quiver in the air. The big man in the yellow suit, tired of the effort to communicate in an alien medium, had also turned away, and, sitting at the upright piano in a corner of the restaurant, was allowing his fingers to draw out handfuls of sound from it. Piling the handfuls on top of each other like square bricks, he began building, building, making the thing he knew best how to make. It was the only way he could talk to Mirabelle; let her read here, if she could, the secret of the force that had lifted him out of the taxi-cab garage and carried him to this morning on the so lately virgin crest of the Alp.

Yes, Edgar thought as the notes bounded almost tangibly, almost visibly, about the room, this, in its limited way, was life. And Philipson-Smith, also in his limited way, was death. But the physical death which should have accompanied that death of the spirit had, meanwhile, been baulked afresh. Mirabelle's self-abnegation had been rewarded; Hammer had a distaste for being

136

interviewed, and she had been lucky to stumble on him in an unprotected moment. Having exchanged a few words with him, the ethics of her business would permit her to make up a complete interview with him, writing in a loquacious set of answers to questions ranging from world politics to how he liked Switzerland. She had her reward, McWhirtner had a scratched face, Philipson-Smith had enjoyed seizing an excellent opportunity to crack the whip. A very successful outing, from all points of view. Except the one that mattered.

Savagely humiliated and depressed, Edgar knew that only a prompt and heavy dose of solitude could save his reason. When the cabins had clanked their way to the lower shed, and the party emerged, he muttered some excuse and hurried away from the others, head bent, hands in pockets, slouching like a moody schoolboy. Indeed, a few weeks previously, when he was still at work, it had been his pedagogic duty, on seeing a boy shambling along in any such manner, to rasp mechanically, "You there, straighten your shoulders." But who was there now to tell him to straighten his own shoulders? Who was there who cared a rap what became of his shoulders, or any part of his body, or of his soul? What, in any case, did the whole silly business matter?

This wave of self-pity was too intense to last for more than a few minutes, and was replaced by a jumble of specific ideas, like an unassembled jigsaw puzzle. What had he expected anyway? Had he imagined that the télésiège restaurant would be perched on the edge of a ten-thousand-foot cliff, with no fence along its edge? In any case, the sacrifice he had demanded of Mirabelle had been rewarded. And if Philipson-Smith was still alive, so was he, Edgar, the instrument of vengeance.

His short upward swing towards cheerfulness, brought on by this last reflection, was quickly checked by another downward plunge into depression. Yes, he was still alive, but what use was he, how much progress did he seem able to make? He had failed in London, he had failed in Geneva, and he had failed here. Were his elaborate schemes too difficult? Would it end simply in stabbing Philipson-Smith to death, in broad daylight, with Roger's clasp-knife, and being led away, smiling and joking bravely, to the condemned cell? Perhaps that was, after all, the only way;

perhaps he had simply been over-reaching himself by wanting to make too neat a job of it.

Without being fully conscious of doing so, he had been making his way, as before, up the hillside, towards the receding tide of sunlight that lay gleaming on the upper slopes. Now he halted at the point where the path divided. On one side was a bridge over the quick spluttering stream, and beyond it, a path winding upward through a deep narrow ravine. A finger-post said, "Gorges du Torrent." He did not, consciously at any rate, want to see the Torrent—what could natural beauty have to say to him in his state?—but nevertheless he ambled slowly across the bridge and began following the path of packed-down snow. Deeply, perhaps, he was motivated by a sympathy with any manifestation of the rage, the bad temper, of this country of violence and suddenness.

At all events, as he moved onwards, the gloomy magnificence of his surroundings gradually muffled his egocentric emotions. He felt, as he had felt on the mountain path the previous afternoon, that thoughts and feelings relating solely to oneself were not merely ridiculous, but outright impossible. Overhead, the sky was still full of sunshine, but most of it was caught and held by the thick pines above him; only in sharply defined patches could it spill down to light up the steep walls of the cleft or the hurrying water. Blinking as he entered the harsh areas of sunlight, groping as he left them, and with the torrent shouting endlessly in his ears, Edgar moved upwards in a world of secrecy. Round each sharp corner, a view of renewed virulence confronted him; the stream, relatively innocent-looking in the shallows further down, was gaining in savagery as he traced it higher, and its roaring became more and more threatening. Once or twice he glanced over his shoulder, unashamedly aware of the nervous dread of a child on a dark staircase, half expecting to see a bear or wolf, or even some nameless demoniac creature, spawned by the rocks, water and brushwood, stalking at his heels.

Climbing a dozen rough steps hewn out of the rock, he went round a shoulder of the hill and stopped, appalled. There, facing him, was the waterfall, a single half-opened fan of mist and thunder. In that confined space it seemed like the lowered head of a charging mammoth. In the crashing torrent underneath it, the gorge had bitten more deeply into the rock, so that the bed of the stream was twenty or thirty feet below the path. To go any further he had to cross a rickety wooden bridge; then the path ended at a stout wooden hut where visitors of romantic tendencies could sit and watch the fall without being soaked in its endless whipping spray.

Edgar walked on to the bridge. In contrast with most things Swiss, it seemed frail and unsafe. Looking down, he saw the whirling water through the wide gaps in its planks. There could be no more certain death than to fall from there into the nerve-centre of pile-driving water and jagged rock.

So this, after all, was the setting! He felt relieved that the episode of the télésiège had been no more than a meaningless false start. All the time, waiting for him, there had been this perfect man-trap. The incessant noise would enable one man to follow another in absolute confidence that he would not be discovered until it was too late; it would be easy to keep a few yards behind, always screened by some twist in the ravine; and then, when the victim stood upon the bridge. . . . It would be so quick, so effective, so merciful to both of them.

His heart pounding, he crossed the bridge and hurried on to the hut, with no clear motive except to survey the ground as fully as possible. Grasping the iron rail, he swung himself up the three wooden steps and burst in. Immediately he spun round and burst out again; inside were a youth and maiden wrenching themselves apart, and throwing him a murderous glare of re-proach. Poor things, he thought; to choose so frightening and death-haunted a place for their dalliance must argue a pathetic shortage of places to go. Imagine kissing and murmuring tender vows in the face of the dreadful crashing water. But perhaps it was an extra *frisson*; he wondered what Baudelaire or Donne would have found to say about it. Ah well, that sort of literary parlour-game was over for him, had been over for a long time. Quickly, purposefully, he stumbled and slithered his way down the path, pausing only for a backward glance at the tiny fragile bridge which represented his fourth coconut-shy at death.

"Immediate action essential to avert world-wide Communist coup," Edgar tapped out on Mirabelle's typewriter. "Secrecy and speed of the essence. Your co-operation, in a sphere of activity not hitherto assigned you, will now be necessary for some days or weeks. Agent bearing precise instructions and vital documents will await you at 1500 hours to-morrow (Sunday). Rendezvous: wooden cabin at top of path signposted "Gorges du Torrent", on hillside above Les Glissades. Destroy this communication."

Unrolling the paper from the machine, he inserted an envelope and typed "R. Philip Smithson" on it. This, he felt, would convey a nicely blended impression of haste and panic on the one hand, and, on the other, a brusque hint that Philipson-Smith was not sufficiently important in the hierarchy to have his name correctly remembered. He folded the letter and sealed it in the envelope.

"That didn't take you long," said Mirabelle; she had been lying on her bed reading a magazine when Edgar had come in with a request for the loan of her typewriter, and now folded her hands behind her head and watched him putting it back into its case.

"No, just a short business note," Edgar answered. "But they always look better when they're typewritten, don't you think?"

"Depends on what they are," she said flatly, and for the first time he was aware of a note of hostility in her voice. She was hurt, of course, at his lack of confidence in her. Well, it hurt him too. After openly enlisting her aid, to the extent of making her go through a series of piercingly unpleasant moments, he had, to all appearances, no further use for her, and did not even respect her enough to go on including her in his counsels. Damn it, why did living in the present involve treating people so badly? This final stage, of course, had to be carried through in solitude; if he let her into the secret, goodness knew what absurd impulses might drive her to interfere and prevent it. As it was, she already knew uncomfortably too much; yet he could not, because of his remorse and his minimal but real respect for her, begin the weary process of hypocritically soothing her, telling her a pack of lies, allaying her suspicions.

As he thought all this he realized that she knew what he was thinking; the substance of it had, telepathically, communicated itself to her as she lay watching his face.

"Mr. Sherlock doesn't need a Watson now, does he?" she asked. Edgar had never expected to hear a note of contempt in that voice, but he heard it now. In anguish, he seized her hands.

"Look, Mirabelle," he said urgently, "you don't understand now—but you will. Just wait a little, and——"

140

She took her hands away from him and crossed them behind her head once more.

"I understand *now*. At any rate, as much as I want to understand."

"But you don't . . . please. . . ."

She looked at him stonily. "I'm not interested, Mr. Holmes. Whatever you're doing, you want to go ahead without me; well, *go* ahead."

Hopelessly, Edgar turned away and left her alone. After a solitary glass of beer in the crowded bar, he went to bed, pausing only to leave the note for Philipson-Smith lying on the table where he would find it at breakfast. That was that; the preparations were complete. Sleep was slow in coming; and when it came he was falling off a high bridge into the oily waters of a harbour, he was sinking under the churning screws of cargo-boats, and from the deck of a tug Mirabelle looked down, saying into a speaking-tube to the engine-room, "I'm not interested, go ahead, full speed ahead, not interested, not interested," until he drowned into consciousness and it was morning.

It was two o'clock. Edgar stood tensely at his window, a point from which, without being exposed to view, he could keep an eye on the street immediately in front of the house. Philipson-Smith would soon be setting off. There was only one way for him to leave the place, and Edgar would be sure to see him. Then he would allow five minutes to go by—his watch was wound up and ready—before beginning his pursuit. So once more, here he was, standing on the diving-board ready to swoop down, finally, into destruction. It was all incredibly horrible; he faced it frankly, trembling at the knees and dragging on a cigarette. The hard crumb of scepticism, which had previously obtruded itself on similar occasions, seemed to have melted at last. This time he really believed that he would die.

A wave of panic brushed across him, and his hands were suddenly as wet as if he had plunged them into the wash-basin. Oh, God, if only he didn't have to do it! He felt an overpowering urge to lie down on the bed and cover his eyes, or hide his face deep in the pillow; but if he did so, even for a moment, Philipson-Smith might go out unperceived. He had to keep standing where he was, and keep his eyes open and his mind clear. Fear choked

141

him like a gas. Why had he never felt this before? All the other times, he had been so calm; realizing intuitively, he now supposed, that something would intervene at the last minute to save him and spoil his plans. Spoil! the word was ironical. It was this time he was going to be spoiled. His body would be smashed into a bag of splintered bones, his heart would be flailed to a standstill, he would never be Edgar Banks any more, walking about, talking, reasoning, smelling, seeing, hearing; it was over. Because this time it was going to happen.

In his mind's eye he saw the rickety bridge and the bounding water. Oh, God, let me off, let me off. But the wish, or prayer, formed itself with a horrible lack of conviction; he did not really want to be prevented again. His resolution had become possessed of a grim life of its own, an identity which pressed upon his own identity and suffocated it. Deeply, under his feverish desire to live, under his raging panic, lay the broad, tranquil foundation of his death-wish. At that moment even his hatred of Philipson-Smith, even his desire to be avenged on him in the name of life, had withered away, and he was left only with the numbing reality of his need for peace. Oh, get it over, get it over!

He tried to take another cigarette out of the packet, but his hands were shaking. Savagely, he tore at the paper, so that the three remaining cigarettes tumbled on to the floor. Groping, he picked up one and lit it, allowing the other two to lie on the carpet, useless and wasted, like the rest of the life that might have been his. Oh, why was everyone else luckier than he? Why did the others feel so assured, so ready to go on taking whatever punishment life could dish out, why were they immune from this terrible drive towards oblivion? It would *hurt*; the water would be cold, the rocks would be sharp, he would not die straight away, but would feel himself being bounced and smashed by the bitterly scornful torrent. Why did this have to happen to *him*?

The other person to whom it would have to happen now appeared in the street below him, muffled in an overcoat. After glancing rapidly up and down the street, as if taking his bearings, Philipson-Smith set off rapidly, his long body swaying purposefully above his short legs, towards the path that led away up the hillside. Edgar looked at his watch, registering the time; four minutes past two. For a moment his brain seized up, and he was unable to add five to four. He began to count on his fingers: five,

142

six, seven, eight, nine. He had to leave when the finger pointed to nine minutes past. In other words, he had to wait out an eternity even longer than the one that had gone by since he came up here after lunch. That had been only four minutes, and yet there had been time for him to experience æons of fear and despair. But at least he could now lie on the bed. He flung himself down and pressed his interlaced fingers over his eyes.

His mind emptied, and he lay for a long time without thinking anything, only seeing a procession of images; himself going shopping with his mother, when, as a little staring boy, the walk down the hill to the shops had seemed a long journey, and the village street a dangerous foreign territory, peopled by weird dogs and big, rude boys kicking at stones and whistling. He had not, after all, been so wrong; the village street, which so soon afterwards had come to seem ordinary and harmless, had really been a dangerous wilderness, and he had got lost there and never found his way again. It seemed to him that his mother had no sooner allowed him to go for walks by himself than he had taken a wrong turning, and never again been at home, so that the very idea of home had withered away inside him. Images of school followed; his prep. school where they had taken folding desks into the garden in hot weather, and done their lessons in the shade of the dark yew hedge; the smell of sun-warmed varnish had always brought back those mornings to him, and by one of the familiar trick effects of memory his time at that school had seemed, in retrospect, to have been spent almost entirely out-of-doors, smelling the varnish, the hedge and the lawn, hearing the cars go past along the road outside, though in fact they had probably not moved the desks out-of-doors more than half-a-dozen times during his three years there. Then the Grammar School with big, roaring masters a hundred feet high, and fights in the changing-room, and endless hours separating lunch from tea, and grasping for a wet egg-shaped ball in the biting wind. As if unwilling to trace his biography further, his mind petered out, leaving the story unfinished in mid-adolescence, with a confusion of books, girls, family rows, long bicycle rides, immense lonely walks on rainy nights. He swung his legs off the bed and sat up. The watch pointed to seven minutes past two.

Two more minutes. He picked up the two cigarettes from the carpet, put them both at once into his mouth, and lit them. A

143

good way of finishing them up—quite easy to smoke two at once. A pity he could not do that with his life, running through forty years in five minutes. That was what people tried to do, he supposed, who lived short, insane, iridescent lives and died in their thirties. They were wrong, of course; you couldn't live like that. Either live or leave it alone; they were trying a half-way solution. Well, he was leaving it alone.

Another minute. Madly he drew on the two cigarettes, filling the room with smoke, gasping like a man nearly drowned. Suddenly the idea of retribution flashed into his whirling brain. He was suffering so much, surely it must be *for* something? What had he done? "He must be wicked to deserve such pain." That was Browning, talking about an ugly animal, a donkey or something. How had he, Edgar, been wicked enough to deserve this?

His mind slowed down again. Partly, of course, it was Philipson-Smith's wickedness he was paying for. Evil was paid for with pain, but not necessarily one's own evil with one's own pain. As long as it worked out in an overall balance, they were satisfied. They? Who were they? Or was it he? It? What was behind this ghastly ledger-balancing that went on—such and such an amount of wickedness must produce, let me see, where's the slide-rule?—*this* much pain. Order it up, men, shower it about. And see that that bastard Banks gets a good share.

It was time. He carefully crushed out the two burning tubes, only half consumed, and went out to crush the burning lives, half-consumed, of himself and his enemy.

During the early stages of the walk, he had to keep a long way behind, dodging and peering round the corners of sheds and the trunks of trees, for the open field, spread with clean snow, afforded no cover. But presently Philipson-Smith reached the bridge, paused for a moment looking at the signpost, and then marched away into the roaring gloom of the gorge.

Hurrying frantically to close the gap, Edgar followed. With no time for any emotion or thought—so that in this sense his life was already over—he ran across the bridge and began to climb the twisting path, stumbling over the stones and brushing heedlessly against the rough wall of rock at his side. His eyes constantly trained on the next bend, his brain alert for the sight of Philipson-Smith's figure moving on ahead, he was oblivious of the possible presence of anyone else, so that a couple of weather-beaten middle-aged ladies, obviously English, seemed grotesquely startling and unreal as they swept towards him round a corner, on their way down from seeing the torrent: they were wrong in the landscape, like giraffes or sandwich-men. Nevertheless he muttered "Good afternoon" as he clawed his way past them, and was aware suddenly that these were the last words he would ever address to a fellow human being; he might use his voice again, but it would be in an incoherent cry, not in anything resembling conversation or greeting. As the thought swirled into his mind, his haste and preoccupation swirled it out again, and he hurried on as mindlessly as the current below him.

Philipson-Smith must be walking quickly. Why did he not come into view? Had the mocking spirit of this place turned him into a fox, his animal counterpart, and sent him scampering up the slope into the gloom of the mountain-side? Panting, sweat breaking out on his face, Edgar ran forward, up the rough-hewn steps, and round the shoulder of rock. There was the thundering curtain of spray, there was the wooden hut and the spidery bridge, and there was Philipson-Smith walking deliberately, shoulders hunched, twenty yards ahead.

Scorning caution and concealment, Edgar sprinted along the path. His mind emptied completely as he ran, and he became a machine, fuelled and adjusted for a mechanical purpose. Of their own accord, although it was still too soon, his hands went out in front of him, fingers crooked, ready to seize his enemy. The pines bent forward like spectators at a gladiatorial contest. Philipson-Smith, still not turning round, set foot on the bridge, with only its unevenly spaced planks, its rickety wooden railing, between him and the dashing water.

Edgar darted forward murderously, then froze. Mouth open, eyes strained wide, he stood staring across at the opposite cliff, above Philipson-Smith's head. Then, with the voice that a moment before had spoken its last human message, he shouted wildly.

"Get back, you little fool!"

Philipson-Smith spun round, staring angrily, but Edgar did not heed him. His eyes were fixed on the swaying branch of a pine that clung to the shelving soil of the cliff in front. A small, struggling figure, hands and knees clenched round the rough wood, was inching its way outwards, over the water. It was the boy Roger.

"What the hell are you doing here?" Philipson-Smith shouted to Edgar above the roar of the torrent.

"The boy! the boy!" Edgar yelled in a shaking voice.

The other swung round to look where Edgar was pointing. Instantly he began waving his arms in a threatening way.

"Go on, break your neck, you little devil!" he shrieked. Edgar remembered English lessons at school where they had had to learn a definition of irony: *saying the opposite of what is meant.*

The boy gaped at them for a moment, then began to crawl backwards, speeding up as he reached the lower and thicker part of the branch. At the same instant the distraught, gesticulating figures of Mr. and Mrs. Crabshaw appeared on the skyline, and they could faintly be heard shouting to their offspring. Groping his way backwards, he scowled at them over his shoulder. Philipson-Smith walked on over the bridge. Edgar followed, still refusing to recognize that the opportunity to kill him had gone by. But when they faced each other, they were on solid ground, protected by a stout iron railing from the steep fall and the disappointed water.

"Well?" Philipson-Smith asked.

At the sound of his wet, arrogant voice, Edgar's accumulated determination ebbed away, and he knew suddenly that this attempt, like the others, had failed. He might still have had an opportunity, but now that he no longer held the advantage of surprise it would mean a long struggle, and he no longer had the spirit to undertake it. He stared heavily, gloomily, into the face of his enemy.

"Well?" asked Philipson-Smith again.

"Well, what?" Edgar muttered lamely.

"You know what. Following me again. Spying, prying again. Let's have the explanation, Banks."

Despair, as usual, gave its own form of inspiration. Edgar felt an expression of astonishment creeping over his face.

"The message I had was addressed to me alone," he said wonderingly. "How was I to know you would be here as well?"

"The message? What message?"

"Look here," said Edgar, adopting the tone of one making an almost bemused effort to clear up a senseless mystery. "The first thing I must know is whether you're here simply by chance, simply because you want to take a walk, or whether it's because you've received the same kind of message as I have."

"Well, damn it, man," Philipson-Smith shouted, "what kind of message *have* you received?"

Edgar looked at him narrowly, as if weighing the chances of his being trustworthy enough to hear the secrets of the Movement; then, after an obvious moment of hesitation, he said, "Perhaps we're both needed."

"Both needed for what?"

Edgar smiled calmly and with a hint of conspiratorial intimacy. "You know, don't you?" he said, and nodded towards the hut. "In there at fifteen hours, waiting for us. You had it—didn't you? The message?"

Philipson-Smith's expression, in spite of his attempt to stifle it into impassiveness, showed traces of both astonishment and fear. He opened his mouth to speak, then shut it, staring uneasily.

Edgar looked at his watch. "Come on," he said. "It's twenty to three. We might as well be waiting inside the hut when he comes."

Silently they moved along the path and climbed the steps into the shelter. Philipson-Smith was the first to swing himself up the three rough steps, and it was clear from the way he stopped short at the top, blinking into the shadowy interior, that something altogether unexpected had confronted him. For a moment Edgar felt a head-spinning, knee-loosening twinge of pure fright; what if the mysterious "agent", with his instructions, really did exist, was actually there awaiting them? Had he called some hideous reality into existence by imagining it? He gripped the hand-rail and pulled himself up the stairs. At once, like a gramophone needle stuck in a groove, he was back in a previous moment of experience; there were the same young couple agitatedly drawing apart, with the same glares of reproach and anger. Flustered as he had been the first time, Edgar was about to bounce down the stairs and make off, when he remembered their situation, and became aware of the figure of Philipson-Smith, erect, immobile and unyielding, at the top of the steps. Of course! With the agent due to arrive at any time, they must have the shelter to themselves. He braced himself to join Philipson-Smith in the task of braving it out, but it was hard to find the resources, to muster the necessary ruthlessness and urgency. Philipson-Smith, apart from the fact that such actions came naturally to his character, so that he would have enjoyed the situation for its own sake, had a genuine

147

motive; Edgar had none. As he lounged against the wall of the
shelter, scraping his feet on the floor, he tried to convey by his
attitude that he saw no reason why the shelter, which was a public
one, should not be enjoyed as such; but inwardly he was a huge
raw mass of apology and insecurity. He felt sorry for the youth
and the girl, driven up here on a Sunday afternoon because they
wanted to be alone together and then intruded upon by a couple
of insensitive English oafs. If only it were possible to signal to
them, to convey to them somehow that the situation was not of
his choosing and that they were suffering in a noble cause! He
stood there woodenly, staring down at his feet, stunned by the
humiliation of it and by the nervous shock, which now began to
make itself apparent, of having keyed himself up to a sacrificial
death and found himself, instead, tossed into a situation of silly
lying and boorish behaviour. That evening in London, centuries
ago, when he had decided to live in the present—how could he
have foreseen that it would lead to this hut, these scowls, this
painful farce against a backdrop of thundering spray?

The girl was sitting bolt upright, staring at the torrent; the deep
flush which had suffused her face was ebbing patchily, creating a
mottled effect. The young man was leaning forward on the bench,
rubbing his clenched fist into the palm of his left hand. Philipson-
Smith, with a passable imitation of an English tourist of the
eighteen-nineties, was standing rigidly, only his head moving as
he swivelled it from side to side to take in the landscape. One
could imagine the instructions in Baedecker: "Les Glissades
(1500 metres); See: Gorges du Torrent (charming view from
shelter at top)."

Unable to meet the eyes of any of the other three, Edgar chose
the landscape. His gaze flickered over the broad front of the
waterfall, bounced on with the current, and suddenly in imagination he was down there, where he had expected to be, swirling
and crashing and coming to pieces in the shallow white water.
He turned abruptly towards Philipson-Smith, struggling to speak,
but between himself and every living person he felt the smoothness of plate-glass, cutting off sound and contact. It was no use,
he had too recently come back from the threshold of death, he
had not yet completely rejoined those who were alive, and in
any case he did not want to speak to Philipson-Smith, he had
nothing to say to him; the thought came pleasantly, with a kind

148

of relief, as he pitched forward into the black emptiness of a dead faint.

"The height sometimes does it," Mr. Crabshaw said professionally, "but I should have expected it to happen before if it had been going to happen."

Edgar looked up at the eager, happy face of Mr. Crabshaw, the dark-stubbled face, twisted in disappointment and uncertainty, of Philipson-Smith, the interested, forgiving faces of the young Swiss and his girl. After a little shifting, they kept still and the scene was intelligible. Ashamed and angry, he began to struggle to his feet.

"Easy now, easy now, old man," Mr. Crabshaw admonished. "No good jumping up straight away . . . you must have been out about five minutes, and that's a good long time."

"As long—as that?" Edgar muttered. Shame gathered in him once more at the thought of his weakness. A fine one to take upon himself to be the avenging soldier of Life! A nerve-shaken weakling who fainted in an ordeal! But he was going on with it, nothing would shake him, he was going on with it.

"Oh, yes, it must have taken us at least five minutes to get here, and it seems you blacked out more or less as soon as you got into the shelter," said Mr. Crabshaw. "We followed you on, naturally, to thank you about Roger."

At the word "Roger", the head of his wife came jutting over his shoulder, and echoed, "Yes, Mr. Banks, to thank you about Roger. It's most unusual for me not to have my eye on him . . . we were picknicking . . . suddenly noticed . . . I think you saved his life! Yes, really, saved his life! If I ever come to these awful mountains again," her voice drifted away, either because she was moving farther off or because his own hold on consciousness was loosening again.

Closing his eyes, he heard the voice of the youth. "I ketched him, le monsieur, he fall. Fell. He fell. He has—you sink—the trouble with art?"

Opening his eyes, he said, "I'm all right now. I can walk—I'll go down to the hotel."

"Bed for you," said Mr. Crabshaw firmly. "Bed, and a good rest before dinner. Come along, we'll all go together."

They helped him up. He felt a terrible desire to be in bed, to

149

pull the clothes up over his face, to hide in the pillow, to be nothing, to flow away.

Philipson-Smith had not yet spoken. Now he said, "If you think he'll be all right with you . . . I'll stay here."

"Stay here?" Mr. Crabshaw asked, puzzled.

"Yes," said Philipson-Smith woodenly. "Stay here. I feel like sitting down and resting a bit. I—feel a bit queer myself."

Edgar tried to feel enjoyment at having involved Philipson-Smith in an embarrassing situation. Obviously he could not, without being thought to have gone mad, admit that he was waiting in the hut to keep an appointment. It was splendid, but he did not feel it as splendid. There was a wall of plate-glass round him, hard, smooth, and cold. He was not properly alive.

"Look here, old chap," said Mr. Crabshaw seriously. "If you're feeling a bit wonky yourself, you'd better come down with the rest of us. I should have it on my conscience if I left you up here to make your own way down. Good gracious, what an afternoon! First Roger tries to make an end of himself, then Banks here throws a faint, then you . . . then you . . ."

"Then I what?" Philipson-Smith cut in coldly. "Never mind about me. I just want to sit here for ten minutes. The whole thing's tired me, that's all."

"You'd much better——"

"Oh, go away and leave me *alone*!" Philipson-Smith yelled. He was obviously in an acutely nervous condition. Even now the agent from Sir Rufus, bearing vitally important instructions, might be peering round the trunk of some nearby pine, wondering angrily what Philipson-Smith was doing with a gang of chattering idiots in the hut with him. It was the end of his career as a trusted member of the Movement. And beneath it, as Edgar guessed, lay a substratum of doubt as to whether the whole thing were not some fantastic hoax. But strong as this doubt was, he did not dare rely on it and wash the arrangement out. Edgar could read Philipson-Smith's mind as never before, so clearly as not to deny him a certain sympathy. Their eyes met for an instant, and Philipson-Smith flashed at him a message of pure hatred that would have been unnerving had it not been for the plate-glass that insulated his spirit from all human contact.

Mr. Crabshaw, after looking at Philipson-Smith for a moment in a way that clearly conveyed a grave sympathy for his over-wrought condition, shrugged, put his arm round Edgar's shoulders, and helped him down the steps. The cortège began to wind slowly down the path, Mrs. Crabshaw holding the children firmly at her side as if afraid that they might fly away by centrifugal force, and the young Swiss couple, talking animatedly and happily, bringing up the rear. What made them happy was the excitement of having seen a group of English people behaving in a really classic fashion, with all the oddity and lack of balance that was traditionally expected of them—fainting, shouting at one another, giving one another first aid, building up tension after tension and still not leaving one another alone. It was wonderfully interesting; their Sunday had not been ruined after all.

"Well, what the hell happened?" Mirabelle asked.

Edgar picked up his glass and drank a generous mouthful of Cinzano before answering. They were sitting in the bar before dinner. Looking at her, he wished there were some way to soothe her, to admit her to his confidence and flatter away the anger she still felt. But the plate-glass was terribly in the way. The events of that afternoon had thrown him too far beyond the reach of the most persistent antennæ of human feeling.

"The Crabshaw guy says you happened along just in time to save the kid from doing a death-dive. Then the next thing was you were out cold. And your pal Smith was there. You'd followed him up that path to the waterfall."

He was silent. His heart cried out to him to unburden it, to speak to her. She knew already so much about him, why did he hesitate now to fill in the gaps, to be human, to hear her friendly comment on the whole terrible mess? She was not trying to claim him, only to understand: *why are you holding back*, he asked himself, *why, why? She knows your body; speak, talk to her, let her know your mind!*

He leaned forward. But there was the plate-glass, cold, invisible, squarely built round him. That day had been too much. After a long time-lag, he had finally caught up with the resolution he had made that evening in his flat, with the white paper staring up at him. It had finally got inside, his decision to make an end of himself. Queer, how these things worked. All along he had acted as if it were not true, even while he had been physically working towards its consummation. Now he knew that it *was*

151

true. No one could call back across the barrier, the barrier he had crossed intellectually at the beginning, and had now crossed spiritually.

"You can't speak to me, can you?" she asked. "Something's happened inside you. Something's gone, hasn't it?"

He stared at her, filled with a dead anguish, as if watching another person in pain. She spoke again, without anger.

"All right, I shan't try any more. I know it isn't anything personal you've got against *me*. You just can't come alive any more. I wish I could help you, Edgar, but you know yourself that's not possible."

She stood up. He reached forward and touched her hand. It was warm and soft, the living flesh of a real person, alive and carrying on.

"Good-bye," she said.

Edgar nodded like a jointed wooden doll. He tried to speak, but the person who made the doll had not put a larynx into its round hard throat. As she turned and walked out of the bar, he knew that he would never speak to her again. The last strand was cut.

VIII

EDGAR was still not quite anæsthetized. As he stepped out of the little grey train at the foot of the mountain, he took note, probably for the last time, of the fact that his existence seemed to have room only for the unexpected. Soon he would cease to have any sense of normality left, and unexpectedness, in a world where nothing was definitely expected, would no longer be a quality. But this morning he was still able to feel the strangeness of it all.

The train drew in and gathered them up. Slumped in a corner, Edgar watched the margin of the lake sway towards him and recede again, saw the neat towns slide past them, the bigger places standing still for a moment to make the introduction a formal one: Lausanne, Montreux, Vevey, places whose identity he would never explore, the whole journey a tapestry which had here and there its focus-points of drama: a glimpse of mountains, a blinding rush through a tunnel, an old prison, that had had a poem written about it, standing thrust out into the water.

As they approached Geneva he forced himself out of his trance and went in search of Philipson-Smith and McWhirtner. It could not be for long now; very soon he would succeed, they would both be dead, and he would have peace on the other side of the plate-glass. In spite of the failure of his previous attempts, Edgar felt quite certain that success could not elude him indefinitely *now*: now that he had caught up with the idea of suicide, possessed it imaginatively and spiritually, and had thus, in every respect except the physical, died already. He remembered someone quoting to him the definition of "life" in the *Oxford Dictionary*: "State of ceaseless change and functional activity, peculiar to organized matter." Well, the functional activity went

153

on, but the ceaseless change was over. Except in the sense that he would not actually decay, he was a corpse by this time, as every determined suicide is a corpse. The crisis of fear through which he had passed in his bedroom at Les Glissades had ended the preliminary or skirmishing period of his battle, and now it was seriously joined. He had overcome that fear—in other words, strangled the last of his desire to live—and since that moment the plate-glass had surrounded him.

Thinking on these lines, he paused in the corridor, staring fixedly at the rushing landscape. "Death destroys a man," he began, aloud, but could not continue: was it true, that second half of the statement? What was the idea of death saving him from? Death had already destroyed him, shutting him away from any touch or sound of humanity, that was true enough; but the rest? He shivered, then shrugged and moved on, peering into the compartments for his enemy.

When he found him, it was at once obvious that McWhirtner had won another battle, for the two of them were sitting in the restaurant-car with an almost-empty bottle of white wine before them. Edgar guessed that Philipson-Smith had begun by trying to keep McWhirtner away from the drink, so as to prevent any rebellious behaviour, but that he had been compelled once more to step aside before the bull-rush of the Scot's appetites. A strained half-smile, which not even the most casual observer could have connected in any way with mirth, lay at anchor along the tense muscles of his jaw as he watched McWhirtner emptying, refilling, and re-emptying his glass.

Edgar, having approached undetected, bent over their table with a polite, "May I join you?"

Immediately on recognizing him, Philipson-Smith stood up. "We shall be in the station in a few minutes," he said coldly, seeming to address no specific person. "We must get back to our compartment."

"Oh, come, we've got ten minutes at least," Edgar said coaxingly, his words intended for McWhirtner. "What about joining me in a brandy to batten that wine down?"

McWhirtner raised his head like one of the dogs assembled by the axiomatic Russian. "Tha' soons laik a guid," he began.

"No!" cut in Philipson-Smith with a yap like a collie's. Swinging round, he faced McWhirtner across the table, eyeing

154

him narrowly. Edgar saw that he had been wrong to go on assuming that the Scot would always be the winner: it was clear that Philipson-Smith was about to put his foot down, with all the strength of a pent-up nervous fury, to prevent any kind of sociability between the three of them. Why? Just for the sake of discipline? Or was it terribly important just now that they should not communicate? Was there something that McWhirtner might reveal?

Taking no notice of him, the pair fixed each other with their eyes for a full half-minute. Then McWhirtner slowly reached out for the bottle, poured what remained of the wine into his glass, and drank it. It was a gesture of defeat, and clearly understood as such by all those present. He stood up.

Philipson-Smith turned to Edgar with a triumphant smile. This show of strength had elated him. Edgar saw this, but even so he was taken by surprise at Philipson-Smith's next words.

"Sorry to disappoint you. You really must come round to our hotel one evening, now that we're all back in Geneva."

"Come roun'—why, wha'——" McWhirtner began in a tone of pained surprise. Philipson-Smith rounded on him like a lion-tamer.

"I'm making the arrangements," he said quietly. After a long, wounding stare to drive his words home, he turned to Edgar again.

"Come round to-morrow evening," he said. "We'll be free after eight."

Some instinct made Edgar turn towards McWhirtner. He wanted to read in the Scot's face his reaction to this invitation. But McWhirtner was thoroughly on his guard, and it may have been just imagination that saw a gleam of malicious pleasure dying away from those pale eyes as quickly as it had come.

"Thank you, I'd love to," he answered impassively.

Philipson-Smith half-bowed in a parody of politeness, and they separated.

The next evening, at half-past eight, Edgar was walking by the lake and talking to himself. For a long time he said nothing but, "Serves you bloody well right," over and over again. Then he stood still, glaring down at the rippling surface of the water, and, after a moment's pause, burst out: "Well, what else did you expect? What else could you possibly expect?"

"You didn't think he'd take all that phoney stuff about the agent lying down, did you?" he went on. "You could hardly expect him to associate with you on normal terms . . . at the very best he must think you're mad, and probably very dangerous too."

Some people walking by heard Edgar talking to himself, and gave him curious and pitying glances. One middle-aged woman, who must have been more tender-hearted than the rest, even slackened her pace for a moment, as if wondering whether to go up to him and ask him what was the matter, but her husband caught her arm and hurried her along.

"Mad!" Edgar continued, oblivious of them. "Well, what about it? Are you going to contest that, by any chance?" He snorted loudly with contempt. "Are you going to say that your conduct has been *sane*?"

Leaning forward on the parapet, he gave a short, bitter laugh.

"The most unexpected thing, of course, is that you should show surprise," he said. "As if it weren't the most natural thing in the world. Of course he's going to take a rise out of you. Obviously he's going to invite you round to the hotel—once they're safely away. And of course you're going to go round there and find them not there and the whole place under instructions not to say where they've gone—not even knowing, probably. And of course," he finished, sneering, "you're going to be surprised. As surprised as hell."

He walked on, turned away from the lake, and began to thread his way among side streets.

"And where does that put you?" he asked himself abruptly, pausing in the pool of light outside the windows of a café. "I'll tell you. It puts you in the position where the man you're looking for might be anywhere, anywhere in Switzerland or in the world, for that matter. In the position of having wasted your money and time coming here at all. In the position where you might just as well have stayed in London and waited for him to come back."

He began to walk very quickly, almost running, turning corners blindly, and talking to himself more and more loudly, in snatches interrupted by heavy panting, till in the end he was not talking but fragmentarily shouting.

"Had any *sense*—you'd *drop it*—just kill *yourself.*"

Plunging into the doorway of his hotel, he whirled round twice in the swing doors. "You're the one that deserves it, after all," he said to himself on the second circuit, dropping his voice a little.

As he stalked across the carpet to the lift, blinded by misery and frustration, he almost bumped into the hall porter, who was showing a degree of attentiveness in excess of what he was paid for, so that to collide with him would have been a poor reward. He was moving forward to intercept Edgar and hand him a note that had been left for him in his absence.

"It came by 'and. A leddy," he said.

Edgar found it very hard to break through to reality, to realize that someone was speaking to him, to understand why there could be any point in his opening the envelope and reading the note, sent by some person still living to him, the corpse. It was as if there were some kind of dazzle on the plate-glass, making it almost impossible to see through.

Finally he had surmounted all these barriers, had thanked the porter, taken the note, opened it, and focused on the writing.

"Dear Sherlock: I knew you'd want to know where the next move was to, and that you wouldn't be smart enough to find out without me. Well, it's to Conasta, near Locarno. Go there if you want to—that is, if you're still too dumb to go home and take care of yourself."

The writer had begun to sign the letter "Mirabelle", for the first four letters of that name had been written; but they were crossed out, and "Dr. Watson" written impatiently, almost savagely, underneath.

Mechanically, while reading, Edgar had been walking towards the lift. He had reached it, it was empty and waiting, he was inside it and climbing upwards to his floor, before the letter filtered through to his comprehension. Then, for an instant, the plate-glass dissolved and he was alive.

"Mirabelle!" he shouted, as if calling her. The lift, seeming to take this as a signal, stopped; they had reached the right floor.

As he walked down the main street of Conasta, a hint of gathering richness in the sun made Edgar realize that February had turned into March and that just down the road lay Italy, the sun, flowers, grapes, and a life lived out of doors. His spirits lifted a little, but only a little; the prevailing grimness of his mood was not to be shaken. Drearily, he turned in at the door of a café which had huge windows like those of a shop. All he could do was to keep his eyes open: if they were here, he would see them walking about before long, and this seemed a convenient point of vantage. He sat down heavily at a table on which there was a round basket of hard-boiled eggs.

"Well, stack me sideways," said a voice from the middle of the room.

Edgar had only known one person in his life who used the expression "stack me sideways" in moments of surprise or emotion. This had been a man named Tom Straw, whom he had not seen for three or four years. With the aid of this fact he might have been able to prepare himself, as he turned round, for the sight of this man's face staring at him across the café; but it still came as a surprise.

"Come over here," Tom Straw called, in an expressionless tone that might have conveyed either invitation or challenge.

"No, you come over here," said Edgar. "I wanted to sit by the window."

Tom Straw was putting on flesh. He had always been squarely built, but now, as he approached, Edgar fancied that his broad frame seemed more bulky. He carried his glass of coffee in one calm rectangular hand.

"Not nearly so comfortable over here," he said, sitting down opposite Edgar. "My table was much better."

"Oh, for God's sake don't let's be so ruddy *English*," Edgar burst out. "We haven't seen each other for years and now we run into each other in this hole—can't we relax the code just for *once* and register some kind of feeling—if it's only surprise?"

"Things don't surprise me any more," Tom Straw answered shortly. "Anyone might turn up anywhere—don't you know that yet?"

"I know it, damn it, but that doesn't stop me from being human," said Edgar indignantly. "If it comes to that, you yourself——" he stopped, aware that Tom Straw was reaching across and offering him something. It was an egg out of the basket.

"Make a start on this," he said. "You must be getting hungry."

Edgar obediently began to peel away the shell, at the same time ordering some wine and bread from the waitress. Eating the egg, he realized how easily and quickly Tom Straw had rolled the two of them over the threshold of their meeting. It would be

158

absurd now to do anything but go ahead with a normal conversation, exchanging news, without wasting any more time on preliminaries.

Looking across at the man, he realized how much, without knowing it, he had missed him since they had last met. Before his life had crumbled into an unshapely heap of fragments, before his vision had contracted until it could no longer range beyond the confines of his own situation, he had been fairly frequently in Tom Straw's company, and had never failed to benefit from contact with his undramatic, self-sufficient character. It was the only example he knew (were there any others?) of a character really built up and nourished from within, really independent of circumstances.

"Well, what are you doing here?" Tom Straw asked. "It must be work of some kind, I take it; you wouldn't be here out of season if it were a holiday."

"Well, as a matter of fact it *is* a holiday," said Edgar, feeling weary and soiled at having to resume the eternal lying and evasion. Still, it must be gone through. "I've left my job, and before taking another I'm just knocking about for a bit. Not very nice here out of season, I know, but—well, it's my whim, I like to see these places before they get into their stride. There's a kind of repose about them. But never mind about me," he went on quickly, to defend his unlikely story from being picked to pieces, "go ahead and tell me your news. Last thing I heard, you were doing something about art history."

A deep gloom settled on Straw's prognathous features.

"Yes," he said mournfully, "I was already bound to that wheel the last time we met, wasn't I? And now, of all things, they go and saddle me with a grant to investigate the Ticinese school. Bundle me out here, if you please, to look at a lot of damned frescoes and murals. Churches, wayside shrines, all the lot." His tone was that of a soldier on fatigue duty.

"In other words," said Edgar, "you're a success in your profession, you've been awarded some money to carry out research in a new field, and you'll write a massive study and be settled in the museum and gallery racket for life. Congratulations."

"Well, I've got to do something, haven't I?" Straw demanded aggressively. "How can I afford to turn it down, I'd like to know? In any case, it's more than likely that the whole subject will turn

159

out to be a mare's nest. That's what I said when they offered it me. I wouldn't take it at first. I as good as accused them of taking the Michael."

Edgar remembered, with affection, that Straw had always used the expression "taking the Michael" when his suspicions were aroused, and that this arousal had been frequent and predictable. His trust in his own instinctive wisdom and sufficiency, a trust that was perfectly justified, had produced, as a harmless by-product, an almost ludicrous unwillingness to accept the good opinion of others, or to admit the practical value of any concrete action he might undertake. He had grumbled his way through the university, jeered at the immense weight of solid work he had produced, and generally complained bitterly about every rung on the ladder while setting his foot on it. Now, it was clear, he was well on the way to becoming a famous art-historian, and his self-defensive doubting and protesting were more pronounced than ever. He sneered at himself as if he were his own unsuccessful rival; perhaps hoping, by this means, to mask his invariable kindness towards others. It was this same compulsion towards wryness and self-deflation that accounted for his oddities of manner. There was, for instance, his extraordinary vocabulary. The combined forces of nature and upbringing had endowed him with the vocal equipment of the successful, respectable man; his enunciation was precise, his voice clearly audible at some distance without being loud, and his general manner of speech rather dry and clipped, as if among the influences of his early years there had been a dash of something military. Hearing him pronounce any simple sentence, a stranger would immediately recognize Tom Straw as a person of, at any rate, potential authority: not seeking prominence, but naturally fitted for it. The knowledge that he created this impression was evidently a perpetual annoyance to him, representing as it did the ever-present danger of being inveigled away from his lonely self-sufficiency and thrust into a position of having to direct others, impose his will on them, and generally assume importance. With the temperament of the lonely philosopher, Straw had the calm and directness of the man who inevitably finds himself in authority; he felt the tide pulling him, and his protest expressed itself in a constant reaching out towards informality and ordinariness. Hence the careful avoidance of anything flamboyant, the playing-down of heightened situations,

160

and the comically incongruous rash of demotic expressions which studded his precise, level conversation.

As if to illustrate this point without delay, he now glanced through the window and said with pedantic clarity: "Well, I'm a Charley."

Remembering, with renewed affection, that Straw had always used the word "Charley" to indicate a foolish and incompetent person (usually himself), Edgar followed the direction of his eyes. A girl in a grey dress, with darkish blonde hair brushed simply from left to right, was crossing the street outside, evidently making for the door of their café.

"I'm a Charley," Tom Straw repeated. "I forgot to tell you about Catherine. And now she's here and it's too late."

Edgar opened his mouth to ask what it was that he ought to have been told about Catherine, but it was, as Straw had said, too late. She had entered the cafe and was coming over, smiling slightly in greeting, to their table. Both men stood up.

"This is Edgar Banks, an old friend of mine," said Straw. "Says he's here on holiday. That proves he's mad, doesn't it? Always was a Charley," he enunciated precisely, as if clinging to the foolish little word to protect the situation from any hint of importance. "This is Catherine Whitmore," he said to Edgar.

Conventional greetings were murmured, and they were seated. Noticing that the girl's eyes were grey, and her skin pale and very clear, Edgar was aware of annoyance at his inability to avoid gathering foolish scraps of detail about casual acquaintances.

The waitress was at their side, and Catherine turned to Straw with: "It's rather late just for drinks and things, isn't it? We ought to start on some lunch if we're going to catch the bus at a quarter to two."

"Quite right," he said, allowing illumination to dawn on his face as if she had shown him the answer to an obstinate crux in a crossword puzzle. One fact about the relationship between them, whatever it might be, was clear to Edgar; she possessed the same kind of unstrained efficiency as he did, and he welcomed the opportunity to lay his own efficiency aside, to pretend to himself that he was inefficient and depended on her. It allowed him a seeming truce in the battle against his own capability.

Dishes were brought, and they started on eggs, salad and wine. As they ate, Straw and the girl made conversation, but Edgar's

161

participation in the talk became more and more spasmodic and moody. The plate-glass seemed oppressively thick, and yet uncomfortably tremulous, as if vibrating under a hail of unseen and silent blows. His heart was always, as it were, leaping forward, trying to rejoice; meeting Straw, and being reminded of his goodness and dependability, was the first positive thing that had happened to him for years. But it had come too late; nothing positive could reach him in his doomed, insulated state. Falling for a moment into reverie, he wondered dimly what would have happened if, on going out to the restaurant when he had decided on his plan, he had met Straw instead of Philipson-Smith. Might they not have eaten together, gone somewhere for a drink, talked a little sense, and might it not have ended in his deciding not, after all, to . . . oh, nonsense, nonsense, that was the kind of thing that didn't happen, and in any case he had gone too far along his road for such vague speculations to be of any value.

"How's your Italian coming along?" Straw was asking Catherine. "You know I shall be lost without you to translate for me when we get to some of these outlying villages. If I explain in dumb-show to the village priest that I've come to give his murals the once-over, he'll think I've got an urgent confession to make, or perhaps that I'm just waiting my chance to strip the lead off the church roof and scarper with it in a lorry."

"Don't worry," she soothed him. "You look too English to be a suspicious character, and not speaking Italian adds to the guileless impression. Anyway you *do* speak Italian, quite well, and anyway they all understand German, and you speak that too: don't start denying it."

She smiled, and Edgar, hating himself for being open to such trifling impressions, noticed that her smile was a little crooked. It was not exactly that she lifted one corner of her mouth and dropped the other, but the effect was something similar.

Perhaps fortunately, he had only a few seconds in which to study it, for Catherine suddenly became serious, even grave. She turned her grey eyes on Straw with a look that was full of compassion.

"By the way, Tom—I'm afraid it's come."

"What's come?" he asked, replenishing her glass carefully.

"The invitation," she said, bringing out the word with a slight struggle, as if it were an obscenity, normally inadmissible to her

162

vocabulary, which she was compelled to utter in a police court. "I could see it coming, ever since he knew where we were staying. And it came through the post, so I couldn't make any excuses as I might have done if he'd come in person to ask us."

"Oh, well, we've always got one way out," Straw countered with a false ring of cheerfulness in his voice. "We can always just stay away."

"Darling, are you quite sure that's wise?" she asked him. Edgar felt disproportionately startled at her opening word. She was not the kind of girl to throw terms of endearment about, and obviously had only come out with this "darling" because the gravity of their discussion, whatever it was about, had momentarily blinded her to the presence of another person. Normally, it was difficult to imagine her calling any man "darling" in company. Edgar naturally did not waste time in trying to imagine any such thing, the whole matter being no business of his, but for some reason his attention became fogged and he missed the next half-dozen sentences of the conversation, tuning in again in time for, "surprising how many English people he's managed to rake up, unless he's exaggerating," from her.

"I don't see why he should be exaggerating," said Straw in a tone of flat, grey courage, like a man facing some bad news given him by a famous surgeon. "You can always muster a lot of English in a place like this. There's all the acquaintance of his protector, for a start."

"Tom, I don't think you ought to call that man his *protector*, in that way," she said warningly. "After all, the word has exactly the associations——"

"Exactly the associations I want it to have," he murmured.

"——and it could be actionable, and in any case you've no proof——"

"No, my love," he interrupted her. "Not those reasons. Neither of them are real reasons, are they? It's actionable, it's not susceptible of proof—neither of those are reasons for not saying something nasty about a nasty man. What's the real reason why I shouldn't say it ? You know it, don't you: let's hear it." He looked at her challengingly and possessively, daring her to step outside his influence, to deny that her mind belonged to his. Edgar realized that they must have been in love for some time. "Let's hear it," he repeated.

6*   163

"Because it's not our business," she said without hesitation.

"Because it's not our business," he repeated. They continued to look at one another for a few seconds more, and in doing so allowed a change to come over their expressions, a change that only a close observer would have noticed. Edgar began by being a close observer, then dropped his gaze to his now empty plate. The whole interlude, during which the couple had been intensely aware of each other's presence and oblivious of his, had lasted only while one could count ten; but from the sudden zeal with which they swung their attention back towards Edgar, as if stricken with guilt at neglecting him, and generally ashamed of their behaviour, it might have been a quarter of an hour.

"Yes, and you too," Straw half-shouted, building up a tremendous geniality so as to make Edgar feel that he belonged and was welcome. "You don't know what we're referring to, but if you only knew—it does concern him, doesn't it?" he appealed to Catherine.

"Certainly," she said, stiffening the word with a mock sternness, "particularly if he knows Fr——"

"SHHHH!" Straw waved his hands in gleeful admonition. "I'm going to get something out of this. I'm going to take him along to the party when we go, and watch his face when he sees who's the host. It'll be worth the couple of hours that follow."

She looked from Straw's grinning face to Edgar's uneasy one, then gave a slight, let-him-have-his-own-way shrug.

"D'you mean he knows—do forgive us, Mr. Banks——"

"Edgar," he said sullenly.

"—do forgive us, Edgar, for talking about you in the third person—do you mean he knows . . . the man who's giving the party?"

"Yes," said Straw with a great calm joy. "He knows the man who's giving the party."

Edgar suddenly felt the truth burst in on him. Of course he knew who was giving the party. How could it be anyone else? So this was to be the manner of his tracking-down the enemy! So Mirabelle's directions had been right, and here he was, actually being taken along to a party given by the man. He felt boisterously relieved.

"All right, don't try to fool your uncle Edgar," he said, grinning waggishly. "I know who's giving the party."

164

"Oh, you've met him already, then?" Straw asked, evidently disappointed.

"No, I haven't actually met him, not here, at any rate; I only got here last night and you two are the first people I've met. But I know by means of—call it clairvoyance." He dropped his eyes modestly, then looked up full into Straw's face, enjoying his advantage. "It's Philipson-Smith, isn't it?"

"Who the hell's Philipson-Smith?"

At first Edgar was tempted to meet the question with a knowing laugh, but this failed to rise further than his throat as he looked at the absolute honesty printed across his friend's face.

"You really don't know who Philipson-Smith is?" he asked anxiously.

"I'm not taking the Michael," Straw said simply. The statement was enough. He did not, obviously, know any person of that name.

"One more guess," Edgar pursued. "The person giving this party—he isn't Scotch, I suppose?"

"Not as far as I know."

That ruled out McWhirtner in the most effective of possible ways.

"You'll just have to wait and see," Straw grinned. "And it won't be long. The party's to-night. Where are you staying?"

Edgar mentioned his hotel.

"Good, it's on our way. We'll pick you up. But I should have a couple of brandies, before setting out. You'll need bracing up."

The girl was looking at her watch. "Tom, the bus. We've got to be there in five minutes."

"Stack me sideways," he said clearly, as if dictating to a class. There was a short whirl of bill-paying, chair-arranging, mackintosh-finding, and they were leaving.

"See you later, Edgar," the girl said, smiling at him with one corner of her mouth a trifle lower than the other. He smiled back with the corners of his own mouth absolutely level and his lips tight.

Straw was half-way to the door, then suddenly turned back. "Eight o'clock," he said conspiratorially, "with two brandies inside you. You'll need bracing up. Don't say I didn't warn you. Bracing up," he repeated, following Catherine towards the door.

Edgar, left alone, smiled in pity at this unconscious innocence. What shock did they imagine could be strong enough to touch a man in his condition? What could a man in his condition have to do with the little surprises of everyday life? What could a man in his condition have to do? What could a man in his condition have? What could a man in his? What could a man? What could?

"Darling, are you quite sure that's wise?" he muttered. The waitress, catching his eye and seeing his lips moving, brought him his bill. It seemed the only possible comment.

At eight o'clock that evening, Edgar, with two recently swallowed brandies smouldering inside him, was standing in one of the side streets of Conasta with Straw and Catherine. They were waiting for someone to answer the door; Straw had just rung the bell, morosely and violently, like a man who has been kept waiting a long time, though in fact they had only just arrived. It was raining and rather windy, rather like a night in London except that the air was not actually poisonous.

Edgar glanced at his companions. They were silent, standing close together: not actually touching, just near each other. This was the utmost their good manners would permit them in the presence of a third person. In the presence of this silent, magnaminous abundance of life, Edgar felt more than ever a corpse. He drove his thoughts savagely along the narrow channel of his hatred for Philipson-Smith. That at least was *something*; as long as he could feel that he had a mission, that he was an avenger and the emissary of justice, he had something to cling on to. All the same, this was a bad moment. Why didn't the others speak? Why didn't whoever it was come down and open the door?

To break the silence he read aloud the name printed beside the bell they had just rung. "Nadia Pilsener," he said, as if musing aloud. "If that's the person who's giving the party, I'm afraid I don't know her."

"No, no," Straw chuckled. "The party's being held in her studio, but she isn't the hostess. That's almost a clue in itself, by the way."

Who cares about your blasted clue, Edgar thought. *What can it matter to me?* Outwardly he said, "After this build-up it's bound to be an anti-climax, whoever it is."

166

On the word "anti-climax" the door was jerked open, and a figure confronted them in an attitude of welcome, which stiffened almost immediately into one of astonishment. It was McWhirtner.

"Whaur the deil did ye spring from, Banks?" he rasped.

This sentence represented a considerable improvement in McWhirtner's linguistic equipment. His fluency and naturalness in his "native" speech were already much better than when Edgar had first met him; back in London he would certainly have said, in a moment of shock, "where the devil" and not "whaur the deil." For this reason Edgar said affably, "Congratulations. Spoken like a man."

"We rang Fraulein Pilsener's bell," Straw said to McWhirtner, politely, as if inviting him to explain his presence on the scene.

"Aye, come up," said McWhirtner listlessly. He seemed dazed. "Francis asked me to come doun an' open the door."

Francis?

"Quick," Straw was saying urgently. "I can see from his face that he hasn't guessed yet. Get him up the stairs and let him find out before he rumbles it. I must see his face—it's my one compensation for being here."

McWhirtner's torpor increased. The shock of finding Edgar standing in the street had evidently dwarfed all his other impressions for the moment. He followed sadly as they hurried up the stairs.

At the top, a soft light shone from a large open door. Evidently the room was lighted by candles. They could hear a good deal of subdued chatter, as if the party were just beginning, and people had begun to talk but not yet to shout and bluster.

They entered. Immediately inside the door was a hollow-cheeked young woman with flowing dark hair, dressed in a tight black jumper and Dirndl skirt. Her personal appearance was evidently built round a conception of herself as an artist; but the effect, large ear-rings, accentuated cheek-bones, and all, was subtly overdone, so that it contradicted itself. It was like a confiding whisper to the onlooker, behind the hand, of "You're not taken in, are you? You know that no woman who was really an artist would dress like this, don't you?" She looked like the daughter of a wholesale ironmonger who has enrolled at the Slade School of Art.

With her, the recipient of her animated conversation, was a

a very big young man with fair hair and long side-whiskers; perhaps an out-of-work actor who had decided to refrain from shaving his cheeks on the off-chance of getting a walking-on part in a film about Edwardian England or some similar past epoch and setting.

Tom Straw halted at her elbow and remained standing, calm and immobile, until she noticed him. Catherine and Edgar, dominated by his confidence and precision of movement, stood still beside him.

"—zo finally I said, eef you are not eenterest, vy you come here at all?" the girl said vehemently, then appeared, but only appeared, to notice for the first time the presence of the three newcomers. Turning, she smiled invitingly at Straw.

"Eet's Tom. Off course. He's every vair. Paris, Berlin. Now Conasta." She fixed him with her eyes, possessively. Edgar took a step backwards to get out of firing range; a battle was imminent. Whoever this woman was, she was now formally at war with Catherine; her very first sentence was an attempt to establish a prior claim over Tom Straw, by hinting at a long record of shared experiences, in Paris, in Berlin, which Catherine had missed.

"And how comms the thesis, professeur?"

Tom Straw bowed slightly and made a formal, minimal gesture with both hands. "This is Mr. Banks, a friend of mine. I'm afraid he is here on my invitation, rather than the host's, but I'm sure it will be all right, aren't you? Miss Whitmore, on the other hand, is expected: this," he said to both his companions, "is Fraulein Pilsener, in whose studio we are standing."

"Already a professeur," said Fraulein Pilsener, fixing Tom Straw with her gleaming eye. "Zo formal. Meeting viss old friends like ceremonies in Bucking Palace."

Edgar stole a glance at Catherine. Her face was quite impassive, but beneath its expression of repose and unconcern a second expression was, as he had expected, forming itself. He had expected this second impression to be one of anger, of fierce competitiveness, but to his surprise, it was simply one of almost concealed amusement. How sure she must be of her ground!

At the same time he had to admit that this serenity was amply warranted by Tom Straw's behaviour. He was giving a classic performance—easily and decisively conveying by every look, every word, the utter impossibility of admitting Fraulein Pilsner's claim

168

to priority. Without embarrassment or rudeness, he was fending her off as if with a flame-thrower. What an object-lesson! This was how you did it: this was how you won and kept the affections of girls like Catherine. To a living man, useful knowledge; to a corpse, knowledge come too late.

The big young man, obviously feeling left out, began craning round as if in search of an excuse to leave them. "Where's Francis?" he mumbled.

"Francis who?" Edgar asked him in an undertone, forgetting until it was too late that an accomplished gate-crasher does not have to question fellow-guests about the identity of the host. The big young man eyed him severely without speaking.

For a moment there was a stalemate. Nadia Pilsener, some examples of whose childish daubs Edgar now noticed lining the walls of the studio, was barring their further advance into the room while she rallied her forces for a renewed attempt to detach Tom Straw from Catherine. This automatically placed the others in the position of the ranks of Tuscany. The big young man shuffled off, throwing a suspicious glance over his shoulder at Edgar; the four of them were left staring at one another.

McWhirtner appeared in the doorway. "Yes, Banks," he said sternly, as if there had been no cessation in the interview they had begun downstairs, "What's it a' aboot? Tell me that, eh? Rollo!" he called across the room.

This meant that Philipson-Smith was present, doubtless in the shadowy centre of some candle-lit group at the far side of the room. Naturally he did not come across to them at McWhirtner's summons—dignity is dignity even in the worst of crises—but Edgar knew that it could not be long before they came face to face, and the prospect filled him with a shuddering depression. His existence seemed so terribly static. The same situations repeated themselves as if the whole march of events had determined to mark time. Was this what happened when one decided to live in the present? No, no, it was simply his own inefficiency. Well, inefficiency or not, he was here, and he would see to it this time.

"A suppose it was the lassie tipped ye off whaur we were comin' to," said McWhirtner accusingly. He had advanced a few paces from the doorway and now dominated the grouping which, a moment before, had been presided over by Fraulein Pilsener;

Edgar was rather grateful for this, and he could see that Straw was decidedly so. Straw, indeed, was so glad of McWhirtner's intervention that he actually said, "Do introduce us to your friend, Edgar," as if seriously desiring his better acquaintance.

Edgar said gravely, "Mr. McWhirtner," but while performing the introduction he felt his social poise rather shaken by the fact that Straw and Catherine were obviously fighting off a shared urge to shriek with laughter. Catherine even turned her back for a moment; Straw glanced sidelong at McWhirtner's face with twitching movements of the lips and eyebrows. Conversation dried up, Fraulein Pilsener retired sulking, and after a moment McWhirtner muttered some excuse and left them, doubtless to confer with Philipson-Smith. As soon as they were left alone, the three subsided into a corner, where Edgar had to wait as patiently as possible for the other two to become coherent.

"I might have known he'd look like that," moaned Tom Straw at last, wiping his face.

"You know about him, then?" Edgar asked.

"Well, doesn't everybody? After all, the thing was the joke of Paris for a few days. Well, that's an exaggeration, of course, but it was the joke of the circles we were moving in. How many times were we told that story, Catherine, d'you remember?"

"Oh, about ten times in three days," she said.

Edgar was beginning to feel thoroughly irked by the number of small, not-worth-solving mysteries that were springing up. First the Francis business, now this. "What story?" he asked impatiently.

"Why, about him and the lift," said Straw, beginning to laugh again. "Don't you really know? Well, it was last summer in Paris. It seems this McWhirtner was over there trying to scrape up funds to start a magazine, or something, and he was staying——"

"Tom," Catherine interrupted, "you'd better tell him afterwards. Here's the host." She nodded towards the door.

Straw and Edgar turned. Bearing down on them, smiling derisively, was a pallid obscene face balanced on a pole of a body.

Edgar gave an involuntary groan, subdued but still plainly audible. Francis Jollet! Since inscribing the man's name on his list of possible candidates for sacrificial destruction, he had ceased to think about him; the action had, as it were, exorcised the spirit of Jollet from his life. And now here he was! And in the role of

170

host, to be tolerated, to be treated humbly! How far had one to travel before one shook off the detritus of one's idle associations?

"Tom!" Jollet cried, as if about to make ill-natured fun of Straw under the pretence of welcoming him to the party. Instead of doing so, however, he switched his attention to Catherine. "Hello, sweetie," he said, dropping his voice to a lubricious undertone, "enjoying yourself in Conasta?" He took her hand between both of his.

"I'm here too," said Edgar harshly. "I wasn't invited."

"No, you weren't, but it's heavenly seeing you," Jollet leered. "I didn't know you were here, but I'm glad you've come to-night —there are such perfectly fascinating people to meet. You'll meet *everybody*," he sniggered, his feverishly bright eyes wandering round the room.

Edgar stared at him with the old mixture of pity and nausea, but at the same moment found time to confirm the rightness of his original decision not to choose him for a victim. Jollet did not *represent* enough. His life was squalid and worthless, but at least he did not carry this squalor and worthlessness into any setting where they might infect anything that was capable of being destroyed. He had his existence, from beginning to end, in such places, and among such people, as one saw here. Indeed, from the moment when Jollet had first perceived the advantage of turning himself into a human butterfly, he had withdrawn from real life altogether, and the effect of this withdrawal was startlingly obvious. Everything about him, including his few shreds of talent, had become, from that hour, magically preserved against change and development. To the end he would go on, "meeting everybody", trading on a slowly hardening and drying immaturity, as cut off from progression as an onion in vinegar.

Such destructiveness as he could, in these circumstances, exercise, Jollet would nevertheless continue to enjoy. He was now about to turn away from them and continue his tour of the room, when a pleasing thought evidently struck him.

"Oh, yes, by the way, Edgar," he said, smiling like a boa-constrictor. "I ran across a dear friend of yours at a party, just before I came away."

Edgar, silent, looked interrogation. Straw and Catherine listened without expression, suffering the man politely, waiting for him to go away.

171

"Phyllis," said Jollet, smirking. "Yes, Phyllis. And she had such a *nice* young man with her. I think all the girls there really envied her. Very young, but *very* nice. And he was a pupil of yours, from your school."

Edgar tried to look unconcerned, but the thrust had gone home. So this was the next chapter in the Benton story, was it? Phyllis had really got her claws into him, to the extent of showing him off as her own property at loathsome parties where such people as Jollet were to be found. Oh, why did everything decent get spoilt, before it had a chance to develop? And why did he, Edgar, have to remain on earth long enough to hear about it? With luck he would have been safely dead, and past caring about Benton's ruin, by this time.

"I had quite a long talk with him," Jollet went on. "It really surprised me to find that he was still at school. So *mature*. I think Phyllis is doing him good already."

"Splendid," said Edgar viciously. "But let me get you something to drink," he said to Catherine, and plunged forward to a nearby table. Anything to get out of Jollet's immediate proximity.

When he got back, the three of them were alone again, and Straw was looking at him with grave sympathy. He tried to begin an ordinary conversation, but Straw cut in, speaking on a note of serious regret.

"Look here, Edgar, I'm awfully sorry I got you into this. I did it for a joke, I admit—I didn't think there would be anything to upset you as badly as this."

"What do you mean, upset me?" Edgar said bluffly. Straw, disregarding the defensive gesture, laid a hand on his arm.

"Come off it, china. I knew you didn't like Jollet, but when he said that about the boy, whoever it is, I could see you turn pale. You didn't like having to listen to him. Not to speak of this queer business with this lift man. There's something upsetting you in relation to him, I can see that as well. I'm sorry, really I am."

"Why d'you call McWhirtner the lift man?" Edgar asked with a heavy, meaningless persistence. He wanted at least to tidy up the edges of the situation.

"Oh, that," said Straw, refusing to allow his new seriousness to be disturbed. "It's not funny really. Just some fool thing he did when he was in Paris. He was staying with some friends who

172

lived in a big block of flats, and coming home one night by himself, drunk, he lay down and went to sleep in the lift. The first person to use the lift the next morning was a nervous old music-master, going out to an early class, who more or less screamed the place down and called the police. It's not funny really," he said again.

Catherine said quietly, "We'd never have swept you into this if we'd known, Edgar."

"Known *what*?" he rounded on her.

"That there were so many unpleasant associations about," she said.

Edgar was silent. He could not fool these people. If his circumstances had been different—if, as he had told Straw in the café, he had simply been taking a holiday here—then of course it would simply have been a joke to get him along to the party and watch his expression when confronted with Francis Jollet. So it was his own fault for lying. And yet, what could he have done? He felt a surge of annoyance, which he welcomed for its power to blot out the sadness of thinking about Benton.

"What about you?" he said, almost spitefully, turning to Straw. "Do you like this mob so much that you come here as a matter of course?"

"Ah; now there, Edgar," Straw replied slowly and deliberately, "you lay your finger on the heel of Achilles. It's not the pleasure-instinct that drives me here, not even the herd-instinct, it's purely the business instinct. I want to get hold of a man called Wercingues, the local patron of the fine arts, very rich—I'm here to thrust my acquaintanceship on him."

"But why? Can't you get along without him?"

"I can get along without *him*, but not without his pictures. I want to look at them. Yes, Edgar, there's a certain amount of dung-eating associated with the career of every professional man, and before you stands one in the act of taking a mighty swallow of the stuff. This man Wercingues is a china of Jollet's, hence the party, hence our presence here. Before I can go home I must wait for the man to turn up, grab him, spray him with charm, and get an invitation to go and look at his collection. It's part of the reason why my employers have sent me down here. I can only hope the man isn't as repulsive as he sounds."

"Repulsive? He's a friend of Jollet's," Edgar reminded him.

For a moment the three of them stood silent, brooding on the probable character and habits of this Wercingues.

Meanwhile, the party was beginning to quicken its pace. A central cone of noise had formed round the main group in the centre of the room, and subsidiary but determined cells of uproar were established on chairs and divans along the walls. Edgar felt that without Straw's presence he would be quickly sucked in to some vortex of idiocy, soused in the atmosphere, robbed of his identity and purpose, and made a fool of, as he had been at Geneva. But Straw evidently numbered among his gifts the power of being present at such occasions as this without being drawn under. He had fought off Nadia Pilsener, and in the same quiet way he fought off any other stray figures who came along in the hope of entangling the three of them in the general mess. They stood quietly together in their corner, watchful and patient, exchanging a few words among themselves now and again, and all three waiting. Edgar was waiting for the next round in the Philipson-Smith battle, Straw was waiting for this Wercingues character to manifest himself, and Catherine was waiting for Straw.

After a while one of the smaller groups at the far end of the studio underwent a short convulsion and split into its component parts. Edgar, glancing across, saw the face of Philipson-Smith, dark-jowled and simian-eyed, glaring fixedly at him. They stared at each other for a moment before a fresh wave of people deposited themselves in the way and the contact was broken. Edgar felt the challenge of the situation, but he had no resources with which to meet it. Reasoning quickly, he could see only two alternatives: to go up to the man and begin again the endless humiliation, the lying explanations, the begging for a job, however humble, in the Movement; or to wait passively until he left the party, shadow him, and find out where he was living as an essential preliminary to forming plans. Weariness and disgust combined to recommend the second course. Anything, anything, was better than starting the old horrible game again in the midst of this crowd and under the piscine sneer of Jollet.

Sunk in gloom and hatred, he roused himself at the sound of Straw's voice, speaking in an urgent undertone.

"He's here. That's him coming in. Wish me luck, both of you. Look after Catherine for a bit, would you, Edgar?"

He was gone, discreetly shadowing a man who had entered and begun to cross the room. In the vague light Edgar could only see that the newcomer was tall, thin and apparently well-groomed.

To make conversation he said to Catherine, "Tell me more about this man. And can you tell me how to spell his name while you're about it? I never heard such a queer-sounding one."

She produced a pencil and wrote for him on the back of a cigarette packet, "Tollemache de Wercingues." Her writing was clear and decisive.

He stared at it. "What on earth—what nationality is he?"

"Franco-American," she said. "But apparently he was brought up in England, made most of his money in Italy, and spends it in Switzerland. I don't know anything much about him, but I suspect his artistic interests are partly a way of investing money, and partly because he finds something that amuses him in mixing with the sort of artistic set you get in a place like this."

"I suppose Jollet's finding the association a useful one, anyway," said Edgar morosely.

This brought the conversation, he realized, to a dead end; naturally the nature of Jollet's dealings with Wercingues was not a pleasant subject for speculation, and she was silent, waiting, not reproachfully but with perfect good-humour, for him to start some other topic.

Feverishly Edgar searched his mind for something to say, but the deadness and coldness inside him seemed to have reached the point of utter paralysis. The plate-glass went up once more; he was alone. It was the Mirabelle situation again, but this time there were no short cuts, no easy comradeship based on a casual approach to serious problems. This girl was a real person, living consciously and steadily, moving towards definite objects. In his inability to communicate with her he realized afresh, with a shock of terror, how far he had already moved towards death. She was patient, intelligent, full of goodwill, and he had nothing, nothing to say to her.

"Oh, God,—I'm sorry I'm such a bore," he burst out.

The warmth and kindliness of her smile made him feel both better and worse simultaneously.

"Please don't worry," she said. "You're not a bore. But you're not very good at hiding your feelings, and it's plain that something's terribly on your mind. I don't expect you to put on an act to amuse me—I didn't expect to enjoy this evening much anyway, and you aren't making things any worse by not being bright. Whatever the trouble is, it's something you don't feel like talking about, and yet you can't think of anything else to say instead. D'you think I don't understand? We all get like that sometimes."

"D'you mean to say *you* get like that sometimes?" he asked incredulously.

"But of course. Everyone does."

"I bet Tom never does."

"Tom?" She turned, half smiling, but deeply serious beneath it. "You've known Tom for so many years and you still think he's immune from feelings like that?"

"Oh, but Tom——" he made a helpless, half-annoyed gesture, "Tom's so definite—he always knows where he is and where he's going."

"You think so?" she murmured, half to herself. Once again the conversation halted, and once again Edgar scrambled in search of firmer ground.

But he could not find it. He was conscious of only one thing: a huge and glaring idea that filled his mind so as to blot out every crumb of miscellaneous thought and sensation. This idea was not, as yet, concrete. It was simply a great mass of dissatisfaction. Something was terribly wrong with the plan he had been working on. It simply wouldn't do. Standing dumbly by Catherine's side, an empty glass clutched nervously in his hand, he struggled to drag the thing upwards into consciousness. What had happened? That evening in London, when he had begun to live in the present, everything had seemed settled. He had formed his plan, and it had seemed a magnificent one, complete and satisfying. Now, with swift and absolute certainty, he knew that it was so no longer. A really artistic suicide, balanced by a farewell present to life: why had it seemed good then, why did it seem bad, small and empty now?

Tom Straw came bearing the answer in his face, carrying it with the strength of his square body, across the room towards him. He was scowling irritably, but the central core of his goodness and honesty was as plain to Edgar's vision as if it had been made of some tangible substance. In the presence of this man, the selfishness, the isolation, the foolish theatricality of his

176

original idea stood out revealed. He remembered undergoing a test for colour-vision; you looked at a page of dots, in various colours, and if your colour-vision was normal you saw a number written there; if it was subnormal, you saw only a swirl of dots. Tom Straw had done something to his colour-vision; in place of the dots, he saw a sign: the sign of his own self-absorption and weakness.

At the same time, Philipson-Smith must go. Whatever he had to do, it must include both the main components of the original scheme: his own death and that of Philipson-Smith: that was certain. It was just that something, some vitamin, was still missing. He must think: he must go away from here and walk about by himself and think.

"I can't get hold of him," Straw grumbled, coming up to them. "Not only is our dear little friend Francis J. hovering about all the time, so that the great man can't keep his mind on anything that's being said, but there's another fly, or rather a damned great cockroach, in the ointment: this blasted Ferguson-Jones man, your pal."

"Philipson-Smith, you mean?"

"That's it," said Straw, sighing heavily and reaching for a drink. "He's a positive menace. I had to stand there, on the edge of the charmed circle, listening to him trying to interest our friend Tollemache in some blasted crack-pot political party he seems to belong to. At least, he was being very mysterious about it—more or less taking the line that he and Tollemache could have a whale of a time arranging to kidnap the Pope, restore the Italian monarchy, blockade the Scandinavian countries, and rule the British Isles from Dublin with death-ray guns, only of course they couldn't discuss anything important with this riff-raff, meaning me among others, hanging about, and what about a nice cosy chat in his bullet-proof hotel bedroom some time. It all sounded like something out of Anthony Hope. And here's me with one simple request to make, please, Uncle Tollemache, may I come and see your etchings? having to stand there and be ignored like the head gardener waiting for orders. Ffffffoooooo-eeeeerrrrrgh," he ended, words being no longer adequate for his disgust and disappointment.

"That's a splendid noise. Do make it again," said a voice over his shoulder, a slightly nasal, slightly over-cultivated voice.

Tollemache de Wercingues had crossed to their side of the room on his tour of inspection.

"I said, Fffffoooooooeeeeerrrrrgh," Straw replied, reproducing the sound with great fidelity. Edgar gave a loud bray of nervous laughter.

Wercingues took a white handkerchief from his sleeve and shook it open. For a moment it looked as if he were waving it to signify his wish for a truce, so dazzling was its whiteness, so compelling the gesture to the eyes of everyone around. But he merely dabbed his unusually broad nostrils with the handkerchief before returning it to his sleeve. The action completed, he fixed Straw with his protruding eyes.

"You were disturbed about something, to make this charming noise?"

"Well, since we're talking about it," said Straw with decision, "I was disturbed about your collection of paintings."

Wercingues looked with an air of suave enquiry from one face to another, as if hoping that someone present would help him to fathom this person's motives; finding nothing in Edgar's face except a slowly fading residue of blank distress, and nothing in Catherine's except polite attentiveness, he turned back to Straw.

"Tell me more," he intoned. "What is it about my collection that you find disturbs you?"

"Simply that I haven't seen it."

"Ah, I understand," Wercingues breathed, allowing a smile to spread across his face like a stain over a tablecloth. Edgar stared with guilty fascination at the watch-chain strung across his waistcoat, the new canvas shoes, the handkerchief peeping from the sleeve. "It is the unseen that disturbs . . . once we have seen, we are at rest." He smiled at Catherine as if to indicate that his remark had a sexual significance. Straw did not appear to notice this, but his next remark had a touch of curtness in its tone, and Edgar knew what an effort it must cost him not to swing his fist into Wercingues's face.

"Not at all—you make the whole situation sound much too interesting. It's purely bread and butter, I'm afraid," he began, and went on to a brief explanation of his purpose, the name of the institution who had provided his funds, and so forth. Edgar's attention wandered back to the huge burning idea of dis-

178

satisfaction in his mind: it claimed attention like a blazing haystack in a small farmyard.

Then he heard Wercingues say, "But by all means come and make notes in a little book about my pictures. I'm not sure at the moment when it will be convenient to invite you to my house—my secretary keeps the engagement book and rules me with an iron hand," here he smiled for an instant to convey how absurd was the idea of anyone's ruling him with an iron hand, "but if you telephone him, I have no doubt that he'll see to it."

Tom Straw was opening his mouth to speak, doubtless with the object of expressing his thanks, when a new voice cut in.

"If it wouldnae be troublin' ye too much, Mister Philipson-Smith would like to mak a definite appointment for that little, that little confab-ulation we were discussin' jist noo."

Wercingues took the handkerchief out again and passed it several times across his nostrils before turning to look at McWhirtner.

"Why doesn't Mr. Philipson ask me himself?"

McWhirtner shrugged his shoulders.

"We didnae think it made ony difference who asked ye."

Wercingues flickered a quick glance in McWhirtner's direction. Then his heavy eyelids came down, half-concealing the protuberant eyes.

"I shall be at my villa next Sunday, out in the country," he said briskly, beginning to turn away. "If Mr. Philips comes over, I can spare him a couple of hours in which to initiate . . . or should we say, infect me?"

"An' whaur is this villa?" McWhirtner demanded brusquely. He was evidently living up to a principle, formed early in life, that politeness was wasted on millionaires. Or was he trying to impress the man with a sense of the powerful and dangerous nature of the organization he represented? Yes, Edgar reflected, that was probably it. Talk turkey with us, and then we'll spare you when we come to power.

Wercingues had turned away to remonstrate with Francis Jollet, who was beginning to wail loudly.

"But, Tollemache . . . that was to be *my* day."

"But how charming it will be, my dear boy, to entertain these friends of yours . . ."

"Whaur is it?" McWhirtner rasped, as if he suspected

179

Wercingues of having picked his pocket and hidden his wallet somewhere.

"Well, *I* don't think it's a good idea *at all*. How are they to get there, for one thing?"

"I'm sure they can arrange that for themselves," said Wercingues shortly; he was beginning to tire of the conversation, and Jollet, who was acute enough to see this, immediately switched on another mood, having played up as required to the suggestion that their quiet Sunday was to include a visit from Philipson-Smith.

"My secretary will give you details," said Wercingues over his shoulder to McWhirtner. His millionaire's manner was beginning to replace his lover-of-the-arts manner. Soon, no doubt, he would leave the party.

McWhirtner crossed over to where Philipson-Smith waited. Edgar watched him go with a stomach-tightening sense of being on the brink of some decisive action. This must be where he stepped in. Fate had put the situation before him on a plate; all it needed now was a strong digestion. Tom Straw had spoken of dung-eating. Well, here was his helping.

He walked over and openly confronted Philipson-Smith with a challenging stare.

"Hello," he said.

"What do you want?" Philipson-Smith asked. He sat stiffly in his chair, glaring up at Edgar like an orang-outang. He must have shaved before coming to the party, but no observer would have thought so. By his side McWhirtner stood servile but suspicious, like a ticket-collector in rush hour.

"I expect you know what I followed you down here for," said Edgar.

"I don't know and I don't care."

"Now really. You may not care, but damn it all, you do *know*. You know that I'm still indulging my hope of being allowed to serve the Movement in some capacity."

"What is that to me?" Philipson-Smith asked. The question sounded oddly stagey, as if he were quoting from some poem instead of talking in his own words.

"What it is to you is this. I want to convince you, once and for all, of my good intentions and my wish to be useful. So I'll try to put it in the form of a concrete offer of service. For instance.

180

I couldn't but hear McWhirtner, just now, fixing up for you go to and see this Worm-hash man at his country seat. Probably somewhere miles up in the hills. He was leaving to you the problem of getting yourself there. Well, if you like to accept help from a man you don't approve of—I'll drive you there."

"For hoo much?" McWhirtner put in. Edgar ignored him.

Philipson-Smith stared at Edgar without expression. "You're a puzzle, aren't you, Banks?" he said. "There's no shaking you off. I don't, of course, attach any weight to this absurd story of wanting to get yourself into a job with the Movement."

"That's just what I'm trying to make you do. Accept the fact of my intentions. This offer isn't much, I know—I was thinking of having a day in the country myself, and it wouldn't be any trouble to——"

"You've got a car?"

"Yes," Edgar lied.

Francis Jollet came up behind him and said, "Now what are you all discussing so earnestly? Not politics again? This is supposed to be a party!"

"No," said Edgar. "We're talking about pleasure. We're each trying to remember how many women we've slept with."

"A vulgar habit," Jollet said, wrinkling his nose.

"Are you really serious?" Philipson-Smith asked Edgar.

"Of course."

Philipson-Smith turned and looked up at McWhirtner. "It might be as good a way as any of saving time on Sunday."

"Och, let him do it if he's daft enough."

"Let him do what?" Jollet asked petulantly.

"All right," Philipson-Smith said to Edgar.

"I'll call at your hotel at midday. Which is it?"

"No," said Philipson-Smith. "We'll be waiting on the piazza."

Edgar grinned. "Why don't you want me to know where you're staying? Afraid I'll get into the kitchen and poison the porridge?"

Philipson-Smith gave him the orang-outang look, with narrowed lids for extra effect. "You might," he said.

Suddenly gay, Edgar raised his glass.

"Here's to a pleasant day on Sunday," he said brightly.

The toast was ignored.

IX

A Ticinese hotel and a decaying block of flats in London represent very nearly the polar extremes of human habitation, and this fact struck Edgar with peculiar directness on the following morning, when, after breakfast, he sat down full in the shaft of sunlight that slanted in through the wide-open window, pulled the little table towards him, and took out his fountain pen and a sheet of paper. The difference in physical surroundings, so obvious in every detail, was an ironic commentary on the sameness of human situations, their power to perpetuate themselves in the face of any degree of restlessness. That February evening in London, with the racket of Flannery's party jabbing upwards through the floorboards, and the fog milling outside, had found him arranging the details of his exit from life. This March morning here, with a dazzling and inciting clarity of sky and air, with real warmth already in the sun and handfuls of diamonds shifting up and down on the surface of Lake Maggiore, found him once more in conference with himself over those same details. Everything surrounding him had changed, but the necessities of his situation had not; he knew that. It was his attitude towards them, his perception of them, that had developed, first slowly, then at increasing speed, until now, this morning, it was time to overhaul the entire strategy.

As before, he clung to the pen-and-paper method, the only means he had of giving a touch of impersonality to his thoughts in a crisis. Gripping the pen masterfully, like a Controlling Shareholder signing a cheque for a million, he wrote the heading: DISSATISFACTION OF ME, EDGAR BANKS, WITH METHOD OF PROCEDURE RELATING TO SUICIDE.

Underneath he wrote: "Reasons for dissatisfaction: (i) rational
182

—slowness of progress. (ii) irrational—emotional distrust of validity of procedure."

For a few minutes he wrote no more, but sat staring at the paper as if paralyzed, his hands lying clumsily, palms uppermost, on the table. Then, deliberately, he added: "N.B.—(i) largely product of (ii); not vice versa."

Immobile again, he began brooding over this last point. Yes, it was obvious that his annoyance at the impossible amount of time it all seemed to be taking, while natural enough in any case, was raised to an enormously higher tension by a sense, pressing upwards from below, of distaste for the scheme itself. Yet this distaste was not easy to drag out into the light. What was wrong with the scheme? It had seemed good enough back in London. Was it just a simple case of the failure of his nerve? He had read somewhere that the suicidal impulse was never prolonged for more than twenty-four hours; if people were still alive after that time, they gave up. This, however, was not his case. A simple suicidal urge might wear itself away after a day and a night, but a sense of dedication and self-sacrifice did not; in war, men very often volunteered for duties in which they would be more or less certain to get killed, but the fact that they accepted this, and that the situation included concrete action and habit-forming routine, made them able to carry on for months without cracking. This, and not the position of the ordinary suicide, was the parallel to his own case.

Why, then, had it turned sour on him? His desire to be rid of the world had not faded; the idea of taking a passenger with him still seemed an excellent one, and Philipson-Smith the best candidate. It was simply that the glitter, the *élan*, had gone out of the thing. Instead of a triumphal exit, it was beginning to seem like a mere escape; the extinction of Philipson-Smith, which had presented itself that night in the restaurant as a crusade, now appeared more like a necessary but boring piece of destruction, like fixing up a rat-trap. It all seemed so worn and old. He felt like a burglar slinking away with his swag. It was true that the house he had burgled would be all the better for the loss of the thing he was taking away, and none the worse for his own departure, so that the act had a certain quality of usefulness; but it had no longer the high, almost Shakespearean, quality which had sustained him at the beginning. "Some vitamin is lacking," he

183

wrote on the paper, then crumpled it nervously into a ball, pushed his chair back, and got up. He needed change, action, diversity; life would supply the answer if he simply went out into the street and looked about him as he walked.

Going down the stairs he was suddenly aware of the personalities of Tom Straw and Catherine. They were not present, but the idea of their presence flooded into his mind at a certain point in the train of thought.

"Vitamin. Tom Straw," he said to himself, going out through the restaurant on the ground floor. "Catherine. Vitamin." The attempt to identify the missing element had something to do with these two—it must have, for his mind to push forward the linked ideas so strongly; but what exactly this connection was, he could not yet be sure. One thing was clear: it was not simply a feeling of inadequacy, a misgiving at the thought of how silly his idea would seem to a man who, like Straw, had successfully made his terms with life. The idea of a comparison, even a remotely implied comparison, between Straw and himself, was entirely unthinkable. It was excluded by the whole framework of reference within which he had placed himself. Straw was one of the fortunate; he, one of the lost. But this in itself offered a clue; why, in that case, did he feel no envy of the man? Why did he accept, without a hint of rebellion or impatience, the fact that Straw was clear of the clinging mire by which he himself had been sucked down?

Hands in pockets, frowning heavily, Edgar halted in the street and stared out across the flat field of water. With his back to the town, the landscape before him was reduced to a few very simple elements. The flat lake, and the humped grey-green hills which contained it, could have been modelled in plasticine by a child; the sky could have been represented by a half-cylinder of stiff paper, painted bright blue and stood on end. The villages perching on the steep slopes were too distant to be more than a few spots of colour, easily flecked on with a water-colour brush. This simplicity, coming after the huddle of detail in the streets he had walked through, brought its luminous calm into Edgar's mind, clearing away the litter of unrelated thoughts and impressions. Blinking as if actually trying to focus the problem with his eyes, he allowed its new outlines to dawn on him. In the same instant he saw what was lacking.

"It's all been tilted too much one way," he said aloud, wishing

184

he had the pen and paper before him. "Too much towards—that . . . but the other's important, the other's important . . ."

He began striding rapidly along the waterfront. He had the answer, and now he must work at its implications. The entry of Straw had altered the scene, not merely by introducing another significant character, but a character who was significant in a new way. Driven by an urge to codify his thoughts before they ran away with him, he dragged out an old envelope and a stump of pencil, and began writing with the paper held against a wall.

"I have been reminded of a responsibility towards life," he wrote. "Formerly aware of the responsibility of hatred. Now of the responsibility of good-will."

Underlining this, he went on immediately: "Dislike of Philipson-Smith (embodies evil) balanced by liking for Tom Straw (embodies good). Responsibility extending both ways."

A seagull perched on a post and looked at him attentively. In his reaching out for the concrete, his hankering for something that would make his interior debate seem external and real, Edgar welcomed the bird as an audience.

"I knew what to do all right," he told it, "as long as I was only reckoning in one of these two elements. As long as I was making it all centre on my hatred of Philipson-Smith, it was easy; get rid of him, get rid of myself, and Bob's your uncle."

The seagull seemed to acknowledge that Bob was its uncle.

"But what about the new situation?" Edgar said fiercely. "Meeting Tom Straw made me realize something I'd forgotten—how nice he is, how much I like him—and that it's perfectly possible he'll miss me when I depart. That he'll even feel extra sorry that I killed myself, instead of waiting for my body to die of its own accord."

He was silent for a moment, then, under the expectant eye of the seagull, launched out with, "So I shall have fallen a long way short of the perfect suicide, with the perfect farewell present to to life. I shall have left a wound, rather than healing something by what I do."

The gull flew away, perhaps indicating a sense of the difficulty of Edgar's position. He crossed the road and stood gazing into a shop window as if the perfect suicide might be on sale. Certainly, it would no longer suffice to follow the old plan. By causing Tom Straw to feel uncomfortable, to miss him when he was dead and perhaps even to experience real grief at the manner of his dying—this would be to leave an unsightly mess behind, a mess that would not be compensated by the removal of Philipson-Smith. His plan had been incomplete. Instead of setting himself one simple task, he now faced the fact that another and complementary job would be necessary.

"Easy enough," he said into the shop window. "Easy enough at the best of times to get someone to dislike you."

He moved a few paces away. "Often dislike you whether you want them to or not," he whispered to himself. "Should be quite easy to get a person to dislike you, to feel glad when you're not about any more."

The street seemed unreal, like a street in a dream. He came to a café whose owner had decided to put a few tables out of doors in honour of the early sun. A negro was sitting at one of the tables, reading *Howard's End*.

Edgar looked down at the pages. "I'll tell you something it says in that book," he said. "It says, *Death destroys a man, but the idea of death saves him.*"

"You know it too?" asked the negro in a Kentucky accent.

Edgar moved on, sure that he knew it, quite sure that he knew it for the first time.

Catherine and Straw had already started eating when Edgar got to the table. Unusually, it was Catherine who spoke first, beginning her sentence while he was still on his feet.

"Sorry we've started, Edgar. Tom had an unexpected invitation this morning, by telephone. He's got to start out very early after lunch."

"To a monastery," said Straw, helping himself to salad.

"Yes, he's looking at murals there," said Catherine. She seemed to have taken over the job of explaining the situation; once again Edgar had a glimpse into the heart of their relationship, a vision of the man gratefully withdrawing from his own solidity and presence of mind, half-consciously asking the woman to intervene before he turned into his own nightmare-figure, the successful administrator. In ten years, if they married, Straw would have carried this so far as to pretend forgetfulness of dates and the names of acquaintances; in twenty, with luck, he would be genuinely forgetting them. And Catherine, realizing what was needed from her, would quietly take upon herself the burden of his competence, so that, between them, they would find it supportable.

"So our trip's off, this afternoon?" he asked.

"It is for me, anyway," said Straw. He assumed a rueful expression, from which Edgar could deduce that it was probably a great triumph to be invited to examine the *objets d'art* at this monastery. "The first bit of real sunshine we get," he went on, moodily, "and Joe Soap has to go to and work."

"I'll look after Catherine for you," said Edgar. As the words left his lips he savoured their falsity, suddenly, like a mouthful of soot. It was exactly the remark that the interloper, the seducer, the sharp point of the eternal triangle, always makes in second-rate fiction and cinema. Straw's answering "Yes, do," and his turning to Catherine with, "You'll be able to enjoy yourself till I get back, won't you?" were, on the other hand, like a clever parody of the trusting-husband stock role from the same kind of source. Why had the atmosphere suddenly turned odd and false? Edgar sighed heavily. He knew why. It was all part of the mess he always created when he began to put his schemes into action.

Catherine smiled, her mouth not quite in a straight line. She turned her grey eyes on Edgar.

"Why the deep sigh? Is it going to bore you to tears?"

What a chance, Edgar thought. *A chance to do six months' damage in ten seconds*. He leered politely, holding her gaze. "Bored?" he fluted.

Then silence. In panic, he searched for some roguish piece of flattery, something that could not fail to pierce Straw's armour of goodwill and convince him, against all the probabilities, that his old friend, Edgar Banks, was really making a pass at his girl.

But why wouldn't the words come?

"Bored?" he repeated, with a hint of a groan behind the word. Straw and Catherine burst out laughing.

"You are *sweet*, Edgar, the way you can't ever hide your feelings," she said, dabbing at her eyes, and ready to laugh again at the thought. "Yes, poor Edgar, you'll be bored."

"No, I won't," he suddenly said with complete sincerity and naturalness. Then, once more, his speech was halted, this time by wonderment at himself. He had not meant to say "No, I won't," in that tone. It sounded—and indeed, *was*—much too much the tone of one who genuinely looks forward to an outing and cannot understand why he should be bored. His real self had unexpectedly spoken up, thrusting his play-acting self out of the way for the purpose. Still too startled to revert to falsity, he glanced again at Catherine, registering this time the clarity and smoothness of her skin, the easy simplicity of the way her dark blonde hair lay across her head from left to right. His real self took in these details and stored them for its own purposes before his fake self took over again, this time putting on a performance as a cynic, muttering jauntily, "If I've got to do it by means of pretending to go for the girl, at least she's attractive—turns it into quite a pleasure."

"Anyway, you do that, Edgar," said Straw, pushing back his chair and rising. "You look after her, even if you *are* bored. You're on holiday, you can spare the time."

Another ideal opening! Now for something on the lines of, "I can always spare the time for a beautiful——" no, too crude; "Just what makes an ideal holiday, I always say", too vulgar; what about something like, "I know I'm on holiday, but when you entrust me with a girl like this, the strain of keeping my hands off her is so great that I might as well be working"?

Yes, something like that. "I know I'm on holiday," he began, "but——" then realized that Straw had said "So long" and was half-way to the door.

"But there's a limit to everything, is that it?" Catherine asked, no longer laughing. He stared at her.

"Look, Edgar, if I really . . . if there's really something you'd rather be doing, please say so. Or rather, don't bother to say anything—I'll just——" she was rising from the table.

"My God!" he cried, horrified, "you're angry!" The note of fear in his voice was so urgent as to compel her attention, and she sank down in her seat again. With another stab of amazement at his own duality, he realized that his natural self had spoken once more.

Catherine was looking at him in silence; not a harsh, scrutinizing stare, but rather a means of allowing her sympathetic concern for him to manifest itself quietly and without imposing demands. Edgar felt calmed and strengthened. With most women this would have been that maddening outrage, "a look of sympathy"; as Catherine managed it, the impression was wholly

188

different: not sympathy, not "understanding", but a readiness to produce these qualities if they were genuinely called for.

Edgar allowed himself four or five seconds in which to bathe in these and similar thoughts; then, inevitably, self-disgust overtook him. Up to the old game again, eh? Seeing everything as grouped round the sacred camp-fire of Me. Treating this girl as if her personality had meaning only in relation to Me, as if she lived in terms of her responses to Me, this damned, thrusting, insolent, suffocating tyrant. This Me that was marked down for destruction, that had already been pushed out of any conceivable foreground—remember that, Me, damn you—you're out of it, see?

Especially out of it where this girl is concerned. Especially.

Edgar took a grip on himself, pushed the brawling components of his mind back to their separate corners of the ring, and focused once more on the practical. All he had to do this afternoon was to take Catherine out on an excursion and be over-gallant towards her, if possible offending her so much that she told Straw about it and thus broke the link between them, the hampering link of kindness and goodwill that held him back from suicide. He would soon be able to tell, from Straw's manner, whether Catherine had complained to him or not. And good gracious, it ought to be easy enough.

But as he helped her into her mackintosh and led her into the street, he knew, with a rush of the old helplessness, that it was not going to be easy. With every tie cut, with every reason for wanting to keep his self-respect swept away, he still knew that it was going to be hard to behave like a cad and get Catherine to despise him. Not that Catherine came into it, he reminded himself, one way or another. It was Tom Straw's feelings that were to be worked on; she was merely the instrument. He forced himself to think of her as an object, inhumanly.

"Shall we stick to the original plan for the excursion?" Catherine was asking. "Or shall we wait till Tom can come with us?"

"Oh, let's go this afternoon, just the two of us," said Edgar, trying to load suggestion into his tone. "You can go with Tom some other time." As he spoke he watched her narrowly, to see whether she seemed shocked or offended. But no change came over her. Why was she so infuriatingly calm? Empty inside, probably; yes, empty, that was the answer.

Then they were sitting in the midget bus, climbing out of the town along serpentine unmade roads, stopping at villages to pick up parcels at the post offices. Their objective for the afternoon was a hillside village, said to be of more than usual picturesqueness, about three miles from the town, and towards this the bus ground its way with a peculiar mixture of national styles; smoothly, because this was Switzerland, but quickly, with a kind of suppressed violence that threatened to slide them over the edge and down the slope into the lake, because this was the Ticino, almost Italy itself. Edgar had a sudden, vivid mental picture of what would happen if the driver misjudged one of his corners: a bounding lurch, a long drop, the bus somersaulting heavily, flames breaking out from the split petrol tank, a heavy confusion of flailing limbs, bodies and parcels, and then a hissing splash as they disappeared into the water. Or perhaps they would be caught and held by a solidly built house, or a strong tree or two, on the little border of level ground by the edge of the lake. In any case, most of the passengers would be dead, or fatally injured, by that time. In a car—any car—the effect would be much the same. An open one would be best—less protection—or would it be easier to get thrown out and perhaps saved? No, a closed one would be . . . he began to work out details.

Then the bus lurched round a descending hairpin into the village street of their destination. The driver, working his elbows like Fangio, swung them round on the outside edge of the curve in the evident hope of running over some children who were playing in the gutter; but his luck was out, and the game managed to leap to safety. To console himself the driver infused more than usual *brio* into his braking, and they bounded to rest within three inches of the post office wall.

As he got out, Edgar suddenly saw the afternoon stretching ahead of him like a malarial swamp, full of poisonous snakes and sniping riflemen. Catherine smoothed her grey dress with a few deft movements, then stood quietly awaiting his suggestions, looking about her with unhurried enjoyment of the colours and shapes of the village. The task he had set himself became more odious the more closely he looked at it.

Odious, but not difficult. They would walk about and see the place first—no need to rush things—and then he could suggest some refreshment, manœuvre her into a secluded café, and begin

190

to insinuate, making the act as much like George Sanders as possible. Catherine was the kind of girl, he decided, who would not be impressed by George Sanders, particularly in *ersatz* form.

The sun was shining. They stood on the terrace in front of the village church, gazing down at the blue of the lake. Edgar searched wildly for a neutral topic of conversation.

"I think Italy begins just about *there*," he said, pointing away to their right. "Just where that little village is . . . of course, the lake . . . the lake . . ."

"You needn't, Edgar," Catherine said gently.

"Needn't what?" he blustered.

"Make conversation."

His conventionally-indignant protest died away before it reached his lips. Oh, damn, if only she had been a "normal" girl, normally vain, normally silly and self-centred! Why was she so ready to keep her attention for the important things and let the trivial things, such as flirting with Tom Straw's friends, go by?

"Has anyone ever told you," he began wearily, hoping to push things to a crisis and be done with it; but before reaching the words "that you're beautiful," he was overcome by a stifling sense of the utter silliness of the *cliché*. So, stuttering, he ended, "the one about the Englishman, the Irishman and the Sc——"

She turned to look at him in alarm and amazement.

"Look here, Edgar, what *is* the matter with you?"

"Matter?" he parried, inanely.

"Why are you acting so strangely?"

Looking her full in the eyes, he rapped out, "Because I'm in——" then came to a halt with his tongue quivering like a diving-board. Something outside his control had begun to spit out the sentence, and something else outside his control had cut it in half. What had he, or it, been going to say? His mind racing, he once again fished up a totally new ending. "I'm in—need of a cup of tea and a sit down. It's hot."

"It isn't hot. I really don't think I ought to let you get away with a silly excuse like that. It's so obviously not the real reason. Edgar, what is it? Are you ill?"

In utter astonishment, he heard his own voice bawl suddenly, "Oh—for God's sake leave me *alone!*"

"Certainly."

She turned on the heel of one grey shoe. He watched her walk

191

away up the street, staring at her back like a man who knows he will go blind in sixty seconds.

She vanished between the houses. He sat down on a stone bench, groping for a cigarette and swearing under his breath. All the time he was smoking the cigarette he swore at the birds, at the sunshine, at the lake, at the mountain opposite, at the cotton-wool smoke of a distant train crawling along by the shore. Then he went to look for her.

She was sitting, motionless, in the shadowy interior of a little café that smelt vaguely of vinegar and olives. He went across to her table and sat down, without waiting for her to show any sign of recognition.

"I'm sorry," he said. When she looked up he could see that she was not angry, only puzzled.

"What is it?" she asked.

The shirt-sleeved proprietor, carting his belly with difficulty across the stone floor, came and asked what Edgar required. Seeing that Catherine had an untouched glass of tea in front of her, he ordered the same. But the question still hung in the air between them: the interruption had done nothing to clear it away.

"I'm behaving strangely because I'm trying to hold myself back," Edgar said with what he hoped was a rather repulsive smile, "from making a pass at you."

She looked searchingly into his face, wondering whether to believe him.

"If that's how you're placed, why did you take me out? You must have known it would be awkward for both of us."

"Well, I didn't foresee it," said Edgar bluffly. "I hadn't any conscience pangs when we started out. It just looked like a good opportunity. They've—developed since."

(How the car would splash into the lake! He wondered if he would be dead already by that time.)

"I don't believe you," said Catherine. She gave two shakes of her neat head. "That isn't true to what I know of your character."

"My character!" he mocked. "What do you know of my character? You don't know the first thing about me."

"Yes, I do." This time she nodded. "I don't know the other things, but that's just what I do know—the first thing. And the first thing in your case is that you're just not the type who would

192

play this particular dirty trick on Tom. And on me," she added.

"Why is it a dirty trick to play on *you*?" Edgar said quickly, seizing the easier point with a kind of relief. "Surely the situation's quite a simple one as far as you're concerned. All you've got to do is to tell Tom, when you see him this evening, that I've been trying to cut him out, and it's all finished. Tom'll never speak to me again, and *ipso facto* neither will you."

"And that's what you want, isn't it?" she flashed.

"Want?" he goggled, nonplussed. Damn her and her penetration! Yes, damn her penetration, and her dark blonde head, and her grey dress, and her smile that went up a millimetre on one side and down a millimetre on the other. Why the hell couldn't Tom have had a normal, ordinary girl who would simply have enjoyed being "offended", or, alternatively, given herself to him behind a wall in the sunshine and then "confessed" to Tom, and so grabbed herself the best of both worlds? Why did he have to pick one like this?

And if this went on, what would happen to his basic assumption that all women were so many Phyllises and Mirabelles? It was intolerable.

Catherine drank her tea, waiting for him to speak. When he did not, she spoke for him.

"Now, Edgar, we're going to be quite sensible. We're going for a walk, to see the village and enjoy the sun, and you're going to behave sensibly, and not talk if you haven't anything to say. And if you want to pick a quarrel with Tom, you can do it perfectly well on your own, without bringing me into it. Understood?"

"But what if I can't prevent myself from——" he began, but she interrupted him in a tone half contemptuous, half affectionate.

"And I give you only one alternative. If you don't fall in with my suggestion, you can just sit down and explain your motives to me—give me a full account of what you're up to and why you're behaving so stupidly."

"I can't do that," he said sharply. Fool! He ought to have kept up the pretence that there was nothing to explain, that he was simply an unscrupulous pleasure-seeker with an occasional stab of conscience. She did not comment, but he knew that she had noted his self-revealing answer. Oh, why did this have to happen when all he wanted to do was to live in the present?

However, there was nothing to be done about it. After making their contribution to the upkeep of the proprietor's belly, they were outside, off on their walk, before he could think up any move, offensive or defensive. "Walk" was, in any case, a euphemism; short of going back along the road they had travelled in the bus, there was no path to choose that did not go more or less perpendicularly up or down the mountainside. Catherine, having the casting vote, chose the upward direction, and for twenty minutes neither of them had breath to spare for anything but the climb. They mounted at a steady three miles an hour, through the woods still smelling of winter rain and leaf-mould but floored with fresh spring grass and primroses, past wayside shrines decorated with paintings about which Tom Straw doubtless knew everything there was to be known, higher and higher until the village below them had dwindled to the scale at which all villages look unbearably picturesque—about one inch to a yard. Halting, they looked down at it in silence.

The climb had caused Edgar's pulse to accelerate a good deal. With the idea of giving it a chance to slow down, he suggested that they should turn aside from the path and sit down on a flat strip of grass that ran, terrace fashion, along the hillside. The grass was not quite dry, so he spread his jacket on the ground for Catherine to sit on; he himself, still thinking in terms of his pulse rate, made no attempt to share so small an area with her, but sat on a tree-stump six feet away. They sat and rested for several minutes, but, to Edgar's disappointment, his pulse did not slow down.

"There's the bus," she said, pointing to the tiny oblong scurrying like a frantic beetle along the road to the village. Even from this height it was evident that the driver, like all artists eternally dissatisfied with his performance, had modified his style to something like that of Gonzalez.

"Yes," said Edgar. "Good old bus," he added, feeling that something ought to be said to gild the bare affirmative.

His heart had not slowed down yet! Was there something the matter with it?

"I think I'm suffering from valvular disease of the heart," he said conversationally.

She looked up at him quickly, but his appearance seemed to dispel any anxiety caused by his words, and she merely asked in the same conversational tone, "What are the symptoms?"

"Accelerated pulse-rate, even when sitting still," he answered.

"Oh." She thought this over. "That doesn't sound valvular to me. Just functional."

They were silent again.

"I wonder what this Wercingues cove really is like," he started up again.

"Yes, I do too."

"Not that it's him I'm interested in."

"No?"

"No, I'd just like to hear his reaction when Philipson-Smith starts spouting politics to him."

"You're interested in politics, then?"

"Some politics."

Long silence.

"Are you cold without your jacket?"

"Not in the least."

"It's very kind of you."

"Don't mention it."

Pause dragging out to eternity.

"Well, I suppose we'd better go down."

"Yes," he said.

As he helped her over the low, crumbling wall, it occurred to him that her waist was conveniently placed for encirclement by his arm, and that this was a good opportunity to offend her once and for all, to make her loathe the sight of him, to go running to Tom and spill out a lot of spite against him. He drew her to him and kissed her mouth, roughly at first, then, when she did not move away, more softly, then when she still did not move away, more softly still, then, when she still did not move away, more softly still, then, when she still did not move away, suddenly more violently again, then, when she still did not . . .

&c. Ad lib.

Finally she twisted away, pushing at his shoulders with what seemed the strength of real hatred, and went down the path, back towards the village, without speaking and without looking round. He leaned against the wall for a moment until his legs stopped shaking, then began to totter down after her like a drunk.

He caught her entering the village. Between two houses she stood still and faced him.

"Why did you do that?"

"Why did *you* do that?" he asked.

"Why do you want to make me hate you?"

"Why do you think I want to make you hate me?"

With a great shrug of hopelessness, she turned away and went down to where the bus was standing. The driver had the engine running already, and as soon as they were aboard he got away to a fine start, using his clutch in the manner of Ascari, but unfortunately again missing the children. The bus was rather full and they could not sit together; this gave Edgar some twenty minutes alone with his thoughts. Or rather, with his thought, for he had only one. Escape! Escape! The situation had become too much for him. If he hung on and allowed things to develop, they were going to develop in a way that would knock the bottom out of everything—he could see that. It came down to this: that his next attempt to engineer the joint destruction of Philipson-Smith and himself would have to be (*a*) soon, and (*b*) successful. He simply could not afford to hang about any longer, getting into more trouble. Death would solve his problems, and it looked as if there were getting to be more problems to be solved with every twenty-four hours he lived. There were moments during the journey back to Conasta in which he thought that death was going to save him the trouble of going to seek it, for the driver had now reverted to the Indianapolis style of Mauri Rose, which he could only have studied through newsreels and had therefore imperfectly grasped. By some thousand-to-one chance, however, they rolled into the town and stopped without incident.

He waited for Catherine to get off. Her skin looked very pale as well as very clear.

"I'd better not see you both again," he said. "It's bound to be awkward after what you're going to tell Tom."

"I'm not going to tell Tom anything," she said quietly.

"Why not?"

She turned to face him with a twist of the body that was both angry and graceful, making the word "leonine" flare across the dark vault of his mind in crimson letters of pain.

"Because that's what you want me to do, and I'm not, I'm *not* going to do what you want me to, because I——"

He knew that "hate you" would be the next words, and suddenly wanted to shriek loudly to prevent himself from hearing them. But she had stopped. The sentence was left in its amputated state.

196

"Please don't, please don't be upset, it's all right really," he mumbled confusedly, trying to soothe her, without any idea of how to do it. "I don't want you to do what I want you to do, if you don't want to."

This sentence so obviously represented the outside limit of contemptible gibberish that a silence naturally supervened, and lasted until they reached the door of her hotel, where he left her. Some unteachable instinct made him wonder, as he walked away, whether she was watching his back as he had watched her back when she walked away down the village street; but when, on an impulse, he swung round to look, the doorway was empty.

X

THE hotel porter had recommended Angelo's garage, but it was hard to see why. Angelo could hardly have tipped him off that he wanted customers, because, patently, he didn't want customers. He stood moodily on the oil-streaked floor of his dark, low-ceilinged garage, staring out of the door at the sunlit street, plainly not wanting to be disturbed by crazy Englishmen asking to hire cars.

Edgar had, in any case, hesitated for some time before addressing Angelo, who obviously spent so much of his time studying how to avoid looking as if he owned a third-rate garage business that he had brought the deception to a fine art. With his handsome oval face, neat lounge suit, and contemptuous boredom, he looked like what he wanted to look like—a rich customer whose car, for some reason not quite ready for him when he called, was being feverishly worked on behind the scenes by the entire staff, who would wheel it out for him at any moment now.

After circling round him a few times, wondering if he knew where the proprietor was, and if so what would be the best language to ask him in, Edgar managed to provoke Angelo into asking him, curtly, what he wanted. Angelo spoke in German because he could see Edgar was an Englishman, so Edgar answered in French. Finally, by dint of repeating, "Je voudrais louer une automobile pour dimanche," over and again, while obstinately refusing to listen to any rejoinders, Edgar drove Angelo to the point of nervous tension at which anything seemed worth while to get rid of him, even if he had to do business with him to achieve this end. Flicking his long, slender fingers dramatically, he led the way through a small door at the back of his shed and on to a plot of waste ground. Halting, he pointed like Cortez at a rusting black saloon which stood inoffensively among the nettles.

"Schön bequem," he said.

Edgar walked round the car, wishing he could think of something to say. It had been a good car twenty years ago. Some great Italian factory, throbbing with power, one of the apples of Mussolini's eye, had proudly sent it rumbling out on to the road, a symbol of social solidity for a bank manager or solicitor—or perhaps it had taken some family doctor about on his rounds, spreading comfort and ease. From owner to owner it had spiralled downwards, rattling and squeaking a little more each year, but always bearing itself with dignity—even, as the years multiplied, with a kind of grandeur, like an erect keen-eyed old gentleman, not yet played out. And it had finished up among the nettles at Angelo's, with a few months of life ahead in which to be hired out to customers who didn't matter: then the scrapheap.

It was exactly what Edgar had hoped for. Tense with a solemn excitement, he wrenched open the door, got in and started the engine. As the starter whirred ineffectually a few times, Angelo stood looking on, a faint sneer painted across his handsome face, establishing in advance his unwillingness to do anything to remedy the car if it proved unable to start. Edgar hated him and felt, obscurely but deeply, that the car hated him too. "Come on, Dad," he muttered to it (pieces of machinery were masculine in Edgar's mind, not feminine), "let's do the sod one in the eye." As if in answer the motor suddenly coughed into life and began a deep, drumming roar.

Waggling his foot up and down on the accelerator, Edgar stared with unconcealed malice at Angelo. The car was running, and what was more, on Sunday he was going to take it away, out of Angelo's clutches for ever. Three people would sit in it and be killed. The car would end its life as a principal actor in this sacred tragedy, and Angelo would be left out of it, not consulted, looking a fool.

He stopped the engine and got out.

"Dimanche," he said triumphantly.

Moodily, flicking his fingers, Angelo answered, "Sonntag."

As the car rumbled to a halt there were three figures waiting on the piazza, not two.

199

"I hope you can find room for me," said Francis Jollet. "Tollemache was going to have driven me over himself yesterday, but he couldn't manage it. I shall have to come with you! I hope you don't mind!"

His tone suggested that he hoped Edgar did mind, because in any case he would not be able to refuse.

"I'm delighted," said Edgar with feeling. "The idea of taking you along really appeals to me."

"In that case," Jollet fluted, "I shall sit beside you. I shall ride in the front seat."

Neither Philipson-Smith nor McWhirtner had yet spoken. Edgar, scorning politeness now that the need for it was past, jerked open the rear door and curtly motioned to them to get in. It was too late for them to start looking for any alternative means of transport out to Wercingues's villa.

"We might 'a' known it'd be a bluidy antique ye'd get hold of, Banks," McWhirtner grumbled. He seemed to be suffering from a hangover. "We shall get there wi' our teeth rattled oot o' the gums."

"You'll be lucky if that's all that happens to you," said Edgar with a light laugh, starting the car rolling down the street. He glanced up into the driving-mirror and met Philipson-Smith's eyes, full of tense hostility. Suddenly light-headed, he laughed again. "Off for a day in the country!" he sang, emphasizing the refrain with a burst of acceleration.

"Be careful!" Philipson-Smith ordered sharply, gripping the back of the driving-seat.

"Don't worry," Edgar cooed. "You'll get where I'm taking you. It's a point of honour with me. I wouldn't for the world be the cause of your not arriving at your—destination."

As the words left his mouth he felt slightly worried. He had, for some reason, given the word "destination" an unbelievably malignant ring; a kind of Satanic sneer. What on earth was he doing? Did he want to arouse their suspicions before they had even left Conasta?

"What the hell's the matter with you?" Philipson-Smith demanded. "Are you drunk, or what?"

In his present over-wrought state, the question seemed to Edgar excruciatingly funny. He gave a groaning bellow of laughter.

"He isnae safe!" McWhirtner complained. "Luik at him drivin' on the crown o' the road!"

Edgar slowed down and took a grip on himself. Cautiously he eased the car into the right-hand side of the road and began to trundle along sedately at twenty miles an hour.

"All right, the joke's over," he said calmly. "I'm not really going to take any risks with such a distinguished cargo aboard. We shall go at this speed all the way. And for your satisfaction, Smith, I'm not drunk."

"I wish I were sure of that."

"A bloke's back brake-block broke," Edgar suddenly shouted. "The Leith police dismisseth us. A cracked cricket critic." The three sentences were all familiar exercises to him, and he uttered them correctly and at an impressive speed; but the effect was spoilt by the strained, cracked note of tension that he could not keep out of his voice, and by its absurd loudness.

Once more he took a hold on himself, striving to analyse the source of his strange behaviour. Something inside him was pressing him in the direction of failure, trying to stop him from getting the car up to the mountain road and then giving that final, decisive twist of the steering-wheel. What was that something? Fear? Probably, and also a new element that had not been present at his last attempt: a new kind of deep misgiving, a hard root of distrust that had somehow formed itself in the very heart of his resolution. Did he still want to kill and die? What did it matter whether he still wanted to or not, he asked himself savagely—he was here, he was committed, and the only thing left to do was to get it over.

Unconsciously, he had speeded up. Now they were out of the town, and curving upwards past the immaculate villas and hotels. Soon they would be on the mountain road with its loose surface and thousand curves, where any death would look like an accident.

Breaking through the cloud of his preoccupation, he became aware that Jollet was addressing him. It was a few moments before the words became intelligible, but even before grasping any of the man's meaning he realized, from the expression on his face, that Jollet was engaged in scoring off him in some way.

". . . seemed to be having a splendid time in Paris," he was saying. "Phyllis is just the person to take care of him, of course."

That was it. He was reverting to the Benton business again.

"You like watching anything get broken, don't you, Jollet?" Edgar asked, giving Jollet a chance to condemn himself out of

201

his own mouth before being executed. "You know quite well that for a boy of his age, and impressionable at that, to get mixed up with . . ." here he fell silent while wrestling the car round a steep curve in the face of some oncoming traffic, "that it's likely to do lasting harm—tragic harm," he finished.

"Oh, but they were both *enjoying* themselves so much!" Jollet protested, his voice leaping up the scale on the word "enjoying". "Phyllis herself told me she'd never had such a nice holiday."

"And you believed it."

"Wha's goin' on?" McWhirtner demanded in a strident, irritable voice. He could not quite catch the drift of the conversation, but had heard a feminine name uttered and was afraid of missing some information relating to one of his major interests. "Why don't ye try to keep the conversation general?"

Jollet gave a hooting laugh. Squirming round in his seat, he began some meaningless exchange of repartee with McWhirtner. Edgar relapsed into his private trance. Another half-mile, and they would be on the right stretch. The car chugged onward with a massive steadiness; the long climb was heating the engine, and a strong whiff of hot oil, rising through the floorboards at Edgar's feet, added to the vividness and urgency of the occasion.

It was interesting to see how his passengers were spending their last few minutes on this earth. Philipson-Smith was silent, tensely staring forward at the driving-mirror above Edgar's head; he was trying to see Edgar's face in it, but Edgar had forestalled this by twisting the mirror to one side. Jollet and McWhirtner seemed to be discussing some absurd proposal to publish McWhirtner's poems with illustrations by Jollet.

"But my illustrations would be *quite certain* to get the book *banned*."

"Weel, isnae that jist wha' we want? Think o' the sales o' the Paris edition. Noo, my idea is——"

"Does it matter *what* I draw? I can't *understand* your poems. All those queer words."

The road began to level out. Edgar shifted from first gear into second, and began to tread heavily on the pedal. Let the old machine finish up in style—let them all finish up in style. The hot smell through the floorboards, the song of the pounding engine, the keen bright light of the sun through the windscreen, all exhilarated him. Here was the beginning of the mountain road;

round this bend they would see the lake beneath them. He pressed the pedal quite flat, swung the wheel over, and—suddenly there was no time to do anything but dive inwards on to the rock-strewn margin of the road, no time even to apply the brakes, no time to fling up an arm to protect one's face from the glass, no time for anything but one wild hauling twist on the wheel, nothing in his ears except the harsh outcry of brakes and a strangled yelp of fear from Jollet beside him.

Straight in front, riding them down like an avalanche, was a bus. And even in that instant Edgar knew that it was not just a bus, but *the* bus, the one in which he and Catherine had ridden over this very road the other day. The driver, a dead cigarette in the corner of his mouth, was sitting well back from the wheel and keeping his arms straight. It was one of his Fangio days.

They had stopped. The bus had passed them and was already disappearing down the road. A cloud of dust hung in the air, but otherwise the landscape slept in its noonday peace.

Edgar gave a tense, forced laugh. "I suppose we ought to keep these things in perspective," he said, breaking the heavy silence. "To all of us, that seemed a very close shave, but by local standards it probably . . . it probably . . ."

The silence weighed down on his voice and crushed it out like a cigarette-end.

"Well, what's the matter?" he demanded irritably, twisting in his seat to stare at the others. "You don't think I was *trying* to have a collison with that bus, do you?"

Philipson-Smith jerked on the door-handle, threw the door open, and climbed out, followed by McWhirtner. Jollet, seeing the general idea, opened his door and got out too. Edgar gaped at them through his open window.

"It was kind of you to offer to drive us out, Banks," said Philipson-Smith with venomous precision, "but we're not tired of life, if you are."

"Tired of life?"

Jollet gave a loud giggle, but the sound was almost drowned by Philipson-Smith's fierce yelp of, "Good God, man, don't say you didn't *notice* how you were driving!"

Edgar tried to look back over the last few minutes. A chill trickle of anxiety wavered down his spine. What had he done *now* to mess things up? It had been the bus driver's fault, not his. He might have speeded up a little as they approached the corner, but—oh, it was all absurd. If they were now refusing to go any further with him, it must be because they sensed in some metaphysical way that he meant to kill them. It *couldn't* be because of anything he had. . . .

"Oh, come now," he said coaxingly. "Jump in and let's get started. We've got a long way to——"

Philipson-Smith shook his head, and McWhirtner came in with, "We'd be better off on our ain feet than locked in that rattrap with you." Even Jollet added, "It really was getting *sinister*. I felt I'd *never* get out *alive*."

Philipson-Smith came up to the car and grasped Edgar's doorhandle. "I'm afraid there's only one way out of this," he said in his curtest voice. "You offered to drive us out for this interview with Wercinques, and that means you're committed to helping us to get there. We didn't make any other arrangements, and now it's too late. So there's only one thing to do. It's out of the question for you to drive us there, after that exhibition, but fortunately that still leaves the car."

"Leaves—the car?"

"Certainly. We're going out to Wercingues's place in this car, but one of us three will be doing the driving. Preferably myself. Yes, *I'll* do the driving."

Rage flooded Edgar's veins. He began to see everything through a red mist.

"Is it all right for me to come along as a passenger?" he asked, choking back his passion, but with a tremble in his voice. "Or does my mere presence constitute a danger?"

Philipson-Smith shrugged. "It's your car; you hired it, at any rate. Come on," he said to the other two, "let's get in."

Suddenly Edgar knew he had had enough of this. White with fury, he snatched at the starter, knowing only that he had to get away, to get out of sight and earshot of this loathsome trio. It was hard enough to have to carry his own blundering, impulseridden, uncontrolled self along with him; but another moment of the company of these three, even for the sake of murdering them—no.

As he dragged at the starter, the engine turned over feebly a few times, then stopped. Again and again, under the coldly reproachful stare of Philipson-Smith's simian eyes, he struggled to get it to start. No result. Sweating, he threw open the door and leapt out.

He knew nothing about cars, but, impelled by the urge to do something, to act on the situation in some way, however futile, he snatched open the bonnet to see if anything looked obviously broken. It all looked more or less as he had expected it to look, but this meant nothing to him. Then Jollet, who had been nervously wandering round in circles, called "Look at this!" and pointed.

Edgar walked over. There, in the dust, were the wheel-tracks which showed the course they had followed when leaving the road to escape the bus. In between these tracks was a jagged out-cropping of rock, higher and sharper than its neighbours, with a freshly scored gash showing white across the grey of its upper edge.

He looked back at the car. A thick blue rivulet of oil was beginning to wander out from beneath it.

"Ay, that's it," said McWhirtner sagely. "Ye've broken it," he said to Edgar, accusingly.

Philipson-Smith stumped across, his legs and arms moving jerkily; he resembled a figure in an old silent film, photographed at sixteen frames per second. He was genuinely beside himself with rage. It occurred to Edgar that he had often read in novels the expression "so-and-so's face was *working*", but until this moment he had never understood it. Philipson-Smith's face really was working; the muscles had got out of his control and were causing his eyebrows to jerk up and down, his chin to slam backwards and forwards like a bureau draw, and his cheeks to bulge out and then contract again.

"You God-damned fool, Banks," he choked. "This is—this is nothing more than I deserve for being fool enough to trust you to——" his voice soared upwards in a kind of wail "—do-oo-oo anything."

"Och, it wasnae an accident," said McWhirtner. "Ye've been right a' along, Rollo. Banks's interest in the Movement has never been onythin' else than a pure an' simple desire to bitch it up."

Philipson-Smith's eyes narrowed. "I believe you're right," he grated. "You've not heard the last of this, Banks. When——"

"Oh, don't be such a pair of melodramatic fools!" Edgar shouted. "You saw the bus coming towards us, with your own

205

eyes. Do you think I came up here yesterday and timed the bus with a stop-watch and then went and put that rock there? It's time you woke up to everyday reality, you histrionic—you——" he searched for a telling description, but in the heat of the moment could do no better than, "pair of squawking self-important geese."

"But what about Tollemache?" Jollet burst out, pettishly. He seemed suddenly to have realized that his day at the villa had become impossible. "He'll be expecting us—what are we going to *do*?"

"Ring him up and tell him you're not coming," said Edgar shortly, turning away. "Tell him you've found a nest of plover's eggs and you're sitting on them to keep them warm, so you can't spare the time to visit him till they hatch out."

"We shall tell Wercingues exactly what has happened," said Philipson-Smith icily. "We shall tell him that we were the victims of a deliberate piece of obstruction on your part."

"All right," said Edgar over his shoulder. "And the next time you make an appointment to see him he'll send his servants round to carry you in a basket. I thought you were trying to pass yourselves off as a couple of tough political tycoons."

"Yes," he cried, wheeling round as it struck him that this was a good vein to tap, "and I can tell you that *my* confidence in the Movement has been ebbing. I was impressed by your principles and aims, but after a study of you two at close hand—I tell you frankly, I despair of ever seeing the thing work properly. If your methods are typical——" he snorted with contemptuous rage. "Who gave you instructions to get hold of Wercingues? Who left an important job like that to you two bunglers?"

"The Movement doesn't have to consider criticism of its members from people like you," Philipson-Smith snapped.

"No, and apparently it can get along without any help from anyone who isn't a certifiable lunatic . . . well, I'm finished. To hell with trying to help you—to hell with the Movement and with you too!"

As he stormed the words he wondered why he was still keeping up the pretence of ever having been interested in the Movement. The only explanation seemed to be that he had got involved so deeply in a false situation that there was no time, now, to try to work his way back to the true one. Here at least was a ready-made

206

dramatic role he could play in order to give Philipson-Smith an uncomfortable five minutes, before the next round could begin seriously.

"Oh, *where* is there a 'phone box?" Jollet moaned, scanning the sun-baked rocks as if hoping to find one tucked among them.

"Come on," Philipson-Smith snarled. "We'll just go along to the nearest house and use their 'phone. And we'll leave you, Banks," he added in a tone of concentrated loathing, "to enjoy the results of your endeavours."

"Good-bye," said Edgar cheerfully. "Tell Sir Rufus from me to tie a can to the Movement and put his energies into playing golf. McWhirtner'll do for a caddy."

When they had gone, he wearily pushed the car back on to the road and started it coasting down the hill the way they had come. In silence, apart from the ominous clanking of whatever it was he had broken, the veteran rolled smoothly back to its duties, cheated of the flaming, sacrificial end he had planned for it. As for Edgar, he felt too flat and exhausted even to be disappointed. What was the use of his efforts, when he seemed just as futile in death as he had been in life?

The road levelled out, the car clanked a few more times and then halted, and Edgar crossed the road to a telephone-box and dialled Angelo's number.

"All right," Edgar said savagely. "I can't stand it and I don't see why I should pretend that I *can* stand it. I've been dishonest enough for long enough."

By the word "it" he referred to his own company. He was going back to London the next day; if he could have arranged it, he would have set off that minute. Having written "FAILURE" in gigantic letters across one more piece of the Swiss landscape, he hated having to spend even twenty-four more hours being reminded of it. Spend them he must, but there was no need to keep up any idiotic pretence of calm or self-sufficiency. He had gone up to his room after dinner with a book, but had barely sat down and allowed his eye to trail over the first few sentences, without extracting any kind of meaning from them, before he knew he had to talk to somebody.

Down the stairs and out. "Pity it has to be them," he muttered, but insincerely; he knew that, on any terms, even quarrelling terms, Tom Straw and Catherine were the only two people left in the world who could do him good.

It took him about twelve minutes to walk to their hotel. During the first four minutes he felt confident that Catherine would have made the necessary complaint to Tom, painting a black picture of his behaviour the other afternoon, and that what lay ahead would be a straight man-to-man quarrel, perhaps even a fight, culminating in the final break which would allow him to take his own life in peace. He felt grimly pleased at this prospect; it was what he had wanted, what he had planned for, and he had no doubt of having achieved it. She had *said*, of course, that she would say nothing about it to Tom; but of course a woman always . . . During the second four minutes this confidence ebbed away and was replaced by a nervous uncertainty and dread. *Why* did he want her to have told him? Because of the plan. Well, to hell with the plan. Yes, but it was a *good* plan. But it would mean never seeing Straw again. Well, that was all right, wasn't it? He was going to die anyway, wasn't he? Yes, but it would mean never seeing *Catherine* again. But exactly! When had he ever counted on seeing Catherine again? What was it to him whether . . . Oh, no you don't! I know what you were trying to make me admit. Well, I'm not, see? *You know you are.* Go to hell. Go to hell. *Yes, but you are.*

"I'm not!" he shouted in the darkness. "I'm bloody well not and I'm not going to be!" he added in a lower voice.

Oh, yes you are. You're in love with Catherine.

The idea was so preposterous that he burst into a loud snigger, which somehow turned itself into a violent snort, half-way between a laugh and a sob. On this note he entered the third four-minute stretch, during which his mind was increasingly swamped with one single emotion—panic at the thought that they might have gone out for the evening and that he might not see them at all before going back to London. In that case the last words she would ever have spoken to him would be the unfinished sentence at the bus stop, the bitten-off one that was going to end with "I hate you".

"It didn't, though," he said.

Here was their hotel. He wondered if they had rooms near one another, on the same landing. They could hardly have the same room unless she did not give in her passport. Perhaps after all they were just . . . they were only . . .

What the hell should I care what arrangement they make anyway? Their own business is their own . . . *But you do care, you know you do care.* Oh, shut up, for God's sake, don't *you* start.

He went in and looked into the bar. They were sitting in a corner together, smoking.

Constricted and gagged by nervous tension, Edgar stood to attention before them, absolutely unable to move or speak. Everything depended on the reception they gave him, which in turn depended on whether Catherine had made her complaint, which in turn depended on . . .

"Well, stack me sideways," Tom Straw said genially. "Come on, Edgar, and have a drink of something. We'll make room for him, won't we?" he said to Catherine.

"Yes, of course," she said, and moved over on the bench with one of her supple, relaxed movements, like a lioness making room for the lion to enter the den. Edgar noticed, however, that she manœuvred so that the empty place was next to Tom Straw, not to herself, and he entered the den like a jackal snuffling for offal. Fortunately Straw began the conversation at once.

"Well, how did the ride go, Edgar?"

"The car got broken," Edgar said shortly.

The other two both laughed, then quickly assumed expressions of sympathy, and Tom Straw said "Stack me sideways" to cover up his embarrassment at having laughed. How *good* they were!

"Yes, we got forced off the road by that damned bus driver," Edgar said vehemently, re-living his rage and frustration at the thought of his failure. "So I didn't get a chance to . . . a chance to . . . we never got anywhere," he ended lamely.

"Were the others very disappointed?" Catherine asked.

"Oh, pretty well," Edgar muttered indifferently, sinking once more into his morass of gloom and preoccupation. The old rectangle of plate-glass had formed round him; he felt increasingly unable to hold any communication with another being. Realizing this, he recognized also that one of his motives in coming to seek them out had been the hope of some sort of violent action, something explosive to shatter the glass, so that, for a few brief moments before it had time to re-form, he might breathe the common air again and feel the presence of something human.

But their equanimity had disappointed his hope. Full of

209

resentment and self-pity, he glared at Straw. Damn the man! Why did he persist in behaving decently?

"Catherine and I had a very pleasant outing the other day," he sneered, in desperation.

"Yes, she told me. I was very sorry I couldn't come," Tom Straw answered. He was, or seemed to be, perfectly unconscious of the malice in Edgar's voice.

"Very pleasant," Edgar pursued in a loud, aggressive voice, almost a shout. "We——"

He dropped his voice as some member of the hotel staff came towards them. It seemed that Straw was wanted on the telephone. He went away, leaving Edgar and Catherine staring grimly at one another.

"All right," he said rudely, as soon as Straw was out of earshot, "don't bother to tell me that I'm behaving like a fool, and a boor, and a spoilt child, and an imbecile, and all the rest of it. I *am* those things, all of them, and I can't behave in any other way and it's too late to change me." He scowled at her, then noticed the grey of her eyes, the unbearable smoothness of her skin that he would never touch, and all at once her beauty hit him like a policeman's truncheon. He wanted to lay his head on the table and bawl.

She leaned forward with her elbows on the table and her fingers interlaced.

"I suppose all this silly idiocy is because you're still trying to make me loathe you, Edgar. Well, you can stop it. It's boring and in any case you're not succeeding."

"Not succeeding?" he jeered. "I suppose the more I insult you the more amiable you think I am."

"I didn't say anything about being amiable. You're certainly not *that*. But that's not the same thing as saying that you're making me hate you. I just feel sorry for you. You're behaving—not so much like any of the things you mentioned—as like a person who's ill."

He shrugged. "Don't think I like behaving in this damned silly way. I don't enjoy putting on a half-baked immature Byronic act. I've—well, I've got my motives, that's all. You'll understand them in due course."

"That's it, be mysterious," she said in a bored, let-it-go tone of voice.

"Well, what if I *am* mysterious?" he blazed, sending the ash-tray spinning to the floor with a convulsive movement of one hand. "You don't think I enjoy that either, surely, do you? What right have you to assume that everything can be made clear all at once?"

She looked at him exactly as the lioness would look at the jackal if he came too close. Her calm, her beauty, her indifference, were like three gallons of icy water flung over him. The keen, hidden blade of her pity, invisibly active behind them, was like a stab from a scalpel.

"What *right*?" she asked. He stared at her in utter misery, knowing that he had made the worst mistake of all: he had offended her so badly that she would simply not bother to mention his name, to Tom or anyone else, but merely despise his memory for ever. "What right have you to thrust the whole business on to me if you don't want me to understand it?"

"Oh, for God's sake," he groaned thickly. "Doesn't everyone—don't all the men who are in love with you behave stupidly?"

She looked at him wearily. "Now please, Edgar, don't just switch from one act to another. Don't start a lot of rubbish about being in love with me. You've already explained all about that, when we were out the other day. You've already told me that all you wanted was to enjoy yourself at my expense and start up a quarrel with Tom at the same time."

"I never told you anything of the kind," he snapped.

"Well, you more or less did. You made it sufficiently obvious. Whatever it is, it's something between you and Tom. You're not in love with me at all."

Surely the best thing would simply be to tell the truth and be quite open about it. Then she would be bound to tell Tom about it and he could go away and kill himself and everything would be all right because he would be dead.

"I am in love with you," he said coldly. "Not that it matters. I'm in love with you and it doesn't matter what you think about it because I'm not trying to get anything out of you and I just don't care whether you care about me or not, do you see?"

"It seems a pretty funny way of being in love," she commented, neutrally, as if talking about some character in a film they had just seen.

"Yes, it is," he said. "A damned funny way. You'll understand when—it's all over."

211

Unexpectedly, she began to laugh softly.

"You're awfully clumsy, aren't you, Edgar? I suppose this is just your way of putting over some terribly well-tried gambit, something on the lines of I'm-going-away-and-you-won't-be-seeing-me-for-a-long-time."

"I'm going away," he said, "and you won't be seeing me for a long time."

Tom Straw had come up in time to hear the last words. "Going away?" he asked. "Really, Edgar? Where?"

"Back to London, in the first place."

"Well, that doesn't mean we shan't be seeing you, necessarily," said Straw, fitting himself comfortably into his corner again. "We'll be going back next week. I've finished with all this business here."

Exhausted, unable to think of anything rational to fill in the next blank in the conversation, Edgar said indifferently, "Well, we must get in touch. Give me your 'phone number."

"I'm not on the 'phone at my place," said Straw. "But if you want to get hold of us, you can ring Catherine at the place where she works. It's Welbeck something-or-other, isn't it?" he asked her.

Edgar momentarily hated him for knowing her so well that he did not even have to remember her number, for being able to count on her presence whenever he wanted it; but his spark of hatred was swamped by a wave of pure astonishment as Catherine uttered the number. Was Straw mad? Was she mad? What were the pair of them up to?

"Well, go on, write it down, man," Straw was saying. "You know how to use a telephone, I suppose?"

"What was it again?" Edgar asked, unscrewing the cap of his fountain pen. He felt as if his own head were being unscrewed from his shoulders. How idiotic it all was! What would he be doing with her number?

Writing it down, he discovered that he was using the same scrap of paper on which he had scribbled his thoughts the other morning. "I have been reminded of a responsibility towards life," it said. He crossed it out savagely.

"You'll lose that," said Straw, nodding at the crumpled paper. However much he, personally, hankered for inefficiency and hated his own capacity for remembering everything and having his

212

information in neat order, he could not repress a slight annoyance at Edgar's lackadaisical method.

"I'll have it microfilmed," Edgar sneered, "and two thousand copies made." He put the paper in his wallet. "There. Is that all right?"

"Go on, take the Michael," Straw sighed. "I can't help being a ruddy bureaucrat."

Edgar felt, suddenly, that he must get away; he had looked forward to spending an hour or two with Straw and Catherine, but now he felt, overwhelmingly, the need to escape from this situation. There were too many pressures on him, from different sides: too much that was puzzling, or dangerous, or just needing to be watched. He felt tired and limp.

"Well, I'll be going now," he said, standing up. "I've got a long . . . I must get an early . . ."

"Going? But, stack me sideways," Tom Straw enunciated, "you've only been here a few minutes."

Edgar seized his opportunity. "That may be," he said with an idiotic leer, "but I've got what I came for."

"What you came for?"

"Catherine's telephone number," he said.

Tom Straw smiled genially, Catherine looked up quietly and watchfully, and Edgar took himself off, wondering, as he went, whether the last remark would suffice to arouse Straw's suspicions and do the necessary damage, and whether, if not, there was anything more he could do about it, and whether, in any case, he still cared.

XI

"WHAT is it, Flannery?" Edgar asked.

"I just wanted a few glasses," Flannery said in the same tone that he would have used if he had been buying glasses in a shop. "Not many, about half a dozen. And to welcome you home," he added.

"In that order?"

Flannery shrugged. "What order did you expect?"

Edgar crossed to the cupboard.

"Would my second-best glasses do? Or must it be the Jacobean ones with my family crest on them?"

"I didn't know you had two qualities. In any case the usual ones are quite good enough; they might get broken."

Edgar handed over the glasses. "I haven't really got any Jacobean ones," he said, "but surely, if I had, you wouldn't let a little thing like that deter you from borrowing them? I mean, wouldn't there be a heightened pleasure about breaking something that was irreplaceable?"

"No," said Flannery. "You're confusing me with those people who have a thing about virgins. Now, as far as I'm——"

"All right," Edgar put in hastily. "As far as you're concerned anything'll do. And you're the same about glasses. Fine. Fine. Only just don't stand here explaining it all." He hustled Flannery towards the door.

"It's been very inconvenient having you away," said Flannery as he went out. "I've been short of all sorts of things."

"Why didn't you break the door down?" said Edgar with a light laugh.

"I was afraid you'd prosecute me when you came back," said Flannery, going down the stairs with the glasses.

214

"What? For a little thing like that?" Edgar called after him savagely. "What's a little housebreaking and robbery between you and me?"

"When you go to prison," he shouted down the silent stairs, "it'll be for something much more interesting."

There was no answer, and he heard the click of Flannery's door closing without haste.

Going back into his living-room, he sat down. The flat looked exactly the same, his relations with Flannery were the same, the view out of the window was the same except that it was light later in the evening and the trees and shrubs were beginning to be lightly powdered with fresh green. Well, what was *not* the same?

The answer to this question, "myself", was so obvious, and so disturbing in its implications, that he switched his attention to something else. It was two or three hours since he had entered the place and dumped his suitcase in the bedroom; during that time he had avoided opening the half-dozen letters that had accumulated during his absence, but now he turned to them and resolutely tore them open in rapid succession. A bill for gas, a bill for electricity, a bill for rent, a circular or two, and a curt type-written note from Stimms: his dismissal. The combined effect of these missives, especially the last, was to fill Edgar with rage against himself for having bungled his suicide and forced himself to come back to this squalid muddle. Gas! Electricity! Stimms! Exactly the weary old routine that had driven him to seek the exit in the first place!

And yet . . . the thing that was changed *was* himself. Uneasily, with a kind of nagging embarrassment, he found himself beginning to see that these people had a point to make, after all: he *had* used gas and electricity, so why not pay for it? He *had* walked out of his job, so why should Stimms not sack him? Groping back to find and re-assemble his original frame of mind, he recalled that its foundation had been the sense of futility. Why go on bothering with these things? he had asked; what is there to keep alive *for*?

As the thought formed itself he had a quick mental glimpse of Catherine's clear skin and grey eyes. The kiss he had forced upon her, up on the hill above the village, once more shot through his veins like brandy.

"Not enough, of course," he said, going over to the door. "You can't set a woman over against the whole dingy mess and call that *enough*."

As he went down the stairs and past Flannery's door he heard the familiar party-sounds. Pausing for a moment to identify the several strands of noise, he realized that Flannery had managed unobtrusively to borrow, beside the glasses, his record of Jimmy McPartland and his orchestra playing "The World is Waiting for the Sunrise."

"Not even if it were *that* woman, not even if it were her," he said, going down and into the street.

The next day, it rained. As if to mark Edgar's homecoming, and to leave him in no doubt as to where he was, the London sky opened and poured down the first of its spring rainstorms.

The effect it had on him was one of paralysis. All day he sat limply in a chair, listening to the surge of raindrops on the window-pane, sometimes opening the window to stare down at the flooded gutters and hurrying pedestrians. Fatigue, despair, confusion, all conspired to rob him of any strength and chain him to the arm-chair; but without the rain he might have beaten them.

As it was, the day passed like a drugged dream. Now and again he made himself a cup of tea or coffee, or ate a slice of bread or an apple; but when the few odds and ends of food he had hurriedly gathered in on the previous night were finished, he did not go out for more. The grocery on the corner might have been a thousand miles away, for all the inclination he had to set out and go there.

During the afternoon, his musings thickened into images, images as keen and insistent as physical presences. Tom Straw scowled genially and paced the carpet; Philipson-Smith sneered, McWhirtner cackled; Catherine smiled, with one corner of her mouth a millimetre higher than the other.

Suddenly, at about six-thirty, the trance snapped. The rain had ceased, the pubs were open, and he was a damned fool to have wasted his day. Flinging on his coat, he went out for a drink.

Once out in the street, he had expected to feel normal and ordinary: but something of the same unreality clung to his thoughts and sensations. The tangle of little streets round about where he lived, which he had known intimately for several years, seemed unfamiliar, and he walked down each one with a curious uncertainty as to where it would lead. Of course it was only the

216

usual thing, the usual slightly queer sensation that one had on coming back to familiar surroundings after an absence; but normally that feeling wore off in a few minutes, and here it was persisting in a way that he found distinctly uncomfortable. As if he were already a ghost, he thought suddenly, as if his plans had succeeded and he were already a ghost.

Ghost or not, here was a pub. His wanderings had taken him outside the small area he usually frequented, and he did not remember having been in this one before. Going into the Public Bar, he looked round with a certain amount of distaste. It was one of those "funny" pubs. There were vulgar post-cards pinned on the wall beside the bar, where you had to see them as you waited to be served, and behind the landlord's head a large notice in a gilt frame: O LORD, HELP ME TO KEEP MY BIG MOUTH SHUT UNTIL I KNOW WHAT I'M TALKING ABOUT. And the landlord said, "Give it a name, mate," instead of "Yes, sir?"

"Half a pint of your cheapest beer," said Edgar.

"Cor," said the landlord. He drew the beer. "You must be celebrating," he said.

"How much is it?" Edgar asked.

"Seven and a half. You must have won something at the races," the landlord said.

"I'm a teetotaller," said Edgar. "When I've drunk this I want you to carry me home. My address is sewn into my clothes." He drained the beer and said, "Same again and two cheese rolls."

"Blimey. You must have won *big*," said the landlord. "You must have cleaned out."

As Edgar turned to carry his beer and rolls over to a chair, he noticed a very broad back turned towards him. A youth had come in and was studying the vulgar post-cards while he waited to be served. When the landlord said "Name it, mate," the youth presented his profile to Edgar. It was his ex-pupil, the full-back.

"I didn't know you were a drinker," Edgar said to him severely.

"Well, I never," said the full-back. "A small glass of water, please," he said to the landlord.

"Not here," said the landlord. "I'm not serving any drunks. You've had enough already." He drew a pint of beer and passed it over. "One and threepence," he added.

When they were sitting down, Edgar asked, "What's the news from school? Or have you left?"

217

"No, I'm still there for one more term. Then the army," the full-back rumbled. Picking up his pint, he swallowed half of it, then turned to Edgar: "You're not going to take me up about breaking school rules by coming in here, are you?" he demanded.

"How could I? I don't work there now."

"Oh," said the full-back ruminatively. "We didn't know. We just thought . . . well, we wondered . . . we didn't know what to think, as a matter of fact."

"I'm sacked," said Edgar. "I sacked myself first by not turning up, and then they obligingly made it official."

"Why did you do it?" the full-back suddenly asked.

"Why does one do anything?" Edgar said evasively. The conversation was blocked; they both stared pensively for a moment at the notice above the landlord's head.

"Have you seen this?" the full-back asked as if wishing to change the subject. Taking out his wallet, he produced a carefully folded cutting from a newspaper.

"Schoolmaster on Assault Charge," Edgar read. "An action for assault and battery was to-day brought by Mr. S. V. Stimms, headmaster of," &c.

"What on earth's been going on?"

"Well, nobody actually witnessed it, but I suppose this chap just couldn't take Stimms—at any rate, he seems to have gone for him and blacked his eye."

"But it says here," Edgar bent over the paper, "it says here that it was a member of Stimms's own staff. But how could it be? I don't know this name."

"It was the temporary man they got in to replace you," the full-back explained. "Didn't you know they'd done that? You must have been away, have you?"

"Yes," Edgar said tonelessly, suddenly feeling bewildered. "Yes, I've been away."

"Well, anyway," the full-back concluded, "this other chap didn't stick it for long. He hung one on Stimms and walked out into the night. We're thinking of presenting him with an illuminated address, if we could only trace him."

For a moment they sat in silence; the youth, as if perceiving that Edgar would be embarrassed by questions about what he had been doing, kept off the subject, and neither of them had anything else to talk about. Edgar reflected gloomily that, since the Phyllis

218

episode, they had probably all taken it for granted that he had found his true level in some slough of vice. In their eyes, it must have seemed only natural that such a character should disappear without warning from normal life. He owed that to Phyllis: but, as he tried to feel the familiar surge of resentment against her, he realized that this time it would not well up. He had been perfectly aware of what he was doing; it would be more honest to take the responsibility squarely instead of pushing it on to the woman.

Ah, but there was another responsibility that rested on Phyllis. What had she been doing with Benton? He turned to the full-back, meaning to ask some leading question, but found that he could not think of any words to frame it in. "What's the low-down about Benton and that bint you met over at my place?" was unthinkably crude and direct, but at the same time he could think of no roundabout way of approaching the subject that sounded anything but silly.

Then, while he pondered, the situation moved forward without his aid. He had often noticed that nearly every conversation between two people is to some extent guided by a rudimentary, but evident, telepathy, and now the full-back gave an instance of it.

"Benton's going up to Oxford next term," he volunteered.

Edgar tried to make his answer sound pleased. He tried to conceal his deep conviction that Benton's soul was in stronger hands than those of the educational authorities.

"Good. Excellent. He was making his arrangements when I . . . left . . . and it's nice to know that everything's completed. Now he's free to leave the school, at least."

"And not before it was time," said the full-back unexpectedly, turning to look Edgar in the face for a moment before dropping his gaze to the stained wooden table in front of them.

Edgar got out a packet of Swiss cigarettes and lit one with deliberation.

"You mean what I suppose you mean, I suppose?" he asked.

"I suppose so," said the full-back, half defiantly.

Edgar felt as if he were standing in the dock. There was no need for him to tolerate this impertinence from a former pupil, a boy still at school, but, equally, there was no need to delude himself by trying to clamber up to a height from which to rebuke him. The full-back was one of those very honest men who can begin to be morally impressive before they are mature or have anything that could be described as wisdom.

Sadly they both stared in front of them. The landlord leaned on the bar and called across to them: "He'll be here in a minute."

"Who will?" Edgar asked, wondering if this was more telepathy and it was Benton who would be here in a minute.

"The undertaker," the landlord said. "So the funeral can get started."

"You'll have to have the swing doors taken out," said the fullback, standing up to go. "They're too narrow for a coffin."

Nodding politely to Edgar, he went out. The landlord turned his attention to tightening the drawing-pins which held the vulgar post-cards, and Edgar sat thinking.

So his successor had found Stimms too much for his patience. Of course, it had only been a matter of time before Stimms was assaulted by one of his underlings, and a young temporary master was the most likely to do it: some impetuous youth who had not yet resigned himself to the life of a yoke-animal. He wondered whether the man was in prison. It would have been pleasant to meet him and offer congratulations and thanks based on a shared experience of Stimms. In any case, this heroic unknown had set him, Edgar, an example, and at the very moment when it was needed. His resolution had been wavering; the clear-cut outlines of his intention had been losing themselves in a fog of complication and indecision. But this was the clarion-call! Action! If some callow youth, fresh from the university, could flare up at Stimms and use his fists on him, thereby sacrificing himself for the public weal, then the least he, Edgar, could do was to play his part and carry out his plan. Was he, with his greater maturity and experience of life, to be put to shame by any raw stripling? It was a time to put personal considerations aside. He felt a kind of sad dignity creeping into his expression and bearing as he sat with his elbows on the wooden table: his face became furrowed, respectable, with a kind of restrained geniality about the eyes, but a geniality that contained within itself a hint of the tragic. He looked like an elder statesman or a racehorse.

"It is a far, far, better thing that I do," he muttered, "and a far, far better rest that I go to . . ."

Then, as his mood changed, he became the young master who had assaulted Stimms. Hurrying out of the pub into the street, to give himself more freedom of action, he began to immerse himself in the noble images of courage and self-sacrifice. "You sent for me, sir?" he asked quietly. "That is correct, Mr. So-and-so, I did send for you," he croaked, staring with a glittering reptilian eye. "I have a few things I wish to say to you." He paused ominously, walking about ten yards in silence. "When you first joined my staff," he began, with an air of leisurely enjoyment, "I believe I made it clear to you that the disciplinary spirit . . ."

Muttering, he walked through the twilit streets. In the last twenty yards before reaching his own door, the explosion came. Straightening up, a cold rage flashing from his eye, he asked in a quiet but distinct voice, "Is that all, Mr. Stimms?" "All—all— what d'you mean," he blustered. "I mean have you finished?" he asked. "Because if so, I've got a piece of advice for you too. *Stuff your disciplinary spirit.*" "How dare you talk to me like that?" he gobbled, outraged. "You insolent young——" "Stand away!" he thundered. "or I won't be answerable for what I do to you!" "You're dismissed," he choked, purple with fury, "dismissed *as from this minute.*" Clenching his fists, he moved forward like a boxer. "Very well then," he hissed, "there's one satisfaction I'll have before I go—you bloated toad."

He jabbed a left to the body and followed it with a tremendous right uppercut. "Try that for size!" he panted.

"Edgar!" came a voice from beside him. "Edgar, what on earth's the matter?"

Slowly he lowered his fists and looked round, blinking like an owl in the day-time.

"The matter? Nothing," he said "I'm . . . all right . . . Catherine."

She caught him as he fell forward.

"Drink, as usual, I suppose," said Flannery. "So sordid, I always think."

Edgar stared up at them. He was lying on his bed, and they were talking in the doorway. Flannery was in his shirt-sleeves. How had he got here? What was Flannery doing here?

"I really hate to see a girl like you," Flannery went on, switching over to his oiliest tone of voice, "associating with a wreck like . . ."

His voice tailed off. Something in her eye must have stopped him.

"Just you leave him to sleep it off," he tried again, "and come down and have a drink with——"

"Thank you, but I'll stay here. I shall be quite all right. Thank you very much for your help, Mr. . . . ."

"Flannery's the name, Humbert Flannery. My friends call me Hum. Why don't——"

". . . for your help, Mr. Flannery, but everything will be all right."

"Banks won't know you've gone. He'll be asleep for hours."

Edgar opened his eyes and sat up. "Leave her alone," he said.

Flannery turned towards him, leering with mock sympathy. "Well, well, the sleeping beauty," he said. "What were you celebrating? How many did you have?"

"Goodnight, Mr. Flannery," said Catherine.

Flannery bowed to her, then turned to Edgar again. "I'll just leave you with a thought for to-night," he said. "It's just this: did you ever think you'd live to be carried upstairs by me?"

"No, I didn't."

Flannery bowed once more and went out.

"I didn't," Edgar said again.

Catherine came towards him.

"You'd better lie down again, Edgar. Did you know you fainted in the street? I'm sorry I had to get help from that awful man, but I did the only thing I could—I just held you up with one arm while I pressed all the bells in turn. And he was the only one who answered."

"I needn't lie down," said Edgar. He passed his hand over his forehead and eyes. Suddenly he felt quite well. "Let's go into the other room," he said, standing up.

They sat in armchairs, but almost immediately she stood up again with, "Wouldn't you like some coffee or tea or something? May I go into the kitchen and make——"

"So you do think I was drunk," he said.

"I do think what?"

"That I passed out because I was drunk. Flannery thought so, and I suppose it was inevitable that you should think so too, and offer to make me some coffee to sober me up. But Catherine," he said earnestly, leaning forward and taking her hand, "I wasn't. It—it wasn't that that made me . . ."

222

"I know it wasn't," she said. "What sort of a fool do you take me for?"

"No sort. But how did you know I wasn't drunk? I had been having a glass of beer, which would be quite enough to make me smell like a brewery, and after all it was a reasonable assumption that——"

"From your eyes."

"Uh?" he said, stupidly, the thread of the conversation slipping away from him.

"I saw your eyes when you caught sight of me. I knew what it it was that knocked you over."

"Shall I say it in words?" he asked.

"If you want to."

"Because I didn't expect to see you and because I love you."

"Coffee," she said. "Or tea? which would you rather?"

"There's not much milk. It'd better be tea. It's terribly kind of——"

"You'll have to let go of my hand first," she said: but she spoke gently, not brusquely, and one corner of her mouth wandered upwards a millimetre and the other downwards.

How could he have held her hand all that time without knowing that he was holding it? But then, the whole situation was full of mysteries, was entirely made up of mysteries. He sat staring in front of him while Catherine moved about in the kitchen. Why had she come here? Why, in any case, was she not still in Conasta? Why did he love her so much?

And where was Tom Straw?

He was still revolving these questions—or, more accurately, they were revolving him, for they seemed to twirl his mind aimlessly over and over on some kind of hub or axis—when Catherine came back with the tray. As she set it down, she glanced at his face, and he could see that she read his perplexity there. Straightening up, she stood looking at him with the clear skin of her forehead slightly puckered, and her lips parted as if she were on the verge of speech but could not find the necessary opening words. He felt her embarrassment and doubt as a tightening in his own chest.

"Please, Catherine, don't bother, "he said. "Whatever it is that you're thinking of saying, let it go for the time being. There's enough in the situation without filling it any more. You're here, and you came at a bad moment for me and made it a good moment, and now I just want to let it all exist—you'll only spoil it by starting to explain yourself."

"No, don't run away from it, Edgar," she said with an edge of determination in her unhurried voice. "You might manage to blink it for a few minutes, but you couldn't go on doing that. Of course you're surprised. You thought I was going to stay in Conasta with Tom for some days yet. And you thought that when you next saw us, and every time you saw us, we should be together."

"Whereas in fact?" he asked.

"Whereas in fact I came back yesterday by myself."

He drank from his cup, waiting.

"I didn't tell Tom. I just came home. Suddenly."

"You must have hated it, to do that," he said.

"Partly I hated it, yes. But partly—I just couldn't bear to see the way he'd suffer. When I told him I . . . couldn't go on with it."

Edgar drank from his cup again.

"I've been an awful coward, Edgar."

"Nonsense, you haven't. If you couldn't stand being with Tom any longer—and mind you, I'm as astonished to hear that as he could possibly be—well then, you were right to get away. Think of the frightful journey back, if you'd travelled together after telling him you weren't going to see him again. It would have been more than flesh and blood could stand. Though, mind you," he said again, "the simplest thing would have been to wait until you were safely back. After all, the trip wasn't going to last much longer, and then you could have——"

Catherine was shaking her head, not quickly, but with a determination that was all the more unmistakable because of her deliberation.

"If you knew—I couldn't have waited. It was getting . . . getting . . ."

"Well?" In his excitement, Edgar challenged her almost brutally. "What was it getting?"

She looked up at him with a heavy, tired movement of the head, and for the first time he saw clearly that her face was drawn and lined with fatigue.

"It was getting intolerable. Because—because logically I couldn't put off sleeping with him any longer."

224

"Oh—you——" Edgar jerked out "—hadn't been . . ."

"No, we hadn't been. Tom seemed to be all right without it, and as for me, I wanted to postpone crossing that particular Rubicon until I felt . . . right about it. For me it *is* a Rubicon—something tremendously important and——"

"You needn't explain," he said.

"Well," she went on after a moment, "somehow the longer I postponed it, the more I wanted to go on postponing it. You see, at first it seemed just the usual thing—one always has difficulties of adjustment to another person, little things that have to be arranged for each other's mutual comfort—and usually it takes some time before you even know whether you could be happy with them, even with a person who's terribly attractive to you . . . Why am I telling you all this?" she asked suddenly.

"If you must have an answer to that question, let's be satisfied with a simple obvious one. Because you need to talk to someone and tell them about it, and I'm as good as anybody."

"All right, we'll put it like that . . . anything as long as I can go on now that I've got started. Well, the time went by, and it looked like a fixture between Tom and me, and we were terribly attached to each other. And then . . . it was queer, but suddenly—I began to realize that I just couldn't take him. I loved him, but I just couldn't stand it."

Edgar poured out more tea, fitting himself snugly into his role of kindly old Uncle Edgar, the comforter. There might, he felt, be a more important role waiting for him if he made good in this one, but meanwhile he did not feel capable of planning his moves with the usual cold strategy of the male. He wanted simply to help her in any way he could.

"Do you feel like trying to make that clearer to me, Catherine? I mean, would it help you if you explained something of how you felt, in more detail?"

"Well, I think I *understand* it all right, myself," she said slowly, "but it's a bit difficult to explain it to another person without sounding like something out of a text-book of psychiatry. But—well—I always felt Tom was subtly forcing me to play an unnatural part. You know how capable and efficient he is: well, it frightens him, you know that too. You've seen how he pretends to be vague sometimes when it's obvious that he's in complete command of everything that's going on."

"Yes, bless him, and how terribly hard he tries to pass himself off as a failure because he hates his own success."

"Exactly. Well, you know, the sort of demands Tom makes on a woman—the sort of *needs* he has—are quite understandable, if one looks at it from that point of view, but . . . well . . ."

"But it takes a special kind of woman to supply them, and you're not that kind."

She looked at him and smiled easily; her tension and fatigue were going.

"Could you really see that at the time? Or are you just being wise in retrospect?"

"I could see it at the time," he said slowly, "only I wasn't in a position to be impartial and judging about other people's situations. I was too wrapped up in my own. And in any case I was trying to give the thing a twist that would be useful to me, so I never really tried to think about it straight. But I could see what Tom was up to. He was trying to get something that you didn't want to give him."

"I wasn't speaking of bed," she said.

"I wasn't either. He was asking you for something that most women have got plenty of and usually try to give whether the man wants it or not. He wanted to act as if he couldn't look after himself, and make you live up to that too, even though you knew he could look after himself and he knew you knew it and knew you knew he knew it."

"Keep on explaining," she said. "You're making it clearer every minute. How many knews does that add up to?"

They both smiled, but he persisted: "It adds up to as many as there are. And you know how many that is. Because you couldn't stand it although you loved him."

"Yes," she said so quietly that he hardly heard the words. "I loved him."

"I envied Tom," Edgar said half to himself. "I thought he had the secret of holding on to a girl like you. A man who had that secret would have nothing much to worry about."

"He'd have me to worry about," she protested.

"That's easy. Plenty of other people might worry about you without your knowing anything about it. They'd worry about not having you."

"That would be silly of them, wouldn't it?" she asked.

226

"Let them be silly if they want to," he said harshly.

The conversation halted. Edgar reached down the box of cigarettes and offered it to Catherine, but when she declined one he put it back unopened.

"Anyway," he said, "You've come home without Tom. In short, you've had all you can take and now it's finished."

"Yes. There it is. I've said it at last and got it off my chest. And the only thing I regret is that I walked out on Tom and left him to it, such a long way from home."

"Did you leave him a message—a letter or anything?"

She shook her head. "I just *couldn't* have explained it all. I couldn't even see it clearly enough myself. It was just pure panic— I ran away and that's all there is to it." She paused, then added, "I suppose he'll think I did it to avoid sleeping with him. Which would be true up to a point—but not the right point."

Edgar felt that the time had come for the situation to be helped forward, for some definite dividing-line to be crossed. Catherine had said her say, he had listened, and the danger was that they would reach a stalemate, with everything frozen up. And he didn't want that. What, then, did he want? Did he want death? Did he want revenge, sacrifice, oblivion, release?

He wanted Catherine.

She was the answer. Not this nonsense about killing and dying. Things would make sense, life would fall into a coherent pattern, if he had her. Sanity could be mirrored in her grey eyes, and nowhere else.

"Why did you come to see me?" he asked.

"To tell you."

"You knew I'd be interested?"

She looked at him almost defiantly. A strand of hair had come loose and fallen over her forehead. He wanted to smooth it back, and then ruffle the rest of her hair so that it would look untidier than before.

"I didn't care whether you'd be interested or not. I just wanted to tell you."

"But you did know I'd be interested: didn't you?"

She said nothing.

"I've just realized something," he said. "I could be all right if I had you."

"I could be all right if I had you, too," she said.

As if he had not heard her, he went on: "And it wouldn't be possible any other way. Making me all right, I mean. There was such a lot that wasn't all right."

"Yes, I could see."

"Everything," he said.

"Tell me about it," she asked him.

"I was going to kill myself. And another person too."

"Someone who'd done something to you?"

"Not to me particularly. Just someone who ought to die."

She smoothed the strand of hair without waiting for his assistance.

"It sounds silly," she said.

"Yes, doesn't it?" He paused. "It more than sounds silly, it *is* silly."

"So I should have thought," she said. "D'you feel like explaining about it?"

He pondered. "It all seems a long time ago. I doubt if I could still remember what it felt like."

"Still, you could try explaining."

"I could try explaining," he said thoughtfully, "or I could put my arms round you. I could do one of those two things, but not both."

Looking up at her, he half expected to see one corner of her mouth a millimetre higher than the other. But she was staring at him almost grimly, almost fiercely.

"You're sure you couldn't do both at once?"

"Positive."

"Then you'd better not bother to explain," she said, and came over to where he sat.

XII

THE next morning, Edgar woke up with the feeling that something was wrong. His sleep had been blissful and dreamless; after Catherine had gone, he had undressed and got into bed in a state of pure tranquillity. But now, like a man who has an appointment with the dentist, he felt in his bones, before arriving at consciousness, that something unpleasant was in store. Rolling over on to his back, he searched for definition.

Of course. Tom.

Getting Tom to hate him, so as to leave the way absolutely clear for suicide, had been a clever idea—once. Now that the context for that idea had been blotted out, it seemed merely squalid. He loved Catherine and was loved by her. All was perfection and light, it was the dawn of creation, it was Paradise. But there was the snake, coiled waiting round its tree. His betrayal of Tom. The man who, by his example, had started the right seed growing in the first place; the man who had appeared on the scene when he had been sunk in wretched folly and confusion, and had begun to lead him towards sanity—and this was his thanks. To steal his girl. For a moment Edgar allowed himself to imagine how he himself would feel if anyone took Catherine away from him now. It was not, strictly speaking, imaginable at all, of course: she never would, she never could, nobody would dare. But if someone even tried . . . It would be a case for murder, a genuine one this time, and not a mere figment of a disordered psyche like the Philipson-Smith case. Philipson-Smith! At the thought of the man Edgar gave a great hoot of laughter. Then he got out of bed and put the kettle on.

But the Tom business was really serious. He was in a mess, not the less squalid because it was the one dirty spot in a clean, new

229

landscape. Putting on his dressing-gown, he went into the sitting-room and sat down to consider.

The telephone rang.

"I'm at work, I can't talk for long," said Catherine.

"At *work*? Why, whatever time is it?"

"Nearly ten, darling."

For several minutes they discussed the state of their feelings towards each other. Then she said again, "I can't talk for long."

"But I haven't nearly finished telling you——"

"No, but listen, Edgar. Something dreadful."

His stomach contracted. "Don't tell me. Something about Tom."

"He's sent a telegram. *Coming home now*, it says."

"What else?"

"That's all."

His kettle began to whistle, as if in derision.

"I don't know what to do," she said.

"Well, don't do anything. After all, you did nothing but what you had to do. I ought to be the one to deal with Tom. If he wants to discuss it with anybody, let him discuss it with me."

"Yes, Mr. Wilson," she said.

"Mr. What?"

"I've got to ring off. Good-bye for now. See you to-night."

"Right."

Edgar made some tea, poured out a cup and began to drink it. The prospect of meeting Tom Straw seemed to form a road-block across the immediate future. He had all sorts of things to do to-day; think about Catherine, start looking for work, buy food and other things for the flat, think about Catherine, try to get some of his property back from Flannery, go to the bank, write some letters, and think about Catherine. It was the first day of his real life, and yet he could do nothing. What was he to say to Tom? What was Tom going to think?

While he was shaving, it struck him that this sort of thing represented the complete success of his scheme to get Tom to dislike him. To have been the apparent cause of Catherine's sudden desertion of Tom and her return to London—it would have been far beyond his rosiest dreams as the perfect method of arousing the man's loathing. He sneered ironically at his reflection in the mirror.

The sense of betrayal followed him about all morning, spoilt his lunch, and dogged him back to the flat. He sat there in a stupor until, towards four o'clock, the telephone rang.

"This is it," he said to himself, going over to answer it. "This is Tom."

Normally this would have been the cue for some absurdity, such as a voice demanding why four thousand mixed nails had not been delivered at his address as promised, or a burst of oafish laughter from some stockbroker who, a moment before, had been talking to a colleague on an internal line. But normality was dispelled; or perhaps it was merely that Edgar's life had become related to a different and more valid norm.

He had expected it to be Tom, and it was.

"I need to talk to you," Tom said when he had established that it was Edgar he was addressing. "Can I come round straight away?"

"Of course. Is it anything important? Have you been back long?"

"Twenty minutes."

"Good gracious," said Edgar feebly. "Then it must be something very . . ."

"I'll be round as soon as I can. You might have a drink lined up for me if you've got any handy. And some good strong coffee. You'll just have time to make it before I get there."

"Don't organize me."

"I'm not organizing you, I'm organizing my coffee and my drink. I need them badly."

"Come round," said Edgar, and rang off.

While waiting for Tom to arrive he made a large pot of strong coffee and put a small bottle of sherry, the only alcoholic drink he had in the house, in readiness on the tray. With his hands occupied in this task, he hoped that his brain might be free to compose some suitable defence against the storm of reproaches he would soon be greeted with.

By the time the bell rang and he went down to open the door, he had got as far as, "It was like this, Tom. Catherine's a sensitive girl."

"Come along up," he said.

Tom looked untidy; his eyes were pouchy and he had not shaved that morning. He was silent as they climbed the three flights of stairs.

231

Once inside Edgar's flat, with the door shut behind them and Tom's coat over the back of a chair, they faced each other.

"Well?" Edgar asked.

"I came to ask you if you know anything about Catherine."

"If I know what in particular about her?"

"In particular, where she is and what she's doing."

"She's in London," Edgar said flatly, "and I don't know what she's doing at this moment, but to-night she's coming here."

"Coming here? To see you?"

"Nobody else lives here."

Tom Straw sat down and poured himself a cup of coffee. Then he poured out a small glass of the sherry, sniffed it critically, and, after an instant's hesitation, poured it into the coffee. This he drank.

"Well," he said contentedly, setting down his cup, "thank God everything's turned out all right."

"All *right*?"

Tom Straw looked up, holding Edgar's eyes steadily. One square hand moved backwards and forwards across his jaw.

"You and Catherine have cottoned on to each other, haven't you?"

"Yes, Tom."

"Well, that's what I mean. Everything's all right."

Edgar took a gulp of his sherry. "I suppose you're just being ironical," he said.

"Ironical? Why should I be? If you and Catherine are getting on fine, then she's happy. Right?"

"I suppose so."

"Well then, that lets me out."

Edgar laughed weakly. "Things sometimes get a bit fast for me to follow," he said, pouring out more sherry. "I thought for a minute you said 'that lets me out'." He laughed again and poured sherry for Tom, tilting the bottle recklessly so that some of the contents poured on to the tray. "Damn," he said and laughed weakly again.

"That's what I did say," said Tom Straw stolidly. He lifted his glass and drank. "I can see you're surprised," he said.

"Not at all. It's perfectly natural. When you've been drifting about Europe with a beautiful girl, the two of you obviously very devoted to each other, and then she whisks away suddenly and attaches herself to another man—well, what is there to get excited about?"

"Oh, I see," said Tom Straw. "Sarcasm. Irony. But you don't quite understand the position, Edgar."

"Well, if you do, what about lowering me a rope?"

Tom Straw produced from his pocket a cigarette-packet that appeared to have been run over by a train. As far as the naked eye could perceive, it was absolutely flat. This, however, must have been an illusion; for, as Edgar watched, he produced from it, like a conjuror, a perfectly round and fresh-looking cigarette. This he lit and began to inhale earnestly.

"Well, the fact is that I was in a damned awkward position. I don't know whether you've ever had the experience of starting off with some woman who seems absolutely ideal, and everything going on like an oil-well on fire for a long time, and then suddenly finding it beginning to fold up?"

"No. I needn't even go beyond the first sentence of that. I've never had the experience of starting off with a woman who seemed absolutely ideal. Except—until last night."

"Oh, well, we'll leave that out of it," said Tom Straw. "It's a little early to start talking about what's going to happen between you and Catherine."

"No, it isn't. I'm going to hold on to her for the rest of my life."

"You mean you're going to marry her?"

"If she'll have me, yes."

"Well," said Straw, "stack me sideways."

"I don't see what's funny about it."

"Well, perhaps I don't either," said Straw, looking pensively across at him. "Probably you two would make a very good pair." He paused.

"Well, if I don't seem impatient," said Edgar, "I'm still waiting to hear why you and Catherine didn't make a good pair."

"It's a bit difficult to explain, really," Straw began slowly.

"Without sounding like something out of a text-book of psychiatry, you mean?"

"That's about it. But you know, I felt . . . well, it would have been awfully hard to explain this to Catherine without hurting her feelings, but . . ."

"Oh, come on!" Edgar almost shouted. "Cough it up in papa's hand!"

233

"Well, it began to seem to me as if she were forcing me—subtly, and little by little—into a false position."

"Playing a false role, you mean?"

"I suppose so. I suppose you've noticed that I'm a reasonably self-sufficient kind of person? I mean, I generally know when the train's due to leave, and what platform it is, and where I've put my ticket, and that sort of thing."

"It hadn't escaped me."

Tom Straw laughed shortly. "No, and it didn't escape Catherine, either. You know, it's my belief that women don't really like too much of that. Some of them do, of course, the clinging type who want you to shelter them. But most of them like a man all the better if he's a bit vague about things. They like to feel that the Almighty gave them a corner in common sense."

"Well, didn't He?"

Straw leaned forward. "Not on your life, Edgar. That's just a yarn they put out. It's all bullshit."

"Well, go on about you and Catherine."

"Yes, it's pretty important to you, isn't it? Well, damme if she didn't start trying to manage me. Always coming out with the time of the next train before I did. Stepping in. Doing the responsible-woman stuff and even, at times, the you-silly-old-clever-darling stuff."

"Oh, nonsense, Tom. I was watching you and I never saw her doing that. If you ask me, you——"

"If I ask you, I what?"

Edgar thought for a moment. "Nothing," he said.

"It began to get quite oppressive," Tom Straw went on. His unshaven cheeks shone dully with perspiration. "Of course, it may have been because I didn't sleep with her. You'll pardon my mentioning that in front of you, but I had the feeling she was getting impatient."

"Oh, yes?"

"In fact I was wondering how to avoid coming to the point when we were in Conasta."

"It must have been quite a relief," said Edgar, "when you found she'd scarpered."

"Well, to tell you the truth it was. Hell, I know you don't mind my putting it frankly, like this," he smiled across at Edgar with all the old honesty and kindliness. "What I mean is, you can

234

talk to a man about a woman in a way you can't . . . Of course, if you're in love with her you must think I'm absolutely crazy."

"I do."

"Well, I can't give you the *tu quoque*. I don't think you're crazy. In my opinion, Catherine's only got to find the right man, the man who really suits her, and she'll be——"

"I don't need you to tell me about it."

They smiled at each other.

"All right, you opinionated bastard. You'll find out all about her soon enough."

"Don't talk as if you'd sold me a car."

"It's not such a bad parallel at that. Run her in carefully, won't you?"

"I hope to do better than you did."

For a moment it almost looked as if an expression of pain had flickered across Tom Straw's face. Edgar, suddenly contrite, leaned towards him.

"I'm sorry, Tom."

"That hurt."

"God knows I'm sorry, chum."

Tom Straw shook his head. "Don't give it another thought. It was me that started all the silly joking. And I'm quite sincere about its being a relief to me. I really did want to get out of that situation, and I was only worrying about doing it without hurting Catherine. That's where you did me such a wonderful good turn, you know."

"Oh," said Edgar, staring at his glass. "I didn't do much."

"I don't know so much. Of course, you were keeping it in check. I could see, you know, all the time we were at Conasta, that you were very drawn towards Catherine."

"Could you?"

"Yes. You didn't want it to appear, because she was mine and you didn't want to walk on the grass. But it was pretty obvious. Of course, women can always tell these things, you know."

"I suppose so."

"But in this case, I could see it myself. In fact, come to think of it," he began to laugh, "the only person to whom it wasn't as obvious as daylight was yourself."

Edgar laughed with him.

"That's funny."

"It's damned funny," Straw cried.

"It's bloody funny."

They laughed for a long time, then wiped their eyes.

"Well," said Tom Straw, standing up, "I'll have to blow. I need a wash and change. We'll be seeing each other about, shan't we?"

"Of course. Often."

"Well, make it soon. And if Catherine says she'll feel embarrassed at having me about, tell her not to be a fool."

"She isn't a fool."

"All right, all right," Straw said, and grinned. "Come to think of it, I don't believe any of us are fools, do you?"

Edgar considered this, but briefly.

"Not now," he said.

Tom Straw nodded several times. With one hand on the door-knob, he stood for a moment nodding his head slowly, as if summing up the situation in his mind. Finally he raised his eyes to Edgar's, at the same time opening the door.

"Well, cut me into lengths," he said, "and stack me sideways."

"All right," Edgar answered.

Tom Straw nodded again and went out.

Catherine would be round in about an hour and a half. He tidied the flat, went out and bought something for them to cook for dinner, and sat down to wait it out. The time went by slowly but deliciously. Waiting, he discovered, is all right when there is something to wait for. He wandered over to his bookshelf and began pulling out books and reading snatches here and there. How wonderfully interesting they all seemed: full of comments on this marvellous new invention, human life. Even where the writer didn't seem to be getting much out of human life, he was always interested in analysing the things that came his way. There was none of this shallow talk of walking out and leaving it all; or, if a character did talk in this strain, you were usually given to understand pretty clearly that he was off his trolley. Like Hamlet. Like himself up to a couple of evenings ago.

The bell rang. Edgar bounded down the three flights of stairs, unable to wait one unnecessary second till he could fling the door open and see her standing there.

She was standing there. So was Stimms.

236

They stared at each other, with Catherine looking from face to face.

"Ah, Banks," Stimms began. "Banks," he added.

"I found, ah, this young lady ringing your bell," he began again.

"She was expected," said Edgar crisply. Catherine was looking pathetically bewildered, so he turned to her and explained, "This is my former employer. Miss Whitmore—Mr. Stimms."

Catherine looked at Stimms as if the fact of his being Edgar's former employer made him interesting to her, and even gave him the right to sympathetic consideration. "How do you do?" she asked. "Was it something important you wanted to see Edgar about? Because if so, I could . . ."

"You could what?" Edgar asked her. He could feel himself slowly turning purple with annoyance. Had he not, over the years, had enough to put up with from Stimms?

"Well, if it's something professional," Catherine said and hesitated. "I could go into the kitchen and be making some soup or something, while you . . ."

That was helpful. Now Stimms was certain to think she was his mistress. It was the Phyllis story all over again, only this time it didn't matter.

"Miss Whitmore is my fiancée," he said to Stimms.

"But you haven't even proposed yet," she put in.

"I'm proposing now. Mr. Stimms doesn't mind. It's probably not the first proposal he's witnessed."

"I assure you it is, Banks, I assure you it is," said Stimms in a tone which Edgar had never heard him use before; rather embarrassed, but kittenish at the same time. "Except at the cinema, of course, on the, ah, screen," he added, making himself clear. He looked carefully at Catherine, as if considering making her a proposal himself.

"Oh, for goodness' sake, Edgar, ask us *up*!" Catherine suddenly cried plaintively.

"Yes, do come up," said Edgar to both of them. He held the door open.

"Well, really, Banks," said Stimms. He seemed nonplussed. "I—er—I hardly know whether Miss Whitmore's business and mine, ah, can be, er, satisfactorily mixed."

"Why, Mr. Stimms? What was yours?" Edgar asked him. It was an entirely rhetorical question; he knew that Stimms could

237

have only one motive in coming round to see him after getting wind that he was back. He had intended, perhaps still did intend, to reinforce his note of dismissal with a little bullying. He had doubtless seen it as his duty to bring home to Edgar the baseness of his conduct in walking out of the job and leaving it open to any whippersnapper who was ready with his fists.

"What was mine?" Stimms asked in his turn. For a moment his face stiffened into the kind of Emil Jannings look which he wore when sitting behind his desk. Then he glanced sideways at Catherine. She was giving him both barrels of her grey-eyed look. His face began to lose its outlines like a pat of butter on a heated plate.

"Won't you come up, anyway, and just make it a social call?" she asked him. Edgar looked at her in surprise. Surely the moment had come for Stimms to be dismissed so as to let the evening begin. But after all, as he had told Tom Straw not long before, Catherine was not a fool.

Stimms wavered. "Come up . . ." he pondered aloud.

"Yes, come and have a drink with us," Catherine pressed him. "It isn't every day I get proposed to."

"I can't think why not," Stimms said half to himself, passing into the house. Edgar turned and met Catherine's eyes, without attempting to wipe off his own expression of bewilderment. He had never heard Stimms say anything so human and natural before. Perhaps he never had.

Stimms went ahead of them up the stairs. Catherine halted beside Edgar on the mat.

"Don't kiss me," she whispered. "He might turn round."

Edgar kissed her several times.

"You've got to marry me," he said.

"I'll think about it."

"No. You've got to do it without thinking about it."

She drew herself away. "I must think about it. I'll think about it till we get to the top of the stairs and then tell you."

"Which floor is it, Banks?" came the voice of Stimms. He had turned a corner and was invisible to them.

"Straight up," Edgar called. "We're behind you. Only till you get to the top of the stairs, mind," he said to Catherine.

She smiled at him, and for a moment he had to lean against the wall. Then they began to climb.

238

Stimms was waiting for them outside the door of Edgar's flat. His face seemed to be making intermittent efforts to re-form itself into its headmasterly expression, but once more he caught Catherine's glance and the stiff severity was wiped off. This time, as if to make quite sure of the effect, she had lowered one corner of her mouth by a millimetre and raised the other the same distance. Was she vamping him? Edgar wondered. Then, as he followed her through the door, he realized that she simply couldn't help looking like that. Whether it was Stimms she was looking at, or the gas-meter man, or the Inland Revenue man, or a policeman in the street, or Stimms, or even another woman, she just had to look like that—she was happy. In the same moment he knew the answer to his question.

"Is it yes?" he asked her, openly, crudely, in front of Stimms.

"Yes," she said.

"Sit down, Stimms!" Edgar shouted. "Make yourself at home! What will you drink, sherry or sherry? There's nothing but sherry, but I can recommend the sherry."

"Ah, not, perhaps, a difficult problem," said Stimms weightily. "In view of everything, perhaps, ah, a little sherry." He seemed happy, and to have grown younger and more humanly accessible.

"Here it comes," Edgar burbled. He sloshed liquid into the three glasses. "Now. Join us in a toast. I don't care what you came round for—I'm sure it was something unpleasant—but now you'll join us in a toast, won't you?"

"I hope," said Stimms as he raised his glass, "that you and this young lady will marry and that you will be happy throughout your life together."

The door opened and Flannery came in.

"Could I borrow——" he began, then looked at Catherine in what seemed to be unfeigned astonishment. "So you really came back for more?" he asked her.

"More what?" Edgar asked roughly.

"Came back a second time," Flannery corrected himself. Then he noticed Stimms. "You're having a party," he said almost accusingly.

"Not exactly," said Edgar. "Miss Whitmore and I have just become engaged. Mr. Stimms here obligingly acted as a witness to make it more difficult for her to go back on it."

"I'm sure she won't go back on it," said Flannery with his

satyr's smile. At first it seemed that his intention was to insult Catherine by implying that she looked silly enough to go ahead with marriage to a wreck like Edgar. But, as he held the smile, it seemed to grow more genuine. Something in the atmosphere seemed to be working on him. Edgar did not know what this something was, but he knew that Catherine had put it there, and that he and Stimms had both begun to add to it in their smaller ways. Now even Flannery seemed to be adding to it. He gave a great leer of *bonhomie*.

"I came up to ask for the loan of a few glasses," he said. "But while I'm here, as this is a special occasion, why don't you all come down and join my guests?"

"Ah, really, I must be," Stimms began, but Catherine turned the grey-eyed look on him again, backing it up verbally with "Now really, Mr. Stimms, you can't leave us just yet."

"Have you a telephone?" Stimms asked, glancing round with the grasp of significant detail that had put him where he was.

Edgar, in spite of his efforts to repress it, gave a loud snigger as it occurred to him that Stimms had good enough evidence on that point. Just in time he merged the snigger into a furious spasm of coughing.

"He's got one unless the Post Office have cut it off for non-payment of the bill," said Flannery, taking charge of Stimms as if, for some reason, he particularly wished to have him at the party. "Ah, yes, here it is."

"I'll just ring my," said Stimms, "ah, wife. I'll tell her I shall be a trifle later than usual."

"Tell her to come over," Flannery suggested.

"Don't be ridiculous," said Stimm's glance, but his voice remained silent. It was astonishing to see how tolerant and polite everyone was becoming. He dialled and spoke his message crisply.

"Well, come on," said Flannery. "Bring the glasses, of course,"

"And the records?" Edgar could not resist adding.

Flannery looked slightly embarrassed, but roguish at the same time.

"Well, I've more or less got most of those, haven't I? The best ones, anyway. I must have forgotten to . . ."

"Never mind," said Edgar largely. "We'd have had to take them down anyway."

They trooped downstairs, carrying glasses in their hands.

240

Stimms looked like a butler; or rather, Edgar suddenly realized, some kindly old uncle playing the part of a butler in a charade.

"Well, come along!" Flannery cried as he threw open the door. The room was already fairly thick with smoke and chatter, though his guests had probably not all arrived. "I don't know whether you know everybody here, but you can circulate and introduce yourselves."

"Ah, Benton," said Stimms in a voice which attempted a reversion to his Emil Jannings manner, but not successfully.

Edgar, following his glance, saw Benton and Phyllis standing together in a corner. It was a difficult moment: Benton was staring at Stimms as if utterly unnerved, but he was scarcely less so than the headmaster. They were like a curate and a bishop meeting in a disorderly house.

Before Edgar could do anything to break the tension, Phyllis moved forward.

"Oh, do introduce me, Roy," she said to Benton. Her voice seemed to have gone huskier since Edgar had last heard it. She walked forward swaying like a charmed python.

"Oh, Phyllis, come over here a minute," said Edgar suddenly. "I want to speak to you." He caught her arm and dragged her over into a corner, nervously aware of Catherine's eyes on the back of his neck.

"You might have some *manners*," she was beginning in an indignant undertone, but he cut in urgently with, "Look, Phyllis, do something for me. Do something nice for me. You will, won't you?"

"What is it?" she asked curiously.

"Just this. Don't queer that kid up with his headmaster. That grey-haired trout is the Head. And the boy hasn't left school yet and probably depends a good deal on the old man's opinion."

"Do you mean," she asked, drawing herself up into an attitude of offended respectability, "that his headmaster's opinion of him is likely to go down just because he sees that he's a friend of mine?"

"Well, isn't it?" Edgar asked simply. She was wearing leopard-skin trousers and a pair of ear-rings that could have done duty on the front axle of a Ferrari. Her low-cut blouse revealed a cleft between her breasts big enough to hold a bundle of firewood.

For a moment he thought he had been too tactless this time.

241

It seemed that she would turn on her heel, go over to where Benton stood talking to Stimms, and start an act that could only lead to a telephone message for the Fire Brigade.

Then, unexpectedly, Phyllis softened. "Oh, dear, I suppose I see what you mean, Edgar," she sighed. "Oh, dear, I am an awful old bag, aren't I?"

"You needn't be," he assured her warmly. "You're easy enough on the eye to get along without all the props."

She shook her head. "You don't understand," she said owlishly; she had been drinking fast already. "When a girl gets to my age, it's *femme fatale* or nothing."

"Nonsense," Edgar shouted jovially, so that several people turned and looked at him curiously. He went on in a lower tone: "Just wipe the Unconditional Surrender from behind your ears and go back to the demure act. You were such a success at it."

"It's not Unconditional Surrender," she said. "It's Scandal in Montmartre."

"Well, I don't care if it's Sit-Down Strike at Covent Garden," said Edgar, talking fast to get through this and go back to Catherine. "Just do this one thing for me. Make a bid for somebody else, and let the old man see you do it. Not me," he added hastily.

"Well, who then?"

Edgar looked round wildly. Catherine was standing by herself, holding an empty glass. Her face was beginning to wear the expression it had probably worn as she walked away from him up the village street on the afternoon of their excursion. Unless he hurried, she would be walking away again.

"Well, I don't care who," he said. "It won't do the lad any harm. It'll shake him—make him stop taking you for granted."

"He *doesn't* take me for granted," she insisted.

Edgar passed his hand over his brow. "Look," he said. "Watch that door, and the first man who comes through it, give him the treatment."

"That's the *bedroom* door you're pointing at," she giggled, loudly enough for several people to turn round again and look at Edgar for a long time.

"Well, damn it, the *other* door," Edgar grated in desperation. "The first man to——"

As he spoke the door opened and three men came in. The

242

second and third were Philipson-Smith and McWhirtner. The first was Francis Jollet.

Phyllis walked straight over to Jollet without even waiting to be introduced.

"You're a brick," Edgar hissed at her retreating back. He went over to Catherine.

"I heard that," she said. "Why is she a brick?"

"Look, don't worry," he said earnestly. "I was just averting a dangerous situation. Really, it's all right, honestly, darling, it's all right—I tell you it's all right. It's all——"

"I take your point," she said. "It's all right."

"Look, honestly," Edgar began hoarsely, "I can't explain just now, but I do assure——"

He stopped. She was laughing at him. For a moment they giggled, silently, then gave each other the first of a series of long looks.

In the middle of one of these, Philipson-Smith came up to Edgar.

"It was you I came to see," he said sternly.

"Why, what have I done wrong?" Edgar asked.

"Don't be flippant. I wanted to see you and then we found your place empty and heard voices, so we came to see if you were down here."

"Quite right," said Edgar amiably. "I'm down here."

"I can see that. Do try to behave reasonably for just one moment. After all, this is a pretty big occasion for you."

Edgar was startled. "You know that, do you?"

"Know it? Of course I know it. It's *you* who doesn't know it yet."

They stared at each other.

"You *can't* know it," Philipson-Smith insisted. "I haven't told you yet."

"Well," said Edgar wearily, "tell me."

"That's just what I'm going to do. If you'll kindly give me one second." Philipson-Smith paused impressively. "It's about that job. I've fixed it for you."

"Job?"

"Oh, for heaven's sake, man," Philipson-Smith cried. "The job you followed me all over Europe trying to get. With the Movement!"

243

Before Edgar could answer, Flannery had come up and was standing beside Philipson-Smith. The expression on his face made Edgar decide to postpone less important business and let the host do the talking.

"You told me you thought I'd recognize you when I saw you again," Flannery said into Philipson-Smith's ear.

"A reasonable prediction, if I remember," said Philipson-Smith coolly. He began to turn away, but Flannery put out a large, plump hand and gripped his shoulder. The hand, in spite of its plumpness, must have been surprisingly strong, for Philipson-Smith's turning movement was decisively arrested and he was jerked back with his face staring into Flannery's.

"I remember something else about you, too, besides your identity," Flannery purred. "Some remarks on the subject of my racial antecedents."

"I never said anything about that," retorted Philipson-Smith uneasily, flushing dully and trying to jerk his shoulder free. "It was my companion who——"

"It was your companion who actually voiced the sentiment. And it was yourself who sat by and gave us all to understand how fully you agreed with him."

"Just let go of my shoulder," Philipson-Smith said sharply.

"And now you walk into my flat as if it were the waiting-room at a station. Just the way you're hoping to do when your party comes to power, isn't it?"

McWhirtner lunged over from the other side of the room. "Tek yir hands off him," he shrilled.

The blood began to mount in Edgar's head. This moment of drama had been a long time coming; partly because the right instrument of chastisement had not been ready. He had seen himself as the instrument of chastisement, but that had been a mistake: he had been too confused, too self-centred and self-pitying. And now the jigsaw was filled in. Flannery was the instrument of chastisement.

He grasped McWhirtner by the elbow before he could interfere. The other guests had still not moved, except to swivel their heads. It was all too sudden.

"Since you make it so clear that I'm not welcome in your flat," said Philipson-Smith with an attempt at haughty politeness, "I'll leave it."

244

Flannery put out the other hand. Now he was holding Philipson-Smith by both shoulders. He was the shorter of the two, but his body, normally flabby-looking, seemed suddenly to have become squat and powerful.

"You'll leave my flat," he said, "when I've given you a message to take to your friends. The people who run the group you belong to."

"I'm not an errand-boy. And I don't carry messages."

"You'll carry *this* message," said Flannery. Releasing Philipson-Smith's left shoulder, he swung his right hand first backward, then forward. The sound of the two slaps rang out like rifle-shots. As Philipson-Smith staggered, his face, under its dark smear of stubble, was suddenly marked with two angry patches of dull red.

Flannery, absolutely silent, stood looking at him. Edgar gripped McWhirtner's arm convulsively. Surely, now, it would come to a fight: fists, chairs, bottles, everything would be thrown in. In that case he must get Catherine into a corner and stand in front of her.

But he had, as so often before, misjudged Philipson-Smith's mind. The man was not a physical coward, afraid of putting up his fists. He was, on the other hand, a moral coward. The atmosphere was against him: there was a crowd present, but it was not behind him; Flannery was the host, on his own ground, and he had the moral initiative. Even so, things might have been different with McWhirtner playing his proper rôle. But Edgar was standing guard over him. Swerving aside from Flannery's steady gaze, Philipson-Smith turned his eyes on Edgar with a maniac blaze of hatred.

"This is the end of your chances with us, Banks."

"Something tells me you're right," Edgar smiled.

Baffled by the situation, Philipson-Smith twisted his head swiftly this way and that, staring into Flannery's face, into Edgar's, into Catherine's. Then, suddenly, he turned on his heel. The path was clear to the door.

As he went out, Edgar released McWhirtner's arm. Flannery swung round to face his second adversary.

"Are you going to take a message too?" he asked in his silkiest voice.

"Oh, no," Edgar interrupted in mock terror. "Don't start anything with him. He might retaliate."

"Retaliate?"

"He might read us some of his poems."

In the background Benton gave a wild snigger.

"Ay, laff," McWhirtner said. "Ye'll laff on the ither side o' yir face when——"

"When your epic gets published," Edgar put in. "Go and write another canto."

"Yes," said Flannery. "Call it, 'The Night the Worm Turned'."

"A'll write wha' A bluidy well please," McWhirtner said sullenly. He walked to the door, stumbling, but with his back straight. After all, he had, in this moment, more dignity than his master.

They had gone. Flannery walked over to the gramophone and put on Edgar's record of Fats Waller playing 'Short'ning Bread.'

Edgar, a slow smile of relief breaking over his face, turned towards Catherine. Before he could say anything, however, he was sent stumbling forward by a violent thrust between the shoulder-blades. "Sorry!" carolled a voice: it was Phyllis, who had seized Francis Jollet in a hungrily powerful grip and was whirling him round the centre of the room. "That's the way!" she was shouting. "Nothing like a good dance to loosen you up!" The other guests stood back nervously; among them, Edgar saw Benton, staring at Phyllis in a way that did nothing to convey that he hoped she was enjoying herself.

This opportunity must not be lost. Strolling across to the boy, he stood at his shoulder. Benton did not see him; his hands thrust tautly into his jacket pockets, he was staring angrily at Phyllis, who had now laid her cheek against Jollet's and backed him into a corner. Always pliable, Jollet had yielded himself momentarily to the rhythm of the dance and the urgency of her presence, and showed every sign of enjoying it.

"What's the matter, son?" Edgar asked, his voice cutting into Benton's angry trance. "Is this the first time a woman's left you standing while she treads a measure with someone else?"

Benton coloured. The whole situation was crammed with embarrassment for him; he could not forget, as easily as Edgar could, that Phyllis had once been Edgar's girl. "I . . . it's . . ." he brought out, then stiffened into silence.

"I understand you," said Edgar, nodding easily, like an uncle. "It's not just being left standing. It's the thought of being left standing for the sake of a human polecat like that, isn't it?"

Benton must have driven his teeth sharply together, for the muscles at the sides of his lower jaw stood out suddenly. "If it had been anyone else——" he snapped.

"Listen," Edgar rumbled sagely, feeling himself more and more wrapped up in his part as the benevolent uncle, a pure piece of type-casting, "if it had been anyone else, no matter who else, the effect wouldn't have been any different. Not in the long run. She's . . . she's like that."

Benton swung sharply round to face him. "You really think I ought to break away from her ?" he asked excitedly.

"Ah, Benton," said Stimms again, coming up behind his right shoulder. But already Edgar felt he detected a little more warmth in the headmaster's voice: the sight of Phyllis straining Jollet to her bosom had evidently made him feel he had wronged Benton in supposing the boy to be mixed up with her. "Just be good enough, my dear fellow, to excuse us a moment," he went on, laying his hand paternally on Benton's shoulder. "I, ah, have a word to say to our friend," he looked meditatively at Edgar, then repeated the word firmly, "our friend Banks here."

Benton glided away, and Edgar found himself staring defensively into Stimm's protruding eyes. Our what? Our *what* Banks here?

"Banks," said Stimms. Again he looked at Edgar meditatively, "I evidently, ah, evidently find you in—shall we say, hem, erm, altered personal, mmm, circumstances." He seemed to be finding difficulty in expressing himself; where, of old, the punctuation of his discourse with 'ah' and other sounds had been obviously rhetorical, it now took on a quality of genuine hesitancy.

"Let me get you a drink," Edgar said swiftly. He dived over to a table, came back with two glasses of something alcoholic, and handed one to Stimms. He was finding some likeable qualities in the man; of course, it took Catherine to bring them out fully, but even without her, there were moments when Stimms seemed able to manage an approach to the human. Of course, it was because the relationship between them had changed. He no longer depended on Stimms for anything.

"I was going, armm, to ask you if, ah, considering, in view of your approaching, your impending, imminent," Stimms went on, slowly. "Your approaching nuptials," he brought out, eyeing Edgar narrowly. "I was going to have asked whether you had found any new, any, ah, any new post. Employment," he added to drive his point home.

"At the moment, as it happens, I'm quite free," said Edgar lightly. "I haven't exactly made any concrete . . ." he stopped. Stimm's hesitation was catching. Besides, the conversation had forced his mind to turn towards a subject he did not want to bother with on this golden evening. He supposed he had about five pounds left in the bank; it might even be ten; therefore why give it a thought—until, at the earliest, to-morrow morning.

Stimms suddenly lowered his eyes and scowled fiercely. Raising his glass, he drained it like a methylated-spirit drinker, avidly and guiltily. Suddenly he barked in a harsh, rapid monotone "No objection taking you back byegones be byegones, always found your work satisfactory."

"But I——" Edgar began. He had been going to say, "I don't want to come back," but the muscles of his throat tightened and closed over the words. *Didn't* he? He caught sight of Catherine, on the other side of the room, smiling as she made some remark to another girl. "I don't—I don't know whether Miss Whitmore— I haven't asked her whether she'd want to be a schoolmaster's wife," he stammered.

"Rubbish!" Stimms barked. "Wants to be *your* wife, doesn't she? *You're* a schoolmaster, aren't you?"

Edgar looked at him. "Am I?" he asked simply.

Stimms turned away. His embarrassment must have been considerable; this was the first wave of genuine human feeling that had broken over him for forty years. "You're a schoolmaster. From Monday," he snarled over his shoulder. "See me in my office to-morrow morning. Fix the details. Settle on an explanation of your absence. Think up a good story."

"A good story, yes," Edgar said weakly, feeling light-headed. He had a job, a salary, a place again: he *did* something for a living. What do you do? I'm a schoolmaster: 1679 Habeas Corpus Act passed, get in line there, no talking, I said *no* talking. What fun it would be! "A good story," he repeated.

"Make it a good one," said Stimms brusquely. He stalked away, and Edgar watched him go over to Flannery and say something, evidently in valediction, for he walked out of the door and vanished.

Edgar walked across to Catherine and, taking her arm, led her into a corner.

"Do you want to be a schoolmaster's wife?" he demanded.

"What schoolmaster?" she countered suspiciously.

"Well, suppose it was me? Suppose I was one?"

She looked at him wide-eyed. "Edgar! Was it—did that funny old Mr. What's-his-name——"

"Stimms."

"Did that funny old Mr. Stimms offer you a job?"

"Not just *a* job. *My* job. The one I had before . . ."

"Yes," she said, "Before."

Before was a funny little word, and it was queer that there should have been a *before* when he had been mad and stupid and thought he couldn't do things and go on living. What a lot of mistakes he had made *before*, and carried them about with him after making them! The second generation of universal scepticism— phooey. The great and noble idea—phooey. Farewell present to life—phooey. The best way to make a present to life was to be happy. He had never understood about that before, but now he knew enough to give the necessary definition. Happiness meant not having to fool yourself because you were all right and did not need to; it meant being able to relax because you did not have to prove anything. Happiness meant waking up every morning with someone dear to you. And other things he had not yet had time to find out, but that he would find out as he went along.

"Death destroys a man," he said slowly, "but the idea of life saves him."

"What a funny thing, darling," she said, smiling at him, "to say at a party."

"I altered the quotation," he explained.

The door was open. Hardly noticing that they did so, they had slipped out on to the darkened landing.

"Put your arms round me," Catherine whispered.

Holding her to him, gazing eagerly over her shoulder at the darkness, Edgar gave a long, silent shudder of laughter at his own happiness as he thought of the bad yesterdays and the wonderful to-morrows. It was over. He was tired of living in the present.

THE END